Train Man

Train Man

Nakano Hitori

Translated by Bonnie Elliott

ROBINSON

London

Constable & Robinson Ltd
3 The Lanchesters
162 Fulham Palace Road
London W6 9ER
www.constablerobinson.com

First published in Japan by Shinchosha Publishing 2004

First published in the UK by Robinson,
an imprint of Constable & Robinson Ltd, 2006

Permission for this edition was arranged through The English Agency (Japan) Ltd

Copyright © in English translation: Constable & Robinson Ltd 2006

A copy of the British Library Cataloguing in
Publication Data is available from the British Library.

ISBN-13: 978-1-84529-351-2
ISBN-10: 1-84529-351-7

Printed and bound in the EU

1 3 5 7 9 10 8 6 4 2

Contents

Mission
1

Emergency Request
[Help me with dinner]

Comments posted by a Geek thread netizen: <OK, I admit it. At first,
I thought Train Man was a wimp. I mean, he was taking forever just to
work up the courage to call and thank her but I thought we should stick
by him and cheer him on. But now he's gone further than I could have
imagined.>

731 Name: Anonymous Post Date: 14/03/04 21:25

Sorry. I may end up betraying you guys.
I'm no good at writing so don't know how well I can tell this story.

Damn. This thread's got something going on . . .
May the force be with you . . .

No way could anybody have known that this board, commonly composed
of banal postings, was about to morph into a support group and fan club for
Train Man.

732 Name: Anonymous Post Date: 14/03/04 21:27

freakinfrakinfreakinfrakinnnnnnnn

733 Name: Anonymous Post Date: 14/03/04 21:28

what's goin' on man?

734 Name: Anonymous Post Date: 14/03/04 21:28

>>731
did you get a girlfriend?

737 Name: Anonymous Post Date: 14/03/04 21:33

>>734
sadly no. But something really big came up. This kind of stuff sounds
too much like I'm making it up. Anyway, the point is that you guys
really need to get out more . . .

738 Name: Anonymous Post Date: 14/03/04 21:35

sorry. Ok, I thought about it some more and it's actually not such a
big deal . . . _| ̄|O
Deep breath . . .

---

739 Name: Anonymous Post Date: 14/03/04 21:36

>>737
how many times have I typed this,

       d.e.t.a.i.l.s por favor

---

740 Name: 731 Post Date: 14/03/04 21:38

>>739
It's gonna come out all weird.
But I'll try anyway.
I'm usually the one reading, not posting . . .
So don't take the piss . . .

749 Name: 731 Post Date: 14/03/04 21:55

I went to Akihabara today. Not that there was anything I wanted to buy.
Anyway, on my way back there was this old drunk guy on the train.
Other than the old geezer and myself, all the people sat in our car
were women.
20s–40s I reckon.

Anyway, he started harassing the women in our car.
First he tried to harass this girl but she wasn't having it and got off
at the next stop. I watched him out of the corner of my eye thinking
what a creep he was.

Then the guy comes over to where I was, right in the centre and leans
over a group of older women. 'Don't even think about using your
mobiles coz I'll 'ave you!' he goes, scaring the shit out of the women.
They were like (´·w·`) – all silent.

Ok this might turn into a long one.

---

763 Name: 731 Post Date: 14/03/04 22:15

>>761
I'm not sure if it's going to lead to anything but . . .
If only I'd had the balls . . .
All right, I'm gonna write through it. Get it together.

---

766 Name: 731 Post Date: 14/03/04 22:23

The old dears sat very still with their heads down
'Best not to notice him' was the idea.
Then the guy started on about
'Women should shut up and do what a man says' and he pushed his
hand into one of the ladies' faces and grabbed her chin.
I couldn't just sit back anymore so I forced myself to shout 'Hey, stop
it!' My voice was probably shaking.

You know, I've never even been in a fight.
But the guy apparently didn't hear me so there was no response.
'Hey! Mate! I said cut it out ameghrrrghrrr!' I stood up and did my
best to yell out a second time. Then one of the ladies looked
over at me and said 'don't worry, we're fine' trying to calm me down.
The guy finally realised what was going on and turned round.
'What are you staring at me like that for eh?' He glared at me.

He staggered over.
'Hhhow f@*%ing old are ya?'
'I'm 22!'
'I'm f@*%ing 60 arraghrrrgftttt'
I couldn't make out half his words but basically, he was telling me I
was a young punk or something.
'So you want some of this? Eh? Some of this?'
The old geezer was ready to fight.
'Huh? What are you talking about. I'm gonna call the police.'
'Go the f@*% ahead and call the police rrrghh.'
He started swinging his arms around stumbling about. While he
swung his arms, he must have lost his balance because he
side-swiped a woman. It wasn't a major slap or anything but still.

Um, how do you cut a long story short . . . ? (´•ω:;,.:…

(´•ω•`)

---

766 Name: 731　Post Date: 14/03/04　22:37

'Oh!' said the woman as she pulled back.
I jumped up and grabbed the man by his arms.
One of the older ladies got up to call the conductor.
Then a businessman in his late 20s who was in the car in front of us
noticed the commotion and came over to help. Seeing the geezer and me
grappling the businessman got behind the guy and put him in an armlock.
'All right, mate, all right. Just don't take it out on the boy.'
You could tell this businessman was a bit older and knew a thing or
two. I mean he knew how to calm the situation down.
'I'll keep him right here so you can sit down now.'
I was pretty worked up, really pumped, so this business man even
calmed me right down. And wouldn't you know it the old guy didn't even
put up a fight. Maybe he knew he wouldn't be able to beat the guy which
means, damn it, that he thought I was gonna be a pushover. (´Д`)

I sat down next to a woman who said 'What a nuisance' to which I
replied
'Yes, absolutely'
Why I couldn't say something wittier, I've no idea. ＿|￣|○

I'm tired . . . ＿|￣|○

---

779 Name: 731　Post Date: 14/03/04　22:52

>>767
It was really just like that . . .
I'm so lame.
The suit was so cool.

After a while the conductor turned up.
When the conductor told the old geezer 'We're going to have to
release you to the police so you'll have to get off at the next stop' the
geezer threw a fit.

Because of the police, me, the girl sitting next to me, the older ladies and the geezer all got off at the next stop.
Then the conductor said
'I'm gonna go and call the police so hold onto him for me will you?' and rushed off somewhere. Leaving me and the ladies with the old guy. How mad is that. So I grabbed hold of the geezer's arm but he yelled back at me saying 'Don't you grab me, I ain't going nowhere!' and started making a scene. None of the posers that passed us by even offered to help . . . (´·ω·`)

So I just held onto the old man who kept trying to run away and finally 2 or 3 policemen showed up.
'This old man?' they asked me. As soon as I replied yes, they moved mad-quick dragging him into an office. So we all followed.
After we all showed them our IDs they asked all the women 'do you want to press charges?' and they all said 'no, thanks'.
I told them I wasn't hurt in the scuffle.

780 Name: 731 Post Date: 14/03/04 23:06

Even if it wasn't handled as a proper crime there was a load of paperwork that needed to be filled out so we followed them to the police station.
On the way there:
'I'm sorry, it's my fault it snowballed into this.' The older ladies had a while to go before their stop but they all laughed and said 'No biggie, don't worry'

At the police station, the old man got taken to a room in the back.
I heard him yelling and then an angry yap from a cop.
'We're gonna squeeze him dry wrwg' The policeman laughed.

As I watched the women scribble out the police forms I felt guilty again, thinking about how I should have just kept my mouth shut. If I had, we wouldn't be in this mess. I bowed to them and apologised.
'There aren't many young men like you out there you know' said one of the older ladies. And I felt ten feet tall.

Just a bit more.
Tho you guys know how it ends already.

789 Name: 731 Post Date: 14/03/04 23:24

Don't know why or how, but I asked the policeman 'Um, am I allowed to go now?'
To which the policeman replied 'Of course, you've given us all we need. Thank you so much.' I mean, he thanked me. And then the ladies also bowed deeply and thanked me.
'If it's ok with you, could you give us your name and contact information?' said one of the older ladies.
I wrote my name and address in her notepad.
'Excuse me, could I also have . . .' the girl who sat next to me asked.
And then added 'I'd like to be able to return this favour soon'
To which I babbled like an idiot 'no, god no, oh no thank you' and then quickly added 'right then, I'm sorry about all of this, the fuss . . .' and promptly legged it.

That's the end of it.
I realised later on how stupid am I for not asking for their contact information . . . _⌐|O
I've never been thanked by a woman before so . . .
I got so nerrrrrrrrrvousssssss

---

792 Name: Anonymous Post Date: 14/03/04 23:27

>>789
You gave them your address, right?
Then there's no need to worry coz they'll come over to your place with a thank you gift.

---

793 Name: Anonymous Post Date: 14/03/04 23:27

Well your address is probably one in a list of many guys!
Even so, you've scored quite big for a Geek _⌐|O

---

811 Name: 731 Post Date: 14/03/04 23:40

Man, I'm so exhausted from my day. It was filled with stuff I never ever do . . . _⌐|O

And guys, thnx for reading my terrible writing.
I'll let you know if I hear from one of the ladies. Will definitely report.
(ˋ·ω·ˊ)

>>805
I wanted to but it just so happened that there were only women in my car
The suit looked to me like a g-o-d
If he hadn't helped out I'd probably have been beaten to a pulp
Would have been quite a scene . . .

Laters

---

812 Name: Anonymous Post Date: 14/03/04 23:42

I think it was pretty gutsy of 731 to go up against a drunk.
Maybe it's weird of me to say when I wasn't even there but . . .

Isn't it kind of an extension from basic, social, common courtesy, no?

---

815 Name: Anonymous Post Date: 14/03/04 23:45

>>811
I think it was pretty damn heroic of you
Tell us as soon as something new develops

---

762 Name: 731 aka Train Man Post Date: 15/03/04 19:08

thanks for listening yesterday.
It's only been a day so nothing new to report.
You're asking about what the older ladies and the young woman
looked like, any special features
I can't remember very well so I'll write without getting into the
details, ok.

Older ladies
There were three in all and they were in their 40s
But all very classy-looking

Girl that sat next to me
Probably in her 20s. But looked older than me. Between 22 and 25.

Celebrity traits, well, I don't know many celebrities . . . _|⌐|O
She had longish brown hair, was a bit on the skinny side.
Wasn't too flashy or too boring and seemed well put together in a
pretty-pretty kind of way.

777 Name: 731 aka Train Man Post Date: 15/03/04 19:27

>>772
I'm your basic Akihabara roaming techie . . . _|⌐|O
Age = how long I've been without a girlfriend
Definitely a no sexperience virgin
You know what tho, I'm gonna try.
I'm gonna try to use that courage that came to me on the train

But even if something did happen with that girl that sat next to me
No way . . . _|⌐|
No way could we walk around town together or anything

---

780 Name: Anonymous Post Date: 15/03/04 19:32

Putting the calling and no-calling aside, you've really stepped up dude.
I don't have it in me to do what you did, Mr Godman _|⌐|O

---

783 Name: 731 aka Train Man Post Date: 15/03/04 19:36

>>780
Of course I thought that this was my chance

I'll step in to save them
↓
they'll be grateful
↓
they might want to thank me
↓
I'll hurriedly report it to this thread
↓
(ﾟдﾟ) fantastico

I shall report as soon as something happens. Laters.

The Geeks and Train Man himself weren't expecting any great changes in their near future. But . . . the first sign of change turned up in a box.

587 Name: 731 aka Train Man Post Date: 16/03/04 18:58

I received a letter today.
I don't know if it's from an old lady or the girl but from the envelope and stationery as well as the handwriting, I think it's the older lady.

It basically thanked me for the other night and from the sound of it, she was the one that was directly harassed by the old man.
I'm thinking about writing back . . .

But as you know, my writing skills are . . . a bit
shabby . . . ＿⌐|O
I will try me best to write . . .

623 Name: 731 aka Train Man Post Date: 16/03/04 19:43

Just now I received a little package and letter from the girl.
They were teacups. She thanked me in the letter.
She wrote 'I sat next to you that night' so I'm pretty positive about it.

Supa cute envelope, stationery and handwriting! (;゜∀゜)=3 hubbahubba
And it smells kinda nice too (;´Д`) pant pant
Damn. I'm getting all feverish. Gotta take a chill pill.

624 Name: Anonymous Post Date: 16/03/04 19:45

>>623
chill man, the smell is definitely your mind playing trix
do her words smell at all like there may be more to come?

625 Name: Anonymous Post Date: 16/03/04 19:45

>>623
if the package was delivered by courier service then you got her numba?

628 Name: 731 aka Train Man Post Date: 16/03/04 19:52

>>624
more to come . . . ?
let me share a sentence
'I was moved by the courage you displayed.'
That's about it . . .

>>625
you is right, it is on the waybill itself . . . ((((;゙д゙)))
woawoawoa

629 Name: Anonymous Post Date: 16/03/04 19:52

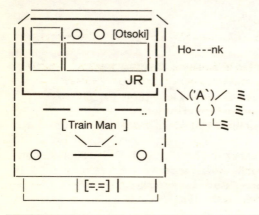

631 Name: Anonymous Post Date: 16/03/04 19:54

ahh . . . yeah . . . well . . .
It seems like a near impossible feat to push the relationship any
further?

632 Name: Anonymous Post Date: 16/03/04 19:54

>>628
you have to call up your courage again. Take two.

643 Name: 731 aka Train Man Post Date: 16/03/04 20:00

Oh no . . .
Things are a bit crazy right now

No way could I call a girl . . . _|￣|○

650 Name: 731 aka Train Man Post Date: 16/03/04 20:03

Seriously, I don't have a clue what I'm supposed to do! ヽ(`Д´)ﾉ
Am I supposed to call right away?

---

653 Name: Anonymous Post Date: 16/03/04 20:04

Calling would be too sudden, no?
But it's a difficult situation so you have to be a bit pushy or it won't go any further.
Why don't you say something like 'Seeing as we met under such unusual circumstances, what would you say to getting together for dinner sometime soon'

---

656 Name: Anonymous Post Date: 16/03/04 20:06

>Train Man
Hold it. How many cups did you get?

---

661 Name: Anonymous Post Date: 16/03/04 20:11

As one who used to hang on the Couples Board allow me to dish out some advice.

Must call. Must make the call!
Call and tell her that you received it.

Tell her something like thank you for the nice cups and compliment her on her taste.
And then slip in something about the train, like do you always take that train? Got it?

665 Name: 731 aka Train Man Post Date: 16/03/04 20:13

you guys . . . thanks a lot

>>660
there are 2 cups
to put it simply, the normal kind _| ̄|O
I have my mobile in my hand but I can't dial the number . . .
This needs much more balls than that day (´ ·ω· `)

---

668 Name: Anonymous Post Date: 16/03/04 20:15

>>665
If you wait till later it's gonna be even more difficult to call.
You should call before 9 at least.

---

669 Name: Anonymous Post Date: 16/03/04 20:16

>>665
_| ̄|O ain't cutting it. Need age, salary, car, family background, looks.
Two cups, just as I thought. So thread it from there. Got it?

---

678 Name: Anonymous Post Date: 16/03/04 20:21

There's no way in hell you can get it on right now so just focus on trying to stay in touch with her.

Sample dialogue
'Thank you so much for the gift. I just received the cups.
They're wonderfully designed these cups. But why are there 2?
I'm alone most of the time so I only use one at a time.
By the way, where did you buy them?
I'd love to go to the shop so could you tell me where it is?'
Like that?

Being a Geek myself, that's all I got

---

680 Name: Anonymous Post Date: 16/03/04 20:21

Call to thank her!

n then,
Thank you so much for the cups--! You really didn't have to.
What a night that was, I couldn't let him get away with that kind of behaviour.
Promote your knight in shining armour side

---

687 Name: Anonymous Post Date: 16/03/04 20:25

Writing a letter is the way to go.
Calling could be too much too soon.
Calling the day the letter arrives, definitely too much too soon.

---

688 Name: 731 aka Train Man Post Date: 16/03/04 20:25

waaaaaaah ─────── ｡ﾟ(ﾟ´Д｀ﾟ)ﾟ｡────────
thanks people
I'm taking all you guys' advice!

>>669
age 22
income £20K
family normal
car none
looks techiecutie ＿|￣|○

am I supposed to use the 2 cups to invite her over for tea?
no way Jose
I'm still holding onto my mobile, no f@*%in' way
Can I call tomorrow? (´･ω･`)

---

690 Name: Anonymous Post Date: 16/03/04 20:25

Is the phone number on the waybill her home or mobile?

---

695 Name: Anonymous Post Date: 16/03/04 20:27

>>688
if you're gonna call, you gotta call today!
Good omens abound when you act immediately upon a thought

698 Name: Anonymous Post Date: 16/03/04 20:27

A call's too pushy, man.
Better to let that great first impression linger.

707 Name: 731 aka Train Man Post Date: 16/03/04 20:30

If I can't call by 2100 then I won't call . . . (´·ω·`)

I'm too worked up anyway . . .
She'd probably hear me breathing heavily or something . . .

709 Name: Anonymous Post Date: 16/03/04 20:31

I was pushing the call earlier but I've got my reasons for that.

If you rely on a letter, there's the chance that this'll end after your reply.
I don't think the relationship would go any further.

If you're looking to explore it further you gotta call and prepare to die an
honourable death.

>>698
If it was me, I'd definitely call.

710 Name: Anonymous Post Date: 16/03/04 20:31

I'm a girl and I wouldn't feel ambushed by a phone call or anything. On the
contrary I'd be like 'great, the cups were delivered safe and sound but
boy, what a nice guy to call to thank me for them'.
Excellent impression

724 Name: Anonymous Post Date: 16/03/04 20:37

I'm also a girl,
And I'd be ok with either letter or call.
I'd pull back if you suddenly stepped over the line and started talking
about personal stuff.
Why don't you call and go with how she reacts?
Whatever, I'd recommend a multi-pronged attack

726 Name: 731 aka Train Man Post Date: 16/03/04 20:37

I've been watching this thread and checking my phone for the last few minutes.
No can do.

---

734 Name: Anonymous Post Date: 16/03/04 20:41

Shit. Why do I have to feel nervous.

---

736 Name: Anonymous Post Date: 16/03/04 20:41

>>726
You say no now but you've got nothing to lose!
You've already got the teacups, right?
Rejection is the name of the game!
Go! You're a man. Put on your gear and go!

---

737 Name: Anonymous Post Date: 16/03/04 20:41

Seriously, this is when you call up your courage. This is it.

---

738 Name: Anonymous Post Date: 16/03/04 20:42

I can't work out if Train Man is a ball-o-courage or a ball-o-dung
You can do it dude! Train! Train! Train!

---

739 Name: Anonymous Post Date: 16/03/04 20:43

>>726
Doh! You are being tested as a man now!
Why would you pull back now?!
Call if it's the last thing you do before you die! Right now!!!!!!!!

---

741 Name: 680 Post Date: 16/03/04 20:43

You didn't make a bad impression on her so she's going to be completely cool with the phone call.

Same thing with the thank you letter.

But as someone wrote earlier, a thank you letter could be more difficult to follow up on so I agree that you should call while you're still buzzing.

If not right away, tomorrow should be fine too!

---

750 Name: Anonymous Post Date: 16/03/04 20:47

Call today!
If you wait till tomorrow you'll say 'I'm kind of busy today' or 'Let's wait another day' and in the end, I can see you'll just give up on the call!

You hear me?!?! Today, today, today. Call today!!!!!!!

---

757 Name: Anonymous Post Date: 16/03/04 20:50

You're standing at one of life's crossroads dude!
Think about it carefully before you act!

---

762 Name: Anonymous Post Date: 16/03/04 20:53

If you don't call, she'll just think of you as what-a-nice-guy-he-was.
Very true.
'I'm so happy that such a nice lady thinks of me that way'
I guess that's a nice thought to have too.
If Train were me, then yeah, maybe he'd be thinking this.
But you know, that woman went o-u-t o-f h-e-r w-a-y to pick out teacups for you.

---

763 Name: 680 Post Date: 16/03/04 20:53

Why don't you just say you'll call tomorrow and we'll practise today, you and me and simulate the actual call.

Will advise as well.

---

782 Name: 731 aka Train Man Post Date: 16/03/04 21:01

I used all my will power and tried a lot of times to call
But no way
Far more nerve-wracking than on the train
My hands are tingling, my face is red, my heart's thumping like
mad

I am a loser __| |O
The letter I guess isn't as effective? (´·ω·`)

---

783 Name: 680 Post Date: 16/03/04 21:01

I'm here to help. For real.
I'll wait for Train Man to reply.

If we're role-playing the phone call, pls start your end.

Or if you need me to I'll jump in.

---

832 Name: 731 aka Train Man Post Date: 16/03/04 21:18

Thank you so much everybody
But I don't think I have it in me . . .
My hands are shaking

Let's go with the letter . . .

---

836 Name: Anonymous Post Date: 16/03/04 21:19

You really are having a difficult time aren't you, Train Man.

---

840 Name: Anonymous Post Date: 16/03/04 21:19

>>832
Everybody's hands shake the first time, yeah.
Mine shook too. But hey, but hey . . .

It's your first time today and they won't shake the second time around.
You'll be stepping up to higher ground.

---

861 Name: ♀ Post Date: 16/03/04 21:26

I think it's better for you to call.
If you write a letter, I don't think it'll lead to the next step.
What're you thinking could follow the thank you letter?
If she doesn't reply, end of story, no?
Just think of it this way. You call to thank a relative for sending you gifts,
right? So tell yourself it's only natural to make the call!

---

864 Name: Anonymous Post Date: 16/03/04 21:28

If you make this call, I think a new Train Man's bound to step onto stage?
It's not a matter of going out with her or not,
I think you'll grab hold of something far deeper.

---

874 Name: 731 aka Train Man Post Date: 16/03/04 21:31

My hands are frozen! ＼(｀Д´)／
Purleeze give me the courage from that day!

---

904 Name: 731 aka Train Man Post Date: 16/03/04 21:37

I'm not gonna do it today . . . ＿|￣|○
I'm gonna read through everybody's comments again and work
myself up for tomorrow . . .

---

910 Name: Anonymous Post Date: 16/03/04 21:39

>>904
Allow me one comment.
'There's only one of her but you've got all us here at 2-Channel'

That's all I've got to say.

---

927 Name: 731 aka Train Man Post Date: 16/03/04 21:42

Shit . . . you're making me kinda teary . . .
I'm overwhelmed by my own lameness and you guys' kindness.
And damn me for not being able to properly say thanks . . .

---

928 Name: Anonymous Post Date: 16/03/04 21:43

You can dooooooooooo it maaannnnnnnnnn!

---

929 Name: Anonymous Post Date: 16/03/04 21:43

You can thank us with your actions!

---

949 Name: 731 aka Train Man Post Date: 16/03/04 21:48

So I'll look though the log and cull the key points and come up with a
plan for the phone call dialogue tomorrow . . .
Thanks people. And sorry for being so lame.

Though most of his fellow Geeks wanted him to make the phone call, this
hurdle was much too high for our Train Man whose age = number of years
without a girlfriend = a squeaky clean virgin.

---

22 Name: 731 aka Train Man Post Date: 16/03/04 22:03

I'm finally feeling back to normal . . .
I don't think my heart's ever raced so much before . . .
I'm throwing in my cards . . . _| ‾|O

---

35 Name: Anonymous Post Date: 16/03/04 22:07

2 cups sounds like an invitation to me

---

47 Name: Anonymous Post Date: 16/03/04 22:13

But wait. We have to analyse this.

Teacups for a techie boy. What is this really saying?

---

48 Name: 680 in prevthread Post Date: 16/03/04 22:14

It's fairly standard to send sets of mugs or any other kind of household goods. Don't think there are any ulterior motives.

I'm going back to being Anonymous from my next post. (·∀·) see ya

---

50 Name: Anonymous Post Date: 16/03/04 22:14

>>45
Yep. I think there are many single-item gifts.
But this was a pair.
Don't want to read too deeply but it smells a bit like she thought it through.

---

55 Name: Anonymous Post Date: 16/03/04 22:16

Well, there really can't be a one-cup situation

---

56 Name: 724 in prevthread Post Date: 16/03/04 22:17

I agree with 680.
Normally, it'd be a set.
Teacups are also a fairly harmless choice.

---

57 Name: Anonymous Post Date: 16/03/04 22:17

It's common. Sending a pair of cups.

---

58 Name: 731 aka Train Man Post Date: 16/03/04 22:17

Just like you guys all kinds of thoughts are swirling through my mind . . .
An endless array of maybe . . . or perhaps . . . couldn't be . . .

66 Name: 731 aka Train Man Post Date: 16/03/04 22:20

All right . . . so I shouldn't read too much into it all, yeah
But I'm gonna treasure them . . .

85 Name: Anonymous Post Date: 16/03/04 22:26

The cups don't mean anything
You're probably reading too much into it
I think that as a thank you gift, it's most definitely a harmless choice

The Geeks ramble on about the meaning of the two teacups. It is 89's quite simple question that ends up leading the thread into a random digression.

89 Name: Anonymous Post Date: 16/03/04 22:27

>>85
Reading too much into the cups are we?
What brand are they? Couldn't we find out a thing or two with that piece of info? Is this old 411?

93 Name: Anonymous Post Date: 16/03/04 22:28

I guess she could have sent a plate or a glass cup as a thank you gift but household goods can get very tricky.
The teacups were definitely the easiest choice.

99 Name: Anonymous Post Date: 16/03/04 22:30

>>89
You're reading too much into it.
One time when I had to send a thank you gift and I asked around for ideas, a lot of people suggested cups.

104 Name: Anonymous Post Date: 16/03/04 22:31

so . . . who makes the cups?

115 Name: 731 aka Train Man Post Date: 16/03/04 22:35

I know I've said this already but guys, really, thanks for thinking all this through for me. I can't say it enough.

>>104

It says Hermes. Guess they're some household goods brand from somewhere.

>>103
thanks, man, really, for supporting lame me.
when I work up the courage . . .

---

117 Name: Anonymous Post Date: 16/03/04 22:35

Hot damn. Herrrrrrrrmes eh

---

118 Name: Anonymous Post Date: 16/03/04 22:35

>>115
You saying they're Hermes!

---

120 Name: Anonymous Post Date: 16/03/04 22:35

>>115
HERMES
Fuel the flames fuel the flames fuel the flames and fan it fan it fan it!!!!

---

121 Name: Anonymous Post Date: 16/03/04 22:36

>>115
Hey, you do know how to pronounce it, right. It's air-mez.

---

122 Name: Anonymous Post Date: 16/03/04 22:36

Can't believe it's Hermes.
She must be rolling in dough.

---

126 Name: Anonymous Post Date: 16/03/04 22:36

>>115
HERMES is the real deal and we're not talking about that spaceship of the same name

---

127 Name: Anonymous Post Date: 16/03/04 22:37

I knew it! The cups have a deeper meaning!

---

132 Name: 731 aka Train Man Post Date: 16/03/04 22:38

Hermes like the bag?
That's like a major brand, dude.
Expensive innit?
They make cups and stuff?

Need Serious Answers Purleeze

141 Name: 731 aka Train Man Post Date: 16/03/04 22:39

(ﾟдﾟ) jaw hangin open
((;ﾟдﾟ)) slightly afraid
((((;ﾟДﾟ))) got the shakes
(((((((;ﾟДﾟ))))))) major shakes and shakes and breaks and shakes

---

146 Name: Anonymous Post Date: 16/03/04 22:40

No matter how much gratitude you have, sending Hermes teacups isn't
your everyday gift.

149 Name: Anonymous Post Date: 16/03/04 22:40

I can't believe she sent you Hermes! To send Hermes teacups as a thank
you gift. Shows you she's got class.

---

152 Name: Anonymous Post Date: 16/03/04 22:41

We're really cookin' now

---

155 Name: Anonymous Post Date: 16/03/04 22:41

>>141
You have to call tomorrow
You have to, have to, have to
I'm not gonna tell you to keep your hopes down
Just call without thinking too much about it.

---

164 Name: 731 aka Train Man Post Date: 16/03/04 22:43

Ok ok ok ok, don't scare me!
My heart's racin' again

---

167 Name: Anonymous Post Date: 16/03/04 22:44

Man oh man.
We still don't know whether she likes you or not . . .
As 149 said, she has class and is mature.
There's no doubt that she feels indebted to you . . .
More reason to pick up the phone and call to thank her.

---

182 Name: Anonymous Post Date: 16/03/04 22:47

You have to take her out to dinner, to thank her.

---

183 Name: 731 aka Train Man Post Date: 16/03/04 22:47

I knew that Hermes was an upmarket brand but
I had no idea they made teacups _| |O

>>168
height 172
weight 68 kilos
face . . . never been told I look like anyone _| |

---

185 Name: 68 Post Date: 16/03/04 22:48

Thanks to the expensive Hermes teacups, now we know how this is
going to go.
'I feel so undeserving of such an expensive gift . . . if it's ok with you, I'd
love to take you to dinner to thank you for the gift . . .'
this kind of flow would sound trés natural.
I'd go if someone asked me like this.

---

234 Name: 731 aka Train Man Post Date: 16/03/04 22:59

I should call today shouldn't I?

---

244 Name: Anonymous Post Date: 16/03/04 23:01

Yeah. But it's too late now.
It's too coupley after 2300

---

253 Name: 731 aka Train Man Post Date: 16/03/04 23:03

I called her mobile but got her voicemail . . .
I'll call again tomorrow

---

260 Name: Anonymous Post Date: 16/03/04 23:04

>>253
What I should say is whatdahelltimeyouthinkitis but way to go,
dude!!
Tomorrow is another day!!!

---

271 Name: Anonymous Post Date: 16/03/04 23:07

Good on you
You went to the next level.

---

292 Name: 731 aka Train Man Post Date: 16/03/04 23:11

I've never, of course, called a girl in my life _| ̄|O
What I wanted to do, more than anything, was to just thank her normally
If she doesn't call tomorrow I'll give her a call!

---

297 Name: Anonymous Post Date: 16/03/04 23:12

Could anyone have ever guessed that Train Man would get this board
going like this?

320 Name: Anonymous Post Date: 16/03/04 23:19

Us Geeks talking amongst our geeky selves . . . that's not the best way of working out how to move things along. We need to get a second opinion.

We won't sit back and cut our geek selves off from humanity. No way.

---

331 Name: Anonymous Post Date: 16/03/04 23:22

>>320
You're right. And in a way, it was nice to have the ladies contribute.
So in that light, ladies, stop by whenever you feel like stopping by.

---

333 Name: Anonymous Post Date: 16/03/04 23:23

I've never felt so encouraged by the ladies, eva eva eva.

Finally, with bated breath, Train Man takes his first step.

---

342 Name: 731 aka Train Man Post Date: 17/03/04 22:13

Just got back from work ＿|￣|
I really wanted to get back earlier . . .

She had called me a couple of times today but I . . .
I'm gonna call her right now . . .

---

344 Name: Anonymous Post Date: 17/03/04 22:14

Y⌒Y⌒Y⌒Y⌒Y⌒Y⌒(｡A｡)!!!
He's ba--------ck!
Welcome back!
Why don't you grab something to eat first.

---

350 Name: Anonymous Post Date: 17/03/04 22:16

(　˚Д˚) < have some tea why don't you

351 Name: Anonymous Post Date: 17/03/04 22:16

forget tea!
Now, now, quickly, you must call---!

366 Name: Anonymous Post Date: 17/03/04 22:20

He's on the phone right now isn't he . . . I guess we hafta hang around
and wait

367 Name: Anonymous Post Date: 17/03/04 22:21

This feeling . . .
I haven't felt like this since my school play . . .

398 Name: Anonymous Post Date: 17/03/04 22:29

I wonder what Train Man is talking about right now . . .

401 Name: 731 aka Train Man Post Date: 17/03/04 22:29

I just hung up.
My hands are still shaking.

She had just run a bath.
Lady Hermes said that she didn't mind. That she'd keep talking but I
told her that I'd call her back.

She said that she'd call me back.

Damn it. I was so nervous.

406 Name: Anonymous Post Date: 17/03/04 22:30

>>401
Good job!!!!!

413 Name: Anonymous Post Date: 17/03/04 22:30

Whoooooooaaaaaaaaa!

You da man! What'd you talk about?

---

414 Name: 731 aka Train Main Post Date: 17/03/04 22:30

I can't ask her out to dinner!

---

432 Name: 731 aka Train Man Post Date: 17/03/04 22:33

>>413
I started out by apologising for not leaving a message yesterday
Then apologised for calling kinda late tonight
Then apologised about her having to call me so much today
Then said how undeserving I felt about the wonderful gift
And apologised some more
And more

What the . . . am I the apology man . . . _|⌐|O

---

437 Name: Anonymous Post Date: 17/03/04 22:33

>>414
Give us a rundown on how the conversation went
I swear I'll analyse it until my CPU explodes into flames, yeah!

---

447 Name: 731 aka Train Man Post Date: 17/03/04 22:34

>>433
Thanking somebody for something they gave you as a thank you gift
is kinda strange, no?
You sure this isn't weird?
Serio-responses purleeze.

---

450 Name: Anonymous Post Date: 17/03/04 22:35

>>447
It's completely fine.
Not weird at all!

451 Name: Anonymous Post Date: 17/03/04 22:35

Invite her out to dinner to thank her for the cups
Invite her out to dinner to thank her for the cups
Invite her out to dinner to thank her for the cups
Invite her out to dinner to thank her for the cups
Invite her out to dinner to thank her for the cups
Invite her out to dinner to thank her for the cups
Invite her out to dinner to thank her for the cups
Invite her out to dinner to thank her for the cups
Invite her out to dinner to thank her for the cups

458 Name: Anonymous Post Date: 17/03/04 22:36

>>436
calm down, heel, heel heeeeeel
'I'd like to thank you in person, that is, if you don't mind'
OR
'I'd like to thank you in person, may I?'
is the way to go
We'll think of dinner or café or cinema later

463 Name: 731 aka Train Man Post Date: 17/03/04 22:37

>>430
She had a normal voice.
First thing she said was 'Ah . . . finally got you on the phone'
Sound good?

Dinner in return for the cups dinner in return for the cups dinner in
return for the cups dinner in return for the cups dinner in return for
the cups

476 Name: 731 aka Train Man Post Date: 17/03/04 22:40

>>458 is the last word, agreed?
And thanks everybody.

485 Name: Anonymous Post Date: 17/03/04 22:41

I'm a girl . . .

I think dinner would be best
458 is too much about the face-to-face which pushed me away
whereas dinner means yummy food and that always works
with me

486 Name: 731 aka Train Man Post Date: 17/03/04 22:42

I'm getting nervous . . . _ˌ⌐|O

492 Name: Anonymous Post Date: 17/03/04 22:42

>>463
'Thank you so much for the lovely gift. It looks like the scale has tipped
too far in my favour. I'd like to be able to do something in return. What
about dinner?'
could you manage that?

501 Name: 731 aka Train Man Post Date: 17/03/04 22:43

Wait! Where am I supposed to take her to dinner?
And would it have to be on a Sunday?

505 Name: 731 aka Train Man Post Date: 17/03/04 22:44

>>492
Thanks for the lines!

510 Name: Anonymous Post Date: 17/03/04 22:45

>>501
Sunday sounds good.
And when you ask her, she's probably gonna say no at first coz she feels
bad about it but just push for more and keep asking her to dinner!

519 Name: 731 aka Train Man Post Date: 17/03/04 22:46

>>510
I'm sure she'll say 'You don't have to feel obliged' when she says no.

Would that be the end?
And how do I push for more?

My mind is all crazy now ＿|￣|○
Anyway, I'm gonna innnnvite her to din-dins

---

522 Name: Anonymous Post Date: 17/03/04 22:48

>>519 Train
You've really . . . matured . . .
better yet . . . are maturing.
Damn. You is shining.

And so a little tug of war between Lady Hermes and Train Man begins. Will Train Man succeed in inviting Lady Hermes out?

---

530 Name: 731 aka Train Man Post Date: 17/03/04 22:49

Ringin

---

531 Name: Anonymous Post Date: 17/03/04 22:49

Call from Lady Miss Hermes------! ——————(ﾟ∀ﾟ)——————!!!!

---

538 Name: Anonymous Post Date: 17/03/04 22:50

Time to take the stage for real!

---

539 Name: Anonymous Post Date: 17/03/04 22:50

I'm praying like mad. Really.

548 Name: Anonymous Post Date: 17/03/04 22:51

I ask you God to provide Train Man with courage and to light his way!

549 Name: Anonymous Post Date: 17/03/04 22:51

If you want the courage I used in primary school when I pissed my pants for the first and last time . . . well I'm giving it away for free!

553 Name: Anonymous Post Date: 17/03/04 22:52

I've never sincerely prayed for a stranger ever in my life.

558 Name: Anonymous Post Date: 17/03/04 22:52

Even if it's just us . . . let's all try to stay calm
Why don't we all join together in some deep breathing.

569 Name: Anonymous Post Date: 17/03/04 22:54

(´ ˆ ` breathe in

(– o – and out

596 Name: Anonymous Post Date: 17/03/04 22:57

Man oh man, I wonder what they're talking about.
I really want him to give it his all.
Train makes me want to be a better man.

600 Name: Anonymous Post Date: 17/03/04 22:58

Oh please please please make it all go well!!!!!!!!

605 Name: Anonymous Post Date: 17/03/04 22:59

Ten minutes on my clock

614 Name: 731 aka Train Man Post Date: 17/03/04 23:00

HELP ME WITH DINNER

616 Name: Anonymous Post Date: 17/03/04 23:01

Ahyeah ahyeah ──♪ o(ﾟ∀ﾟo) (oﾟ∀ﾟo) (oﾟ∀ﾟ)o ──♪

621 Name: Anonymous Post Date: 17/03/04 23:01

Why don't you just say that you don't know too many places and just buy some time?

622 Name: Anonymous Post Date: 17/03/04 23:01

To Sir With Love!!!!!!!!!

627 Name: Anonymous Post Date: 17/03/04 23:02

Just say you'll look into it and that you'll call her back

628 Name: Anonymous Post Date: 17/03/04 23:02

All rrrrrite!

629 Name: Anonymous Post Date: 17/03/04 23:02

First thing is to decide which train station to meet at.
You have till the day to decide on the restaurant.

641 Name: 731 aka Train Man Post Date: 17/03/04 23:02

Got it.

643 Name: Anonymous Post Date: 17/03/04 23:03

>>641
the realism is killin me

649 Name: Anonymous Post Date: 17/03/04 23:03

>>641
ahyeah ahyeah!
────ヽ(∀ﾟ)人(ﾟ∀ﾟ)人(ﾟ∀)人(∀ﾟ)人(ﾟ∀ﾟ)人(ﾟ∀)/──── !!!

652 Name: Anonymous Post Date: 17/03/04 23:04

Train Man two-word post is for real

653 Name: Anonymous Post Date: 17/03/04 23:04

Sir Train Man Sir . . . serious respect

658 Name: Anonymous Post Date: 17/03/04 23:04

>>641

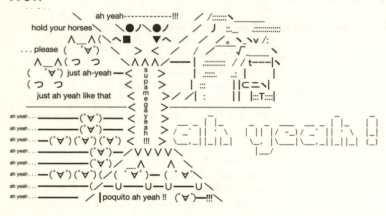

662 Name: Anonymous Post Date: 17/03/04 23:04

this kinda place is fairly harmless and the way to go methinks
Tsuki No Shizuku is a fav of the ladies. whatchu all think?

http://www.sankofoods.com/shop.html

686 Name: Anonymous Post Date: 17/03/04 23:08

No go with the ladies

When the place is too stiff it makes the ladies pull back and affects what
follows, if you know what I mean.
Let's say that food and drink will be split down the middle then it should
be not-too-expensive not-too-cheap a place, nor can it be too fancy so

basically we're talkin about a so-so kinda vibe, yeah

---

690 Name: Anonymous Post Date: 17/03/04 23:08

>>683
Italian or French should do it
Quick search online should pull a couple up
Could ask a guy at work who's popular with the ladies
Could check one of dem local message boards
Techies must act as techies do and use da puter for this!

---

691 Name: Anonymous Post Date: 17/03/04 23:08

http://www.diamond-dining.com/atcafe/index.html
kinda stylish, no

---

692 Name: Anonymous Post Date: 17/03/04 23:08

conveyor belt sushi, family dining, fast food, Korean bbq, yakitori, ramen
places would all be no-go in this case – places that would work would be
casual Italian.

---

693 Name: Anonymous Post Date: 17/03/04 23:08

I'm a girl and I'd have to say that French would be too fancy schmancy and
could present unnecessary problems so Tsuki no Shizuku or slightly fancy
Japanese tapas or ethnic dining could end up being the cool way to go.

---

722 Name: Anonymous Post Date: 17/03/04 23:11

You guys have probably forgotten that Train Man dresses like a techie.

Let's take him shopping! – (´ A `)

---

734 Name: Anonymous Post Date: 17/03/04 23:12

If they're still talking, it's been 23 minutes.

---

765 Name: Anonymous Post Date: 17/03/04 23:14

Girl here. I've overexcited myself and need to grab some tea.
Laters.

767 Name: Anonymous Post Date: 17/03/04 23:15

All right then. Shall we begin our Train Man make-over?

But this Geek cannot be of much help . . .

Ladies, ladies, may we ask for you to step up

Finally, Train Man jumps over his first hurdle.

---

785 Name: 731 aka Train Man Post Date: 17/03/04 23:17

Just hung up.
We agreed to meet for dinner.

Thanks, e-v-e-r-y-b-o-d-y.

---

790 Name: Anonymous Post Date: 17/03/04 23:17

>>785
ahyeah ＊·°˚·＊:.｡.₀.:＊· °(ﾟ∀ﾟ)° ·＊:.｡. .｡.:＊·°˚·＊ !!

791 Name: Anonymous Post Date: 17/03/04 23:17

>>785
spill the details why don't you

792 Name: Anonymous Post Date: 17/03/04 23:18

>>785
Good job! You da man!!

794 Name: Anonymous Post Date: 17/03/04 23:18

>>785

```
  。 ◇◎。o.:O☆oo.
          。:˚ ◎::O☆∧_∧☆。∂ :o˚
       ╱ 。O。 ∂ (´∀`)O◇。☆
     ╱    ◎│⎺⎺⎺U  U⎺⎺⎺│:◎:
    ╱     ☆。│.. Congratulations .│☆
  ▼        。O..io。◇.☆⎽⎽⎽⎽⎽⎽⎽⎽│ 。.:
  ∠▲⎯⎯⎯⎯⎯⎯⎯☆ : ∂ io☆ ˚◎ ∂ :.
```

---

795 Name: Anonymous Post Date: 17/03/04 23:18

>>785
grats!!

---

797 Name: Anonymous Post Date: 17/03/04 23:18

wooooooooooo!!! I'm participating in real time for the first time!

---

803 Name: Anonymous Post Date: 17/03/04 23:18

>>785
Awesome! Way to go!

---

814 Name: Anonymous Post Date: 17/03/04 23:19

>>785

```
        'good job'          ∩   ∩
            __∩         (⌒) (⌒)        ∩__  'good job'
'good job'  (∃,,, i         │ │ ╱ ╱       i ,,E)
    _n         \  \         │ │ ╱ ╱        ╱ ╱
  ( │      _,, -  \ \(<˚ )│ │╱ ╱ ˚J´ )╱ ╱   _,, -   'good job'
   \ \  (<˚´ )  \ \    )(    ╱___( .J´ )   n
    \ \(<˚´ ) │    ╱ ╱ \     │         \  │..E)
```

---

59 Name: 731 aka Train Man Post Date: 17/03/04 23:34

The first call I got from her was about 12 noon. I was working through my lunch break so I could get out of work early. I checked my call log about an hour later at 1 and realised that she had called. I called her back immediately but didn't get through. She called me at around 3 but I was working and couldn't get to the phone. She called again at 5 and then at 7 but again, I couldn't get to the phone. What a loser.

101 Name: 731 aka Train Man Post Date: 17/03/04 23:42

So then I got home a little after 10 and mad rushed to call her.
Pretty sure this was how we kicked off
'Hi. This is Train. Is this Lady Miss Hermes?'
'Oh wow, finally we got through to each other.'
Something like that.

'I'm really sorry I was away from the phone so much and thank you
so much for calling me so many times.'
'No problem. It was my fault for having bad timing.'

Then
'I received the cups yesterday.
Thank you for such a lovely gift.'
'It was nothing.'
And we went on about stuff like this and got to talking about the train
and what happened then.

Oh man, I can't remember it all . . . _| |

---

105 Name: Anonymous Post Date: 17/03/04 23:43

>>101
sounds good sounds good

---

116 Name: 731 aka Train Man Post Date: 17/03/04 23:49

Me 'I'm really sorry for making it such a big deal on the train and
taking up so much of your time.'
LMH 'Please, it wasn't any big deal.'
Me 'On top of it all, I left before anybody.'
LMH 'We all left right after you. I talked with the older ladies about
you, Train Man.'
Me 'Whaaaaat?!?!'
LMH 'We all talked about what a courageous young man you were.'

We talked for a while using all sorts of words
But I'm just reporting the gist of what we talked about

120 Name: Anonymous Post Date: 17/03/04 23:50

I likey likey ------

139 Name: 731 aka Train Man Post Date: 17/03/04 23:54

Then I heard somebody's voice, probably her mother's, yell out from the distance
'The bath is ready!'

LMH 'Sorry. Just give me a second. (and she probably covered the phone with her hand) Later----!'
Me 'I can call back later'
LMH 'So sorry. I'll call you back later'
(Didn't ask whether it was all right or anything)

And then, I quickly returned to the thread to give a little report

146 Name: Anonymous Post Date: 17/03/04 23:56

Train, tho you may be a fugly techie you have the power, and the courage usually reserved for the in-crowd.
I bow in reverence.

(`A`) me here being a combo of fugly and a major chicken should probably be run over by a train or something

161 Name: 731 aka Train Man Post Date: 18/03/04 00:01

So I get the call

LMH 'I hope I didn't keep you waiting too long'
Me 'That was quick'
LMH 'I take quick baths'
Me 'I probably made you take a quick one. Sorry.'
LMH 'Don't worry so much'

So we continued talking like this with her being extra careful with her words not to make me uncomfortable with anything . . . or so it felt

I'm thinking about how best to steer the conversation towards my inviting her to dinner

187 Name: 731 aka Train Man Post Date: 18/03/04 00:18

>>79
Her specs	Which celeb does she look like? > don't know many celebs
Meeting place	Closest station so we can search> Anywhere along the Keihin Tohoku Line
Your specs	height weight, long legs or not, how do you dress usually? _⌐	

---

194 Name: Anonymous Post Date: 18/03/04 00:10

Honestly, re your specs
If you tell us for real and skip the asci stuff then we can give you some honest to goodness advice.

---

198 Name: 731 aka Train Man Post Date: 18/03/04 00:12

>>194
Height	172 centimetres
Weight	68 kilos
Dress	major puter nerd _⌐ |O

---

201 Name: Anonymous Post Date: 18/03/04 00:12

>>198
when you say major techie are you in jeans and sloppy shirt?
First thing, do you have a nice jacket?

---

215 Name: 731 aka Train Man Post Date: 18/03/04 00:16

>>201
You got me exactly.

And glasses. What does outer mean? (´・ω∵∵…

Let's hold off on the next step
Let me finish telling you what already transpired, the results

So we decided that we would have dinner together
Time and place are yet to be decided.

228 Name: Anonymous Post Date: 18/03/04 00:19

>>215
Leave it up to me. I used to dress like you so I've got it all covered.
Do you have a pair of somewhat straight and tight jeans? If you do, that's a keeper.
For your top just wear a light turtleneck and a jacket. That would be enough. Let me go google a few samples for you.

237 Name: Anonymous Post Date: 18/03/04 00:21

I think we need to pretty him up just a bit.

Dress for the occasion then you won't be too nervous about walking into the restaurant.

238 Name: Anonymous Post Date: 18/03/04 00:21

Couple of basics you need to keep in mind
-Cut your hair
-Iron the wrinkly clothes
-Don't go out with bed hair

That's about it. Don't know what your hair looks like now but you should go and get a haircut so you feel put together.

239 Name: 731 aka Train Man Post Date: 18/03/04 00:21

Thanks everybody.
I'll go out and buy some clothes

And for now, no pimples.

269 Name: Anonymous Post Date: 18/03/04 00:26

Here are some sites I studied in order to shed my techie-dom
Take a look and see

http://www.at-fashion.com/
http://www.exiare.net/
http://moc2002.cool.ne.jp

295 Name: 731 aka Train Man Post Date: 18/03/04 00:32

I think I maxed out coz I'm not absorbing any of you guys' words
_⌐|O
This is it for me tonight . . .

I feel bad coz I know my people are thinking it through for me
But I'm too tired.

299 Name: Anonymous Post Date: 18/03/04 00:33

>>295
good job. sleep well

300 Name: Anonymous Post Date: 18/03/04 00:33

Train, there's no need for you to listen to anybody other than yourself!
We're all here to support you so listen closely to yourself and just take our
comments with a grain of salt.

Regardless, good work.

301 Name: Anonymous Post Date: 18/03/04 00:33

good job
I'm sure you're all panicked inside but there's happiness in that, man.
Sweet dreams.

302 Name: Anonymous Post Date: 18/03/04 00:34

>>295
sleep well
you were amazing today (∕∀｀)

399 Name: Anonymous Post Date: 18/03/04 00:53

I'm just reading through the thread and trying to step into Train's shoes but
man, you know what, it's really difficult to incorporate women into your life.
I don't know if I could do it
The hurdles are many and way high

410 Name: Anonymous Post Date: 18/03/04 00:55

>>399
For Train, it's appeared to be easier than we thought, don't you think?
Honestly, I didn't think he was going to be able to ask her to dinner. Laters.

556 Name: Girl 1 Post Date: 18/03/04 10:01

How did Train Man invite her to dinner?
This here Girl 1 would like to quietly, from an all-good corner of my heart
offer some advice to Train Man.
Pologies if I'm way off.

'Thanks for the cups. They must have been really expensive.'
This shows that you are respectful of her actions, of her giving you an
Hermes teacup. Also, it provides an opportunity for her to peek into your
not quite understanding upmarket brands and such.

'Where do you usually go to dinner?'
'What do you want to eat' may be too direct.
Instead, you may want to ask the first question so you get an idea for what
she tends to like and then you can incorporate into the conversation on
the day.

If she answers and it's way beyond Train's territory then, 'Wow, I usually
don't get a chance to go to places like that so I have no idea what to
recommend. Do you know of any places?' And the ball will be in her
court.

If she gets uncomfortable about being in her territory (she could just not want to have to organise the evening so don't worry so much about it) just ask 'Do you have anything you can't eat?' and then 'I'll look around for a good place, But you know, I usually just go to bars with my friends so there's a slight chance that I may not come up with anywhere good. If that happens, can we look for a place together on the day?'
That said, you should definitely check out the area before your date so you have an idea about which restaurants are where. If possible, that is.

---

557 Name: Girl 1 Post Date: 18/03/04 10:01

'What time do you get off work?'
When you ask 'what do you want to do?' the answer is usually 'whatever you want' so it's best to ask questions that are easier to answer and steer the conversation forward.

(if she answers 'a little after six')
'Would meeting at XX at 7 work for you?' shows that you are being very sensitive to her schedule and at the same time it shows that you will not let her get away.

---

558 Name: Girl 1 Post Date: 18/03/04 10:01

Gotta tell you that from my past experiences . . .
1) Not too sexy when a guy is looking around helplessly in a restaurant. It made me think why hadn't this guy chosen a place he was comfortable in. So, combine the frayed nerves from a first date with the frayed nerves of walking into a restaurant you've never set foot in – and you're asking for trouble.
2) 'What do you wanna do?' is not a good question to ask because there's always an awkward silence that follows. Always ask questions that are easier to answer so the conversation keeps flowing.
3) Make sure you don't run out of things to talk about. When you call to arrange the date, make sure you understand that the phone call is not just about the date. You can't keep talking about the train incident forever and ever. Here's an example: 'You mentioned you often go out for Italian but what do you like? I haven't been to the real Italian restaurants so I don't know much about the food but remember back when tiramisu was all the rage? I ate a lot of tiramisu for sure.' It's best to not pretend like you know more than you do because it is bound to bite you in the arse. Stick with what you know.
     But if you really only stick to what you know, the conversation may

not go anywhere so you should do a little research online about some of the stuff she mentioned over the phone.

'You mentioned over the phone yesterday about xx but I think I saw it online as yy. Is that the same thing?'

Man I have so much I want to say but it's getting way too long. This is it for now. I'm gonna be cheering you on. Seriously,

---

559 Name: Anonymous Post Date: 18/03/04 10:07

>>558
I was floored by your posting. The detail. The involvement. Your kindness. Amazing job, you.

---

560 Name: Anonymous Post Date: 18/03/04 10:17

mornin dudes
So things have moved along here haven't they.
This thread has morphed into a warm fuzzy place from the old one where we kept getting shot down in flames. Trust you people are well.

---

561 Name: Anonymous Post Date: 18/03/04 10:25

>>560
losing weight nicely

---

562 Name: Anonymous Post Date: 18/03/04 11:17

>>560
Enveloped in a musky warmth with an endless supply of encouragement until one day you open your eyes and realise that you are a XXXXXX

---

563 Name: Anonymous Post Date: 18/03/04 11:21

>>561
XXXXXXXXXX

---

564 Name: Anonymous Post Date: 18/03/04 11:53

>562
Man, that's exactly me.
I was enjoying myself tracking the thread but this is no place for a real

Geek anymore. It's really turned into this thread where a cool boy and a girl get rescued from the scummy depths of our pond.

Every night Train Man appeared to report, blow-by-blow, his conversation with Lady Miss Hermes.

---

568 Name: 731 aka Train Man Post Date: 18/03/04 19:26

Thanks for staying up late for me (ɔД`)
Let me read the past postings. Be right back.

Do we need to discuss yesterday's phone call anymore?

---

576 Name: 731 aka Train Man Post Date: 18/03/04 19:54

>>534
＿|￣|

I read through all the postings and I grovel if I've neglected to answer some of your questions.

The general flow seems to be that I 'wear a suit and go for Italian' what do you think? I have to go get myself a suit ＿|￣|○

---

581 Name: 731 aka Train Man Post Date: 18/03/04 20:01

This is the first time I'm going out to eat with a girl so
I had no idea where I was supposed to take her . . . ＿|￣|○

To be honest, while I was talking on the phone with her, you guys right here in the thread were all the support I had.

---

608 Name: 731 aka Train Man Post Date: 18/03/04 20:33

t I had forced her to take a quick bath so I apologised
she said 'Really, my baths are usually this short'

I'm gonna return to my story
She and the older ladies talked about the incident on the train

'If he hadn't been there, really, who knows what could have happened'
'Most people just pretend they don't see what's happening so that was an amazing amount of courage it took for him to speak up.'

I don't remember much else _| ̄|....O))

I said 'I'm not sure whether I did the right thing or not. That old man may not have done anything if I had stayed silent and if that were the case none of us would have had to spend any time at the police station. I'm really sorry about all that.'

To which she replied
'You did what was right'
'I really am grateful'
'You risked your own life for strangers. That doesn't happen very often.'
'I told my parents and friends about it.'

Man, I really don't remember much else. _| ̄|

---

652 Name: Anonymous Post Date: 18/03/04 20:58

Being a bachelor myself, I'd like to be your big bro and help you out a bit.
How long has she been working?
What kind of company does she work for?

I'll give you some tips about clothes and restaurants depending on those answers.

---

674 Name: 731 aka Train Man Post Date: 18/03/04 21:14

>>652
Sales. It's her third year on the job.
I'm withdrawing money from my war chest so I think I should be fine.
Not that I have a fortune to spend . . .

676 Name: Anonymous Post Date: 18/03/04 21:16

>>674
got more info about her?

677 Name: Anonymous Post Date: 18/03/04 21:20

>>674
tell me your height and body type.

Your outfit will change accordingly . . .

678 Name: 731 aka Train Man Post Date: 18/03/04 21:20

>>676
I don't know much other than her name and address . . .
She said she would basically go anywhere
But she lives fairly close so we'll go somewhere in Tokyo

679 Name: 731 aka Train Man Post Date: 18/03/04 21:21

>>677
medium height and build suits me perfectly

gotta get to a barber too

680 Name: Anonymous Post Date: 18/03/04 21:22

>>679
Hairdresser! Make an appointment immediately!

681 Name: 731 aka Train Man Post Date: 18/03/04 21:22

>>679
not a barber but a hairdresser
not a barber but a hairdresser
not a barber but a hairdresser

not a barber but a hairdresser
not a barber but a hairdresser
not a barber but a hairdresser
not a barber but a hairdresser
not a barber but a hairdresser
not a barber but a hairdresser

---

687 Name: Anonymous Post Date: 18/03/04 21:24

>>679
You may have already seen it but

lots of sleep
go to hairdresser
clean the brows
clip the nose hairs
clean your ears
day of, shower in the morning (or evening), wash hair
make sure you wash your little willy just in case
xtra mint tablets
packet of tissues and a handkerchief
charge the mobile
keep phone number and address of restaurant on your person
toothpaste
good amount of cash, maybe £100–200
blot oil from face

---

739 Name: Anonymous Post Date: 18/03/04 21:47

Survey
What do you think Train Man should do.
Please answer each of the following.

-Outfit
-Dinner
-How to prepare
-What to take with
-Topics of conversation, day of

812 Name: Anonymous Post Date: 18/03/04 23:06

There's a fairly inexpensive Italian restaurant in Ginza that has pretty good food.
It's got a funny name so . . . well, if you want to use it on your follow-up dates, that'd be cool
http://gourmet.yahoo.co.jp/gourmet/restaurant/Kanto/Tokyo/guide/0202/P000999.html

814 Name: Anonymous Post Date: 18/03/04 23:11

>>812
That name is perfect for me (´–`)

815 Name: Anonymous Post Date: 18/03/04 23:11

What's the story behind that name???

853 Name: Mr Anonymous Post Date: 19/03/04 02:53

Preparations Flow Chart

Day Before
Put tomorrow's outfit on a hanger. From underwear to jacket. All of it.
Febreeze it.
Prepare all personal hygiene items: tissue, handkerchief, mints, oil paper to blot oil.
Can place items in trouser pocket if need be.
↓
charge your mobile (put restaurant number in phone memory)
↓
go to bed early (try to get 8 hours sleep)

Day Of
Wake up, take a shower
Wash body, head, face. Use Men's Biore for the face. Don't rub too hard. Skin gets too red.
If you shave with a razor then this is when you need to shave.
↓
have a light meal
↓

face care
align the brows, clip nose hair, clean the ears, check for eye goop
if you use electric shavers, this is when you shave. Don't forget to use
aftershave.
↓
style the hair
↓

change. If you use cologne, this is when you splash some on. Just a bit on
the stomach. Don't go overboard on the wrists and neck.
↓
Ready to go (check that you have your mobile and wallet. Prepare for
worst case, memorise her number, know it by heart).

---

888 Name: Anonymous Post Date: 19/03/04 13:47

♀ here, thinking that denim and a simple Comme Ça top and jacket
would be fine. First buy a pair of jeans you plan on wearing to the date
(like the one that was recommended earlier) and then go to the shop
and say 'I want a shirt and jacket to match these jeans, nothing too
ostentatious' and I'm sure they'll give you a few options. You'll probably
go through the same headaches for your follow-up dates so might as well
get a couple of tops. You can't help but prefer one style over the other but
I think you should push for something slightly different from your usual
style! Sorry to babble. Go Train Go!

---

114 Name: 731 aka Train Man Post Date: 20/03/04 01:12

**Sorry I'm late. I was spending some time preparing and doing some
research.
By the way, I have not called Lady Miss Hermes today.**

**I will follow up yesterday's story a bit later
I'm basically close to forgetting most of it by now . . .**

---

127 Name: 731 aka Train Man Post Date: 20/03/04 01:27

**In order for me to steer the conversation towards inviting her to
dinner I had the mantra 'dinner in return for the cups' from this thread
running through my mind.**

So I said
'The cups you gave me must have been really expensive. You really shouldn't have'

'Don't worry I have an "in" at work.
It looks like I've made you worry about it unnecessarily.
I'm sorry,' answered Lady Miss Hermes

I thought this was my chance.
'It sounds weird to say "in return for the cups" but I'd like to invite you to . . . rghfnmmb njioio'

choked big time. ＿「｜O

---

129 Name: Anonymous Post Date: 20/03/04 01:29

>>127
sweet (*´∀`*)

---

134 Name: 731 aka Train Man Post Date: 20/03/04 01:35

Lady Hermes said 'What?'

How else could she have responded.

So I repeated myself.
'Umm . . . how about dinner . . . could I take you out to dinner'
Can't remember the exact words but it went something like this.

'You don't have to be so conscientious you know, it wasn't a big deal' ＿「｜O

what-can-I-do popped into my mind

'Well . . . aaaaa . . .'
There may have been a few seconds of silence.

'If you agree to split, then I'd be happy to'
'What?'
I couldn't help but react like a droopy dog ⊥⌐O

---

137 Name: Anonymous Post Date: 20/03/04 01:36

>>134
me like da way it sounds

---

138 Name: Anonymous Post Date: 20/03/04 01:36

>>134

da train is here------------!!!!

---

139 Name: Anonymous Post Date: 20/03/04 01:37

>>134
train's here-- ─*˚ ゜*:.｡..｡.:*˚ (ﾟ∀ﾟ)゜*:.｡. .｡.:*˚ ゜*─!!!!!

---

143 Name: 731 aka Train Man Post Date: 20/03/04 01:42

'When you say split . . .'
I asked even though I knew what she was talking about

'I'd feel bad if you had to pay so . . . what do you say?'

I was about to
Ahyeah-----!!!!
────(´∀`)･ω･) ﾟД゜)ﾟ∀゜)･∀･)￣ー ̄)´_ゝ`)-_)゜∋゜)´Д`)゜- ̄)────!!!!」

Wanted to scream out loud but I did my best to keep it down and
typed with one hand to report back to the thread. I just wanted to let
you guys know pronto

'Are you sure?'
'We're splitting ok'
'Thank you sofyueuyukj much'
I bowed and bowed holding myself together the best I could

'When do you want to meet?'
'Whenever is good with me'
My response would have come under 'desperate' had this been a
2-Ch exchange

168 Name: 731 aka Train Man Post Date: 20/03/04 02:02

'So I guess we should shoot for Saturday or Sunday' was Lady
Hermes' preferred schedule

'That sounds ok with me'
I'd make time for it wheneva but still, had to say something.

'Then where shall we have dinner?'
'Ummmm . . .'
It was here that my mind went totally blank
I haven't even decided where yet __| ‾|O
I quickly turn to the thread and scroll through for any pointers and
then send an SOS signal

'Wherever is fine with me'
'Aaa . . . um . . . oohh k then . . .'
I wanted to shake myself out of it.

'Ask if she has any likes or dislikes, food-wise' I read in the thread. So
I just spoke without giving it much further thought.

'Do you have any likes or dislikes?'
'I can't do really spicy . . .'
'Umm . . . well . . .'

And time slipped away just like that . . . __|‾ |

174 Name: 731 aka Train Man Post Date: 20/03/04 02:13

That's right. There was no need for me to decide everything right
away. I was so nervous I couldn't even work that out.

'Well then, could I call you back when I work out where we should
eat?'

'Sure, no problem.'
'I'll look for a non-spicy place.'
'All right.'

We laughed a bit, or at least I think we did.

'If we're talking Saturday/Sunday then how about next weekend?'
'Sure.'
'All right. I'll call you again to confirm.'
'I'll wait to hear from you.'

And that's how it ended. After which I was completely drained of all energy. ＿｜￣｜○

---

193 Name: Black Ship Post Date: 20/03/04 02:26

I got back late today and it took so much time just read through all the postings to catch up.

I see that things are definitely moving in the right direction for Train Man. Even if she made you promise to split the bill, I think you should excuse yourself to go to the bathroom and quickly pay the bill.
When Lady Hermes realises and says 'you promised we'd split today' answer that by saying 'I was the one that asked you out' to which she would reply 'You'll have to let me pay next time.'

That 'next' means that you could go to another place for drinks immediately after or maybe arrange for another date on another day.

---

213 Name: Anonymous Post Date: 20/03/04 02:33

>>198
I don't know, dude. I mean she was the one who insisted on splitting and you agreed to the conditions so you paying for it may make her overthink the situation, create uneasiness? No?
Well it also depends on how much dinner is . . .

---

219 Name: Anonymous Post Date: 20/03/04 02:35

Even if you have talked over the phone, Train and Hermes are still strangers.

On top of that, Train saved her from a drunken pervert.
Regardless of the teacups, I think splitting is the standard way to go.

The Geeks go on for a while fired up over the splitting vs paying debate. Train Man leaves to go and say goodbye to his techie outfit and welcome in a new train.

---

233 Name: Anonymous Post Date: 20/03/04 02:40

She has class, this woman. She sent him a thank you gift. Said that she would rather pay for herself. If he pays, she's going to feel weird about it.

---

306 Name: Anonymous Post Date: 20/03/04 03:19

Date Dialogue Forecast

Type 1
Train Man 'I thought Hermes made bags but they make cups too?'
Hermes 'There are a lot of other things as well.'
TM 'Do they make clothes and accessories for men too?'
H 'Sure they do. Would you like to see their catalogue?'
T 'Sure. How about next week?'

Scored another date!

Type 2
TM 'Thank you so much for the pretty cups. I almost feel like I shouldn't use them.'
H giggles 'I'm just glad that you liked them'
TM 'Speaking of cups, do you usually drink tea or coffee?'
H 'I like tea so yes, I drink tea usually.'
TM 'Do you make tea yourself?'
H 'Yes. There are delicious teas out there.'
TM 'I usually make instant coffee. If you don't mind, could you show me where I can get good tea leaves?'
H 'Sure. When do you want to go?'
TM 'How about next week?'

Scored another date!

Working with the info we have right now, we can guide him pretty well with these simulations.

307 Name: Anonymous Post Date: 20/03/04 03:21

>>306
you sound like you're havin fun dude

361 Name: Anonymous Post Date: 20/03/04 13:04

I think that since Train Main invited her out to dinner because he thought that the teacups were expensive, he should pay.
If Hermes seems uncomfortable then she can pay for drinks.
If you mention 'I rarely get the opportunity to go out with women' as a reason for paying, then I would definitely pull back. I'd think about what you'd be like if you had the opportunity, you know. I think that since the teacups are the main event you shouldn't mention the opportunity stuff.

435 Name: Anonymous Post Date: 20/03/04 18:23

When's Train getting home?

443 Name: 731 aka Train Man Post Date: 20/03/04 21:12

Just got back . . . (ﾟдﾟ)
Tired . . . ＿|￣|○

I've never spent so much money on clothes
First time using my credit card too

Was charged £30 for my haircut. What da hell is that about . . .
＿|￣|,,,,,,,,,,O))
Though I look kinda hip
Clothes-wise I'm set because the assistant helped me choose

Did you know that you need your insurance card
to get contact lenses made? ＿|￣|

Let me go read the log. Laters.

464 Name: 731 aka Train Man Post Date: 20/03/04 21:48

I had so many bags that I had to come home to drop them off and headed out again. I'm exhausted . . . but I really do feel like I've transformed.
From a long way off you probably couldn't tell that I was a techie. These contacts are so thin

I also went to the restaurant we picked.
The Japanese creative cuisine place recommended in the thread.
Major yum (ﾟдﾟ)

I asked one of the in crowd at work to recommend a hair salon
I was so embarrassed . . . ＿|￣|○
But my hairstyle would definitely not have been possible at the barbershop
First time I've ever had my hair cut this short
My head feels kinda floaty

To hell with the expense ＿|￣|

---

465 Name: Anonymous Post Date: 20/03/04 22:49

>>464
Hey, have you ever worn contacts before?
I don't know if you should be going on a date after only one week with the new contacts.

---

473 Name: Anonymous Post Date: 20/03/04 22:53

What kind of outfit did you buy?
Give us a link

---

475 Name: 731 aka Train Man Post Date: 20/03/04 22:54

>>465
You serious . . .
Push comes to shove, I'll go without my glasses

>>461

I think I still look techie

I'm gonna stick to splitting the bill since we agreed on that already.

---

481 Name: 731 aka Train Man Post Date: 20/03/04 23:03

>>469
>>472
Decided to combine the opinions posted here and the assistant's suggestions

Grey leather-like jacket
Long-sleeved black top (add a shirt and sweatshirt and divide by 2)
Pair of jeans and trousers to match the jacket
Black socks
Big and hard shoes

That be it

I asked the hairdresser to make me look cool
And off my hair went, supa short (´·ω·`)
I can't describe it well

---

485 Name: Anonymous Post Date: 20/03/04 23:06

'big and hard shoes'
that's a strange description
details please

---

493 Name: 731 aka Train Man Post Date: 20/03/04 23:15

>>485
I guess they look like leather shoes
a little different looking
matches the outfit. Yep, I think so.

Didn't know that you could buy shoes at clothes shops these days . . .

506 Name: 731 aka Train Man Post Date: 20/03/04 23:32

>>494
I got the jacket at Comme Ça Du Mode. This one was the priciest.
_|‾|O
Other stuff from Uniqlo.

---

545 Name: Anonymous Post Date: 21/03/04 00:21

I commend you brave soldier for going out in the hail and pouring rain to
get your shoes, clothes and a haircut to boot.

Finally, Train Man seals the deal with Hermes

---

604 Name: Train Man ◆ nm4g8qV1Cg Post Date: 21/03/04 22:01

Ready to seal deal. I'm gonna call her now.

---

605 Name: Anonymous Post Date: 21/03/04 22:02

>>604
You can do it dude!

610 Name: Anonymous Post Date: 21/03/04 22:05

His post is giving off a different aura. I can feel it.
There's no wimpishness there and it looks like he got more confident by
changing the way he looks.

---

617 Name: Train Man ◆ nm4g8qV1Cg Post Date: 21/03/04 22:18

Ok. Just hung up.
Deal has been sealed (;´Д`) **huffpuff** (;´    Д`) **huffpuff**
(;´   Д `) **huffpufff**
But I was still really nervous _|‾|O

622 Name: Train Man ◆ nm4g8qV1Cg Post Date: 21/03/04 22:29

Let me report while it's still fresh in my memory
'Hellowww, sorry for calling so late . . .'
'Hi there, good evening.'

'About dinner, what would you say to Japanese?'
'Sure, of course.'

'Great.'
'Japanese cuisine suits your vibe.'

'Really?'
'Yes.'

'I'm gonna get dressed up but I don't want you to make fun of
me . . .' _⌐|O
'What? You're dressing up?'

'Yes, but I don't want you to expect too much.'
'Really? Well then I GUESS I'LL GET DRESSED UP TOO'

'Sorry to make you feel that way on account of my . . .'
'Don't worry about it so much'

Something like that . . .
I may have messed up a bit . . . _⌐|O

---

623 Name: Anonymous Post Date: 21/03/04 22:30

>>622
No, it sounds real good. For real, Train Man rising.

---

624 Name: Anonymous Post Date: 21/03/04 22:30

Rising for Hermes

---

632 Name: Anonymous Post Date: 21/03/04 22:34

Sounds like your integrity or strength of character is what's doing the
business.

I mean Hermes is already convinced of it to begin with.
I'm getting excited about the date!

---

636 Name: Train Man ◆ nm4g8qV1Cg Post Date: 21/03/04 22:38

Really? You think I did ok?
I thought I dropped so many clangers.
Phew! Thanks, as always.

---

641 Name: Train Man ◆ nm4g8qV1Cg Post Date: 21/03/04 22:48

Thanks people. Really. Really. Thank you.
I'm gonna try my best.

---

651 Name: Anonymous Post Date: 21/03/04 22:58

Man oh man. It's like
Train Man Mega-Rising

---

652 Name: Train Man ◆ nm4g8qV1Cg Post Date: 21/03/04 23:00

Honestly, I haven't really thought about going out, you know,
girlfriend-boyfriend like with Lady Miss Hermes or anything. Though
it is true that I kind of think of it as a 'gotta grab this or I'll never get
another chance at it' type of thing

But I have these feelings for her already
When I heard her voice just now, I felt something that wasn't
nervousness
I'm pretty sure I'm gonna fall for her if I see her . . . ⌐ |○

She could already have a boyfriend
In that case I could be asking for trouble if I fall for her
Kinda tough

660 Name: Anonymous Post Date: 21/03/04 23:06

Train Man, you are shinin
You are no longer a Geek. Don't change what you are.
Don't try too hard to be something you're not and just have a fun night
with Lady Miss Hermes.
Look at it this way. Meeting her gave you the chance to change.
And don't ever come back here, you get me.
Good luck.

666 Name: Train Man ◆ nm4g8qV1Cg Post Date: 21/03/04 23:11

Thank you everybody. Reading your posts I end up feeling
stronger and more confident, like things are going to work out just
fine.

I gotta thank you guys and go suss out my feelings!

667 Name: Anonymous Post Date: 21/03/04 23:12

Train Man seems so sincere and is really . . . budding
Are you going to the place I suggested?
I'm really cheering you on so keep at it!
My instinct says that Lady Hermes already quite attracted to you
I don't think she's going out with you because she couldn't say no on
account of some unwritten social law

677 Name: Anonymous Post Date: 21/03/04 23:17

Watching Train Man, I realise that

it's what's on the inside that counts
not that Train's ugly or anything

759 Name: Anonymous Post Date: 22/03/04 15:47

I think somebody mentioned this earlier but our Train does not need any of
our run of the mill advice anymore.
He's back on track.
Everyone's being so overprotective. So kind.

893 Name: 731 aka Train Man Post Date: 24/03/04 22:36

Hiya. Been a while.
I'm ready to roll. I'm now deep in make-over land as I prepare for the day.

Some of you offered to put the info together for me but
I've already been doing that myself, so thanks.

I wonder if I'll get any sleep the day before.

987 Name: Train Man ◆ SgHguKHEFY Post Date: 26/03/04 14:03

ello-ello. I got a half day today.
I'm feeling jittery . . . ＿「 ｜O

The cool guy at work gave me some guide he thought would come
in handy on the date.

125 Name: Anonymous Post Date: 27/03/04 13:18

wonderin when Mr trainman is gonna pay us a visit . . .
a-wonderin' o(・∀・o)o(・∀・)o(o・∀・)o a-wonderin'

126 Name: Train Man ◆ SgHguKHEFY Post Date: 27/03/04 14:16

just woke up. Will start preparing now

128 Name: Anonymous Post Date: 27/03/04   14:19

preparing must mean that it's today?

129 Name: Train Man ◆ SgHguKHEFY Post Date: 27/03/04 14:21

Today. From now. Few more hours ghiuliliuhjy

150 Name: Train Man ◆ SgHguKHEFY Post Date: 27/03/04 17:53

I'm ready to go.

I wanted to thank everybody for being there for me, the doomed Geek.
I owe it to you guys. Your words of encouragement and
support are what gave me the strength to go for it. Seems like I've only
been here for a flash in time but it also feels like a long, long time.
I will report back when I return.

Laters.

Our techie, age = years without a girlfriend, virgin is ready to go. Will God
smile down on him?

Mission
2

I'll Just Hold on Tightly to You

Unable to contain their nervous energy as they waited for Train Man's return, the Geeks' imaginations run amok and just when they are ready to explode, Train Man returns. And slowly but surely he starts dropping the bombs.

168 Name: Anonymous Post Date: 27/03/04 19:52

Train 'How is it? Is it good?'
Hermes 'Yes. It's got great ambience too. Do you Mr Trainman always eat at places like this?'
Train 'I guess so'
Hermes (blushing) 'How nice'

169 Name: Anonymous Post Date: 27/03/04 19:53

A Geek Mind Trip

Hermes 'Thanks for today. I had a great time.'
Train Man 'The pleasure was all mine. I had a great time too.'
H (giggling) 'Oh, look at the time.'
TM 'Sorry, it got pretty late didn't it.'
H 'It's all right (giggle) Well good night then.'
TM 'Hold on . . . !!'
H 'What?'
TM 'Don't go yet!'
H (!?)
TM 'I don't want to let you go'
H 'What do you mean . . .'
TM '. . . . .'
H '. . . . .'
TM ' . . . . I . . . . . . I . . . . . . love you.'
H '. . . . . . do you really mean it?'
TM 'Sure I do.'
H '. . . I'm a woman with not much to give.'
TM 'That's not true.'
H 'I'm not even that pretty.'
TM 'You are the cutest of the cute.'

170 Name: Anonymous Post Date: 27/03/04 19:54

H 'I'm not a good conversationalist like you are.'
TM 'Your voice is most charming.'

H 'I'm older than you . . .'
TM 'Age has no say in love'
H 'I'm a terrible cook.'
TM 'I'll eat anything you cook.'
H 'I get jealous easily and am deeply distrustful.'
TM 'I swear to you. You are the only one in my sight.'
H 'I dream of weddings all the time.'
TM 'We can get married tomorrow.'
H ' . . . .'
TM 'Hermes . . . . . . I'm being serious'
H '. . . . .'
TM 'Mm? Hermes?'

Hermes jumps into Train Man's arms.
H (wailing) 'Train Man!'
TM 'What happened?'
H 'Don't be so impervious! You must know that I like you too!'
TM '. . . . . . Hermes?'
H '. . . . . . I'm happy! I've thought about nothing but you since that incident.'
TM '. . . . . . let's . . . the two of us . . . walk the path of life together.'

---

180 Name: Anonymous Post Date: 27/03/04 20:29

Right about now Train Man is doing a little bit of this and little bit of that

---

194 Name: Anonymous Post Date: 27/03/04 21:11

('A`) arghhhhhhhhhhwoooooooaaaaaaa

---

195 Name: Anonymous Post Date: 27/03/04 21:14

Medic!!!
The pre-battle pressure has pushed him off the deep end!
Take him away! Now!

---

263 Name: Anonymous Post Date: 27/03/04 22:58

Could . . . it . . . be . . .
While we all root for him on 2-Ch ova here . . .
That it could all be going really really well . . . and . . .
There's no way . . . it . . . could . . . possibly . . . happen . . . no?

---

277 Name: Train Man ◆ SgHguKHEFY Post Date: 27/03/04 23:18

Just got home.
First, let me go get changed (·∀·)

---

279 Name: Anonymous Post Date: 27/03/04 23:18

The train has arrived ───(˚∀˚)─── !!!!

280 Name: Anonymous Post Date: 27/03/04 23:19

All aboard ───────(˚∀˚)─────── !!!!!

---

296 Name: Train Man ◆ SgHguKHEFY Post Date: 04/03/27 23:28

I'm back.
First off, results: massive success!
Will give all the details when my memory comes back.
And thanks, people.

---

299 Name: Anonymous Post Date: 27/03/04 23:30

Here he comes --------!!! Sexcess! Sexcess!!!
───(˚∀˚≡(˚∀˚≡˚∀˚)≡˚∀˚)───!!!!!!!!!!

301 Name: Anonymous Post Date: 27/03/04 23:30

Success is sexcess but is guesses nevertheless

308 Name: Anonymous Post Date: 27/03/04 23:31

Been a while since the last . . . air raid! Air raid! Comrades, take your
positions!!!!

310 Name: Anonymous Post Date: 27/03/04 23:32

Into the dugouts NOW!!!!!

314 Name: Anonymous Post Date: 27/03/04 23:32

I could die just about now.
Excuse me for living.

---

318 Name: Anonymous Post Date: 27/03/04 23:34

Man, why are my eyes watering? Why salt water? Why oh why oh
why!?!?!

---

331 Name: Anonymous Post Date: 27/03/04 23:38

```
                    (´･ω･`)
                    (´･ω･`)
                    (´･ω･`)
                    (´･ω･`)
                    (´･ω･`)
                    (´･ω･`)
                    (´･ω･`)
                    (´･ω･`)
                    (´･ω･`)
      ∧＿∧         (´･ω･`)
    (´･ω･)  (´･ω･`)          Please feel free to use them. I bought tons ...
    ／ヽO==O(´･ω･`)
    ／  ‖_｜(´･ω･`)
    L'(　))　(　))　(　))
```

---

341 Name: Train Man ◆ SgHguKHEFY Post Date: 27/03/04 23:41

Well, sexcess it ain't.

We arranged to meet at 8 pm at the station. It usually takes about an hour
from my house to the station so I gave myself 2 hours. Sure enough, I got
there an hour early and ended up waiting for her for an hour.

As 8 pm approached, I got more and more nervous.
She's a no-show at 8.
She turned up five minutes later. I saw her in the distance.

From the moment I saw her, she picked up speed and quickly walked towards me.
Man, I'm forgetting already

---

347 Name: Anonymous Post Date: 27/03/04 23:43

>341

```
∧＿∧   My heart's a-
( ・∀・)    thumpin'
( ∪ ∪
と__)_)
```

---

364 Name: Train Man ◆ SgHguKHEFY Post Date: 27/03/04 23:49

'I'm so sorry I'm late,' were the first words out of her mouth
To which I replied, 'No worries, no worriezzmng,'
Maybe I was a bit funny. My nerves were crazy.
She was and, dude, I mean she really was a lot cuter than I remembered her . . .
AND SHE REALLY DRESSED UP FOR THE OCCASION . . .
looked a lot younger than I remembered, too.
Quite girly. I could say blooming . . .
Then I said, 'Hello. It's nice to see you again,' and she gave a bow.
'It's nice to see you, too, and thank you so much for the other day.'
I bowed back.

---

379 Name: Anonymous Post Date: 27/03/04 23:54

Hey, where is da bunker?
Where oh where is dat thannnng
I is gettin shot down!!!!

---

383 Name: Train Man ◆ SgHguKHEFY Post Date: 27/03/04 23:57

When we'd got that over with, we decided to head for the restaurant. I was crazy nervous about walking alongside a woman.

When I walked at my usual pace, she ended up a few steps behind. Women walk slower than men. This is news to me. All I know is I felt kind of uneasy trying to pace myself, making sure I was walking in step with her.

Not only that, but the idea of someone like her walking with someone like me . . . I kept thinking everybody was looking at me and thinking about how weird we must look together . . .

I talked with her on the way to the restaurant but I only remember one thing . . .

---

390 Name: Anonymous Post Date: 27/03/04 23:59

Didja brush up against her hand! Didja? Didja? Didja?

---

395 Name: Anonymous Post Date: 28/03/04 00:01

I'll sit back, relax and listen to some cheesy love songs while I wait . . .

---

398 Name: Anonymous Post Date: 28/03/04 00:02

>>395
Stop it! You know they're death-traps for the single Geek!!!!

---

417 Name: Train Man ◆ SgHguKHEFY Post Date: 28/03/04 00:11

What I remember are her words. She said, 'With you, I feel protected on the train.' The moment she said this, I felt my heart skip a beat.

Apparently, women are a bit afraid of taking trains, especially during the crowded morning commute. Take for example that old drunk from the other night. But with me by her side, she said she feels protected. I came out with a stupid whiny laugh. No way could I come up with something cooler to say . . . ⌐|O

We got off the train, left the station and walked towards the restaurant. There were tons of people around the station. Saturdays, I guess. I kept one step ahead of her but kept turning around to make sure she was behind me. I must have been turning around every 15 seconds. It occurred to me then that I've always walked behind people. Never ahead. It was weird to be walking ahead.

---

420 Name: Anonymous Post Date: 28/03/04 00:12

'With you, I feel protected on the train.'
Quote numero uno. Decided.

---

439 Name: Train Man ◆ SgHguKHEFY Post Date: 28/03/04 00:21

'Boy it's crowded today, isn't it?'
'I suppose it's because of the weekend.'
We made our way through the crowd.

I kept turning around to check she was behind me.
She noticed and said, 'Don't worry so much.'
To which I wittily replied 'Really?' _⌐|O
THEN she said
'I'LL JUST HOLD ON TO YOU TIGHTLY'
and reached for my wrist.
I was so freaked out that my body twitched in response. _⌐|⌐
This could very well be the first time a woman actually touched me . . .
And what's that softness all about . . .

'Oops, I'm sorry'

She let go of my wrist as soon as she felt my body twitch.

---

440 Name: Anonymous Post Date: 28/03/04 00:21

ahyeah ahyeah------ ───────(ˇ∀ˇ)─────── !!!!!

---

441 Name: Anonymous Post Date: 28/03/04 00:22

Ok. I'll just hold on tightly to you.

Risingggggggg

450 Name: Anonymous Post Date: 28/03/04 00:23

```
  /‾‾‾‾‾‾‾‾‾‾‾‾‾‾‾‾‾‾‾‾‾‾‾‾‾‾‾‾‾‾‾‾‾
 | Upham! Upham! I need more bullets! Uphaaaaaaaaaaaaaaaaaam!
  \‾‾‾‾‾‾‾‾‾‾‾‾‾‾‾‾‾‾‾‾‾‾‾‾‾‾‾‾‾‾‾
              V
                          /‾‾‾‾\ Mr No Bulletman
     /\       _./‾‾\     |___|
    /  \   |\/ _ \ |      |∩(・∀・;||￢
   /    |\/_\ `\ |   (`д`; ||￢  _ｪ_Ⅱ
  /      |     |( " つつ[三三 _[------°
 /          \__/ \\ \    ||
/          |      ] \_)_)..|||
```

---

456 Name: Anonymous Post Date: 28/03/04 00:25

```
              (´A`)(´A`)
              (´A`)(´A`)
              (´A`)(´A`))
              (´A`)(´A`)
              (´A`)(´A`)
            (´A`)(´A`)
  ∧＿∧     (´A`)(´A`)
 ( ´・д・)   (´A`)(´A`)    I've brought you tons of ammo. Feel free to use
 /＼O==O (´A`)(´A`)              as much as you like
/  ||_  |(´A`)(´A`)
L'  ()) ̄ ()) ̄ ()
```

---

458 Name: Anonymous Post Date: 28/03/04 00:26

I can't keep up with the demand …

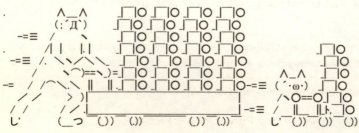

459 Name: Anonymous Post Date: 28/03/04 00:26

Even after the reconstruction, in the end, a Geek desperate to be a Train
hides inside.

525 Name: Train Man ◆ SgHguKHEFY Post Date: 28/03/04 00:57

'Oh, no. I'm sorry. It's all right'
It was too late by the time I said this.
'No, it's my fault for grabbing you so suddenly.'
Well, could you please grab my hand. Or better still, hold my hand, I
wanted to say. ＿￢|O
In the end she never grabbed my hand after that. ＿￢|.............O))

We get to the restaurant. Of course since I made a reservation, we
glide right in.
It feels cool to walk through a crowded room. (·∀·)
Once we're sat down she says
'this place has great ambience.'
'It's nice isn't it. I like it too.'
Sorry. It's only my second time there. ＿￢|

The menu arrived and she asked
'What do you recommend?'
So I recommended what I ordered the last time I was there.
Since I thought it tasted all right in a basic kinda way.

526 Name: Anonymous Post Date: 28/03/04 00:59

(·∀·) and then and then

527 Name: Anonymous Post Date: 28/03/04 00:59

>>525
keep it goin' man, keep it goin' . . . (´Д`) all right, you're movin it along. I'll
shut up now.

531 Name: Anonymous Post Date: 28/03/04 01:01

I've got no probs cheering Train on for some reason . . .

532 Name: Anonymous Post Date: 28/03/04 01:01

Everybody, this is what a date is
Everybody, this is what a date is

540 Name: Train Man ◆ SgHguKHEFY Post Date: 28/03/04 01:14

We were ordering our drinks and when I ordered a beer she quickly took another look at the menu and ordered a beer too.

'Sorry. Didn't think you were going to drink.'
'No, no, sorry I must have forced you into a drink.'

No idea what we talked about while we waited for our food.
No surprises, she kept mentioning the train incident.
'Just as I thought, you are such an earnest guy.'
Or
'Are you the type that can't sit back when confronted by some kind of "wrong" behaviour?'
I think it went something like that.
Once the food came out,
'This is delicious'
and stuff like that . . . hmm, don't know if I managed to keep the conversation jumping . . .

552 Name: Anonymous Post Date: 28/03/04 01:23

Damn that Lady Miss Hermes sounds like a find, dude!
Rise.

563 Name: Train Man ◆ SgHguKHEFY Post Date: 28/03/04 01:31

There's some heavy stuff coming up so let me get it straight.

566 Name: Anonymous Post Date: 28/03/04 01:31

Did she comment at all on how well dressed Train Man was?

574 Name: Train Man ◆ SgHguKHEFY Post Date: 28/03/04 01:34

>>566
slipped my mind ＿｢｜Ｏ
'Hmm. You look a little different?'
or something like that. When we were moving about.
I said
'Yes . . . I did my very best'
I figured I had to reply. At least
She replied 'I think it's a good look.'

587 Name: Train Man ◆ SgHguKHEFY Post Date: 28/03/04 01:43

After we scoffed our food
'Do you come to places like this a lot?' she said. We were done with
the food and it was turning into a we're gonna talk kind of vibe,
weighing heavily on me as she glanced over, making me mad
nervous . . .
'It's only recently that I've taken an interest in places like this' I came
clean.
'Really? I love hunting around for places like this,' she replied.
'Is this the kind of place that's hot nowadays?'
I think some of the info from the guide came in handy . . . I think?
She started talking about some restaurants she liked.

Apparently she likes searching for hip new restaurants.
Maybe that's just a chick thing?

But one of her best mates who she used to go restaurant hopping
with just got a boyfriend so she hardly ever goes out anymore. So she
really enjoyed her time out with me, she said.

592 Name: Anonymous Post Date: 28/03/04 01:44

>>587
sssssssssssssshit
da vibe is too good it's makin we wanna puke blood. ('A`) arrrrgh

593 Name: Anonymous Post Date: 28/03/04 01:45

>she really enjoyed her time out with me
>she really enjoyed her time out with me
>she really enjoyed her time out with me
>she really enjoyed her time out with me

goodvibesgalo--------------re ——————(ﾟ∀ﾟ)———— !!!!!

---

605 Name: Train Man ◆ SgHguKHEFY Post Date: 28/03/04 01:54

We were finally getting used to chatting but the place was really
crowded. There was a slight shift in the air that seemed to point at
the commotion in the place and she seemed to sense it. 'Well shall
we,' she said and called the waiter over.
I didn't know what I was hoping for but inside I was let down thinking
that the night was going to end . . . or so I thought.
When the waiter came over she said
'I only have large bills so let me just pay for it' and quickly took
care of the bill. My plan was to quickly slide my big bill over to her
but . . .
'I'll pay you for my portion later then' I told her.

After we left the restaurant, we started walking to nowhere in
particular not saying anything. I tried to suss out whether she was
thinking of going home.
We walked for a while then
'It's still early isn't it?' she said.

Inside, I was all
Ahyeah------! ———ヽ(ヽ(ﾟ∀ﾟヽ(ﾟ∀ﾟヽ(ﾟ∀ﾟ)/ﾟ∀ﾟ)/ﾟ∀ﾟ)/ﾟ)/))/———!!!!

---

606 Name: Anonymous Post Date: 28/03/04 01:55

mo and mo goodvibes comin at yaaaaaaaaaa
————(ﾟ∀ﾟ)———— !!!!!

616 Name: Anonymous Post Date: 28/03/04 02:00

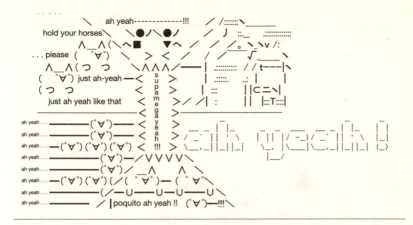

627 Name: Train Man ◆ SgHguKHEFY Post Date: 28/03/04 02:09

I checked my watch and it was only a bit after 9.
I asked her 'Um, do you have a curfew?' I thought I was being considerate.
'Aha-hah-hah' she laughed. ＿冂○
But I got to see her smile so it was all good.
'I'm way past curfew age but thanks for asking' she replied.
Damn it. Did it again. ＿冂￢

'There's a place nearby that I like. Do you want to go there for a bit?'
ahyeah comin atcha! ─────────(ﾟ∀ﾟ)───────── !!!
'Sure. That'd be great.'
So off we went.
'Let me pay my share for dinner' I said and handed her about 70% of the total bill. She took it and said
'This is a little too much' and gave some back
'But I was the one that asked you out . . .' I said, urging her to keep it.
'I guess you won't listen even if I argue'
and she quickly (?) took all the money. I may have been too persistent.

637 Name: Anonymous Post Date: 28/03/04 02:13

It's ahhh . . . basically . . . the BEST possible dialogue innit?
Lady Miss Hermes just a little bit of the older lady and Train Man on his
tippy toes trying to act mature

A match hand-selected and hand-drawn. _|‾|O

641 Name: Anonymous Post Date: 28/03/04 02:16

Train Man, take me now.

663 Name: Train Man ◆ SgHguKHEFY Post Date: 28/03/04 02:24

Since we were already full we went to this place where we would be
able to just do drinks and snacks and man, this place was much
hipper-looking than where we had just come from. I thought I
wouldn't even be allowed in. She had been there a few times. I
thought that the place matched her vibe.

We sat down and looked through the menu. She was going to order
wine and some appetisers. I looked through the menu and couldn't
find anything I could order so I ended up with wine and a cheese
thing, both of which I'm not used to eating or drinking. _|‾|O

'This place is so cool-looking.'
I said it hoping to sound like I was admiring her taste.
'Yeah it is. I kind of like it here.'
She seemed to be enjoying herself. I was very uncomfortable. _|‾|

We milked the restaurant topic for as long as we could then
'Are you ever told that you look like a celebrity?' I asked, even though
I don't really know many.
'What? No, not really. But my friends say I look like a Moomin.'
I almost fell off my chair because cartoon characters are not
celebrities, I wanted to tell her but I kept it in.
'aaaaa . . .'
I made as if I was agreeing.
Moomin . . . hmmm . . . she may in fact, look like Moomin . . .

665 Name: Anonymous Post Date: 28/03/04 02:25

Moomin ahyeah!!!! ————(゚∀゚)———— !!!

666 Name: Anonymous Post Date: 28/03/04 02:25

Moomin-lookalike Lady Miss Eromes . . . pantpant

681 Name: Anonymous Post Date: 28/03/04 02:32

But my friends say I look like a Moomin

729 Name: Train Man ◆ SgHguKHEFY Post Date: 28/03/04 02:58

After the wine she looked like she was a bit drunk
I was feeling a bit drunk as well.

The conversation went back to the train incident
'What were you feeling at that moment? We were a bit pissed so the
questions were more to the point.
'Of course I was afraid.'
Said it just like it was . . . ＿「￣|○

Like I didn't care
'I'd like for all men to become like you'
I was gobsmacked, did not compute (　°д°)
'I'd also like to be more like you'

I couldn't work out why but I was getting nervous.
I always get embarrassed when people around me, my boss or any other guy say how they should be more like me.

It was past 2200 hours by now.
She may have sussed out that she wouldn't be getting any more conversation out of me so we paid the bill and left the restaurant.
We split the basically straight down the middle.

We walked towards the station. There were still loads of people out.
Weird but we didn't talk much on the way to the station.

750 Name: Train Man ◆ SgHguKHEFY Post Date: 28/03/04 03:10

We both got on the Keihin Tohoku Line. We were going in the same direction.
'I'm getting off at the next stop'
She lives here, I thought to myself.
'Thank you so much for today.'
'No, no, the pleasure is all mine.'

A little voice in me was saying I can't let it end like this but I had no idea how to suggest something more. I just couldn't. ＿┌ ○

The train was picking up speed. This is the end. Oh well, good while it lasted. Thoughts were swirling through my head. The doors opened
'Good night then'
She stepped off the train and onto the platform.
She turned around to wave.
The doors are closing. Just as they closed, I yelled out
'I'll call you again!'
I'm not sure if she heard me but she looked like she was nodding.

and that's all folks.

Train Man lies exhausted from the bombing campaign. Fellow Geeks line up for the relentless counter attack.

754 Name: Anonymous Post Date: 28/03/04 03:12

>>750
Man oh man, sounds like a film (*´∀`*) cough cough

756 Name: Anonymous Post Date: 28/03/04 03:12

>>750
like a soap opera

>I'll call you again

Probably better to say
'May I call you again?'
But if she nodded,
That's all that matters. (˘∀˘)

758 Name: Anonymous Post Date: 28/03/04 03:12

>>750
Did you call her when you got back?

765 Name: Train Man ◆ SgHguKHEFY Post Date: 28/03/04 03:14

I'm tired . . . ＿|￣|○
Thanks everybody for hangin with me

>>758
I didn't call . . .
coz I wasn't sure if she had heard me

Does this mean it's over maybe?

775 Name: Anonymous Post Date: 28/03/04 03:16

>>765
Can you let it end this way?
What do you feel in your heart?

It's late. Why don't you sleep on it?

778 Name: Train Man ◆ SgHguKHEFY Post Date: 28/03/04 03:17

>>775

_⌐|O

---

798 Name: Anonymous Post Date: 28/03/04 03:21

I think somebody mentioned this earlier but
dressing up and going to dinner with a girl
in itself is a step up, you know.
It's not like you're pushing it too far to begin with.

If you want to get closer to Lady Miss Hermes then
you can move it up a notch later.
You can do it dude. Good job.

---

807 Name: Anonymous Post Date: 28/03/04 03:24

>Train Man
You definitely have to call her tomorrow!
You got to get another date with her!
It's the man's job to ask women on dates.
That is a moral obligation as well as a rule!!!!

---

810 Name: Train Man ◆ SgHguKHEFY Post Date: 28/03/04 03:25

I tried to tell her that I wanted to see her again but
I couldn't . . .
Not with her right in front of my face . . . _⌐ |O

---

811 Name: Anonymous Post Date: 28/03/04 03:25

>>777
From this point forward you can just ask her out on regular dates, no?
You don't have to look at it as going out-out immediately. Dinner can be
just friends.

Plus Lady Miss Hermes likes going out to trendy restaurants
and she doesn't have anybody to go there with which means
that you need to step up and ask her to dinner
or ask her to take you to one of her haunts
which is totally reasonable and probable and possible.

still got nothing to lose, gotta give it a go, no?

---

824 Name: Anonymous Post Date: 28/03/04 03:27

When Lady Hermes said that she didn't have anybody to go
restaurant-hopping with she probably hoped that you'd jump in
and say 'Then why don't we go together'.

---

829 Name: Anonymous Post Date: 28/03/04 03:31

Lost a friend she checked out restaurants with

She gave you the bait
but you kept your mouth shut
That was a top opportunity

---

840 Name: Anonymous Post Date: 28/03/04 03:31

I think the key is in the parts Train Man has left out
Restaurant-hopping →no one to go with . . . you get me
You can go for it when you call tomorrow.

---

88 Name: Train Man ◆ SgHguKHEFY Post Date: 28/03/04 21:01

Hey people. Where am I?
Phone call . . . haven't made it yet

I'm crapping myself again

---

96 Name: Train Man ◆ SgHguKHEFY Post Date: 28/03/04 21:08

I can't help thinking she's gonna think I'm stalking her ⎯⌐○

99 Name: Train Man ◆ SgHguKHEFY Post Date: 28/03/04 21:10

>>96
I see where you're coming from but you did say you'd call so not
calling would be weird.

100 Name: Train Man ◆ SgHguKHEFY Post Date: 28/03/04 21:11

Since you lost your restaurant-hopping friend, do you wanna go out
again with me?
Is that the final decision?

119 Name: Mr Anonymous Post Date: 28/03/04 21:20

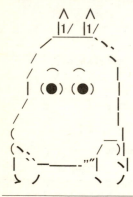

115 Name: Anonymous Post Date: 28/03/04 21:18

>>96
If ur not calling today, when ru calling?
What's going on in my mind

Thank you for last night.
↓
I don't have dinner with girls that often so I was really nervous but I still
had a laugh.
↓
If it's not too much hassle, may I ask you out again?

Suss out her reaction and decide where to go from there.

---

117 Name: Anonymous Post Date: 28/03/04 21:19

>>115
I think instead of inviting her, better to let her pick the place.
Train Man is out of ammo.

---

120 Name: Anonymous Post Date: 28/03/04 21:21

>>117
How about taking turns? 'Could you tell me where you'd like to go?'

---

121 Name: Anonymous Post Date: 28/03/04 21:21

>>115 no way
Thank you for last night ← ✓

I don't have dinner with girls that often ← ✕ too much info
I was nervous but I still had a laugh ← ✓ if you're gonna add to it,
                                        say if you don't have a friend to go
                                        restaurant-hopping with, I'm here for
                                        you . . . kinda thing.

and feel out how she reacts and if she seems ok,
then try for another date ← ✓

This time, Train Man quickly got back on track. Once again he faces the challenge named Hermes.

---

123 Name: Train Man ◆ SgHguKHEFY Post Date: 28/03/04 21:22

Ok! I'll call her now!

---

128 Name: Anonymous Post Date: 28/03/04 21:24

>>123
Excellent! Go for it!

---

133 Name: Train Man ◆ SgHguKHEFY Post Date: 28/03/04 21:25

Didn't get through to her ´·ω∵.∵...

201 Name: Train Man ◆ SgHguKHEFY Post Date: 28/03/04 21:46

That's her

---

207 Name: Anonymous Post Date: 28/03/04 21:47

a call? from her?

---

224 Name: Anonymous Post Date: 28/03/04 21:51

```
+      +
  ∧＿∧  +
 (0°・∀・)    heart a-thump-thump
 (0° U U +    sparkly shiney
 と＿)＿) +
```

lookin like dis now raiseyohandsinda air

laters.

---

234 Name: Anonymous Post Date: 28/03/04 21:53

wooooooohhhhhhhhh
I just can't understand!!!!!
how women feel!!!!!

we are the true Geeks!!!!!! For real!

---

263 Name: Train Man ◆ SgHguKHEFY Post Date: 28/03/04 21:58

just hung up.
what can I say. thank you everybody.

264 Name: Anonymous Post Date: 28/03/04 21:58

how was it?

269 Name: Anonymous Post Date: 28/03/04 21:59

we is all waitin with bated breath innit

282 Name: Anonymous Post Date: 28/03/04 22:00

what is this I see?

is that a new type of Train??!

283 Name: Anonymous Post Date: 28/03/04 22:01

do I need to get ready for the bomber crashing here?

297 Name: Anonymous Post Date: 28/03/04 22:04

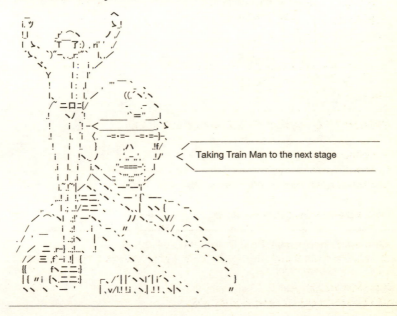

Taking Train Man to the next stage

to cut to the chase, I've got a second date
will get to the progress report a bit later

---

301 Name: Anonymous Post Date: 28/03/04 22:05

train's here train's here train's here------
——('∀˙≡('∀˙≡'∀')≡'∀˙)————-!!!!!!!!!!

---

304 Name: Anonymous Post Date: 28/03/04 22:05

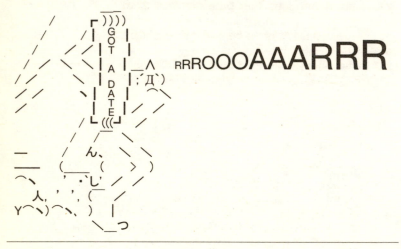

---

305 Name: Anonymous Post Date: 28/03/04 22:05

train's here —*·°˚·*:.｡..｡.:*·° (˙∀˚)°·*:.｡. .｡.:*·°˚·*—!!!!!

---

306 Name: Anonymous Post Date: 28/03/04 22:05

trainhere trainhere trainhere
ah yeah ah yeah ah yeah (·∀·) ah yeah -!!!

316 Name: Anonymous Post Date: 28/03/04 22:06

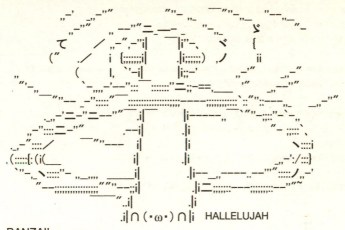

.i| ∩ (・ω・) ∩ |i   HALLELUJAH

BANZAI!

---

317 Name: Anonymous Post Date: 28/03/04 22:06

>>297
Top timing

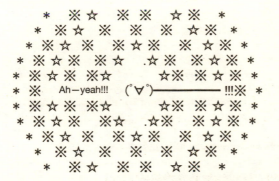

---

330 Name: 297 Post Date: 28/03/04 22:08

>317
No way. Train Man, top timing. I'm falling for you!

335 Name: Anonymous Post Date: 28/03/04 22:08

I'm gonna get it out while there's loads of other posts

I've never had dinner with a woman

Not only that but when I asked a girl out she said 'Why would I want to look at your face while I'm eating?'

339 Name: Anonymous Post Date: 28/03/04 22:08

Unbelievable!!!!!!
I'm feeling kinda teary

343 Name: Anonymous Post Date: 28/03/04 22:10

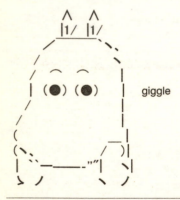 giggle

383 Name: Train Man ♦ SgHguKHEFY Post Date: 28/03/04 22:20

She just called me
our first exchange went something like this

'I'm sorry I was away from the phone earlier'
'No, no, you must have been busy?'
'No no, it's fine'

Something like that
then I thanked her for last night.
I asked her if she heard what I shouted out from the train and she

said she had.

After that I mentioned her losing her restaurant-hopping friend, and I asked if she didn't mind, could I take over.

---

386 Name: Anonymous Post Date: 28/03/04 22:21

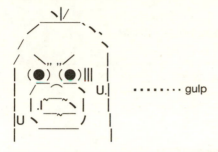 ・・・・・・・ gulp

---

404 Name: Train Man ♦ SgHguKHEFY Post Date: 28/03/04 22:29

'Yeah that would be nice. It would be my pleasure.'
quick answer. I took a deep breath.
'I really wanted to bring this up yesterday but . . .'
'ha-ha-ha, I was teasing you yesterday'
'I'm a bit dim. Sorry.'

(ﾟдﾟ) retardo
just as in the thread

and then she mentioned a place she wanted to go so we decided to go. Next week or the week after.

(ﾟдﾟ) retardo

---

410 Name: Anonymous Post Date: 28/03/04 22:30

>>404
'ha-ha-ha, I was teasing you yesterday'
'ha-ha-ha, I was teasing you yesterday'
'ha-ha-ha, I was teasing you yesterday'

'ha-ha-ha, I was teasing you yesterday'
'ha-ha-ha, I was teasing you yesterday'
'ha-ha-ha, I was teasing you yesterday'
'ha-ha-ha, I was teasing you yesterday'
'ha-ha-ha, I was teasing you yesterday'

---

415 Name: Anonymous Post Date: 28/03/04 22:30

you lucky dog youuuuuu
you are actually living the kind of dialogue
that I dream of under the coverzzzzzzzzz

---

420 Name: Anonymous Post Date: 28/03/04 22:32

How was she teasing?
I really don't understand . . .

---

430 Name: Anonymous Post Date: 28/03/04 22:33

>>420
'There is a restaurant that I want to go to but my friend doesn't want to go with me'

↓

Translation 'I'd like to go to another restaurant with you.'
that's the way to read it.

---

451 Name: Train Man ♦ SgHguKHEFY Post Date: 28/03/04 22:38

all right then . . . I suppose I should get some more clothes . . . ＿l ￢l○
It looks like I'm gonna get everything I had my eye on . . .

---

465 Name: Anonymous Post Date: 28/03/04 22:43

By the way Train Man
Did you ask Lady Miss Hermes = Moomin her age?

---

474 Name: Train Man ♦ SgHguKHEFY Post Date: 28/03/04 22:45

Oh, and I got her e-mail. (·∀·)b

I don't play the sex simulator games much
but I do play the regular ones
got through all of Dragon Quest V ＿|￣|○

---

478 Name: Anonymous Post Date: 28/03/04 22:46

I am the one that said Lady Hermes teased you last time so you could ask
her to dinner. Give thanks yeah.

On your second date you should talk about films.
What have you seen recently? like that
Anything you want to see? etc
and that gives you the chance to ask her to a film.
2 dinner dates squeezes the conversation well dry so
if you go to see a film you'll recharge the conversation.

And don't stress about what to wear. Lady Hermes likes you for you and
she probably sees that you aren't too big on the clothes thing anyway.

---

489 Name: Train Man ♦ SgHguKHEFY Post Date: 28/03/04 22:49

>>465
Didn't ask. But she's old enough to not have a curfew.
I bet she's older than me.

---

539 Name: Anonymous Post Date: 28/03/04 23:07

Who's the one that said it was gonna be difficult to push this story further

---

573 Name: Anonymous Post Date: 28/03/04 23:21

>>563
As far as I can see, from what Mista Train Man has written
he doesn't say much but what he does say is really good

Like
'I'm going to get dressed up'
or

'It's only recently that I've taken an interest in places like this'

I wouldn't call it hip but you're right on target or a bit smart or a bit on the simple side yet really quite attractive
Those words never would have come out of my mouth
And Miss Hermes' replies are great too

---

592 Name: Anonymous Post Date: 28/03/04 23:30

>>585
Just tell me if she has a high or low voice mannnnnnnnnn

not that it means anything but I just wanna know

---

597 Name: Train Man ♦ SgHguKHEFY Post Date: 28/03/04 23:32

>>592
Ummmm . . .
if I had to choose, I'd say she has more of a high-pitched voice

and she has a tiny voice so it's difficult to have a conversation . . .
＿厂|○
I'm guessing at most of her lines in much of the progress report

---

611 Name: Train Man ♦ SgHguKHEFY Post Date: 28/03/04 23:36

Her age remains a mystery.
She looks about 23-25 but she gives off a really settled kind of vibe
it's like she's got some kind of buffer that adds years to her real age

---

619 Name: Train Man ♦ SgHguKHEFY Post Date: 28/03/04 23:37

oh, and I live with my parents.

677 Name: Anonymous Post Date: 29/03/04 00:14

Mr Train Man

Giggle. Just wanted to call your name

682 Name: Anonymous Post Date: 29/03/04 00:24

>>676
hey dude do you have questions you need to ask?
or are you pretty much cool on your own now?

684 Name: Train Man ♦ SgHguKHEFY Post Date: 29/03/04 00:26

>>682
I'm thinking that I need help with keeping the conversation going.
Your comments have been really helpful for me.
I'm pretty sure of it now that I've seen her and all . . .
I reckon I'm falling for her . . .

736 Name: Anonymous Post Date: 29/03/04 03:43

>>735
Is this the thread where Train finally gets . . . de . . . pressed?
it seems to me that there is hope . . .

737 Name: Anonymous Post Date: 29/03/04 04:01

>>736
There is hope therefore we have depression

738 Name: Anonymous Post Date: 29/03/04 04:04

>>737
it's a different kind of hope! for the future! the light!
is the tip I'm on
meaning, da vibe on dis thread . . .

*a glimmer of hope especially for all Geeks

768 Name: Train Man ♦ SgHguKHEFY Post Date: 29/03/04 18:44

Got an e-mail from Hermes!!!! ahyeah-!
────(｡A｡)─(ﾟ∀ﾟ)─(｡A｡)─(ﾟ∀ﾟ)─(｡A｡)────!!!!
Apparently there's someone that wants to meet me so she asked if
she could bring the friend along

770 Name: Anonymous Post Date: 29/03/04 18:47

Wwaaaa? No way

777 Name: Anonymous Post Date: 29/03/04 18:54

There's no reason to say no.

778 Name: Train Man ♦ SgHguKHEFY Post Date: 29/03/04 18:55

Oh . . . right . . . it could be a guy ＿|￣|○

I can't tell her no, tho

---

799 Name: Anonymous Post Date: 29/03/04 19:13

I guess if it were a girl then she'd have said that she has a 'girlfriend' that wants to meet you . . .
I'm hoping it's just my reading too much into it

---

800 Name: Train Man ◆ SgHguKHEFY Post Date: 29/03/04 19:14

>>799
whoops. jogged my memory. She did say girlfriend. (｀･ω･´)

---

801 Name: Anonymous Post Date: 29/03/04 19:15

So it's definitely her girlfriend.

---

807 Name: Train Man ◆ SgHguKHEFY Post Date: 29/03/04 19:34

got a reply from her already! ahyeah---!
————(｡A｡)—(ﾟ∀ﾟ)—(｡A｡)—(ﾟ∀ﾟ)—(｡A｡)————!!!!
quick! way quick Lady Hermes!
not only that
'Woowee, thanks ♪' was her reply
she don't sound like b4 (*´Д`*) **pant pant**

---

828 Name: Anonymous Post Date: 29/03/04 20:23

>Mr Train
You should try to reply quickly to her e-mail
If you let too much time pass there's a chance she won't reply

---

845 Name: Train Man ◆ SgHguKHEFY Post Date: 29/03/04 20:36

just sent my reply

wonder what her friend's like
I can't wait

---

849 Name: Anonymous Post Date: 29/03/04 20:38

well normally in these type of scenarios, Hermes is bringing her girlfriend
so they can gossip about you (sorry for the expression) pretty sure that's
the real story

---

875 Name: Train Man ♦ SgHguKHEFY Post Date: 29/03/04 20:51

another reply from her!!
─────ヽ(∀°)人(°∀°)人(°∀)人(∀°)人(°∀°)人(°∀)/───── !!!
'sorry for the delay'
she says when she's nowhere close!!!?!?!?

she's known her girlfriend since school, she said
and it's now definitely a girl --

---

880 Name: Anonymous Post Date: 29/03/04 20:53

Introducing you to a close friend!!!!!!!
no way!

---

884 Name: Anonymous Post Date: 29/03/04 20:53

if this is the case then >849's theory is dead right

---

886 Name: Anonymous Post Date: 29/03/04 20:54

girls get talkative around guys they're interested in.
well, I'm just sayin this coz of your e-mail exchanges
girlfriends are really bitchy so if she thought her girlfriend wasn't gonna
like you, she wouldn't let her meet you.

---

889 Name: Train Man ♦ SgHguKHEFY Post Date: 29/03/04 20:55

boy it's been a long journey . . . (´ー`)

899 Name: Anonymous Post Date: 29/03/04 20:57

she must have told her friend about being 'saved' by you
and I'm sure that made her ask to meet you.
I hope you can just enjoy yourself without thinking too much

191 Name: Anonymous Post Date: 30/03/04 20:19

and . . .

when are you gonna tell her . . . ?

194 Name: Anonymous Post Date: 30/03/04 22:21

Moomin please explain to us why there will be two of you

199 Name: Train Man ♦ SgHguKHEFY Post Date: 30/03/04 22:24

>>191
if I could, right now . . .
but probably impossible . . . _|￣|O

>>194
the girlfriend insisted, she said

55 Name: Anonymous Post Date: 31/03/04 13:18

>>45
in my mind Moomin has morphed into brainy actress Tamaki Ogawa

101 Name: Train Man ♦ SgHguKHEFY Post Date: 31/03/04 22:34

Hey people. We set our date
first week of April

113 Name: Anonymous Post Date: 31/03/04 22:46

what's the vibe you're goin for this time?

117 Name: Train Man ♦ SgHguKHEFY Post Date: 31/03/04 22:48

>>113
good question
I'm not sure which way to go

142 Name: Anonymous Post Date: 31/03/04 23:06

If you're going for a fresh vibe . . . how about a light green or light blue top with white trousers? Stick with lighter colour trousers and if you're wearing trainers then something with some blue?

this being my sense of style, of course (′A`)

152 Name: Train Man ♦ SgHguKHEFY Post Date: 31/03/04 23:15

>>150
First time we met I had a brown-black thing going on
When I saw her the other day, I was kinda peachy

The first time we met, I looked kind of structured and then the second time, I kind of fluffed out.

196 Name: Anonymous Post Date: 01/04/04 00:46

The other day some girls at work were yapping on about how they 'absolutely don't want a boyfriend that wears Uniqlo stuff'. I'd recommend United Arrows or Ships.
http://www.united-arrows.co.jp/

197 Name: Anonymous Post Date: 01/04/04 00:50

But haven't Arrows gone Uniqlo on us lately?

198 Name: Anonymous Post Date: 01/04/04 00:50

likewise with Beams

199 Name: Anonymous Post Date: 01/04/04 00:58

If it looks good on you it doesn't matter where you bought it

201 Name: Anonymous Post Date: 01/04/04 01:05

a guy at work who's popular with the ladies swears by Uniqlo

203 Name: Anonymous Post Date: 01/04/04 01:05

Let this man speak on behalf of the board
'It doesn't matter which brand you choose'

204 Name: Anonymous Post Date: 01/04/04 01:06

Tho Comme Ça is Comme Ça I'd recommend Comme Çaism for Train
because it's a bit better than Uniqlo and above all, cheap
Remember not to get anything with a logo tho

309 Name: Train Man ♦ SgHguKHEFY Post Date: 02/04/04 20:13

**Respect. I went out and bought all the stuff in preparation for the day.
It's got a breezy cool vibe going on.**

311 Name: Anonymous Post Date: 02/04/04 20:13

>>Train Man
Welcome home.
Sucks that all your money is going out the window.

312 Name: Anonymous Post Date: 02/04/04 20:16

first week of April means . . . tomorrow?

314 Name: Train Man ◆ SgHguKHEFY Post Date: 02/04/04 20:22

>>311
I've spent over £250 ＿|￢|O

>>312
we decided on tomorrow

---

319 Name: Anonymous Post Date: 02/04/04 20:35

>Train
did you guys decide on a place?

---

320 Name: Train Man ◆ SgHguKHEFY Post Date: 02/04/04 20:40

>>319
decision made
it's apparently Western food

---

321 Name: Anonymous Post Date: 02/04/04 20:42

Western . . . watch your table manners, yeah
don't hold the knife with your wrong hand and make slurping noises when
you eat soup.

---

323 Name: Train Man ◆ SgHguKHEFY Post Date: 02/04/04 20:43

>>321
(((((((((;°Д°))))))) shiver shake shiver shake tremble tremble

---

331 Name: Anonymous Post Date: 02/04/04 20:56

Manners . . .

when eating soup, push the spoon outwards away from you to scoop!
bring your mouth forward to the spoon to eat!
do not make any noise (absolutely no slurping!)

use the knife farthest from the plate (for formal dining)
unless it's dessert or coffee, then you start with the one closest to the plate

napkins should be placed on your lap, leaving one third folded over (I think)

I'll write more if I think of anything
But it may be better to not worry about stuff like this and instead be
honest like 'I'm not used to coming to places like this . . . I eat Japanese
most of the time'

---

344 Name: Train Man ♦ SgHguKHEFY Post Date: 02/04/04 21:46

I looked up some info on table manners

I think I've got the conversation end covered . . .
We've been e-mailing over the last few days getting a bit pumped up

---

371 Name: Anonymous Post Date: 02/04/04 22:15

getting pumped up over e-mail? what d'you talk about?
do you know if Hermes has a boyfriend?

---

377 Name: Train Man ♦ SgHguKHEFY Post Date: 02/04/04 22:19

>>371
I'm not sure if she has a boyfriend or not but
we chatted about our selves

every time she mentions me to her friend, the friend says
'I can't wait to see him'
what do you do with that kind of expectation . . . _|￢|O

---

383 Name: Train Man ♦ SgHguKHEFY Post Date: 02/04/04 22:23

we joked over the phone too
'Were you being a hero on the train again?'
and such

387 Name: Anonymous Post Date: 02/04/04 22:25

>>383
'Were you being a hero on the train again?'
I've put that into the Hermes word bank
I'm sure some crafty dude will upload some Tamaki Ogawa pics and link
the word bank to em.

388 Name: Anonymous Post Date: 02/04/04 22:26

what kind of clothes did you buy?

394 Name: Anonymous Post Date: 02/04/04 22:34

The cherry blossoms could be peaking tomorrow. You could probably
take a walk after dinner to check them out.

401 Name: Train Man ♦ SgHguKHEFY Post Date: 02/04/04 22:42

>>388
I think it's what's called a pullover
cherry blossom viewing after dinner
I'll suggest it

402 Name: Anonymous Post Date: 02/04/04 22:45

so you've begun to use words we don't know . . . .
I'm happy for you
and a little sad

403 Name: Anonymous Post Date: 02/04/04 22:45

all right, may seem weird to ask at this point but hey Train Man,
do you

L I K E

Hermes?

406 Name: Train Man ♦ SgHguKHEFY Post Date: 02/04/04 22:47

>>403

I LIKE HER
Apart from that, it's like I'm thinking about whether I'm asleep or awake ＿|￣|○

---

410 Name: Anonymous Post Date: 02/04/04 22:48

all right then you'll be telling her tomorrow
>>406 exact same words only change her for you

---

416 Name: Train Man ♦ SgHguKHEFY Post Date: 02/04/04 22:51

>>410
impossible . . . ＿|￣|○
her friend will be there tomorrow anyway

444 Name: Train Man ♦ SgHguKHEFY Post Date: 02/04/04 23:17

We've already set the time and place
but there's no end in sight for our e-mails

470 Name: Train Man ♦ SgHguKHEFY Post Date: 02/04/04 23:38

'Do you wanna see my dog?'
she asketh. How best to respondeth.

---

474 Name: Anonymous Post Date: 02/04/04 23:40

> she asketh. How best to respondeth.

. . . you is thick

482 Name: Anonymous Post Date: 02/04/04 23:44

OK, I admit it. At first, I thought Train Man was a wimp. I mean, he was taking forever just to work up the courage to call and thank her but I thought we should stick by him and cheer him on. But now he's gone further than I could have imagined. Looks like I'll always be a step behind . . .

---

493 Name: Train Man ♦ SgHguKHEFY Post Date: 02/04/04 23:48

dog pic cometh-----!!!!!
————ヽ(∀゜)人(゜∀゜)人(゜∀)人(∀゜)人(゜∀゜)人(゜∀)/———— !!!
cute looking doggie. (*´Д`*)

as always, I wonder if this is a dream
I've completely changed from what I was a month ago
please don't let me wake up from this dream

---

539 Name: Anonymous Post Date: 03/04/04 00:05

What must it be like to get this much support on 2ch
maybe we'll morph into something special if they get it on.

I reckon we could end up being the unsung heroes (´A`)

---

543 Name: Anonymous Post Date: 03/04/04 00:06

Hey, people!
Don't you get the jitters every time you call a girl?
I do!
I'm not proud of it but I get it bad!
so bad I'm jealous of el Tren's strength . . . .

---

567 Name: Train Man ♦ SgHguKHEFY Post Date: 03/04/04 00:18

Done. Went along nicely. Even talked about films
I turned my phone off

I'm lending her a DVD. (゜д゜)

571 Name: Anonymous Post Date: 03/04/04 00:20

>>567
man, you own a fancy schmancy DVD . . . ..

686 Name: Train Man ♦ SgHguKHEFY Post Date: 03/04/04 11:11

good morning
I reckon I'll leave the house early today

687 Name: Anonymous Post Date: 03/04/04 11:13

>>Mista Tren
laters

your heart ready?

691 Name: Train Man ♦ SgHguKHEFY Post Date: 03/04/04 11:19

just checked to make sure the disc was in the DVD

694 Name: Anonymous Post Date: 03/04/04 11:23

check for random hairs on the case . . .

697 Name: Train Man ♦ SgHguKHEFY Post Date: 03/04/04 11:41

>>694
check.

I actually have to go buy a bag so I can take the DVD.

701 Name: Anonymous Post Date: 03/04/04   11:55

>>697
practicality comes second
design is of most importance

I'm getting a bit worried

---

706 Name: Train Man ◆ SgHguKHEFY Post Date: 03/04/04 12:20

I'm off!
I'll think carefully about the bag!

laters

Train Man's second time out on the battlefield couldn't even compare to his
first time. Even as the clock ticked precariously close to midnight there was
no sign of Train Man's return. While they waited, a heated discussion went
on as the netizens imagined Hermes as a round and soft type or a sharp and
beauty-conscious type. Just as their imaginations were about to take off,
Train Man returned.

---

732 Name: Anonymous Post Date: 03/04/04   19:52

You think the bomb will drop in the next thread?
Is it too soon? Or could it even be today . . .?!

---

735 Name: Anonymous Post Date: 03/04/04   20:01

what are we gonna do if he doesn't come home today?

---

765 Name: Anonymous Post Date: 03/04/04   22:42

Train's late . . .

---

792 Name: Anonymous Post Date: 03/04/04   23:44

. . .something has to be wrong if Train Man's not making his appearance
at this time of night . . .

The bomb shelter ain't ready! What're you waitin for, get movin'!

---

797 Name: Anonymous Post Date: 03/04/04 23:46

hold off on the bomb shelter and focus on piling sandbags . . .
and step on it with the anti-aircraft missiles!
It'd be way too late if we wait for the bombers . . . .

---

804 Name: Anonymous Post Date: 03/04/04 23:52

Shit. I was hiding in the dugout when they came at me with a flame-thrower
Stop it! I ain't who you think I am coz it's my world that's.anlouajhafuhg@;;

---

807 Name: Train Man ◆ SgHguKHEFY Post Date: 03/04/04 23:53

Just got in.
I'll give the full report later

Me tired. _|￣|○

---

808 Name: Anonymous Post Date: 03/04/04 23:53

>>807
Welcome home--!!

---

815 Name: Anonymous Post Date: 03/04/04 23:55

You're back -------! Yeaaaaaaah ————(ﾟ∀ﾟ)———— !!!!
Welcome home!

---

832 Name: Anonymous Post Date: 04/04/04 00:01

attention everybody!!!
Got to survive the first wave of defensive aerial bombing coming our way!
Landing force take your positions! We will not be defeated!

---

852 Name: Train Man ♦ SgHguKHEFY Post Date: 04/04/04 00:13

So, I went out to get a bag to carry the Matrix DVD with me. I basically thought it'd be ok if it was big enough for the DVD so I bought a nice little bag like I've never bought before. I guess it's what's called a tote bag. I bought it and went straight to where we were going to meet.

I got there 30 minutes early.
I waited for 30 minutes in place.
Just like last time, she was just a little bit late.
No joke, she was just as cute as the last time. Made me wanna rise to the occasion if you know what I mean.
She had on a denim jacket and a skirt layered in whites and pinks.
She looked much younger than last time.

. . . and she was wearing pig tails!!!!! ────────(ﾟ∀ﾟ)────────!!!
My favourite
not to mention her make-up which looked much more carefully applied this time . . . (;´Д`)

'Sorry I'm late' she bounced over to me.
'No worries at all.'

Her friend was running late so we decided the two of us should head to the restaurant first.

---

854 Name: Anonymous Post Date: 04/04/04 00:13

I think I just spotted Mr Train's plane in the sky
Was that a reconnaissance plane?

---

857 Name: Anonymous Post Date: 04/04/04 00:14

>>854 he stuck his head out and got shot in the neck

---

859 Name: Anonymous Post Date: 04/04/04 00:14

>>854
look at that. Came out of the dugout only to take a bullet meant for Train Man.

863 Name: Anonymous Post Date: 04/04/04 00:15

pig tails . . . careful make up . . . . . . I think the doors of hell are
beginning to open.. ('A`)

---

893 Name: Train Man ♦ SgHguKHEFY Post Date: 04/04/04 00:29

Since she was the one leading me to the restaurant I made sure I
walked a bit behind her.

It was crowded again so I made sure not to lose sight of her. During
the walk we talked a bit.

'Thanks for humouring me till late last night . . .'
I knew instantly that she was talking about our e-mails.
'I'm sorry for taking ages to reply . . . you e-mail super-fast, don't you.'
She said people reckoned she was on the slow side.
Yesterday in an e-mail she mentioned stressing about her pollen
allergy. She took some pills today to make sure she wasn't going to
get a dribbly nose.

Coz she was walking a bit ahead of me she kept turning around to
look at me all the time.
Then, as she turned to face me, she was heading straight for a metal
pole. She didn't have a clue.
'Oops,' I said and just grabbed her arm . . . .
'Mmm?'
'It looked like you were going to walk into the pole'
'I'm sorry. When I take my pills, I get a bit out of it. Thank you.'

And then we started to walk again.
'Let's walk side by side,' she said.
'Um ok,' I said, stepping forward a bit. I really need to learn how to
be more sensitive . . . ⌐|O

---

899 Name: Anonymous Post Date: 04/04/04 00:31

>just grabbed her arm . . . .
You probably just did it on the spur of the moment but it's something no
Geek could ever do,,,, ('A`)

924 Name: Train Man ♦ SgHguKHEFY Post Date: 04/04/04 00:49

Once we get to the restaurant she says to me,
'I copied you.'
'What?'
For a moment, I had no idea what she was talking about but then I
realised that she had booked.

It was an Italian restaurant. As expected, lots of pizza and pasta.
'Why don't we just go ahead and order.'
'Ah, sure.'
The dishes here were apparently meant to be shared.
'Whatever you like.'
'No, no please go ahead.' Though that's what I said, honestly, I had no
clue what to order unless there were photos of the dishes . . . ⌐|⎺|O

And then,
'Sorry, sorry,' said a girl. Her friend caught up to us.
'I'm so sorry to have kept you waiting.' She apologised to me as she
huffed and puffed.
'It's no problem at all.'
The friend looked a bit more outgoing than Lady Miss Hermes and
was dressed a bit flashier.

946 Name: Train Man ♦ SgHguKHEFY Post Date: 04/04/04 01:03

'We haven't even ordered yet so it's fine.'
'Oh, thank god,' she said, and sat down next to Lady Hermes.
'Nice to meet you.'
'Likewise, nice to meet you,' I answered and introduced myself.
'I've heard a lot about you,' she said as she giggled.

The three of us talked about the menu then decided what to order.
'Mr Train, will you be drinking again tonight?' Hermes jumped right in.
Maybe it was because her friend was there but it was like she had a
different kind of vibe.
'Ah, yeah, sure.'
I ordered a beer. The two of them also ordered beer. ⎍|⎺|O

Dunno why I couldn't figure that one out . . . doh!. ⎍|⎺|

We chatted some more while we waited for the food.
But man can her friend talk . . .
She was pretty funny and not shy, I could relax with her and talk.

958 Name: Anonymous Post Date: 04/04/04 01:07

I'm gonna poke my head out from the trench.

960 Name: Anonymous Post Date: 04/04/04 01:07

>958
Shit! What's that child doing! Get back down!

994 Name: Train Man ♦ SgHguKHEFY Post Date: 04/04/04 01:18

While we waited for the food, it was basically the friend firing
questions and me answering them. About the incident on the train
and about dinner the other night.
'Sounds like you guys are getting along,' she said, poking fun at us.

Even after the food arrived, the friend kept at it without letting up.
Lady Hermes laughed a lot. There were a few jokes I couldn't
understand but I laughed anyway. As I'd been on the receiving end
most of the night, I decided to come up with something myself.
'Lady Miss Hermes, have you ever been told that you look like
Tamaki Ogawa?'
'Tamaki Ogawa?'
They didn't have a clue who Tamaki Ogawa is.
'Is she an actress?'
'Ahh . . . yes, I'm pretty sure she is.'
'I wonder who she is. I'd probably recognise her if I saw her.'

According to her friend, Hermes looks like a cross between YOU and
Ryouko Kuninaka.
'Aha . . . .' I said, but really, I didn't have a clue who they
were . . . ＿￢○

120 Name: Train Man ♦ SgHguKHEFY Post Date: 04/04/04 01:38

'Mr Train, what celebrity do people say you look like?'
'Well, I've actually never been told that I look like anyone.'
I get uncomfortable when the topic of conversation revolves around me.
'Could look a tiny bit like the guitarist from ELT?'
Did ELT have a guitarist??? ＿￢|O
Whatever, I replied by saying that I wasn't as cool-looking.

Then we talked about films. I gave her Matrix 1-3.
'Thank you so much~'
'The story gets a bit complicated, but . . .'
'I'll ask you when there's something I can't understand.'
'Ha ha ha . . .'
But I can't even understand it . . . ＿￢|
Gotta get studying. FYI she and her friend have only seen 1.

The two of them reckoned Lord of the Rings is cool.
I've only seen the 1ˢᵗ of that series . . . ＿￢|O
And some dog film . . . (title slipped my mind)

---

132 Name: Anonymous Post Date: 04/04/04 01:41

>>120
>'Could look a tiny bit like the guitarist from ELT?'
That ain't no compliment dude . . .

135 Name: Anonymous Post Date: 04/04/04 01:42

>>120
The dog film must be Quill

---

185 Name: Train Man ♦ SgHguKHEFY Post Date: 04/04/04 01:57

Her friend kept on mentioning the YOU and Ryouko Kuninaka
likeness but all I was trying to do was remember the names ＿￢|O

'I'm going to the loo . . .'
I went to the loo . . . but since I didn't know where it was and the
directions one of the waiters gave me were wrong, I just walked

around for a bit until I found it.

When I got back after taking care of business . . .
'Umm . . . are you, Mr Train, being innocent for real?'
man, I'm being asked about me again . . . ＿⌐ |O
'I've been told so occasionally.' ＿| ⌐ |
'You mean not all the time?'
This friend of hers machine guns her questions . . . ＿⌐ |O
Lady Hermes laughed a bit.
'I've been hearing all about it but you're a firebrand aren't you?' the
friend quickly followed up with another whammy. What does she
mean . . . having heard all about it . . . and in the end,
'There aren't many like you around, so I think it's a good thing,'
Hermes said, smoothing things over, but . . .
'Well, there definitely isn't anyone like you around me.'
Yet again, the friend opened her mouth.

---

186 Name: Anonymous Post Date: 04/04/04 01:58

being assessed for the rare creature you are?

---

213 Name: Train Man ♦ SgHguKHEFY Post Date: 04/04/04 02:14

It felt like we talked about a lot more stuff but
What other stuff happened . . . . . .
There were a lot of times I had no idea what they were on about . . .
It was after 9 when the friend decided to leave.
She said she had to go to work early the following day.
We all decided to leave the restaurant together.
We split the bill.
'Sorry to be the gooseberry'
The friend's face was lightly glowing from the wine . . .

And when it was just the two of us
'Shall we go to another place?'
'Sure'
This time, I was the one who suggested it.
We didn't feel like walking too far so we decided to randomly choose
a bar close by.

'Sorry for all the fuss today.'
'Not a problem. That was fun.'
She apologised but it was cool with me

Man I'm tired . . . ＿￢|O

---

214 Name: Anonymous Post Date: 04/04/04 02:15

what a thoughtful, sensitive friend to take her leave early,
ah yeeaaaaaa ――――――――(´∀`)―――――― !!!!!

---

221 Name: Anonymous Post Date: 04/04/04 02:16

Emergency! Emergency! Air raid! Air raid! Prepare anti-aircraft missiles and
fire!!

---

224 Name: Anonymous Post Date: 04/04/04 02:18

anti-aircraft fire bombs are flying across the sky!!!!

---

231 Name: Anonymous Post Date: 04/04/04 02:20

By the way, have you found out what Ladyluv Hermes does for a living
and how old she is?

---

234 Name: Train Man ♦ SgHguKHEFY Post Date: 04/04/04 02:23

>>231
ummm, I forgot . . .
we talked a bit about each other's jobs and age.
Sounded like they both earned loads . . . ＿￢|O
As for age, they looked me up and down and said
'We're probably a bit older.'

---

271 Name: Train Man ♦ SgHguKHEFY Post Date: 04/04/04 02:41

lay off, no lip-touching no sex-anything no no!!! ＼(´Д´)／
Well, I wanted to, of course but but buttttwooooaaaaa stop it . . .

The rest of the time we talked about films and
the next place we wanted to go . . .
even talked about fashion which is very rare for me since I know
nothing about it
'I know absolutely nothing about it so I was thinking about trying to
learn a thing or two . . . '
'Really? Come to think of it, you've changed a lot since the first time I
met you, haven't you?' She went for the jugular and made me
nervous. But I told it how it was.
'As I was having dinner with a girl for the first time, I did my research,'
I owned up.

'Reallllllllly?'
I . . . don't think . . . she thought much of that . . .
'I'm not all that bothered about fashion either.'
I wanted to blurt out what a lie that was but I swallowed my words
instead.

It was getting late so we decided to leave the bar
Just like last time, we pretty much walked in silence to the station.

288 Name: Train Man ♦ SgHguKHEFY Post Date: 04/04/04 02:52

For our ride home, we got on the Keihin Tohoku Line again.
I spotted a few drunks in our car.
She looked at them and then looked at me.
'Aah . . . .don't worry, it's fine . . .'
'(laugh)'
Don't think there was any deep meaning to this.

Just like last time, she got off first and waved her hands at me
saying
'I'll e-mail'
'Me too'
'Good night'
after which the doors closed

As soon as I got home I turned on my PC and opened my mail. I sent
her a thank you note and asked if she got home safely and she
replied almost immediately.
'Thank you for today. I just got home too~

Looking forward to going out to eat more yummy food!'

And that's all folks. (´—｀)

Train Man appears to continue to make progress but how the hell could this story evolve? Just you wait and see.

Mission
3

She Pulled
My Hand Lightly

After Train's bombing campaign ended things dragged in the thread.

---

300 Name: Anonymous Post Date: 04/04/04 02:55

>Since I was having dinner with a girl for the first time, I did my research.

Mmmmm . . . . . . I don't know about this one.

---

303 Name: Anonymous Post Date: 04/04/04 02:56

>>300
I reckon it would've been better not to say it

---

304 Name: Anonymous Post Date: 04/04/04 02:56

Train, good job. I ate cup noodles for dinner.
Dats all. (´ — `)

---

306 Name: Anonymous Post Date: 04/04/04 02:57

I think 'Since I was having dinner with a girl for the first time, I did my research' basically is synonymous with 'I'm a virgin.'

---

309 Name: Train Man ♦ SgHguKHEFY Post Date: 04/04/04 02:57

you think it was a bad move huh . . . _|⎺|O

---

337 Name: Anonymous Post Date: 04/04/04 03:03

Hold it!
There is a chance that she might not think too hard about 'Since I was having dinner with a girl for the first time, I did my research' . . .
At the rate Train's going now, anything is possible . . . . . .

---

339 Name: Anonymous Post Date: 04/04/04 03:04

Hermes might actually think it's sweet a man trying to transform himself for her.

---

362 Name: Train Man ♦ SgHguKHEFY Post Date: 04/04/04 03:12

my body's giving out . . . . . . _⌐¡O

thanks again for everything today.
Laters.

---

383 Name: Anonymous Post Date: 04/04/04 03:17

All right. Why don't we all start writing lines for when Train professes his love for her.

---

389 Name: Anonymous Post Date: 04/04/04 03:19

>383 I can imagine the screenplay for their wedding ----'scenes from when they met'

---

390 Name: Anonymous Post Date: 04/04/04 03:19

Me knew from the first moment me saw you

---

392 Name: Anonymous Post Date: 04/04/04 03:20

>>383
'Would you like to go on a journey called life with me? By train . . .'

---

398 Name: Anonymous Post Date: 04/04/04 03:23

'I know I'm younger but I'll do my best not to fall behind . . .'

---

404 Name: Anonymous Post Date: 04/04/04 03:27

'Can I fall in love with you?'

---

433 Name: Anonymous Post Date: 04/04/04 07:01

morning people ´A`))

unlike what we expected, we didn't suffer that many casualties, eh
but Train's battle is yet to come
I think he should wait a bit before telling her he loves her but

He should take her on a hardcore date just to suss out Hermes' true feelings about him. I live out in Chubu so I'll leave it to the sexy Kanto folk to come up with the location . . . ('A`)

---

462 Name: Train Man ♦ SgHguKHEFY Post Date: 04/04/04 15:15

I checked the thread to make sure yesterday really did happen.
Even now I'm not sure . . .

---

475 Name: Train Man ♦ SgHguKHEFY Post Date: 04/04/04 15:58

I just read through the log . . .
Looks like you've written my lines for me . . . _|￢|O nuff nuff nuff

Oh . . . I forgot the cherry blossoms . . . _|￢|O stoopid me stoopid me
I guess I was thrown by her friend . . .

---

486 Name: Anonymous Post Date: 04/04/04 17:07

at an observatory looking out over the city lights at night

Lady Hermes	'Isn't that beautiful . . . '
Train Man	'This is my favourite spot . . . '
Lady Hermes	'Really . . . thank you so much for sharing such a place.'
Rain Man	'Of course, I shared it only because it was you, Lady Hermes'
Lady Hermes	'(laughs) That makes me happy.'

After a moment of silence both hands brush against one another out of the blue

Brain Man	'Oops, I'm so sorry (he suddenly pulls hand away)'
Lady Hermes	'(in muffled voice) . . . you didn't have to pull away'
Sprain Man	'Wha . . . '
Drain Man	'Umm . . . Lady Hermes?'
Lady Hermes	'Y . . . yes . . . '

(both hearts beating wildly)

Grain Man	'I . . . umm . . . I . . . actually . . . have for a long time . . .'
Lady Hermes	'Hold on. Can I please finish that sentence first?'
Plain Man	'Y . . . yes.'

(here, Lady Hermes leans towards Train Man)

| Lady Hermes | 'Ever since you came to our rescue on the train, I've liked you, Mr Train . . . and even though I am older . . . . I'll do my best to keep up . . . so please, will you be my boyfriend?' |

(Train pulls Hermes in close)

| Stain Man | 'If you're happy with a silly thing like me, then I'd ask you myself, to be my girlfriend. |
| Lady Hermes | '(giggles) I'm so glad . . . and looking forward to us being together.' |

They kiss.
The sparkling lights of the city embraced the couple from afar.
As if it were orchestrating a grand send-off . . .
-----
damn it, what da hell am I writing at work . . . ahjkbteouhermesiki

---

488 Name: Anonymous Post Date: 04/04/04   17:10

>>486
How many times has Train morphed?

---

489 Name: Anonymous Post Date: 04/04/04   17:13

>>486
Is it Train or Grain or Stain
But more importantly, we need to clarify the situation

Anyway, have we decided on Maim Man's plan of attack?

---

490 Name: Train Man ♦ SgHguKHEFY Post Date: 04/04/04 17:16

I am also imagining all sorts of scenarios à la >>486

553 Name: Anonymous Post Date: 04/04/04 21:51

I bet while we're calling Train's love interest 'Hermes', Hermes and her friends are calling Train Ikkun, like the children's book character.

Friend	'Ikkun seemed so sweet and nice . . . '
H	'Really? Did you really think so?
F	'It's pretty obvious that he's into you.'
H	'You think so . . . (blushing)'
F	'You're e-mailing every night aren't you? Sounds good to me. Why don't you do the boyfriend-girlfriend thing'
H	'But, but I could have got it wrong . . . Ikkun is kind to everybody . . . '
F	'There is absolutely no way that could be it . . .'

And much more . . .
And here exists an ecstatically happy me, glad to see you budding and leaving the lair and another, really sad and lonely ME . . . you get me . . .

537 Name: Anonymous Post Date: 04/04/04 21:40

If there's anyone here that has ever professed their love to someone or has had someone express their love to them . . . speak up!

578 Name: Anonymous Post Date: 04/04/04 22:17

>>546
sorry, catching up

I was talking to a friend on the phone
And just as I worked myself up to tell her how I felt about her
she sensed something in the air and told me that she 'wasn't interested'.

There was a girl at work who I fancied so one day I got up the nerve to talk to her. 'I'd like to talk to you,' I said, after which she looked at me like I was a worm and walked off.

I fell for this girl, a friend of a friend who came out to a bar with a bunch of us, I kept it simple and just asked her if she'd like to go out with me.
She replied 'I'm not sure about the going out bit but why don't we start out as friends.' 2 weeks later she told me 'I don't think it's going to work out.'

Then there was this girl at college, we were in the same club, she was younger and seemed to look up to me so one day when we were alone, I asked her to go out with me. She refused saying that she 'couldn't see me as a man.'

And that's the way the cookie crumbles . . . ('A`)

591 Name: Anonymous Post Date: 04/04/04   22:28

I just realised but Train's 'Since I was having dinner with a girl for the first time, I did my research,' could be interpreted as 'I dig Hermes'

If he was just being polite it wouldn't mean dinner and doing his research.

I bet you Lady Hermes has figured it out already.

596 Name: Anonymous Post Date: 04/04/04   22:33

Train's pretty innocent but
Hermes is not so different herself
Maybe neither of them has figured it out yet

55 Name: Anonymous Post Date: 04/04/04   00:44

Hermes Lingo Log
'ha-ha-ha, I was teasing you yesterday'
'I'LL JUST HOLD ON TIGHTLY TO YOU.'
'I guess you won't listen even if I argue'
'But my friends say I look like a Moomin'
'Japanese cuisine suits your vibe.'
'I guess I'll get dressed up too'

598 Name: Anonymous Post Date: 04/04/04   22:34

>>596
you think so . . .
I don't think the innocent types end up saying stuff like >>55

599 Name: Anonymous Post Date: 04/04/04   22:35

lineas fantasticas-----!!! ——————(ˊ∀ˋ)——————— !!

600 Name: Anonymous Post Date: 04/04/04 22:37

lineas?

601 Name: Anonymous Post Date: 04/04/04 22:41

>>600
lineas=lines=words out of Hermes' mouth

765 Name: Train Man ♦ SgHguKHEFY Post Date: 06/04/04 20:51

**Hey people. I was focusing entirely on my e-mail yesterday. As I
expected, The Matrix ended up posing some difficulty.**

766 Name: Anonymous Post Date: 06/04/04 20:57

What do you mean?
What'd she say?

767 Name: Train Man ♦ SgHguKHEFY Post Date: 06/04/04 21:03

**>>766
The story gets really complicated from the 2nd one.
I explained it the best I could
She seemed like she enjoyed it tho.**

769 Name: Anonymous Post Date: 06/04/04 21:16

focusing entirely on e-mail . . .
e-mails worth focusing on, eh
('A`) whoa

770 Name: Train Man ♦ SgHguKHEFY Post Date: 06/04/04 21:25

**Looks like it's going to be a while till our next date (week after next)
Kick back till then. Don't know if there's much to discuss so I'm**

thinking we should leave it for a bit and I'll start a thread once there's progress worth reporting.
What do you think?

881 Name: Train Man ♦ SgHguKHEFY Post Date: 06/04/04 22:58

I'll be back to start the thread around the 15th

Moomin and the Pointy Hat Part 3 will be the title

Thanks again.

Laters.

367 Name: Anonymous Post Date: 10/04/04 21:00

sorry to keep you waiting.

I've renewed 'Geek Gets Shot Down in Flames ---- Calls for Back-up'
http://www.geocities.co.jp/Milkyway-Acquarius/7075/

I've compiled both bombings into one big one.
If you haven't already been exposed, be warned. Enter at own risk.

Lately, the thread has split in lots of directions but I've compiled the posts from two locations. If anybody knows of other places where the thread continues and thrives, please let me know.

Thanks for your cooperation, all you hard-working editors out there.

390 Name: Train Man ♦ SgHguKHEFY Post Date: 12/04/04 20:17

>>397
Thanks for all your amazing work. When I think back it was only a month ago that I thought the 125-person compilation page as a far away and unreachable fantasy land . . . and who would have guessed that I would be featured on a compilation page . . .
Straight up, you never know what's coming . . .

I've been e-mailing with her over the past few days . . . but . . . how can I say this . . . it's, I guess . . . .what's commonly known as . . . 'clicking' . . . we're clicking. (´—`)

---

392 Name: Anonymous Post Date: 12/04/04 20:33

Train's here-------
────(#`Д´)´∀`)·ω·) °Д°)°∀`)·∀·)￣ー）´_ゝ`) ────!!
(´—`) premonition of trauma to come . . .

---

399 Name: Anonymous Post Date: 13/04/04 02:29

clicking . . . clicking . . .
Major!! there is no . . . clicking . . . in my pulse!

---

400 Name: Anonymous Post Date: 13/04/04 03:08

Snap out of it soldier!
Remember that your mummy is waiting for you to come home!

---

409 Name: Train Man ♦ SgHguKHEFY Post Date: 13/04/04 21:00

**Sorry I disappeared without a word yesterday.
I think I just nodded off . . .**

By clicking, I mean that we e-mail at least once a day. What we write about . . . well, mostly we talked about films which lead to a discussion about what we believe in then a discussion about romance.

**Then she made a comment and I said
'Not that I would know since I don't have any experience (laughing uncomfortably)'
'You must be joking. How could any woman keep her hands off you? (laughing)'**

Went something like this. (´—`)

412 Name: Anonymous Post Date: 13/04/04 21:07

>>409
Staying humble but being sure of yourself, without getting a swollen head.
I hope that Mr Train, you stay true to yourself . . . . . . so you can coast
into a good relationship.

413 Name: Anonymous Post Date: 13/04/04 21:10

>>409
Hermes saying that means that Train Man's metamorphosis has left no
trace of the techie.
Sounds like the conversation's moving along. I bet you guys will be
cooking next time you see each other.

414 Name: Anonymous Post Date: 13/04/04 21:07

>>409
You lucky dog you . . . .

But it looks like Lady Miss Hermes has Train Man up on a pedestal . . . I
fear for the slip-ups . . .

But when women say stuff like 'the ladies must dig you' or some such
thing, it really means sweet FA. I've even had women say 'you're lying!'
when I mention not really being such a hit with the ladies . . . but basically,
no woman has ever come sniffing at my door.

415 Name: Anonymous Post Date: 13/04/04 21:12

>>409
All the same . . . don't let your guard down just yet!
Not good to let it go to your head
Just keep going slowly but surely.

419 Name: Train Man ♦ SgHguKHEFY Post Date: 13/04/04 21:26

Yes sir. I will continue steadily, sticking to my guns. (｀·ω·´)
All right, will see you in two days.

Laters.

477 Name: Anonymous Post Date: 17/04/04 21:29

Train Man inspired me so much that I went to the hairdresser for the first time in my life! It's nice to have a lady play with your hair and massage you and stuff innit. Kinda sexy, no? (;´Д`) pant-pant
By the way, how do you recreate the hairdo?

478 Name: Anonymous Post Date: 17/04/04 21:38

>>477
Why don't you photograph yourself and use some wax and styling gel to recreate it?

479 Name: Anonymous Post Date: 17/04/04 21:42

>>478
But how do you recreate the hairdo?

Salon Girl: Do you usually use wax?

Me: No

Salon Girl: You should.

Boy did I want honey-girl to scold me some more.

480 Name: Anonymous Post Date: 17/04/04 21:53

>>479
Get some magazines and learn how to use the product.
It all depends on the kind of hair you have and your hairstyle, so it's a bit difficult, but you can do it, dude.

Men's Hairstyle + Hair Care (29)
http://life3.2ch.net/test/read/cgi/diet/1082167933/l50

483 Name: Anonymous Post Date: 17/04/04 22:09

>>480
I read through it but
don't understand a single word

488 Name: Anonymous Post Date: 17/04/04 22:17

>>485
Words I don't understand

Set-Cut
Blow
Styling
Hair Bunch

Looks like 'twisting' is an important action, but what the f@*% does twisting do?

---

492 Name: Anonymous Post Date: 17/04/04 21:38

Set-Cut: ability to get the hairstyle you imagined for yourself, being
              satisfied with it
Blow: Using a hairdryer to style your hair
Styling: Shaping your hair
Hair Bunch: A bunch of your hair

I think . . . sorry if I'm wrong on any of this.
I'm not sure what twisting does . . .
But I reckon it helps style the hair into the shape you want?

Saw this earlier in the thread
http://www.walkerplus.com/hairsalon
http://www.beauty-navi.com/

---

493 Name: Anonymous Post Date: 17/04/04 22:49

If you twist your hair, then the ends kind of stick together then split up in small bunches, going one way or another.
That's it.
It's called Easy Hair --- it looks kind of messy but at the same time kind of cool and styled. You've seen it on the boys from the in crowd.

Probably, that is . . . .

57 Name: Anonymous Post Date: 16/04/04 11:38

I was just at the corner shop thinking about getting some stuff before
heading home when I spotted a woman asking the assistant for directions.
Being a local, I asked where she was headed and since I knew where it
was I walked her over.
Once there, the lady thanked me loads and asked for my name and
address but I told her it was only natural to help out someone in need and
told her that there was no need for her to thank me and just left.
I know, I know, I'm a pussy . . .

58 Name: Anonymous Post Date: 16/04/04 11:44

>>57
You missed your chance to become Guide Man!!!

59 Name: Anonymous Post Date: 16/04/04 12:03

>>57
Moron!
Wimp!
'I'd like to thank you' is code for . . . you know . . .

111 Name: Anonymous Post Date: 16/04/04 23:36

Unbelievable as it may sound I got the numba of anova sexy lady today

Lady policewoman on a bike . . . __ITO

102 Name: Anonymous Post Date: 16/04/04 23:05

You can order a chicken around via a webcam.
http://www.subservientchicken.com/
take a peek if you got nothing else to do

673 Name: Anonymous Post Date: 16/04/04 22:57

I told the chicken 'I love you'
Then it came way up close to the camera and gave me the peace sign

Got me a bit fired up

108 Name: Anonymous Post Date: 16/04/04 23:34

>>102
Just saw it. It's pretty funny. It looks really bored---somebody please tell him to do something

109 Name: Anonymous Post Date: 16/04/04 23:34

How in the world is 102 possible?
Is the chicken live?

113 Name: Anonymous Post Date: 16/04/04 23:37

>>109
It's just a bunch of readied images that pop up according to the keywords.

But still funny.
Try to calm down
or lay down
or hate you

121 Name: Anonymous Post Date: 17/04/04 00:01

It walked over to me when I said 'kill me'
It freaked me out so I shut him off.

123 Name: Anonymous Post Date: 17/04/04 00:06

When I said 'suck my dick' it walked over to me and did something

125 Name: Anonymous Post Date: 17/04/04 00:12

He wagged his finger at me when I said 'sex'

128 Name: Anonymous Post Date: 17/04/04 00:15

'duck' got a funny imitation bit

331 Name: Anonymous Post Date: 17/04/04 17:28

>>102's chicken's command list
http://dev.magicosm.net/cgi-bin/public/corvidaewiki/bin/view/Game/
SubservientChickenRequestList

I'm scared of the chicken now---I think he's gonna appear in my dreams.
I really thought he was going to get me when I typed in 'kill me.'

While the Geeks were getting fired up about the chicken, Train Man focused
on e-mailing Hermes and getting another date.

---

147 Name: Train Man ♦ SgHguKHEFY Post Date: 17/04/04 01:02

Sorry for being late. Today was a normal work day . . . . . .
Since I was e-mailing her from work, couldn't get much work done
We're having dinner tomorrow!

---

150 Name: Train Man ♦ SgHguKHEFY Post Date: 17/04/04 01:06

I'm sorry about the misunderstandings . . . ＿│￣│○
Actually we were squabbling about whether we'd go out tomorrow or
the day after. (´·ω·`)

---

157 Name: Train Man ♦ SgHguKHEFY Post Date: 17/04/04 01:12

I guess it wasn't a squabble but more like her being indecisive.
She kept talking about how she had an early day the next day so . . .
that kind of thing.
we also tried to work out where to go for dinner . . .
We hadn't decided till yesterday where and when we were going to
get together. ＿│￣│○

---

158 Name: Anonymous Post Date: 17/04/04 01:12

squabbling over when to get together . . . this late at night . . .
Damn, I be bombed

162 Name: Anonymous Post Date: 17/04/04 01:15

I can't believe that instead of digging our trenches we were playing with a chicken

---

167 Name: Train Man ♦ SgHguKHEFY Post Date: 17/04/04 01:18

How can I describe it . . .
We're e-mailing all kinds of silliness back and forth lately . . .
What did you eat for lunch or it's hot today or what'd you watch on TV . . .

Doing that kind of back and forth . . . and we forgot to set our date. (´ー`)

---

170 Name: Anonymous Post Date: 17/04/04 01:19

(´ー`) could we be heading towards a distressing event?

---

172 Name: Anonymous Post Date: 17/04/04 01:21

Have you decided when you're telling her you dig her?

---

174 Name: Train Man ♦ SgHguKHEFY Post Date: 17/04/04 01:22

>>172
_⌐○

---

175 Name: Anonymous Post Date: 17/04/04 01:23

>>174
Do you know her birthday?

---

177 Name: Anonymous Post Date: 17/04/04 01:24

>>174
((((;゜Д゜))) what the hell is the _⌐○!!!! Don't tell me you've already . . .
?!?!?!?

---

182 Name: Train Man ♦ SgHguKHEFY Post Date: 17/04/04 01:26

>>175
Neither one of us knows.

Oh yeah, and there's talk of commuting together but the timing is a bit difficult to coordinate . . .

She told me that some perv on the train copped a feel the other day
ヽ(｀Д´)ﾉ

---

184 Name: Anonymous Post Date: 17/04/04 01:26

Commmmmmuting togethaaaaaaaaaaahhhhhhh . . .

---

186 Name: Anonymous Post Date: 17/04/04 01:27

>>182
If I had been there, I would've kept him away

You must've said, no?

---

187 Name: Train Man ♦ SgHguKHEFY Post Date: 17/04/04 01:27

>>177
Didn't mean anything by it. Just that I hadn't really been thinking about it.
What would happen if I told her . . .
but I do feel this situation can't drag on forever . . .

---

189 Name: Anonymous Post Date: 17/04/04 01:28

I think it's cool to just take it slowly.
You guys talk romance?

190 Name: Anonymous Post Date: 17/04/04 01:28

>>186
Didja say that -----?!?! Didja didjaaaaa?!

The more she experiences stuff like that on the train, I sense that the more
the wind will blow in Train's favour . . . . . .

191 Name: Train Man ♦ SgHguKHEFY Post Date: 17/04/04 01:29

>>186
(´—`)

199 Name: Train Man ♦ SgHguKHEFY Post Date: 17/04/04 01:31

>>189

We talked a little bit about it while we discussed films

204 Name: Anonymous Post Date: 17/04/04 01:33

>>
You're pretty sure Hermes is single, right?

211 Name: Train Man ♦ SgHguKHEFY Post Date: 17/04/04 01:35

I was wondering what the deal was when she sent a rare early
morning e-mail.
'Perv copped a feel on train,' it read.

She sounded really depressed so I tried my best to cheer her up via
e-mail.

Then
'Had I been there, it would never have happened'
'But I can't expect that from you'
'Shall I take the train with you? Commute together?'

And we tried to work out how to coordinate timing and train stations but it doesn't look possible. Too complicated.

217 Name: Train Man ♦ SgHguKHEFY Post Date: 17/04/04 01:36

Truth is . . . it'd be impossible for me to dress right every day . . . ＿┌ ￢|O

222 Name: Anonymous Post Date: 17/04/04 01:38

Shit man shit, I'm so jealous I'm gonna go masturbate to a chicken.

223 Name: Anonymous Post Date: 17/04/04 01:39

>>222
Don't do it! It sounds unhealthy . . . kinda . . .

225 Name: Anonymous Post Date: 17/04/04 01:39

>>211
You've really found a self-assurance that wasn't there before.
I don't see the Train Man who couldn't decide whether or not to call Hermes.
You jumped over our heads and took a giant leap forward didn't ya.
Makes me kinda sad but I'm happy for you.

226 Name: Anonymous Post Date: 17/04/04 01:40

I guess Train always had the courage.
He just needed the right opportunity.

229 Name: Train Man ♦ SgHguKHEFY Post Date: 17/04/04 01:42

>>204
Haven't heard directly from her mouth that she is indeed 'single' ..
＿┌ ￢|O

There's a scene in Matrix 2 where Neo kisses another woman in front of Trinity and apparently, that scene gave her a bit of a shock. We talked about romantic relationships and such after we discussed that scene.

By the way, she said that if she'd been Trinity, she would have died from shock. (´—`) And me, I said 'I don't know because I have no experience' _|‾|O → 'You're joking' was how it went, basically.

243 Name: Anonymous Post Date: 17/04/04 01:49

Why don't you just ask her whether she has a boyfriend or not?
Say something like 'I thought it would be wrong of me to keep asking you out to dinner if you had a boyfriend'

256 Name: Anonymous Post Date: 17/04/04 01:57

I guess you're not gonna be telling her how you feel for a while, which means we're in for a long battle-! But it looks to me when I hear what Hermes is saying, that she knows how Train feels and that she's struggling to come to terms with it.
If you tell her now, she may say 'let me think about it' . . . at least that's how it looks to me.

258 Name: Train Man ♦ SgHguKHEFY Post Date: 17/04/04 01:58

Thanks again for all your encouragement.
I will fire myself up for tomorrow.

Laters

273 Name: Anonymous Post Date: 17/04/04 02:14

Honestly, Mr Tren doesn't need our help anymore.
We're gonna fall victim to Tren's anti-depression bombs and get depressed ourselves as we retreat back into our gloomy thread.
It could be that we're finally returning to our true states.

291 Name: Anonymous Post Date: 17/04/04 08:45

. . . blessed us with a visit after some shut-eye Mr Tren, eh . . .

First let me just charge straight into this commuting together bit tho it may get long . . . can't you try . . . even if it's difficult for you . . . to commute with her? You don't have to worry too much about your work clothes. All you have to wear is a basic suit, no? If you don't own a lot of suits, just get 7 or so shirts and that way even if you don't do laundry every day, you 'll have enough to wear something different every day

I think that even if it is a bit on the difficult side, you should step up as a man and be her knight in shining armour. These perverts on the train tend to really terrify women and you can't escape the fact that you've been knighted as the Train Man already. If saving her from a drunk was the reason you met, then why not step up to the task for real!

And as far as boyfriends are concerned, if the conversation went this way it must mean she doesn't have one. Besides, if she had a boyfriend, she would never complain about not having anybody to go restaurant-hopping with. She'd also be asking her boyfriend to protect her from the train perverts, no?

Train, this is your chance!

You can see Hermes every day!
If you do, then you can get to know her better and better!
You figured out last week that you can basically talk about 'anything', no?

Well, I'm sure the story is that Train has to get to work earlier than Hermes but . . . I think you should attempt the first two days of the week by asking your work whether you can come in a bit late on those days.

If you do end up commuting together, I think you will score extra points.

Mr Tren, this is the way to go (plant your flag dude).

---

294 Name: Train Man ♦ SgHguKHEFY Post Date: 17/04/04 10:49

Just woke up. And just made a reservation at the hair salon.

I plan on talking to her about commuting together
The problem is that the station she gets off at and my station are on different lines, not to mention the fact that they're far apart, so if I were to ride all the way with her then I would definitely be late for work. Bottom line is that if we're gonna do this, then we're both gonna have to get up early.

Plus, if we go early then we would be missing rush hour traffic . . .
_⌐|O

---

296 Name: Anonymous Post Date: 17/04/04 10:53

By the way, what are your plans for today.
Whatever you feel comfortable sharing, pls.

---

297 Name: Anonymous Post Date: 17/04/04 10:54

thought I'd just take a peek before I head out and here you are in real time
(´A`)
would like to suggest that you google a bit on how to combat train-pervs
just for general info . . .

---

298 Name: Train Man ♦ SgHguKHEFY Post Date: 17/04/04 10:59

>>296
As usual. Meet up in the early evening then go to restaurant and bar.

>>297
ok, will do.

---

305 Name: Train Man ♦ SgHguKHEFY Post Date: 17/04/04 11:43

still way early but I'm headin out.
will return in the evening.

Laters.

With the wind behind his back, Train Man heads out to face his battle. He
shows no signs of his former self during the first battle as he heads out to
face a new battle.

---

387 Name: Anonymous Post Date: 17/04/04 23:30

Though he may not reach sex, if he returns with a kiss, that's a job well done

. . . if he returns just with a friendly hand-holding, then we can get back to the business of scriptwriting . . . .

---

392 Name: Anonymous Post Date: 17/04/04 23:39

Done with the foreplay . . .

Lady Hermes	'Hey Mr Train . . . I wanna be at one with you . . . '
Train Man	'Ok'
Crane Man	'Lend me a hand . . . with the rubber'
Lady Hermes	'Today's a safe day so . . . you can have a go without . . . '
Main Man	'I can't . . . shouldn't do that . . . '
Lady Hermes	'Ha—ha, I'm just playin' with you again. I'm glad you're a man of integrity.'

But once he enters . . .

Drain Man	'oops . . . I came . . . '
Lady Hermes	' . . . already . . . ?'
Train Man	'(´·ω·`)'
Lady Hermes	'It's so like you Mr Train . . . I'll just hold on tightly (to your thing)
Rain Man	'(´—`)'

---

401 Name: Anonymous Post Date: 17/04/04 23:49

Hey everybody, are you cheering for his success or his failure . . . which is it?

I want him to succeed and become a happy couple with Hermes

---

403 Name: Anonymous Post Date: 17/04/04 23:49

>>401
I'm with ya

---

404 Name: Anonymous Post Date: 17/04/04 23:51

>>401
same here

408 Name: Anonymous Post Date: 17/04/04 23:52

>>401
1 vote for his success

would like him to build another bright lights big city story

---

409 Name: Anonymous Post Date: 17/04/04 23:52

>>401
I'm putting down 10000 Hermes on sexcess, oops, I mean success

---

410 Name: Anonymous Post Date: 17/04/04 23:52

As long as Train's happy, I don't care either way.

---

415 Name: Anonymous Post Date: 17/04/04 23:54

he's way late
does this mean you know what?

---

420 Name: Anonymous Post Date: 17/04/04 23:55

down boys down
this isn't the first time Train's been late

---

423 Name: Anonymous Post Date: 17/04/04 23:55

Train will definitely go online to send Hermes an e-mail once he gets home
and it's only natural that he'll post a quick note to us . . . therefore, I am
assuming that he hasn't gotten home yet.

---

448 Name: Anonymous Post Date: 18/04/04 00:14

I think their 2nd location tonight is a romantic bar atop a fancy hotel.
Just as Train gets ready to leave so they can catch the last train, Hermes
flashes a hotel room key . . .

---

449 Name: Anonymous Post Date: 18/04/04 00:15

>>448
(ﾉ∀`) only from the mind of a Geek

459 Name: Anonymous Post Date: 18/04/04 00:29

I realised tonight that there's no bigger bomb than not receiving a response.
I've hit my limit . . . and am heading to bed.

464 Name: Anonymous Post Date: 18/04/04 00:34

I will wait for him! Till he gets home!
I'm gonna burn the candle!

Unfortunately, there's no sign of Train showing up. But just as one by one people start giving up, Train Man returns. He returned with a secret stash of firepower.

---

476 Name: Train Man ◆ SgHguKHEFY Post Date: 18/04/04 00:42

Hey people. Just got in.
I took her home so . . . it got to be this late . . . (´ー`)
I'm totally exhausted today . . . ＿| ￣|○

Ok, I'm gonna go change. Laters.

---

478 Name: Anonymous Post Date: 18/04/04 00:44

>>476
welcome home and gooood job

479 Name: Anonymous Post Date: 18/04/04 00:44

we're under attttaaaaaaaaaack----!
————(Д゜(○=(゜∀゜)=○)Д゜)————!!!

481 Name: Anonymous Post Date: 18/04/04 00:44

ah yeaaaaaaah-------- ————(Д゜(○=(゜∀゜)=○)Д゜)————!!!!!

took her hooooome-------!!! ————(Д゜(○=(゜∀゜)=○)Д゜)————!!!!!

487 Name: Anonymous Post Date: 18/04/04 00:45

>I took her home so . . . . it got to be this late . . . .
>I took her home so . . . . it got to be this late . . . .
>I took her home so . . . . it got to be this late . . . .
>I took her home so . . . . it got to be this late . . . .
>I took her home so . . . . it got to be this late . . . .

A blow to the body straight off . . . _|￢|O

523 Name: Train Man ♦ SgHguKHEFY Post Date: 18/04/04 01:00

I'm back.

Though we were meeting in the evening, since my reservation at the
hair salon was on the early side, I left way early.

When I got to the salon, the same hairdresser did my hair
She asked 'Do you have a date today?'
So I said, rather cool, 'yeah, kinda.' (´ー`)

Since I had a lot of time to kill, I went to Akihabara, to check out
some electronics. Not that I can afford to buy anything anymore . . .
_|￢|O
When one of the PR girls said to me 'you don't look like the Akihabara
type' I was stunned. (` ·ω· ´)

After killing some time I headed for our meeting place and got there
15 minutes early but she was already there. I quickly ran over to her.

528 Name: Anonymous Post Date: 18/04/04 01:00

>'you don't look like the Akihabara type'

killin me

540 Name: Anonymous Post Date: 18/04/04 01:02

'You don't look like the Akihabara type'
are you serious?

Can people really metamorphose this far?
You must be jokinggggggg!!!!!!

---

556 Name: Anonymous Post Date: 18/04/04 01:06

shit . . . it's too late . . . there's nowhere to hide . . . . . .

---

559 Name: Anonymous Post Date: 18/04/04 01:06

My weapon of choice when it comes to couples is a bamboo pike.
I wonder if I climbed the roof, would I be able to reach Train?

---

563 Name: Anonymous Post Date: 18/04/04 01:07

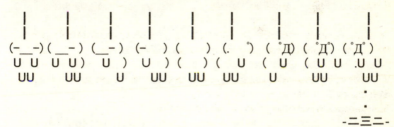

---

573 Name: Anonymous Post Date: 18/04/04 01:08

calm down everybody!!! This isn't even the first wave of attacks!!!!!!

---

582 Name: Anonymous Post Date: 18/04/04 01:09

hold up!!!
enemy aircraft have not dropped bombs yet!!!

---

587 Name: Anonymous Post Date: 18/04/04 01:10

>>582
this is how we are with only a warning shot . . . . . .

This time, Train Man aims his gun directly at the Geeks, who are fretting over
the false alarm.

616 Name: Train Man ♦ SgHguKHEFY Post Date: 18/04/04 01:15

'Hello.'
'Whoa, you're early today'

We say hello casually. She tells me that since she had always been
late she did her best to be early today. She was wearing a very light,
spring outfit.

She was wearing trousers, well, jeans, I guess, which was unusual.
Her legs were so skinny that I wanted to ask if she was eating right.
She had a cute short-sleeved shirt on. Her arms were so white and
thin too (ohyeah)
What can I say . . . the light fabric is . . . really makes a guy smile . . .
(´ ─ `)

We immediately started to walk towards the restaurant.
Again, the street was overflowing with people on either side of us and
we parted the crowds. I had my head turned slightly to look behind
me.
'Crowded again today, isn't it,' she mumbled.
'It'll be ok because I'll hold on tightly to you,' I said, half-jokingly as I
grabbed her wrist.
She laughed, looking down at the wrist I grabbed.
'Make sure you follow me to the restaurant' I said, heading towards it.

Her wrists were so thin (´ ─ `)

---

625 Name: Anonymous Post Date: 18/04/04 01:16

>I said, half-jokingly as I grabbed her wrist.
>I said, half-jokingly as I grabbed her wrist.
>I said, half-jokingly as I grabbed her wrist.
>I said, half-jokingly as I grabbed her wrist.
>I said, half-jokingly as I grabbed her wrist.

New type of bomb rears its headdddddddddd----!!!!!!!
──────────(ﾟAﾟ)──────── !!!!!

630 Name: Anonymous Post Date: 18/04/04 01:17

this was meant to be my last . . . breath . . . . . .

_|⌐|O I'm sorry . . . . . .

635 Name: Anonymous Post Date: 18/04/04 01:18

medic!!!! Med--------dddddddiiiiiiicccccccccc!!!!!!!

636 Name: Anonymous Post Date: 18/04/04 01:18

what a sad sight . . .

640 Name: Anonymous Post Date: 18/04/04 01:18

Does Train have a mobile suit like in Gundam that he slips into??

645 Name: Anonymous Post Date: 18/04/04 01:19

```
      /‾‾‾‾‾‾‾‾‾‾‾‾‾‾‾‾‾‾‾‾‾‾‾‾‾‾‾‾‾
     |  Upham! Upham! ('A`)! ('A`) Bring it over here! upham!
      _____
                     V
                    /‾‾‾‾‾‾\  ('A`) Nuttin'
      /\      ._/‾\   |_____|      /\    /\
     /  \    |\/_`\|___     |∩(・∀・;|├┘  |‾‾\  /‾‾|
    /    |‾|‾|( ´д`; |├┘ _ユⅡ___   |‾|‾‾|  |‾‾|
   /    |_|_|(  "  つつ[三≡_[------°    |_|__|  |_|
  /    |‾|‾|  ︿︿   ‖ /            |‾|‾‾|
 /    |_|_|___] \_)_)..|||   |‾|‾‾|  |_|
```

661 Name: Anonymous Post Date: 18/04/04 01:21

so it's come to this, eh
Train who used to be a Geek just like us, has really transformed . . .

God showered a never-before-seen powerful light on him . . . and
we who have been left behind can only watch his shining aura

Grrulp

663 Name: Anonymous Post Date: 18/04/04 01:21

```
 — —  —  - — — — —  -    — —   — - — — — - — —
      -         -     -     — —      - -    - -
            —  — — — — —  = — — —  = — — —  -
            -     —            -
      Mamah      —   — — — -  — —  — — — — —  — —
            —       —           —          — —
      -  — —   — — —  = — — — —  -
         — —            —
         —   — — — —   — — — — —  — —
```

```
        ∧ ∧
       /⌒＼)   lukewarmness
      ＝＝＝
      ＝＝
```

664 Name: Anonymous Post Date: 18/04/04 01:21

everybody is being enveloped by the light . . .

but me, no, no . . . I must keep going . . . I won't be taken

672 Name: Anonymous Post Date: 18/04/04 01:23

>'It'll be ok because I'll hold on tightly to you,'
>I said, half-jokingly as I grabbed her wrist.
>She laughed, looking down at the wrist I grabbed.
>'Make sure you follow me to the restaurant'

What the!!! What is happening here!!!!???
Is this the new weapon????!!

688 Name: Anonymous Post Date: 18/04/04 01:25

I report!

Our First Anti-aircraft Artillery Unit has been wiped out!
It appears that our enemy has employed a new type of bomb!!!!

689 Name: Anonymous Post Date: 18/04/04 01:25

Amazing how Train's words, one by one enter the sticky-messy place in
my heart and then explode.
What precision. Only with a new weapon is this possible.

One by one the Geeks take flak yet Train Man continues to pull the trigger.

695 Name: Train Man ✦ SgHguKHEFY Post Date: 18/04/04 01:26

I kept holding on to her wrist.
Just as we were waiting for the light, she pushed away my hand then grabbed the palm of my hand.
'This feels much better,' she smiled at me. I was so shocked and have no clue how I looked at that moment.

Her hand was so thin and cold and soft and small.
Even now, I can still remember how her hand felt in mine.

I must have been nervous because as we walked for a while, my palms started to sweat . . . _⌐|O

Even so, thank you for not letting go.

---

699 Name: Anonymous Post Date: 18/04/04 01:27

Waaaaaaaaaaaaaaaaaaaaaaaaaaaaaaaaaaaaaaaaaaaaaaaaaaaaaaaaaaaaa
aaaaaaaaaaaaaaaaaaaaaaaaaaaaaaaaaaaaaaaaaaaaaaaaaaaaaaaaaaaaaaa
aaaaaaaaaaaaaaaaaaaaaaaaaaaaaaaaaaaaaaaaaaaaaaaaaaaa

---

702 Name: Anonymous Post Date: 18/04/04 01:27

this is proof positive no doubt no way yes yes

---

701 Name: Anonymous Post Date: 18/04/04 01:27

another new bomb!
We need to evacuate everybody within a 10-mile radius of the thread!
Hurry!!!!!

---

707 Name: Anonymous Post Date: 18/04/04 01:28

>Just as we were waiting for the light, she pushed away my hand
What?
>then grabbed the palm of my hand.
Neeeeeeeeaaaaaaah, kaboom!

713 Name: Anonymous Post Date: 18/04/04 01:28

>>707
like an attack with a running start or something . . .
shock and awe

The Geeks grumble on, complaining about why couples can't just stand
still at a traffic light, adding preposterous complaints about this or that
ridiculous scenario, expressing anger and frustration as Train Man
continues his attack.

---

715 Name: Anonymous Post Date: 18/04/04 01:29

I can't understand why this hand-holding attack was more powerful than a
plain old sex-attack.

---

717 Name: Anonymous Post Date: 18/04/04 01:29

> then grabbed the palm of my hand.
>'This seems much better,'
> then grabbed the palm of my hand.
>'This feels much better,'
> then grabbed the palm of my hand.
>'This feels much better,'
> then grabbed the palm of my hand.
>'This feels much better,'
> then grabbed the palm of my hand.
>'This feels much better,'
> then grabbed the palm of my hand.
>'This feels much better,'
> then grabbed the palm of my hand.
>'This feels much better,'

2nd wave comin our way!!!!
and a massive one!!!!

720 Name: Anonymous Post Date: 18/04/04 01:29

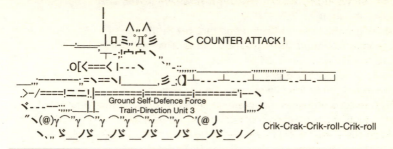

840 Name: Anonymous Post Date: 18/04/04 01:50

What in the world have we . . . created
Could anybody have imagined he'd grow into such a beast?
In the beginning, it was just curiosity and perhaps a bit of sympathy.
Once he accepted our helping hand and heartfelt encouragement he then
powered-up, got stronger and built upon that strength on his own.
And now, he has turned into a monster who has the power to crush us
with his toenail.
I can't tell if this is a victory or a defeat for us . . .
The fact that we have given birth to a monster who has far exceeded any
of our hopes has nothing to do with our achievement as such, for what we
did was merely awaken something that lay dormant in him, an instinct.
And so yes, in fact, yes, we have been defeated, we are forever chained
to the cycle of defeat.

865 Name: Train Man ♦ SgHguKHEFY Post Date: 18/04/04 01:55

The restaurant we went to today really had an eclectic vibe.
Can I say, tinged with horror . . .
'I've been wanting to try this place out~' according to her. Me, I was
way nervous.

Food-wise, it was majorly good. (゚д゚)
Wasn't too expensive either.
She ordered a cocktail and I said 'I'll have one of those too'
'You drink cocktails?'
'Just thought I should try what you're having . . . '
'(laugh)'

Then she handed me Matrix 3.
Though we'd talked about it over e-mail, we talked some more about what she thought.
She's got the hots for Keanu and me, for Smith.
The scene leading up to the Neo-Trinity kiss really pulled her in ((((;゜д゜)))
and got her all anxious
so when they finally kissed, she really freaked. (゜Д゜)
As for me, watching that scene got me going you know where (´ー｀)

---

870 Name: Anonymous Post Date: 18/04/04 01:56

third wave comin'!

---

884 Name: Anonymous Post Date: 18/04/04 01:58

(in the film) and when the kiss happened, she really freaked (゜Д゜)

all right, this threw me. Lol.

---

919 Name: Anonymous Post Date: 18/04/04 02:07

that gap . . . frightens me too

---

922 Name: Anonymous Post Date: 18/04/04 02:08

I've been living in Tokyo for a long time but
I have no idea what restaurant you're talking about

If it was in Nagoya, this is where I'd imagine you went
http://www.kangoku.com/41.htm

---

924 Name: Anonymous Post Date: 18/04/04 02:08

>>922
I imagined something similar, old-school Japanese tapas place only with prison decor

---

933 Name: Anonymous Post Date: 18/04/04 02:10

http://r.gnavi.co.jp/g528910

should be it

---

923 Name: Train Man ♦ SgHguKHEFY Post Date: 18/04/04 02:08

and we talked about commuting together in the morning while we talked, she kept getting sadder and sadder so I kept asking her if she was all right. In the end, it just sounded too difficult to coordinate, time-wise, so we just left it.

Then I gave her a printout of some info I had googled about fighting off train-pervs. I mentioned a few key pointers which I had memorised earlier. She kept thanking me over and over again bowing her head. I bowed a few times too.

Our bookings for the second place were creeping up on us so we left the restaurant a little early. We split the bill.
'Isn't it time you let me take you out?' I asked jokingly to which she replied, quite simply, 'no way.' (´ー`)

---

929 Name: Anonymous Post Date: 18/04/04 02:09

You are so sweet.
For real, you're making me cry.

---

941 Name: Anonymous Post Date: 18/04/04 02:12

hey . . .
people . . . you guys are really melting down into soppiness aren't you

---

942 Name: Anonymous Post Date: 18/04/04 02:12

shit. I'm all restless. I'm gonna eat a banana.

---

944 Name: Anonymous Post Date: 18/04/04 02:13

we ain't got no banana here

---

945 Name: Anonymous Post Date: 18/04/04 02:13

>>933

Three times each day, a heart-stopping performance stirs your inner appetites at this prison-themed tapas bar. (all rooms are private)

(all rooms are private)
(all rooms are private)
(all rooms are private)
(all rooms are private)
(all rooms are private)
(all rooms are private)
(all rooms are private)
(all rooms are private)

953 Name: Anonymous Post Date: 18/04/04 02:16

>>923
I'm not sure what the general vibe was so I may be reading too much into it but from Train's comments, I get the feeling the morning commute situation is on the back burner for now.

And, about fighting off the train-pervs—well, instead of handing her a printout, I think it'd be better if you'd just told her what you knew.

That said, with Hermes' massive good impression of Train, don't think any of this even dents it . . .

960 Name: Anonymous Post Date: 18/04/04 02:19

>>agree with 953 about dropping the morning commute topic
fighting off the train-perv situation, well, receiving printouts, though from good intentions could trigger a pull-back.

966 Name: Anonymous Post Date: 18/04/04 02:20

>>965
Yep! Point taken! But . . .

('A`) No way could something like this break the bond between Hermes and Train . . .

967 Name: Anonymous Post Date: 18/04/04 02:20

This thread is all about digging frantically in search of any remotely

971 Name: Anonymous Post Date: 18/04/04 02:21

>>953
mostly agree
I mean there are train pervs everywhere and even if someone cops a feel,
it's a shock when it happens, but you put it behind you, so if a guy (and
especially a guy you kinda dig) ends up stressing about it, then it blows all
out of proportion and becomes worse than it actually is . . . so we should
drop it . . . . is my advice, after a long absence . . .

56 Name: Train Man ♦ SgHguKHEFY Post Date: 18/04/04 02:29

When we left the restaurant she reached for my hand
so I held hers right back. This time she didn't say anything in
particular and neither did I.

The second place we went to was a fair way from the first so we took
the train.
We held hands most of the time except when we bought our tickets
and went through the turnstiles. Every time, she grabbed me first . . .

While on the train,
'If we could commute like this together . . . it would be
so great . . .' she said, turning up her flirt volume . . .
━━━ヽ(ヽ(°∀°(°∀°ヽ(°∀°)/°∀°)/∀°)/°)/)/━━━!!!!!
I really hate the train company for giving us the damn line problem . . .

We get to our stop and start walking. We leave the station and I
reached my hand out towards hers.
'oh, thanks.'
'of course . . .'
she grabbed my hand, slightly hesitating . . . (´—`)

Man am I sleepy . . . ＿|￣|○

66 Name: Anonymous Post Date: 18/04/04 02:30

You're a full on couple! An avec, as the French say.

73 Name: Anonymous Post Date: 18/04/04 02:31

avec! Haven't seen that word in a long, long while.

90 Name: Anonymous Post Date: 18/04/04 02:33

there's no ifs or ands or buts about it. Done deal.
It's gone way beyond talking about train-pervs or not.
(could be Lady Hermes makes the best dialogue.)

good for you, Train.
You, dude, are supa fly! ('A`)

118 Name: Anonymous Post Date: 18/04/04 02:38

>>56, for me was the ultimate bomb second only to the God 125 Couple
Seat bomb. ＿￢|O

129 Name: Anonymous Post Date: 18/04/04 02:39

It's not Train that's in love with Hermes!
It's Hermes that's fallin for Train!!

156 Name: Train Man ♦ SgHguKHEFY Post Date: 18/04/04 02:45

**The second spot was more café-like and had tons of sweets on the
menu. This place was another one of those spots on her list.**

**Here, I ordered the same cocktail as her again.
She laughed way loud.**

**I usually don't eat sweets but man, was it gooooood (ˊдˋ)
It had a very adult-friendly taste and so even men could eat the stuff
no hassle.**

**Then we talked for the first time about fashion or I guess she just
asked me tons of questions, totally one-way. I also asked her for
some pointers on how to dress.**

This has nothing to do with the above but

She had mentioned having an early day the next day---which was a Monday---originally we had talked about going out on Sunday but we switched it to Saturday because of her early Monday thing.

We had basically decided to discuss the morning commute thing when we saw each other today . . .

---

168 Name: Anonymous Post Date: 18/04/04 02:48

Train, you are maturing at an incredible speed

---

169 Name: Anonymous Post Date: 18/04/04 02:48

>>saw each other today
????

---

172 Name: Anonymous Post Date: 18/04/04 02:49

You, Train Man, are like a completely dried-out sponge that is now doused in water

---

173 Name: Anonymous Post Date: 18/04/04 02:49

People . . . that's not it, no, that's not it, man.
Let Train's metamorphosis be the daily bread we feed on!!!

---

176 Name: Train Man ♦ SgHguKHEFY Post Date: 18/04/04 02:50

>>169
sorry. I'm talking about yesterday's news.
Just in case you were wondering, she's not here sitting next to me or anything.
I'm alone at home now.

---

243 Name: sage Post Date: 18/04/04 03:08

Thanks Mr Train! I figured out why I was Geek-Girl because of you!!!

Next time I catch a train-perv I won't kick him onto the train platform and

give him one of my wrestling moves . . . no, I won't do that, no I won't,
so . . . ＿| ̄|O

I've sustained a slightly different injury from the bomb than the Geeks but
nevertheless am near death . . .

---

246 Name: Anonymous Post Date: 18/04/04 03:08

>>243
 . . .

---

273 Name: 243 Post Date: 18/04/04 03:12

and anyway, I've already given up . . . . . . sorry
I'm not going to post any more
But you know, I don't have a Mr Train in my life . . .
I suppose I'll keep fighting off the train-pervs as usual . . .

Sorry for messing up your thread

---

278 Name: Anonymous Post Date: 18/04/04 03:13

>>273
no worries
O
＼
＿ﾄ| ̄|O

---

301 Name: Train Man ♦ SgHguKHEFY Post Date: 18/04/04 03:18

We were so wrapped up in our conversation that suddenly it was
time for last orders. We decided to leave because we didn't feel like
staying till closing time. It was kind of cold outside. There weren't
as many people out on the streets as earlier so losing sight of each
other wasn't much of a concern anymore but we ended up holding
hands anyway. Don't know who went for it first . . .

On our train ride back home, she seemed a bit moody so I asked
'Are you getting tired?'
to which she replied with a shake of her head in silence. This was the
first time I had seen this particular type of gesture.

'I think I may be a little drunk'
'Rr . . . really . . . ?'
I start getting a bit stressed.

And so the silence continued on for a bit longer and since she still
seemed extra moody with her head hung low, I leaned in and peeked
up at her face. She opened her eyes wide and said 'mmm?' forcing
out a happy voice. Her expression got me all fired up inside.

We were getting close to the station she usually gets off at so I
asked her
'How far do you have to walk from the station to your house?'
'About ten minutes.'
'Then I'll walk you home.'
'What! No, I'd feel bad if you did.'

And so my offer was refused just like that . . . (´･ω･`)

---

306 Name: Anonymous Post Date: 18/04/04 03:19

since she still seemed extra moody with her head hung low, I leaned in
and peeked up at her face.
since she still seemed extra moody with her head hung low, I leaned in
and peeked up at her face.
since she still seemed extra moody with her head hung low, I leaned in
and peeked up at her face.
since she still seemed extra moody with her head hung low, I leaned in
and peeked up at her face.

---

331 Name: Anonymous Post Date: 18/04/04 03:23

there's something that follows the refusal . . .

something big, no?

something so big it may kill every one of us in one go

---

332 Name: Anonymous Post Date: 18/04/04 03:23

a moody Hermes . . . could that be a hint . . . ???

no, it couldn't be . . .

---

342 Name: Anonymous Post Date: 18/04/04 03:25

> On our train ride back home, she seemed a bit moody.
This is key.
Yep, I've got a feeling something scary is about to happen. And what is
that explosive roar I hear coming closer to us?

---

347 Name: Anonymous Post Date: 18/04/04 03:26

'Mmm . . . but I'd really like to spend more time with you, so would you
please walk me home?'

is this it?

---

354 Name: Anonymous Post Date: 18/04/04 03:28

Lady Hermes was playing the sensitive-to-your-needs card only to tease
you and was waiting for Tren Man to say 'I insist, let me walk you home'!!!

Whoooooaaaaaa, lucky dog lucky dog.

---

355 Name: Anonymous Post Date: 18/04/04 03:28

>>332
'I'm sad because even though I want to be with Mr Train forever I can't
avoid the fact that our time to part is approaching . . . '

---

357 Name: Anonymous Post Date: 18/04/04 03:28

>>355
you is too good with the girly talk innit

---

358 Name: Anonymous Post Date: 18/04/04 03:28

>>355
Highly likely that Lady Hermes would say something like that.

---

359 Name: Anonymous Post Date: 18/04/04 03:28

>>355

Judging from how things have progressed so far, it can only go in that direction

---

Train Man pulled out an enormous firearm from deep within, aimed it directly at the Geeks and pulled the trigger.

---

365 Name: Train Man ♦ SgHguKHEFY Post Date: 18/04/04 03:30

We got to her station. I said
'I'll e-mail you again. Good night' as I prepared to part ways, but she softly reached for my hand and pulled me towards the door. I was feeling kind of 'wha—?' but I let myself be pulled.

In the end, both of us got off the train.
She said kind of apologetically 'I've changed my mind . . . will you walk me home?'

She was pleeeeeeading----- ah yeaaaaah-----
———(´∀`)·ω·) ゚Д`)゚∀`)·∀·) ̄ー ̄ ) ´_ゝ`)−_)゚∋`)´Д`)゚ー゚)———

That expression on her face could have lasted through at least three drinks for me.
'Sure. No problem,' I answered, loud and clear.

After the ticket gate, we held hands, both at the same time . . .
After about 5 minutes we hit a residential area where there were hardly any people out. Because there seemed to be lots of dark areas and I sensed a bit of danger, I said
'I'll walk you home from now on'
to which she just nodded.

---

370 Name: Anonymous Post Date: 18/04/04 03:31

hey everybody! She pulled his hand!

---

373 Name: Anonymous Post Date: 18/04/04 03:32

> but she softly reached for my hand and pulled me towards the door
> but she softly reached for my hand and pulled me towards the door

> but she softly reached for my hand and pulled me towards the door
> but she softly reached for my hand and pulled me towards the door
> but she softly reached for my hand and pulled me towards the door

---

386 Name: Anonymous Post Date: 18/04/04 03:33

hey everybody----they've been holding hands all day long today!!!

---

436 Name: Anonymous Post Date: 18/04/04 03:40

Lady Hermes is definitely waiting for Train to tell her he's falling for her!
Most women are the type that just waits to be told coz they can't get
themselves to say it!
They only own up once you're in the relationship! Unfair man, unfair!
Definitely.

---

478 Name: Train Man ♦ SgHguKHEFY Post Date: 18/04/04 03:46

**I think we walked for about ten minutes. We got to the front of her
house, which was a really nice one . . .**

**'Here it is. And thank you for walking me all the way,' she said and
bowed deeply.**
'No problem at all,' I said, bowing back.
'Will you e-mail me when you get home?'
'Um, yes. And tomorrow too.'
'Let's talk over the phone some time.'
'Sounds good . . . '
We talked about random stuff in front of the house.
'Oh, you might miss the last train,' she said, always the thoughtful one.
**'Right, I should get going,' I said and pulled away from her. My hands
were the last to pull away. I walked for a while and turned around and
saw her waving.**

That's about it for now . . . (´ー`)

---

489 Name: Anonymous Post Date: 18/04/04 03:48

Hold on, Train. You mean, you didn't tell her how you feel about her . . . ?
I think Hermes was waiting for you to say it . . .

497 Name: Anonymous Post Date: 18/04/04 03:49

That's about it for now . . . (´ー`)
That's about it for now . . . (´ー`)
That's about it for now . . . (´ー`)
That's about it for now . . . (´ー`)
What's about it? ＿| ￣|○

500 Name: Train Man ♦ SgHguKHEFY Post Date: 18/04/04 03:49

Bottom line, no kiss, no telling her I love her.
Search me how I go about that ＿| ￣|○

501 Name: Anonymous Post Date: 18/04/04 03:49

I think you're ready to go
>>Train

502 Name: Anonymous Post Date: 18/04/04 03:49

>Train
I got lots I want to say but first off, thanks for the report.
You must be exhausted. I really appreciate you filling us in.

530 Name: Train Man ♦ SgHguKHEFY Post Date: 18/04/04 03:53

I'm going to bed.
Thanks again, as alwayzzzzzz-
Laters.

535 Name: Anonymous Post Date: 18/04/04 03:53

>>Train
Good night.
Laters.

536 Name: Anonymous Post Date: 18/04/04 03:53

Thankzzz Train--!
Laters

538 Name: Anonymous Post Date: 18/04/04 03:54

>>530
good job. Best to come clean quickly.
Laters.

539 Name: Anonymous Post Date: 18/04/04 03:54

>>530
you've done another amazing job today. Chill. Laters

541 Name: Anonymous Post Date: 18/04/04 03:54

Good job Train!
Laters

542 Name: Anonymous Post Date: 18/04/04 03:54

>>530 laters. Sleep well!

544 Name: Anonymous Post Date: 18/04/04 03:54

good night . . .

at this point, your time belongs to Hermes.
Get the fuck to bed . . .

546 Name: Anonymous Post Date: 18/04/04 03:54

>>530
good job

laters.

547 Name: Anonymous Post Date: 18/04/04 03:54

how many are we!!!!!

548 Name: Anonymous Post Date: 18/04/04 03:55

>>530
hey
can you let us hang out in your dark shadow for just a while longer . . .

549 Name: Anonymous Post Date: 18/04/04 03:55

laters

550 Name: Anonymous Post Date: 18/04/04 03:49

Laters. Dude, there's a lot of us.

567 Name: Anonymous Post Date: 18/04/04 03:58

Train's definitely got a chance . . . all that's left is the timing for when he comes clean.
Can't do it over the phone or e-mail. Has to be during a date.

570 Name: Anonymous Post Date: 18/04/04 04:00

Best if it happened on the train, you know, where they met.

577 Name: Anonymous Post Date: 18/04/04 04:01

If this doesn't lead to coupledom then
Hermes is ultimately an alien and
I will swear off pussies for real

580 Name: Anonymous Post Date: 18/04/04 04:02

>>570
the best man at the wedding, of course, will be the drunken old fart from the train.

What a story, to have a drunken old fart play cupid . . .

581 Name: Anonymous Post Date: 18/04/04 04:03

lastly, I'd like to offer some words of advice to Train . . .

Women are strange creatures . . .
When you're told to never come round it means that you need to get your ass over to her even during a typhoon or when a nuclear bomb is about to drop, and when you're told you don't need to walk her back, you need to hold her hand even tighter and insist on walking her back.
When you take the words at face value then they complain and pout that you don't 'understand women.'
And when you try to push through something they seriously don't want to do, then they will consider you weird.

This is the way of the woman . . . and I tell ya, it took me a while to figure it out. _⌐⌐O

Most agreed that things were flowing smoothly and that Hermes was going to be an easy catch. The Geeks were now on the offense after a long period of constantly being under attack but what they were lacking was the final bomb aimed at Hermes. Was Hermes really going to fall? Were they all going to quickly withdraw without planning the final blow?

Mission
4

The Time for the Cups have Arrived

'She softly reached for my hand and pulled me towards the door' – a major offensive on Train Man. The words 'Haven't decided on our next date' open the floodgates and lead to an amazing turn of events for the netizens.

656 Name: Train Man ♦ SgHguKHEFY Post Date: 18/04/04 12:09

Good morning.
Damn, I slept well.
The good kind of tired really makes for a good night's rest, huh. (´—`)

658 Name: Anonymous Post Date: 18/04/04 12:13

>>656
when are you getting back out there?

660 Name: Train Man ♦ SgHguKHEFY Post Date: 18/04/04 12:18

Haven't decided on our next date yet.
We just left it that we'd get in touch. That's how it goes.

661 Name: Anonymous Post Date: 18/04/04 12:18

>>656
mornin. What nice weather today.

665 Name: Train Man ♦ SgHguKHEFY Post Date: 18/04/04 12:26

A few posts sounded like I shouldn't tell her how I feel just yet but since last night, I guess there's been a shift! So now I'm supposed to own up . . .
_⌐|O

671 Name: Anonymous Post Date: 18/04/04 12:37

>>665
Well we haven't got a clue what you guys are on about in your e-mails . . .

Sounds like you've got a good thing going.
You should just work out the timing on your own and take it from there.

---

672 Name: Anonymous Post Date: 18/04/04 12:39

The timing should be up to Train Man himself. Don't listen to the opinions in the thread. This is just my opinion but judging from your report yesterday, you guys are seriously clicking which means the opportunity is ripe.
By the way, did Hermes' friend ever give her feedback about Train Man?

---

675 Name: Train Man ♦ SgHguKHEFY Post Date: 18/04/04 12:45

I see . . .
I had no idea . . . 9 __⌐ ⌐
>>672
Didn't get much feedback about her feedback . . .

---

676 Name: Anonymous Post Date: 18/04/04 12:47

The fact that you can't work out the best time to tell her how you feel . . .
is kinda Geek-like . . .

---

679 Name: Train Man ♦ SgHguKHEFY Post Date: 18/04/04 12:52

Whoa, I got an e-mail.
Looks like she's reading the printout about fighting off the train pervs.
She says she's going to try some of it out from early tomorrow
morning. (´−`)
I'm still definitely a Geek . . . . . __⌐ |O

---

680 Name: Anonymous Post Date: 18/04/04 12:52

>>675
When you say you had no idea . . . are you saying you had no idea you
guys were clicking? If so, you are seriously thick.
I thought Hermes decided to get up close and personal because her friend
said it was ok.

685 Name: Anonymous Post Date: 18/04/04 12:55

You know, I was here till 3am last night, and I've been following this from
two previous threads and well, I live with my girlfriend and she caught me
typing away in the middle of the night and basically accused me of
cheating on her . . . and then she kept thinking I *was* cheating on her . . .
and the situation escalated into a discussion about splitting up . . .
anyway, we haven't split up yet but she did leave a while ago . . . what do
you think, is she making me suffer? . . . . . . because I was jealous of
Hermes and Train . . .
I've been blown to bits for real with this bomb.

686 Name: Train Man ♦ SgHguKHEFY Post Date: 18/04/04 12:55

Recently I've been dying to tell her she's cute.

688 Name: Anonymous Post Date: 18/04/04 12:56

>>685
. . . . . .

689 Name: Anonymous Post Date: 18/04/04 12:56

>>685
Bring her to the thread.
Us Geeks will convince her of the truth.

690 Name: Train Man ♦ SgHguKHEFY Post Date: 18/04/04 12:57

>>685
what the . . . _⌐|○

695 Name: Anonymous Post Date: 18/04/04 13:00

Lol . . . yep, she's out and says she's not planning to come home today.
>>621
Sorry . . . as loyal supporters of the same Train, could you please just let
this one go

702 Name: Anonymous Post Date: 18/04/04 13:05

>>686
Say it.

705 Name: Anonymous Post Date: 18/04/04 13:06

>>702
If it feels like the right time for Train then it is the right time.

707 Name: Anonymous Post Date: 18/04/04 13:12

If you held hands all the way through and she pulled you off the train like
that . . . and if she says 'that's not the kind of relationship I had in mind for
us' that'd be a crime. Impossible.

711 Name: Anonymous Post Date: 18/04/04 13:16

>705
Definitely. The best time to say it is when you feel like you want to and can
actually say it.
But I get this feeling Mista Tren's personality is similar to mine . . .
That when you tell yourself you have something to say, then that kind of
scares you and ends up being the reason why you can't say it . . .
(sorry if I'm way off base)
I don't know why but this type basically makes a conscious decision then
wanders off on a tangent.

And then it arrived out of the blue.

---

714 Name: Train Man ♦ SgHguKHEFY Post Date: 18/04/04 13:18

Receiving callllllll.

---

716 Name: Anonymous Post Date: 18/04/04 13:19

Call's come innnnnn------!
——(ﾟ∀ﾟ)——(ﾟ∀)——(　　ﾟ)——(　　)——(ﾟ　)——(∀ﾟ)——
—(ﾟ∀ﾟ)—— !!!!!

717 Name: Anonymous Post Date: 18/04/04 13:19

Comecomecome-----!
They'll get together again today!!!
Wanna do lunch?
Well, I won't force you or anything!!

738 Name: Train Man ♦ SgHguKHEFY Post Date: 18/04/04 13:26

Will meet up

740 Name: Anonymous Post Date: 18/04/04 13:27

> 738 Name: Train Man ♦ SgHguKHEFY Post Date: 18/04/04
> 13:26
>
> Will meet up

ah yeah Ｙ⌒Ｙ⌒(ﾟ∀ﾟ)⌒Ｙ⌒(｡A｡)⌒Ｙ⌒(ﾟ∀ﾟ)⌒Ｙ⌒Ｙ　!!!
ah yeah ah yeah ah yeah ah yeah───(ﾟ∀ﾟ≡(ﾟ∀ﾟ≡ﾟ∀ﾟ)≡ﾟ∀ﾟ)───!!!!!!!!!!
ah yeah! ─(´_ゝ`)´_>`)─·)ﾟ∀ﾟ§ ;;;;)´A`)´−`)·ω·`)`Д´)0皿0)´∀`)·(ｴ)·)─!!!!

742 Name: Anonymous Post Date: 18/04/04 13:27

Ahyeahahyeahahyeahahyeah------
───(ﾟ∀ﾟ≡(ﾟ∀ﾟ≡ﾟ∀ﾟ)≡ﾟ∀ﾟ)───!!!!!!!!!!

743 Name: Anonymous Post Date: 18/04/04 13:28

Seeing her!
Great . . . respect . . . you da man . . . you is shining . . .
Laters.

747 Name: Anonymous Post Date: 18/04/04 13:28

Ahyeaaaah ⌒Ｙ⌒(ﾟ∀ﾟ)⌒Ｙ⌒(｡A｡)⌒Ｙ⌒(ﾟ∀ﾟ)⌒Ｙ⌒Ｙ!!!
supa dupa mega development----!!!!
───(((((ﾟ(ﾟ(ﾟ((ﾟﾟ∀∀ﾟﾟ)))ﾟ)ﾟ)ﾟ)))))───!!!!!!

748 Name: Anonymous Post Date: 18/04/04 13:28

Day time bomb!

```
                          r-,
                     J'‾ 'I-)\
                    T'L l/^/
                     `ᒪ‾\<
########    ##      ## | i_1      ##      ## ####
##     ## ##       ## \_/ /      ###     ## ####
##     ## ##       ## ᒪ_j'(‾_)    ####    ## ####
########   ##       ## | '(—      ## ## ##   ##
## ##      ##       ## | /—,      ## ####
##    ##   ##       ## \_J)=7    ## ### ####
## #       # #   #######  |-i| l/   # #    # #  ####
```

749 Name: Anonymous Post Date: 18/04/04 13:28

Whoa! It's a kamikaze!!!! Train's been possessed by the kamikaze spirit!!!

752 Name: Anonymous Post Date: 18/04/04 13:29

Who could have predicted this attack in broad daylight?

757 Name: Anonymous Post Date: 18/04/04 13:29

They've come at us knowing we were vulnerable in daylight

771 Name: Train Man ♦ SgHguKHEFY Post Date: 18/04/04 13:32

goo hoooos

775 Name: Anonymous Post Date: 18/04/04 13:33

goo hooos???????

779 Name: Anonymous Post Date: 18/04/04 13:33

>>771
Wassup?

780 Name: Anonymous Post Date: 18/04/04 13:33

>>771
What da . . . is this code . . . for what . . . somebody decode it pls. Is he asking for help?

781 Name: Anonymous Post Date: 18/04/04 13:33

goo hoooos??
Somebody decode it pleeeease!!!!

782 Name: Anonymous Post Date: 18/04/04 13:33

Going to her house?

783 Name: Anonymous Post Date: 18/04/04 13:34

>>771
Dpt of Information, Dpt of Information, code charts pls

784 Name: Anonymous Post Date: 18/04/04 13:34

Goo hoooos . . .
   . . .

Going to her house!!!!!!!! Tada----------

785 Name: Anonymous Post Date: 18/04/04 13:34

>>782
You got ittttttttttttttttt!!!!!!
you must be jokkkkkinnnnnnnnggggggggggggggg!!!!!!!

798 Name: Anonymous Post Date: 18/04/04 13:35

I bet you that today, it's just Hermes and her dog at home.

800 Name: Anonymous Post Date: 18/04/04 13:36

Captain! The enemies have launched a sneak attack! We were grossly under-prepared and can not return fire.

813 Name: Train Man ♦ SgHguKHEFY Post Date: 18/04/04 13:37

Just hung up.
So, it looks like I'm going over to her place.
I have to get ready fast . . .
I don't have anything to wearrrrrrr!!
And . . . I'm taking the cups.

820 Name: Anonymous Post Date: 18/04/04 13:38

Daaaaaaaaaaaaaammmmn
Tea for two with Hermes cups!!!!!!
Un-fucking-believable

828 Name: Anonymous Post Date: 18/04/04 13:39

Damn. Teacups!
Your taking the teacups to drink out of for real?!?!?!
You must be joking?!?!
Could this . . . be . . . . . . for real????

830 Name: Anonymous Post Date: 18/04/04 13:39

Could this be what she meant with the teacups?
No, no way could you two have guessed that something like this would
happen for god's sake!

840 Name: Train Man ♦ SgHguKHEFY Post Date: 18/04/04 13:41

I forgot to mention this but we did talk about the cups yesterday. I
told her that 'I didn't have an excuse to use them.'
We were talking about that just now and she said, 'I'm not doing
anything right now. Why don't you come over. I'll make some tea.'
Gotta jump in the shower . . . and oh, she told me that her parents
are gone till the evening.
Seriously. I got nothing to wear.

847 Name: Anonymous Post Date: 18/04/04 13:42

Parents gone till evening . . . here(-_-)..it(_-)..cccc.(-) ccc( )..(゜)comes!
(゜ ∀)comes! (゜ ∀゜)comes!!!!!!

848 Name: Anonymous Post Date: 18/04/04 13:42

>her parents are gone till the evening
>her parents are gone till the evening
>her parents are gone till the evening
>her parents are gone till the evening

853 Name: Anonymous Post Date: 18/04/04 13:43

her parents are gone till the evening
her parents are gone till the evening
her parents are gone till the evening
This is not a drill.
I repeat. This is not a drill.

854 Name: Anonymous Post Date: 18/04/04 13:43

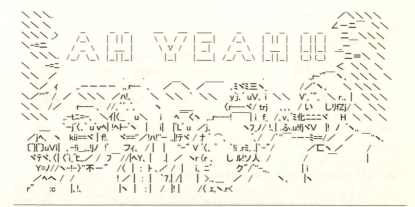

860 Name: Train Man ♦ SgHguKHEFY Post Date: 18/04/04 13:44

And about letting her know how I feel about her . . . It's beyond me today.

866 Name: Anonymous Post Date: 18/04/04 13:45

make sure you scrub your dick clean

867 Name: Anonymous Post Date: 18/04/04 13:45

>>860
It's your decision.
I don't understand stuff from fairyland.

875 Name: Anonymous Post Date: 18/04/04 13:46

>860
If you feel inside that you're ready to tell her, that's when you should tell her.
You know when the right time is for these kind of things.
Make sure you don't let that right time pass by, though. And it's best if you
tell her when your heart says its ready.
From the outside looking in, it may look like you should be ready to tell her
but I'm sure the vibe and mood are different for you guys on the inside.
So . . . pick a number between 1 and 18, will you?

908 Name: Anonymous Post Date: 18/04/04 13:51

Hold on a sec!
I just noticed how the thread suddenly got huge but this, dude?!?!?
An attack in real time?!?! I wanted to get in on it, dude!!!!
This is not the time to be fussing with my own website, dude!
I'm shocked and awed by the responses, dude!
And as I kept reading, I realised I am now hooked on this thread, dude!
To: Train Man
Listen, man.
Remember to take the Rubber Man with. No kidding.

920 Name: Anonymous Post Date: 18/04/04 13:52

Train: 'Umm . . . I have something I want to talk to you about . . . '
Hermes: 'What is it?'
Train: 'By the time I became aware of it, I had strong feelings for you. I'd
really like us to go out seriously. That is, if you don't mind.' Go the
standard way---o.

923 Name: Anonymous Post Date: 18/04/04 13:53

Just realised I've got goose bumps all over ('A`)

948 Name: Anonymous Post Date: 18/04/04 13:57

How come there are so many people here so early in the day?

955 Name: Train Man ♦ SgHguKHEFY Post Date: 18/04/04 13:58

All right. Jumped in and out of the shower at max speed.
Cleaned down there too.
So now, what do I wear?

962 Name: Anonymous post Date: 18/04/04 13:59

Train: 'There's something I need to talk to you about.'
Hermes: Tilting her head a bit, 'What is it?'
Train: 'As I mentioned to you before, I haven't had much experience
            with girls. That's why I need to know how you feel about me,
            why you ask me out to dinner and places.'
Hermes: ' . . . . '
Train: 'But there's one thing I can say for sure.'
Hermes: 'What can you say?'
Train: 'I'm attracted to you.
            At first I thought I was attracted to you just because I wasn't
            around other women. But that's not what it is.
            The more time I spent with you, the more I talked to you, the
            more I came to know that I was attracted to you.
            I know that having somebody like me tell you that could be more
            of a pain than anything. But I wanted to make sure I told you this
            today. I really like you and would like to go out with you.'

966 Name: Anonymous Post Date: 18/04/04 14:00

>>962
Way long!
But maybe, just maybe . . . the Train could fit it all in . . .

969 Name: Anonymous Post Date 18/04/04 14:01

>>962 Add a backdrop of city lights and pack all you got into every single word. She'll fall for it if you lay it on, thick and juicy.

970 Name: Train Man ♦ SgHguKHEFY Post Date: 18/04/04 14:01

Nope . . . can't do it. Just gonna drink some plain old tea.

32 Name: Train Man ♦ SgHguKHEFY Post Date: 18/04/04 14:08

Don't have the time to go out and buy new clothes
I'm spraying nice smelly stuff on yesterday's clothes
Will iron like mad

61 Name: Anonymous Post Date: 18/04/04 14:12

They sit facing each other on a sofa.

Hermes: 'Umm . . . .'
Train: 'Yes?'
Hermes: 'Can I sit next to you? You seem so far away.'
Train: 'Oh, aah, yes. Of course. Please do.'

Hermes walks over to sit next to Train.

Train: 'This is making me a bit self-conscious.'
Hermes: 'Don't you want me here?'
Train: 'God, no. I'm happy you're there.'

Hermes reaches for Train's hand.

Hermes: 'It's the first time I've seen a man's hands so up close and
             personal.'
Train: 'Wwwwell, my hand is not anything special. It's not pretty, nor is
             it strong-looking.'
Hermes: 'No. These are the hands that protected me on that train. They
             are the strongest in the world for me, at least.'
Train: 'Thanks but I really am a wimp . . . '

Hermes sits in silence, peering into Train's eyes intently.
With racing heart, Train meets Hermes' eyes.
Hermes softly closes her eyes.

Train: 'Wha . . . . . . '
Hermes: With eyes still closed, whispers 'You don't want to?'
Train: 'Wha wha wha what, no . . . no, of course I do.'

Train puts his arms around Hermes and pulls her close.
Their lips meet.

---

66 Name: Anonymous Post Date: 18/04/04 14:13

>>61
Man oh mannnn . . . that's some real shit . . .
I'm gonna remember that one. Off for my afternoon nap.

---

67 Name: Anonymous Post Date: 18/04/04 14:14

>>61
For real.

---

85 Name: Train Man ♦ SgHguKHEFY Post Date: 18/04/04 14:17

Off I go!

---

100 Name: Anonymous Post Date: 18/04/04 14:19

>>85
Sally forth! Procession at attennnnnntion! Salute! (`−´)>
(hhhhhhut!)

Knowing that the two were going to be all alone at Hermes' house sets the
Geeks' imaginations on fire.

---

90 Name: Anonymous Post Date: 18/04/04 14:18

'Mummy, where did you meet Daddy?'

'Why the sudden interest?'
'Tell me, tell me. Where did you meet?'
'Oh honey, why are you suddenly so interested? Well . . . Mummy was on the train one evening when a man accosted me and Daddy came to rescue me. That was how we met.'
'Really? Daddy looks so wimpy but I guess he was cool back then'
'That's why your father is my hero. Then and now.'
'Was it love at first sight?'
'Little Train, where did you learn that expression? But yes, yes, I would have to say that when I saw him, I felt like he was "the one"'
'Whoa. You guys are so lovey-dovey.'
'Honey, please don't make fun of us . . . '
Ooooo . . . . . . I can't take it anymore.

---

107 Name: Anonymous Post Date: 18/04/04 14:20

I can see Hermes flashing coy looks at Train at their wedding reception as she tells the story about how they met.

---

114 Name: Anonymous Post Date: 18/04/04 14:21

>>107
As us Geeks gather outside the banquet room preparing flower petal confetti.

---

154 Name: Anonymous Post Date: 18/04/04 14:32

I see a thank you card. It's addressed: All Geeks

---

178 Name: Anonymous Post Date: 18/04/04 14:43

Hermes Lingo Log
'Hee hee, I was actually just hiding that cat in the bag.'
'I'll just hold on tightly to you.'
'Must be that you can't hear when you're told.'
'But my friends say I look like a Moomin.'
'Japanese cuisine suits your vibe.'
'Well then, I guess I'll get dressed up too.'
'It's nice because there aren't many people like that.'
'Do you wanna see my dog?'
'Were you being a hero on the train again?'
'This feels much better.'

'Make sure to follow me.'
'I've changed my mind. Will you walk me home?'
'If we could commute like this together . . . it would be so great . . .'
That's it for now.

---

247 Name: Anonymous Post Date: 18/04/04 16:20

Man, she said that her parents were out till evening but I have a hunch
that the parents know that Train is coming over and will come home early.

Father: 'Well, that nice boy did save our baby Hermes. We have to at
          least see his face.'
Mother: 'You're so silly! Why don't you calm down a bit.'
Her: 'Mum, Dad, please don't say anything silly to my Train, ok?'
Father: 'Oh, he's your Train now is he? Honey, this is getting exciting!'
Mother: 'My word! Little Her . . . my, my . . . . . .

I will continue imagining this family discussion as I hang my clothes out to
dry. ('A`)

---

253 Name: Anonymous Post Date: 18/04/04 16:28

Mother: 'I mean she won't stop talking about the time you rescued her.
          Even now.'
Father: 'So rare to come across your courage nowadays.
          Commendable. I thank you, truly and deeply.
Her: 'Oh my god . . . please . . . you're embarrassing me . . . '

---

257 Name: Anonymous Post Date: 18/04/04 16:34

Father: 'This is the first time our Hermes has brought a male friend to the
          house. Isn't that right, mother?'
Mother: 'Oh, yes, yes . . . our little Hermes keeps all her moves up her
          sleeve. Mr Train, I hope you stay good friends with her for a very
          long time.'
Her: 'Oh my god, you too, Mum?' (red in the face)
\('—')/

---

258 Name: Anonymous Post Date: 18/04/04 16:36

Train: 'Yes . . . I mean no, I mean definitely. I'm so pleased to make
          your acquaintance.'

261 Name: Anonymous Post Date: 18/04/04 16:40

Father: (hearty laugh) 'Just like Her said, you react kind of brusquely.'
Her: 'Oh my god, father!!!??!?!'
Mother: (covers mouth to laugh) 'Don't be so cheeky now. You'll make Mr
          Train uncomfortable.'

---

264 Name: Anonymous Post Date: 18/04/04 16:43

Father: 'Well then, us old folks will take our leave now and leave the
          young 'uns alone. (slaps own knee as he stands)'
Mother: 'Yes, indeed, well, Mr Train, take care of little Hermes for us.'
Father: 'All right then. We'll see you later' (hearty belly laugh)

The two are left alone. Two rabbits caught in headlights.

Train: 'Ummm . . . aahh . . . '
Her: ' . . . y . . . . . . yess? . . . '
Train: ' . . . what are yyyyour . . . umm . . . hobbies?'

---

266 Name: Anonymous Post Date: 18/04/04 16:44

how many fucking times have you asked that question since they met,
dude!

---

269 Name: Anonymous Post Date: 18/04/04 16:45

They've held hands but they're so formal when they talk.
I wonder if they'll be so formal when they have sex.

Train: 'May I enter?'
Her: 'Yes, please.'
Train: 'Does this feel pleasant?'
Her: 'Yes, it is pleasant.' (covers mouth to laugh)
Train: 'I am about to come.'
Her: 'Yes. Please, do.'

Hey, it sounds like royal family sex.

---

281 Name: Anonymous Post Date: 18/04/04 16:59

I left you guys for an hour and THIS is what I return to?!?!?

Damn, how I love all of you.

---

282 Name: Anonymous Post Date: 18/04/04 17:00

Train:	'Wow. This is the first time I've set foot in a girl's room.'
Her:	'Please don't look around so intently.' (averting eyes)
Train:	'It's such a calming room. And so sweet.'
Her:	'Thank you. This is the first time I've let a man into my room.'

---

284 Name: Anonymous Post Date: 18/04/04 17:02

>>282

Train:	'For real?'
Her:	Let's out short laugh in disbelief. 'Mr Train, are you doubting my words?'
Train:	'No, no, no . . . that's not what I meant'
Her:	'I'm kidding. I'm just teasing . . . '

---

285 Name: Anonymous Post Date: 18/4/04 17:04

Her:	'Well, then . . . ' (she crosses arms behind her) 'what DID you mean?' (bends forward, suggestively towards Train)

---

289 Name: Anonymous Post Date: 18/04/04 17:12

Train:	'Miss Hermes, you're just so sweet that I . . . (garble garble)'
Her:	'What did you say? I couldn't hear . . . '
Train:	'You're so cute!'
Her:	'Oh . . . !!!!'

---

296 Name: Anonymous Post Date: 18/04/04 17:28

So then, dinner time rolls around which makes me wonder what
Train & Co. are planning.

- Dine together
- Cooking together
- Hungry after sex, already out at a restaurant together
- Parents return. Hermes and her mother are busy cooking. Train and Hermes' father are sipping brandy, having a man-to-man talk.
- Already buddy-buddy with entire family

Which oh which oh which could it be?

301 Name: Anonymous Post Date: 18/04/04 17:35

>>296
* Being the innocent guy he is, Train goes over and has the tea, then returns home.

Uh-uh, no way. Not an option.

303 Name: Anonymous Post Date: 18/04/04 17:35

The Hermes family kitchen sounds like it could be huge.
Plenty of space for Train Man to fidget around.

Knowing that the two were going to be all alone at Hermes' house light the Poisonoids' imagination on fire.

360 Name: Anonymous Post Date: 18/04/04 19:34

Where the hell is Train . . . and how long is he gonna make us wait around? Could it be some monkey business taking up so much time?

362 Name: Anonymous Post Date; 18/04/04 19:45

The parents are coming home in the evening so how come Train isn't home yettttttt!!!!!!

367 Name: Train Man ◆ SgHguKHEFY Post Date: 18/04/04 20:01

I is back.
Nothing much happened.
Just the way it goes.
Let me go read the backlog.

374 Name: Anonymous Post Date: 18/04/04 20:04

>>367
Don't worry about the backlog. Not much there.
It's just our imaginations exploding. (´·ω·`)

375 Name: Anonymous Post Date: 18/04/04 20:05

Nothing much happened???? Oh NO!!! It can't be!!!!!!

383 Name: Train Man ♦ SgHguKHEFY Post Date: 18/04/04 20:08

There's too much of a backlog so I'm gonna give my report first.
Just a sec.

396 Name: Train Man ♦ SgHguKHEFY Post Date: 18/04/04 20:21

So I quickly got ready and went out.
I remembered how to get to her place pretty easily. It was basically
one straight road from the station.
I stood at her front gate. Being super nervous, it took me 2 minutes
to muster the strength to ring the doorbell. I swallowed hard and
pressed the bell.
'Who is it?'
'It's me, Train.'
'I'll be right there.'
Soon after the large door beyond the gate opened.
She walked over and opened the gate.
'Please, come in.'
I entered.
She wasn't dressed in chillin-at-home clothes but she was dressed
pretty casual.
But even in her hang-out wear, she was well stylish. Casual is goood,
I thought. (´ー`)
'I'm sorry I called you out at such short notice,' she apologised
'I wasn't doing anything anyway'
It was clean and spacious inside. Really different from my house.
Smelled nice, too. She took me into a room and there sat the doggy,
welcoming me.
The furry dude was wayway cute (*´Д`*) pantpant

413 Name: Train Man ♦ SgHguKHEFY Post Date: 18/04/04 20:36

So I stroked the doggy.
The room was spacious and spotless. There aren't any rooms like

that at home.
'Please, sit down.'
I sat down on a large couch.
'Let me make some tea. Which would you prefer? Coffee or tea?'
'I'd prefer tea, please.'
I placed the teacups on the table.
'You really haven't touched them have you?'
'We only drink green tea at home.'
'Would you have preferred Japanese teacups?'
'No, not at all. I'll just put these ones on display.'
We joked for a bit.
'Let me warm up the cups'
She took the cups into the kitchen.
After a while she returned with a tray filled with what looked like coffee
stuff and placed it on the table. When she leaned forward to place the
tray on the table, I got a peek at her cleavage. (;ﾟ∀ﾟ)=3 arruffruff
It was pink.

442 Name: Train Man ♦ SgHguKHEFY Post Date: 18/04/04 20:51

'Do you have a preference?'
she asked as she picked up and showed me the different types of
teas.
'I'm only familiar with Afternoon Tea that I buy at the corner
shop . . . ' ＿┌ ｜○
'So then you'd probably want the ○○○tea'
She mentioned some kind of tea and shook some out into the
transparent teapot.
She brought out the hot water and poured it into the pot. I watched
as the red tea leaves expanded. Boy, she knew what she was doing.
This making tea stuff.
'It's best to leave it steeping for a while' she said, leaving the pot on
the table.
She stood up to go to the kitchen and returned with some snacks.
'My mum baked these . . . ' she said, showing me 4 scones, 'and
here's some biscuits, though they're shop bought.'
'Thank you so much.' I bowed.
She poured the tea and there it was, right in front of me. The Hermes
teacup.
FINALLY, THE OPPORTUNITY TO USE THE CUP HAD ARRIVED.

444 Name: Anonymous Post Date: 18/04/04 20:51

Darjeeling
Earl Grey
Orange Pekoe

450 Name: Anonymous Post Date: 18/04/04 20:53

There's a lot of stuff Train's gonna hafta learn.
I'm glad to be a Geek, I'm glad to be . . . glad to be . . .

452 Name: Train Man ♦ SgHguKHEFY Post Date: 18/04/04 20:54

>>450
Got to remember the details so I can report it all to you guys. _| ̄ |O

455 Name: Anonymous Post Date: 18/04/04 20:54

Home-baked scones? Don't know if it's Assam or Earl Grey but we're talking loose tea leaves and not teabags. I bet you they have a deer head mounted on the wall above their fireplace.

461 Name: Anonymous Post Date: 18/04/04 20:55

And water pours out of a lion's mouth into their bathtub I bet.

466 Name: Anonymous Post Date: 18/04/04 20:59

Dad enters puffing a cigar

467 Name: Anonymous Post Date: 18/04/04 20:59

Definitely no stuffed deer head on wall

490 Name: Anonymous Post Date: 18/04/04 21:06

>>452
Hey man, don't worry about remembering the details for us.
Always remain focused on the person right in front of you.

498 Name: Train Man ♦ SgHguKHEFY Post Date: 18/04/04 21:13

I'm back. I'm e-mailing with her at the same time, so this could take a while . . . ⌐¯⌐O

---

518 Name: Anonymous Post Date: 18/04/04 21:24

Ask her what type of tea it was if you're e-mailing.

---

525 Name: Anonymous Post Date: 18/04/04 21:28

>>518
Type of tea. Yep. Vital info.

---

559 Name: Anonymous Post Date: 18/04/04 21:39

>>452
Just remember whatever YOU find interesting.
I think trying to remember what she finds interesting and to be interested in that . . . that's part of the whole being in love thing.

---

569 Name: Train Man ♦ SgHguKHEFY Post Date: 18/04/04 21:44

'Do you take sugar?'
She brought out the sugar and milk containers but I said
'No, this is fine.'
'You know your teas very well.'
'No, not at all.'
We bantered back and forth as I took the first sip.
I've only drunk tea from the corner shop so I had no idea it could taste so delicious. Not only that but the biscuits and scones went well with the tea. Then again, it was the fact we were drinking out of those teacups that made it so delicious.
'Could I use one of your cups?'
'Of course, of course. Please do.'
She reached for the teapot but I said, 'Let me.'
'Don't worry. It's not like we're drinking alcohol Japanese-style.'
'Please, allow me,' I said, reaching for the teapot. Then I poured her a cup.

571 Name: Anonymous Post Date: 18/04/04 21:45

What a cosy afternoon tea set-up. For couples.

---

573 Name: Anonymous Post Date: 18/04/04 21:47

I shan't partake of such silly afternoon tea matters (˚⊿˚) I jest.
···＿￢｜●

---

594 Name: Anonymous Post Date: 18/04/04 21:55

And why, pray tell, does Train not want to tell her how he feels?

---

598 Name: Anonymous Post Date: 18/04/04 21:56

He's never professed his love to anyone before.

---

601 Name: Train Man ♦ SgHguKHEFY Post Date: 18/04/04 21:57

She took the cup in her hands and slowly sipped the tea
I watched her and thought how natural she seemed . . . sipping tea
was second nature to her.
We talked about tea and baked goods for a bit. I told her that maybe I
would start making tea myself at home. She recommended some tea
companies and also some cakes . . . but I forgot already. ＿￢｜O
There were moments of silence but even that felt natural.
'Do you always spend your days off like this?' I asked.
'God no, I'm usually just lazing around the house,' she laughed.
'Me too.'
Completely out of character for me--it continued on flowery and
flowy . . .

---

615 Name: Train Man ♦ SgHguKHEFY Post Date: 18/04/04 22:00

>>518
She says it's Benoist Tea

622 Name: Anonymous Post Date: 18/04/04 22:03

BENOIST TEA!

623 Name: Anonymous Post Date: 18/04/04 22:03

>>615
The stuff made for the British royal family!

---

624 Name: Train Man ♦ SgHguKHEFY Post Date: 18/04/04 22:04

Aha, Benoist tea . . .
＿￢○

---

689 Name: Train Man ♦ SgHguKHEFY Post Date: 18/04/04 22:34

'I've never spent my day off like this. It's nice, isn't it . . . '
' . . . (ha ha ha) . . . '
We chat for a while and finish the baked goods and tea. I ended up
drinking three cups.
The doggy was hanging around wanting to be noticed so I waved at
him to come over, and sure enough he did.
'He's so well behaved.'
'He just loves people.'
Indeed, he seemed to be enjoying my company.
I've never had any animal like me so much.
'This dog is from that Disney film isn't he?'
'He's a Ω ♥□ φ'
'He's adorable.'
I felt myself falling for the dog the more I played with him.
'He's really into you, isn't he?'
'I think I really like him.'
So we kept on talking about dogs and pets and such.
Apologies for the boring report.
(´·ω:;.:...

---

648 Name: Anonymous Post Date; 18/04/04 22:14

* Hey, how old is she?*

698 Name: Train Man ♦ SgHguKHEFY Post Date: 18/04/04 22:36

>>648
I haven't asked yet. I'm sure she's older though.
I know what she does for a living but I'll keep that to myself.
Probably makes a lot of money.

---

742 Name: Anonymous Post Date: 18/04/04 22:52

Benoist Tea
Manufactured since the 18th century by an upmarket English foods
company steeped in tradition. (Officially launched in 1910). A Master
French Chef nicknamed 'Papa Benoist' started the company. In fact, in
England, the company only makes the tea available to a limited number of
upmarket restaurants and to the British royal family. Japan is the only
place in the world where it's available retail. The tea company is famous
for its tight quality control and being one of the very few tea companies
which holds 3 royal warrants.

---

751 Name: Anonymous Post Date: 18/04/04 22:55

>>742
Good research. Well done.

---

747 Name: Train Man ♦ SgHguKHEFY Post Date: 18/04/04 22:53

'Is this your room, Hermes?'
I reckoned it wasn't, but I asked anyway.
'(ha ha) No it isn't. I can't show you mine. It's too messy,' she replied
all slippery smooth. ＿￣|○
Oh and I guess I kind of influenced her and now she wants to buy a
PC. And no, she does not own one if you can believe it. She emails on
her phone.
I gave her some info about what she can do on a PC.
So we decided to shop for a computer, together. (｀･ω･´)
Blah blah blah . . . time flew by.
'Well . . . won't your parents be back soon?'
'You're right'
'I shouldn't be here, right?'

'It's fine.'
´(´д`)…..aahh…..speeeeechless'
I guess she's already told her parents all about me . . .
About how we've been seeing each other on the weekends and stuff.
That they weren't upset that she had me over, in the house . . .
But I told her that I was kind of anxious and that I'd better get going.

775 Name: Train Man ♦ SgHguKHEFY Post Date: 18/04/04 23:00

She said she'd walk me to the station but I told her to stay put
because I was worried about her walking back home alone (`·ω·´)
As for telling her how I feel about her, well . . . this is our fifth 'date'
and I'm not sure about the timing. But apart from anything, I can't
work up the courage to tell her that I like her. _|￣|O
How do you all work up the courage?

---

791 Name: Anonymous Post Date: 18/04/04 23:03

Train Man: 'When you come across a website you like, you click the
favourites button like this . . . '
Lady Hermes: 'What is this 2-Channel thing . . . ?'
Train: 'Oh, well, you shouldn't go there . . . '
Lady Hermes: 'Moomin and the Pointy Hat . . . ? What is this?'
Yikes!

---

798 Name: Anonymous Post Date: 18/04/04 23:05

>Train Man
A while back, a girl came on to me kinda like this.
I knew instantly that she liked me but it was a first for me and I was afraid
things would change if I said anything so I kept it to myself. As for her, she
couldn't take my lack of response and basically cut her feelings off from me.
For women like Hermes, they can switch their feelings off pretty quickly.
Once they cut their feeling off, there's no turning them back.
Don't make the same mistake I did. All you need to do is tell her you like her.

---

811 Name: Anonymous Post Date: 18/04/04 23:10

I reckon that even after Train gets all twisted up inside and tells her he
likes her, she'll be like

'Oh, thank you so much. I like you too. (smiley face)'
'Aa, umm, ohh . . . . . . well . . . '
There's no doubt that two off-balance people make for a difficult couple.

---

817 Name: Anonymous Post Date: 18/04/04 23:12

>>775
We're not talking about you being courageous or not!!
You like Queen Hermes don't you?
Just tell her your feelings straight up. I'm being sincere.
Don't even think about being turned down.
Don't worry, we've got your back. You can absolutely do it.
On your next date, go somewhere moody and romantic with a nice view . . .
and seduce her. She will react to you just the way you want her to.
And that's when I will reply by lobbing the biggest ball of jealousy at you
to congratulate you from the bottom of my heart.

---

833 Name: Anonymous Post Date: 18/04/04 23:16

If you can't see it turning into a romance, then think of it as an extended
battle.
One of my strategies was to 'move into her life on many fronts'.
Helping her buy a computer is a good thing for you to do.
She will refer to you for all things PC, at least.
Keep introducing things into her life that she depends on you for, little by
little, one by one.

---

877 Name: Train Man ♦ SgHguKHEFY Post Date: 18/04/04 23:27

I was reading Mr Mole's log.
To be quite honest, it was freaking me out.

---

878 Name: Anonymous Post Date: 18/04/04 23:27

>>866
Don't use the Mole card . . .
Though you do have a point.
I mean originally, this thread was about us depressive shadowy types
poking out to read your posts and then retreating into the dark . . .

879 Name: Anonymous Post Date: 18/04/04 23:28

I'm posting this just in case
'Mr Mole, you are really a good person but I don't have those types of
feelings for you. Please don't misinterpret my behaviour.'

881 Name: Anonymous Post Date: 18/04/04 23:28

>879
arghwaaaaarhhhhhhargghhhh

882 Name: Anonymous Post Date: 18/04/04 23:28

>>879
Don't post just in case

883 Name: Anonymous Post Date: 18/04/04 23:29

>>879
Fffffuuuuuuuuuuuuuuuuuuuuuuuuuuu

886 Name: Anonymous Post Date: 18/04/04 23:29

>>879
aaaaaarrrrrrrgHermesssssssssssss

888 Name: Train Man ♦ SgHguKHEFY Post Date: 18/04/04 23:29

>>879
＿厂￣IO

889 Name: Anonymous Post Date: 18/04/04 23:29

It's Train's romance so it can only go the way Train feels.
It's up to Train whether this will be an express or chug along like a local
train.
I could understand if he was still starting off but Train is by now a big
grown man . . . . . . Lucky him, he's havin so much fun. Lucky him . . .

890 Name: Anonymous Post Date: 18/04/04 23:29

>>877
will leave selecting the options to you
love>when your heart is in your mouth, tell her so.
Help me with coming out with it
Is all you need to say for us to rush to your rescue!!!

891 Name: Anonymous Post Date: 18/04/04 23:29

Man, you guys really are some good people.
To get all serious about a stranger . . .
If I had people like you around me . . .
I think my life would have been a lot more fun . . .

914 Name: Anonymous Post Date: 18/04/04 23:34

I cried reading you people's responses.
This social retard is blossoming into coupledom while . . .
It's just so unfuckinfair?!?!

922 Name: Anonymous Post Date: 18/04/04 23:36

>>914
Life in coupledom isn't always that great . . .
Well, umm . . . I'm just guessing . . . . . .

Train Man waivers between professing his love and feeling as if he has
misinterpreted Hermes. The thread splits between two camps – one that
urges him to profess his love and the other to go at his own pace. Can
Train come out with it?

Mission
5

Stop Leading Me on So Much

Fellow Geeks renew their interest in the Benoist tea Train Man drank out of the Hermes teacups. Some went hunting for the tea itself.

126 Name: Anonymous Post Date: 19/04/04 11:55

I asked a tea-lover friend of mine about Benoist tea but
he's never had it either . . .
And apparently it is really difficult to get, not to mention expensive.
She didn't seem like your average person from the fact she sent Hermes
teacups but this really takes the biscuit.

140 Name: Anonymous Post Date: 19/04/04 13:41

Apparently you can buy and drink it at the Matsuzakaya Department store
in Ginza. There's also a salon in Kokoda.

141 Name: Anonymous Post Date: 19/04/04 13:47

I called Benoist.
>>140 is dead right.
All right, I'm going to speed down the Shuto Expressway and check it out.
Over to you . . .

147 Name: Anonymous Post Date: 19/04/04 14:09

located Benoist bunker
http://www.matsuzakaya.co.jp/ginza/service/gourmet.shtml

150 Name: Anonymous Post Date: 19/04/04 14:29

hey hey hey, are you guys under the impression that drinking Benoist tea
is going to bring happiness into your lives????

159 Name: Anonymous Post Date: 19/04/04 14:44

They're going PC shopping together aren't they?
He's gonna get to take her to Akihabara

161 Name: Anonymous Post Date: 19/04/04 14:47

Make sure you don't expose too much of your true techie self at Akihabara –

and don't you dare set foot in the figurine shops or anything!

---

165 Name: Anonymous Post Date: 19/04/04 14:49

Why don't you just get the parts and build one from scratch at her house? That way you can be her full-on tech support.

---

171 Name: Anonymous Post Date: 19/04/04 15:00

Why don't we work out which is the best (·∀·) scenario for Train
Desktop
Laptop
MAC
Self-built
This is one area where we can help

---

178 Name: Anonymous Post Date: 19/04/04 15:19

Turn the tables and make Hermes a techie Akihabara-hag

---

179 Name: Anonymous Post Date: 19/04/04 15:24

And in the end, Hermes becomes a 2-Channeller herself.

---

180 Name: Anonymous Post Date: 19/04/04 15:25

and it all comes out in the open . . .

---

189 Name: Anonymous Post Date: 19/04/04 16:02

Here goes
- MAC (iBook—for some reason, it's convertible)
- Buy the parts (so Train can be the tech support)
- Internet ready
- Choose router, modem, FTTH
- DVD player (burning not necessary?)
- Laptop
- Longhorn compatibility
- Download films (only to get arrested)

All right, so which machine can handle all of the above . . . . . .

195 Name: Anonymous Post Date: 19/04/04 16:36

like a fish in water . . .

---

198 Name: Anonymous Post Date: 19/04/04 17:16

But when it's time to teach her . . . I mean, he is a Geek after all ('A`)

Tren	' . . . and, this is called the motherboard . . . ' breathing heavily through his mouth as he explains, looking extremely happy and nervous at the same time
H	' . . . umm . . . yeah . . . ' (obviously not understanding + extremely bored)
Tren	'this has 7 PCI slots which means it has expandability . . . ' (oblivious, continues to explain with a twinkle in his eye
H	' . . . umm . . . I just remembered I've got something to do so I'm gonna go now. Thanks for today.' (leaves without waiting for a yes or no answer)
Tren	'What? Um . . . I'll take you home----!' (quickly runs after her but trips and falls, leaving him stranded as she runs away home)

('A`) gaaaaarrrrrrrrhhhhhh

---

199 Name: Anonymous Post Date: 19/04/04 17:20

guffaaaaaw guffaaaw har-har-har. Just got back from Matsuzakaya in Ginza
I bought a can of Earl Grey and had a little drink on the 4th floor.
. . . aaaaaa . . . ummmmmm . . . . . . is . . . this . . . .really tea?
It smells great and how can I describe it . . . it's deep . . . .Lalalady Hermesalicious.

---

201 Name: Anonymous Post Date: 19/04/04 17:22

>>199
Whoa, cool?
btw did you go alone?

---

202 Name: Anonymous Post Date: 19/04/04 17:22

>>199
You're a man of action aintcha.

203 Name: Anonymous Post Date: 19/04/04 17:24

>>199
got close to Ginza → got a headache
got to Ginza → severe headache
got close to Matsuzakaya → nausea and dizziness
got to Matsuzakaya → legs shaking, cold sweat
got to floor that has the tea → faint after foaming at mouth

208 Name: Anonymous Post Date: 19/04/04 17:31

>>201
I'd like to go with Lady Hermesalicious arrragh whhhattt rrruuuuu ddddd
←appears to be attacked by Train
All jokes aside, when I got there, there was a man straight out of one of
the Jump mangas wearing silver-rimmed shades and sipping an iced tea. I
ordered an iced Earl Grey and out came two rectangular biscuits with it.
I left the biscuits untouched (for some reason) as I kept worrying about
what the ladies-who-lunch and the Hermesalicious ones were thinking so I
quickly drank one cup and headed to the till. I'm not sure if the tea was at
the till . . . the cans were going for anywhere between £5 and £10 per
100g depending on the tea. They had other things for sale that looked like
some kind of spread and something like a scone.

212 Name: Anonymous Post Date: 19/04/04 17:35

could a techie casual dude like myself pay a visit?

213 Name: Mr Anonymous Post Date: 04/04/19 17:36

Ginza
Curious Spring Affair?
Numerous Single Men Lose Consciousness at Department Store Tea
Salon
<Matsuzakaya>
There have been numerous reports about single men visiting the Tea Salon
in the Matsuzakaya Department Store in the Ginza district whom faint
upon arrival, one after the next.There have been a total of 16 men reported
to have fainted by early evening today but causes have been largely
unknown. Then men whom fainted have no known connection to each
other and the only unifying thread between them seems to be that they

are all single. Amongst the unconscious were some who mouthed incoherent words as 'Hermes' 'Train' and 'Dhalsim' but all were transported to a mid-city hospital.

The Matsuzakaya spokesperson struggled to explain what had transpired. 'They were certainly not the type of customer we are used to seeing in our store and we have no idea what happened or how to even comment on the incident.' The random and wholly unexpected happenings that transpired one after the next in an otherwise peaceful environment gave customers pause for thought as they looked on with concern.

214 Name: Anonymous Post Date: 19/04/04 17:36

does this mean that I should speed off to the Benoist Salon with miniature models of Hermes and Train?

217 Name: Anonymous Post Date: 19/04/04 17:40

>>199 are you falling in love with Hermes?

225 Name: Anonymous Post Date: 19/04/04 17:48

I think it's not just expensive but rare
>>212
Indeed, I think it's best not to go as you are
I put a suit on
>>214
you definitely need to go for a gentlemanly sure of yourself approach or you'll drown in the completely incompatible vibe of the place, and I definitely would not recommend simulating Mr Tren a-panting heavily
>>217
If Mr Tren-tren isn't going to declare his love then I just may have to step up to the task ;y=—(ﾟдﾟ)･∵.

280 Name: Anonymous Post Date: 19/04/04 18:15

but hey, is any of this tea talk gonna come in handy one day?

307 Name: Train Man ♦ SgHguKHEFY Post Date: 19/04/04 18:28

I came straight home today and got here a lot earlier than usual (･∀･)
Come to think of it, I haven't e-mailed her today.

309 Name: Anonymous Post Date: 19/04/04 18:29

if the tea and coffee boards caught a glimpse of our responses here . . .
benwaaaaaaahhhhh ('A`)

310 Name: Train Man ♦ SgHguKHEFY Post Date: 19/04/04 18:30

looks like you guys are having fun.
let me check the backlog.

333 Name: Train Man ♦ SgHguKHEFY Post Date: 19/04/04 18:41

I'll ask her about her budget for the PC and what she plans to use it for.
She mentioned the other day that all she was looking for was net
access and mail capability.

338 Name: Train Man ♦ SgHguKHEFY Post Date: 19/04/04 18:43

I quickly skimmed through –
I see you've been researching Benoist tea.
Better yet, somebody actually went and got some! Amazing!

349 Name: Train Man ♦ SgHguKHEFY Post Date: 19/04/04 18:48

It may just be my mind playing tricks but she looks cuter than
when I first met her . . . (´─`)

352 Name: Anonymous Post Date: 19/04/04 18:49

>>349
if you say anymore I'm going to spontaneously combust

353 Name: Anonymous Post Date: 19/04/04 18:49

(´─`) this face
shit, you lucky dog

369 Name: Anonymous Post Date: 19/04/04 19:00

If you add Princess Hermes+made and poured by her+just the two of you
alone+teacup set all together then if it was me, I'd probably just die from
happiness and yumminess. Hail to Benoist.
Who cares if its dumb or silly or whateva because nothing compares . . .
＿|￢|O

370 Name: Train Man ♦ SgHguKHEFY Post Date: 19/04/04 19:01

>>358
(´д`) yummalicious ?
Apparently I had the Darjeeling variety . . .

377 Name: Train Man ♦ SgHguKHEFY Post Date: 19/04/04 19:05

>>371
I don't think I'm going to Akihabara to get the PC.
Plus, I can't build it myself . . .

376 Name: Anonymous Post Date: 19/04/04 19:05

hurry up and come out with it>Train

381 Name: Train Man ♦ SgHguKHEFY Post Date: 19/04/04 19:10

>>376
I can't stop thinking about it lately.
I mean, she's been so friendly ever since we first met but it's different
when you put it in like girlfriend-boyfriend. And I get thinking about
whether I'm worthy or not.
I'm so not up to her standards but . . .
I think about what would happen if I didn't tell her how I feel . . .
Would we just be friends? That's probably what it'd be but
if I do tell her and it's a no-go, then she'll probably ditch me?
I'm scared about losing our friendship as well coz I may not be able
to see her anymore . . .

And beyond anything, if it's a no-go, then I can't show my face anymore . . . ⌐|○

---

386 Name: Anonymous Post Date: 19/04/04 19:14

>>381
Damn, you think you're a man?
If you really like her then you keep telling her so over and over and over again even when she says no. Go for it!

---

387 Name: Anonymous Post Date: 19/04/04 19:14

Afraid of being dumped and then her distancing herself??? For god's sake, what are you, still in school????

---

394 Name: Anonymous Post Date: 19/04/04 19:17

>>381
don't be rushed
if you're maintaining a steady pace with these dates and have a good vibe going then I wouldn't rush it. Unless of course it's dragging on for 6 months or a year . . . that would be a different story.

---

401 Name: Anonymous Post Date: 19/04/04 19:19

I think you'll reach a point where you won't be able to keep it in any longer.
And that's when you'll tell her how you feel.
Don't force it.
Gotta take it easy, yeah?

---

417 Name: Anonymous Post Date: 19/04/04 19:24

Isn't it your turn to have her over?

---

420 Name: Train Man ♦ SgHguKHEFY Post Date: 19/04/04 19:25

>>417
((((((((;´Д`)))))) shake shake tremble shake tremble tremble

425 Name: Anonymous Post Date: 19/04/04 19:28

You still live at home Train?

426 Name: Anonymous Post Date: 19/04/04 19:28

Let's say that Hermesaloo learns a thing or two about the PC.
And then you guys get to know each other and start visiting each other's house.
And let's say that you start doing the back and forth between each other's places.
Make sure you don't forget to erase your favourites and wipe the history clean.

445 Name: Anonymous Post Date: 19/04/04 19:40

let's stop pushing him any further.
no matter how you look at it, our smelly Geek words of comfort come second to Train's own decision-making.
('A`) benwaaaaaaa

484 Name: Anonymous Post Date: 19/04/04 19:57

I love tea and collect all kinds of tea leaves.
I told a girl once.
Then she said
'Gross. You just spoiled the tea . . . why don't you go and boil some tap water and drink your fucking tea.'
Through it all, even I survive.
Hey Mum, sorry I haven't been home in a while. I promise to visit soon . . .

497 Name: Train Man ♦ SgHguKHEFY Post Date: 19/04/04 20:05

Now that I'm full . . .
Well, I think I'm gonna go send her an e-mail. (`·ω·´)

503 Name: Anonymous Post Date: 19/04/04 20:09

>>484
I think it was the woman that spoiled the tea

506 Name: Anonymous Post Date: 19/04/04 20:11

>>503
sweet words.
sweet and lovely they are.

---

510 Name: Train Man ◆ SgHguKHEFY Post Date: 19/04/04 20:15

done. Sent. (ˋ·ω·ˊ)
>>506
couldn't agree more

If she does come to the house
I think my parents would probably freak out (´—ˋ)
But I can't have her over unless I completely renovate my room
I guess I'll rent storage somewhere . . .

When the topic shifted to fashion, most of the Geeks lost interest but once the topic shifted back to Hermes' PC purchase, the Geeks came to the table with loads of advice.

---

542 Name: Train Man ◆ SgHguKHEFY Post Date: 19/04/04 20:32

got a reply
all she needs is net access and e-mail
her budget is 1K
man, she's rich
she'd prefer a laptop
and Windows for starters
no need for DVD
and
aiming for after payday

---

551 Name: Train Man ◆ SgHguKHEFY Post Date: 19/04/04 20:35

but I guess the laptop and router/modem would put you at that spec

552 Name: Anonymous Post Date: 19/04/04 20:35

Sony VAIO
NEC Lavie
Toshiba Dyna
Are the best buys
Personally, I recommend the NEC

569 Name: Anonymous Post Date: 19/04/04 20:44

Some time had passed after they purchased a laptop together
E-mail from Hermes.
H: 'Mr Train, I don't know how to do this . . . '
T: (since there's no real reason to refuse . . .) 'OK, I'll be right over.'

While Train works on the PC, Hermes falls asleep. Train leaves quietly.

H: 'Mr Train, I want to convert my CDs to MP3s'
T: 'Sure, I'll be right over.'
H: 'Make sure you don't leave without telling me.'

It is midnight by the time set-up is complete.

H: 'How about some more personal stuff support?'
T: (since there's no real reason to refuse) 'I'll support you forever.'

572 Name: Train Man ♦ SgHguKHEFY Post Date: 19/04/04 20:44

>>567
copy+paste bits ringing all kinds of bells!!! Ah yeaaaah!!!
————(｡A｡)—(ﾟ∀ﾟ)—(｡A｡)—(ﾟ∀ﾟ)—(｡A｡)————!!!!

575 Name: Anonymous Post Date: 19/04/04 20:46

NEC has a good warranty and quite good support.
If you buy it from NEC Direct online then you can pick and choose the
software you need. VAIOs are ridiculously expensive but the chicks dig it.

578 Name: Anonymous Post Date: 19/04/04 20:48

Oops, but I guess you can't go buy it together if you get it online.

---

582 Name: Train Man ♦ SgHguKHEFY Post Date: 19/04/04 20:49

>>578
plus she doesn't have net access
I'll use the net access set-up as an excuse for going over to her
house (´ー`)

---

584 Name: Anonymous Post Date: 19/04/04 20:50

strategiser ahyeaaaaaah (´ー`)

---

587 Name: Anonymous Post Date: 19/04/04 20:50

I'll use the net access set-up as an excuse for going over to her house (´ー`)
I'll use the net access set-up as an excuse for going over to her house (´ー`)
I'll use the net access set-up as an excuse for going over to her house (´ー`)
I'll use the net access set-up as an excuse for going over to her house (´ー`)
Benwaaaaaaaah
I'll use the net access set-up as an excuse for going over to her house (´ー`)
I'll use the net access set-up as an excuse for going over to her house (´ー`)
I'll use the net access set-up as an excuse for going over to her house (´ー`)
I'll use the net access set-up as an excuse for going over to her house (´ー`)

---

596 Name: Train Man ♦ SgHguKHEFY Post Date: 19/04/04 20:53

Using the log as base.
I'm gonna write back and tell her that I did some research for her.
What kind of line do you reckon? Might as well do fibre-optic?

---

600 Name: Anonymous Post Date: 19/04/04 20:54

>>596
that's overdoing it
leave it at ADSL

if that's not good enough then she'll come to you with questions

614 Name: Anonymous Post Date: 19/04/04 20:57

don't know if it's a family computer or a personal computer but maybe you'll get to go to her room . . .

621 Name: Train Man ♦ SgHguKHEFY Post Date: 19/04/04 21:00

I just caught a commercial with somebody that looks like her. Hythiol C

634 Name: Anonymous Post Date: 19/04/04 21:03

>>621
Miki Nakatani?????

637 Name: Anonymous Post Date: 19/04/04 21:03

No, no more, please, no no nono. I can't go on now that I've heard that name. I can't be a Train supporter any longer.
I'm dropping out. Of the thread. From life.

640 Name: Train Man ♦ SgHguKHEFY Post Date: 19/04/04 21:05

>>634
Don't know her name . . . ＿|￢|○
But she looks like YOU too.

690 Name: Train Man ♦ SgHguKHEFY Post Date: 19/04/04 21:22

I'm not good with the details but
Her hair is on the long side
Average height
On the skinny side
I like her better anyway. (´ ─ `)

702 Name: Anonymous Post Date: 19/04/04 21:25

I like her better anyway (´—`)
like her better anyway (´—`)
her better anyway (´—`)
better anyway (´—`)
anyway (´—`)
(´—`) this face
goddamn you lucky dog

703 Name: Train Man ♦ SgHguKHEFY Post Date: 19/04/04 21:26

But her responses have been unusually slow today(´·ω·`)

708 Name: Anonymous Post Date: 19/04/04 21:26

>>703
wha— What were you guys talking about?

721 Name: Train Man ♦ SgHguKHEFY Post Date: 19/04/04 21:30

>>708
about PCs
I wonder if she's anorexic . . . ⌐|￢|O
But she did scoff her food the other night . . .

737 Name: Anonymous Post Date: 19/04/04 21:35

Maybe she's getting fleshier because she's happier and that's why 'she
looks cuter than when I first met her' no?

742 Name: Train Man ♦ SgHguKHEFY Post Date: 19/04/04 21:37

Oh, but she did mention that she had tried mega-hard at dieting
>>737
(゜∀゜)

743 Name: Anonymous Post Date: 19/04/04 21:37

Hey Train, dunno what you're thinking
but Hermes ain't your woman yet

744 Name: Anonymous Post Date: 19/04/04 21:37

>>743
Shhh . . .

745 Name: Anonymous Post Date: 19/04/04 21:37

>>the wise words of 743

747 Name: Train Man ♦ SgHguKHEFY Post Date: 19/04/04 21:37

_| ̄|O

748 Name: Anonymous Post Date: 19/04/04 21:38

That's right. So you better move quickly to make her yours >Train

749 Name: Anonymous Post Date: 19/04/04 21:38

This may sound harsh but don't forget that Hermes has you placed up on
a pedestal as her 'saviour' so maybe she won't turn you down even if she
wanted to

750 Name: Anonymous Post Date: 19/04/04 21:39

>>749 adding the extra bite

762 Name: Train Man ♦ SgHguKHEFY Post Date: 19/04/04 21:41

Are we talkin Sista Kikuko

772 Name: Train Man ♦ SgHguKHEFY Post Date: 19/04/04 21:45

there goes a stray bomb . . . _⌐|O
I'm acting like I've got my shit together but when I see her 80% of me
goes fluttering away somewhere . . . _⌐|O
When I'm here in the thread, somehow I feel like I can do anything.

---

781 Name: Anonymous Post Date: 19/04/04 21:47

> 762 Name: Train Man ♦ SgHguKHEFY Post Date: 19/04/04 21:41
> Are we talkin Sista Kikuko

Train! Is that really you!

---

789 Name: Train Man ♦ SgHguKHEFY Post Date: 19/04/04 21:50

Mail here-------! ──────(ﾟ∀ﾟ)────── !!!
She says there's so much she doesn't know so
she's looking forward to learning from me!

---

792 Name: Anonymous Post Date: 19/04/04 21:50

Kikuko Inoue
http://www.office-anemone.com/image/photo_kikuko.jpg

---

803 Name: Train Man ♦ SgHguKHEFY Post Date: 19/04/04 21:54

>>792 (;´Д`)

---

805 Name: Anonymous Post Date: 19/04/04 21:56

hmm . . . Tren Boy likes Sista Kikuko . . .

The debate continued over when to tell her, how it would probably go
well and how it would be best if Train went at his own pace. But most
responses, including Train Man himself, relied on conjecture when it came
to Hermes' feelings. Then suddenly it changed.

827 Name: Anonymous Post Date: 19/04/04 22:05

Don't try to speed things up on account of us.
It wouldn't pay to see you fall flat on your face.

828 Name: Anonymous Post Date: 19/04/04 22:05

hey people, why don't we keep up the support even if it looks like a
long-term battle?

829 Name: Anonymous Post Date: 19/04/04 22:08

It'd be weird if it went on like the past two dates . . .
Plus, she was basically a complete stranger until a while ago . . .
you know what, Train, just go with what you feel.

830 Name: Anonymous Post Date: 19/04/04 22:10

I guess being used to the unbelievable drama that Train's been feeding us
so far makes us hope against hope.
Even I get a bit dizzy when I read Train's posts, yeah.
But we'll lose out if we look for that everytime.
Basically we're just gonna feel let down if we think that's the norm.
What I mean is instead of mulling over our feelings, let's try to be
considerate and coax Train along at his pace.

831 Name: Anonymous Post Date: 19/04/04 22:11

you guys are so kind

873 Name: Anonymous Post Date: 19/04/04 22:45

But at first he said
'But even if something did happen with that girl that sat next to me
No way . . . . _| |'
 . . . what a major lie that was! He's holdin' hands and shit now! _| |O

879 Name: Anonymous Post Date: 19/04/04 22:47

Oh yeah, now that I think of it, a woman dropped her mirror on the train so
I picked it up for her and she thanked me. But after our eyes met she

quickly got off at the next station, as if she were running away. Umm . . . yeah. (´A`)

---

938 Name: Anonymous Post Date: 19/04/04 23:06

Sorry. I gave my girlfriend the URL for this thread.
I talk about the thread at least once every time I see her.

---

944 Name: Anonymous Post Date: 19/04/04 23:08

>>938
My girlfriend told me about the thread. I can kinda understand why women are interested.

---

947 Name: Anonymous Post Date: 19/04/04 23:09

>>938
Me too. My girlfriend told me that somebody told her to leave her pussy and get the fuck out.

---

165 Name: Train Man ◆ SgHguKHEFY Post Date: 20/04/04 21:27

Today we e-mailed about Benoist and other kinds of teas. She apparently is a tea person and was worried about how to answer if I'd asked for coffee that day. (´ー`)

183 Name: Train Man ◆ SgHguKHEFY Post Date: 20/04/04 21:40

I'm feeling a cold wind that says we aren't seeing each other until after the holidays.

188 Name: Train Man ◆ SgHguKHEFY Post Date: 20/04/04 21:44

To be more specific, it looks like the second week of May. She says she's going to be busy during the holidays. (´·ω·`)

255 Name: Anonymous Post Date: 20/04/04 22:25

Seriously, she's the one who started the hand-holding on the date, not to mention pulling him off the train and well. If the relationship has already reached this level, then whyohwhyohwhy can't he tell her he likes her?
If Lady Hermes is kind of a tough girl then her behaviour basically points towards her really being into Train, and if she's not so tough a girl then we're talking about her getting a bit vulnerable if we attack.
But from what we know, she's bound to be the first type,
I mean, for god's sake Miss Hermes, Miss flirtatious hand-holder who invites him to her house! If this is still a no-go then you better give up on the chicks if you know what I mean. ('A`)

---

303 Name: Anonymous Post Date: 20/04/04 22:51

I think you've got a point there . . .
As far as Train has told us, Lady Hermes is prettier than Miki Nakatani, well put together but not stuck up, feisty, stylish, a great conversationalist with a strong sense of justice which basically makes her a total superhuman being.
But if this amazing person really gets together with Train . . .
Do you think it's ok to decide there is hope for Geeks?

---

315 Name: Anonymous Post Date: 20/04/04 22:56

No way dude.
Let's take a look at reality.
I was on the train and gave my seat up to a woman who had some heavy bags.
After a while, the seat next to her was free so I sat down but then she deliberately shifted away from me, making a huge space between us.
Let me just say that after yesterday's mirror story and this as a follow-up, guys, the end of the road is near. ('A`) Benoist

---

389 Name: Anonymous Post Date: 21/04/04 10:51

I'm thinking that all should go well even if he doesn't come clean
you know, while watching the skyline
H: 'I think I'm a bit drunk . . . '
T: 'Are you all right' (he says, peeking into her face)
H: (soft laughter) 'Mr Train, you always peek into my face like that'
T: 'Oh . . . a . . . umm . . . sjhduhkdfy:kyu'
H: (continues soft laughter)

They go on staring at each other awkwardly
Suddenly, Lady Hermes closes her eyes

T: 'Whh . . . www . . . what happened? Are you feeling all right?'
H: 'Oh, Mr Train . . . '

Lady Hermes pouts a bit and then smiles.

T: 'Aah . . . aa . . . I'm sorry. I'm not used to this kind of thing.'
H: 'Don't be a such a sap . . . '
T: 'Wha . . . ?'

---

409 Name: Anonymous Post Date: 21/04/04 21:17

Today on the train, I booted a drunk off but I didn't even end up talking to
the people nearby . . .

---

410 Name: Anonymous Post Date: 21/04/04 21:25

>>409
That's the way things usually go.

---

411 Name: Anonymous Post Date: 21/04/04 21:26

>>409
Good job! Supa-dupa! and I love ya!

---

412 Name: 409 Post Date: 21/04/04 21:48

>>410
It was kind of a big deal for me but it's not interesting enough to talk about
here. Seriously, it's pretty average.
It's not like the idea of being like Train didn't cross my mind but I needed
to share.
>>411
thanks, dude. love ya right back.

---

413 Name: Anonymous Post Date: 21/04/04 21:50

another romance blossoms . . .

443 Name: Anonymous Post Date: 21/04/04 22:59

Wouldn't you say that e-mailing every day makes them a couple already?
And if they're holding hands, each initiating . . . well then.
I don't know how people feel about it but if he's gonna say it, might as
well say it as soon as possible so they can enjoy couple-time for longer. At
least that's the way I personally see it.
Everything's cool if he succeeds but . . . damn, pass me the poison if he
doesn't.

444 Name: Anonymous Post Date: 21/04/04 23:08

But that period of time just before the relationship is official . . . isn't that
when it's most fun?
It should be . . .
said I, who's just bullshitting . . . ('A`)

445 Name: Anonymous Post Date: 21/04/04 23:12

>>443
I think the most exciting time is right before you actually tell her you like
her.
Holding her hand and then having her squeeze right back or having her
smile at you when your eyes meet, that's all fine but you haven't heard
exactly how the other feels yet. When I think back, that time when you've
got all these feelings growing inside, well that was when it was most fun. It
doesn't last long so I'd really like Train to enjoy it, right before they make it
official.
Plus, if they start prancing around in their birthday suits, I'm not gonna be
able to watch. __|￢|O

446 Name: Anonymous Post Date: 21/04/04 23:14

>>445
I've spotted an enemy combatant!
Everybody, aimmmm, fire! ╲(｀Д´)/

448 Name: Anonymous Post Date: 21/04/04 23:16

O|￢|_ －3O|￢|_

449 Name: Anonymous Post Date: 21/04/04 23:17

>>444-445
well done

451 Name: Anonymous Post Date: 21/04/04 23:32

I also went to Benoist
Difficult to explain . . . it was a place I was not meant to be.
There were lots of classy-looking ladies and classier older ladies.
I stood out big time.

And then the tide shifted.

591 Name: Train Man ♦ SgHguKHEFY Post Date: 23/04/04 22:11

Hey. I've got quite a harvest today so let me give a report.

First, we e-mailed about clothes (fashion).
She said that she didn't like it when it got hot because she had to
wear less clothes which meant that she couldn't hide her body. I told
her that she was thin so there was nothing she needed to hide. This
was how we got to talking about body size and shape. And then she
told me that her friends and family say that she 'isn't sexy because
she's too skinny.'
 . . . then
she added
'do you think me being so skinny has something to do with me not
having a boyfriend? (×_×)'

She's single. It's confirmed.

594 Name: Anonymous Post Date: 23/04/04 22:13

ah yeaaaaaaaaaaah ——————(˙▾˙)—————— !!

Way to go, Train Dog!

595 Name: Train Man ♦ SgHguKHEFY Post Date: 23/04/04 22:16

I'm going to follow up on that note . . . (´ー`)
All right then, I'm going to focus on e-mailing today
I'll stop by if I have anything to report (×_×)

laters

---

598 Name: Anonymous Post Date: 23/04/04 22:20

> with me not having a boyfriend-? (×_×)'
All right kids, how best do we read into that line?

---

600 Name: Anonymous Post Date: 23/04/04 22:23

>>598
I'm betting 1,000 on teasing

---

601 Name: Anonymous Post Date: 23/04/04 22:23

This is just the best.

---

635 Name: Anonymous Post Date: 23/04/04 23:02

Hey, listen up. I may be worrying over nothing but . . .
maybe, just maybe, since Lady Hermes has been about three steps ahead
of us all from the start and bombing us all without fail, well, it's probably
impossible but . . . maybe, you think she'll spring a bomb on us today?
You think we're ok?

---

649 Name: Anonymous Post Date: 23/04/04 23:08

Air Raid! Air Raid!
All hands evacuate!
Search crew what are you doing!
Lay down a barrage!
In your positions, Unit 1!

---

654 Name: Anonymous Post Date: 23/04/04 23:10

you guys really rate Train don't you?

665 Name: Anonymous Post Date: 23/04/04 23:15

>>664
love im

671 Name: Train Man ♦ SgHguKHEFY Post Date: 23/04/04 23:19

ok

'Don't lead me on so much' (laughing)

I will use every inch of my power to lead her on, I will. (´ー`)

laters

672 Name: Anonymous Post Date: 23/04/04 23:19

o . . . . hhhhhhhhhhhhhhhhhh
kaaaaaaaaaa . . . . yyyyyyyyyyyyyyyyyyyy
eeeeeeeeeeeeeeeeeeeeeeeeeeeeee

iuahjsakkkkkeeeeeeeaaaaaaaaayyyyyyyyyyyy

673 Name: Anonymous Post Date: 23/04/04 23:20

You can't see this any other way----she is teasing him.
It looks like Train has picked up on it too . . . . . ('A`) Benwa

674 Name: Anonymous Post Date: 23/04/04 23:20

g . . . .aaaassssp

675 Name: Anonymous Post Date: 23/04/04 23:20

>>671
whose words are they!!!????

676 Name: Anonymous Post Date: 23/04/04 23:21

(´A`) Bennnnnnwaaaaaaaaaaaaah!!!!

684 Name: Anonymous Post Date: 23/04/04 23:22

Run everybody runnnnnnnn! They're attacking ussssssss

705 Name: Anonymous Post Date: 23/04/04 23:26

　　　O Hm?
＿∏￣|

　　Σ. .. . .O ta-dah!
＿∏￣|

706 Name: Anonymous Post Date: 23/04/04 23:26

I'm a lancer and I have guarded you with my gigantic shield!!
Plusminuszero, man

724 Name: Train Man ◆ SgHguKHEFY Post Date: 23/04/04 23:33

'I have to say that you're hot enough for me'

729 Name: Anonymous Post Date: 23/04/04 23:33

nooooooooo waaaaaaaaaay

730 Name: Anonymous Post Date: 23/04/04 23:33

>>724
damnnnnnnnnn-----------!
you sexy beast you!!!!

732 Name: Anonymous Post Date: 23/04/04 23:34

hot enough? said Hermes??

733 Name: Anonymous Post Date: 23/04/04 23:34

cluster bombs coming atcha----- ! ——————(ˇ∀ˇ)—————— !!!

734 Name: Anonymous Post Date: 23/04/04 23:34

whoaaaaaa
here it comesssssssssssssssssss

735 Name: Anonymous Post Date: 23/04/04 23:34

>>724
>>724
>>724
>>724
>>724

damn yoirouh just stoooopidajklheio (×_×)

736 Name: Anonymous Post Date: 23/04/04 23:34

>>724
wwwwhooooaaaaaaaaaaaa!

737 Name: Anonymous Post Date: 23/04/04 23:34

>>724
enough already enough already-!

746 Name: Anonymous Post Date: 23/04/04 23:35

This is really too much for a sneak attack

764 Name: Anonymous Post Date: 23/04/04 23:38

*Train, you guys are definitely cookin'. It's confirmed. But make sure you don't come clean over e-mail. Gotta tell her when you see her.

A switch from conjecture to conviction.

775 Name: Train Man ♦ SgHguKHEFY Post Date: 23/04/04 23:39

Let's just say that for now, I've settled things.
How can I say it, it's like we both know that the next time we see
each other, we will be facing the final battle. It's as if we both know
what the other's thinking so all that's left is to see each other and
confirm face to face.
I'll report on today's e-mails tomorrow.

laters

thanks everybody

---

776 Name: Anonymous Post Date: 23/04/04 23:39

It is an honour to have experienced first hand the sneak attack . . .

---

788 Name: Anonymous Post Date: 23/04/04 23:40

thanks

thanks

thanks

let me die now

---

790 Name: Anonymous Post Date: 23/04/04 23:40

>>775
It's a bitch that I can't explain the depth of my despair with words
a depression deeper than the deepest sea!!!

---

791 Name: Anonymous Post Date: 23/04/04 23:40

>>775
uh-huh, yur right
you still toying wit us eh (´A`) Benwah

Train Man the final chapter, in the next instalment!

792 Name: Anonymous Post Date: 23/04/04 23:40

>>775

ah yeaaaaaaaaaah ——————m9(ˊ∀ˋ)——————!!!! >>775

795 Name: Anonymous Post Date: 23/04/04 23:40

can't breath . . . . . . the world is . . . turning white . . .

whaddaya say, would you guys like to join me as I walk towards the light . . . ?

796 Name: Anonymous Post Date: 23/04/04 23:40

thanks everybody!
(ˊAˋ) Benwa

797 Name: Anonymous Post Date: 23/04/04 23:41

hold up! does this mean it's ending soon?
when and where are we to digest it all with friend-o-Hermes?

801 Name: Anonymous Post Date: 23/04/04 23:41

If Train:
'I have to say that you're hot enough for me' --- basically coming clean
in that Train would be telling Hermes that she has control over his
love-o-meter.

If Hermes:
'I have to say that you're hot enough for me' ---Hermes digs Train.
If these words came out of Hermes, then it's a dead cert.

802 Name: Anonymous Post Date: 23/04/04 23:42

so all that's left is to see each other and confirm face to face.
so all that's left is to see each other and confirm face to face.
so all that's left is to see each other and confirm face to face.
so all that's left is to see each other and confirm face to face.
so all that's left is to see each other and confirm face to face.
so all that's left is to see each other and confirm face to face.
so all that's left is to see each other and confirm face to face.

so all that's left is to see each other and confirm face to face.
damn it, what's up with all this cool and calmness?
is this, could this, straight up, is this really Train?
We have created a monsterrrrrrr!!!

807 Name: Anonymous Post Date: 23/04/04 23:42

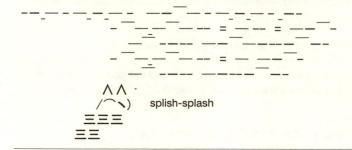

splish-splash

873 Name: Anonymous Post Date: 23/04/04 23:54

damn right . . . he's really grown up.
and it's not like they met at a speed-dating party or anything.
it started with a techie helping some people out.

the Geek miracle . . . is that what it's about?

No, not a miracle. It's more like hard work producing results!

874 Name: Anonymous Post Date: 23/04/04 23:55

Probably the God of 125 is the Great God but in addition to not being a
virgin he's fashionable and pretty much a smooth talker which meant that
he basically wasn't a Geek to begin with. In other words, he was a trained
mercenary.

But Train's different. He's a techie who was keen on voiceover actresses.
which meant that he was indeed a Geek. But now, with confidence and
composure, he goes on the attack.

This, my friends, is the stuff legends are made of. The man who
became the legend of the single male board is no other than Train Man
himself.

806 Name: Anonymous Post Date: 23/04/04 23:59

Aha. And here I was contemplating which porn video I was gonna rent at the video shop. Wondering whether I should stop choosing based on the actress and lean towards genre. Like role-playing. Cheerleaders. Nurses. Great, I'm feeling all worked up. Let me go keep myself busy.
 . . . to think that while I sat around puffing up my imagination, a nice cherry-coloured cloud was being created here . . .

56 Name: Anonymous Post Date: 24/04/04 00:50

So if the god of figuring out the teacup brand and the god of pushing Train to call to thank her for the cups weren't around . . . this miracle wouldn't have happened . . .

78 Name: Anonymous Post Date: 24/04/04 01:44

>>56
Hey, you've forgotten one key player.
The drunken geezer.

I'll give it to you, without the ones >>56 mentioned, there wouldn't be a story here.
But in the end, what really made it all happen was Train Man's courage.
If he'd just watched and pretended it wasn't happening, then none of this would have happened.

Let's drink to having this courageous soul amidst our kind! Cheers!

Japan's not all that bad if you see it in this light.
Way to go, Train!

95 Name: Train Man ♦ SgHguKHEFY Post Date: 24/04/04 09:56

morning.
sorry for dropping out in the middle of it all last night.
I was taken over by the sleep monster.

I'm gonna give you the details about my e-mail exchanges

98 Name: Train Man ♦ SgHguKHEFY Post Date: 24/04/04 09:58

Awoof! Give me some time to finish watching Keroro.
slipped my mind, completely . . . 凵￢|○

---

99 Name: Anonymous Post Date: 24/04/04 10:01

was thinkin'
Train's here-------------! ——————(ﾟ∀ﾟ)———————— !!

but then hey, Tren! you still watching anime?
but of course it brings me joy as a Geek . . .

I gotta leave before 11 so quick with the details, please

---

100 Name: Anonymous Post Date: 24/04/04 10:01

>>98
glimpse of the true face of an anorak ah yeah----!!
＊ﾟ゜・＊:.。..。.:＊ﾟ(ﾟ∀ﾟ)゜・＊:.。. .。.:＊ﾟ゜・＊!!!!

---

101 Name: Anonymous Post Date: 24/04/04 10:05

>>98 love you for still checkin in with your anime at this point in the game

---

106 Name: Train Man ♦ SgHguKHEFY Post Date: 24/04/04 10:24

Man, Keroro is way cool.
Got to be flavour of the month. (´ー｀)

ok, so finally, here I go.

---

110 Name: Train Man ♦ SgHguKHEFY Post Date: 24/04/04 10:30

'do you think me being so skinny has something to do with me not
having a boyfriend? (×_×)'
first off, how I followed up this comment

'When it comes to you, Hermes, it doesn't matter whether you're thin or fat. It's probably that the guys around you don't know what they're missing.'

on top of which I said that my body type, sense of style and looks are no good, therefore, I never seem to be able to find a girlfriend. (×_×)

---

111 Name: Anonymous Post Date: 24/04/04 10:30

All in position----!!!!! We're under attack! Under attack!!!!

117 Name: Anonymous Post Date: 24/04/04 10:33

It . . . . it's coming down from above . . . some scary thing is coming for us---

118 Name: Anonymous Post Date: 24/04/04 10:38

It's tough to get down to the nitty gritty at this time of day . . . because there aren't so many people here . . .

119 Name: Anonymous Post Date: 24/04/04 10:38

>>118
This is when, in light of lax security, the enemy likes to attack

---

123 Name: Train Man ♦ SgHguKHEFY Post Date: 24/04/04 10:40

In response came
'Stop leading me on so much (laughing)'
and
'I have to say that you're hot enough for me'
ah yeah------------ ────ヽ(ヽ(ﾉ`ヽ(´∀ヽ(´∀ﾟヽ(´∀ﾟ)ﾉ´∀ﾟ)ﾉ∀ﾟ)ﾉ´)ﾉ)ﾉ──── !!!

In response to that, I said
'Leading you on meaning . . . what? I have zero experience with this stuff so I don't have a clue (laughing)'

'I have to say that you, Lady Hermes, are hot enough for me too.'

125 Name: Anonymous Post Date: 24/04/04 10:41

bring it onnnn Y⌒Y⌒Y⌒Y⌒Y⌒Y⌒(｡A｡)!!!!!

129 Name: Anonymous Post Date: 24/04/04 10:43

watch for what's comin' from above

141 Name: Train Man ♦ SgHguKHEFY Post Date: 24/04/04 10:49

she replies, yet again
'Leading me on . . . ? It probably means that we should meet so I can
explain it to you?'
and with that sentence, I could tell that the fun and light banter we
had going was gone. Straight away, my hand holding the mobile
began to sweat.

To this, I replied
'I wonder what that is, something you can't tell me unless we see
each other. I may have something that I need to tell you too . . .
something I have to tell you next time we see each other . . . '

To which she replied immediately:
'Until next time . . . (laughing)'

Think that's about it. (×_×)

142 Name: Anonymous Post Date: 24/04/04 10:50

I guess this slippery lukewarm vibe is very Hermes and Train.

148 Name: Train Man ♦ SgHguKHEFY Post Date: 24/04/04 10:52

you think I'm just being toyed with?

149 Name: Anonymous Post Date: 24/04/04 10:52

Words will no longer seem necessary from the moment you see each other next.

Ahem, tho I've only come accross this kind of thing . . . in my virtual games.

151 Name: Anonymous Post Date: 24/04/04 10:53

>>148
don't go there. that's definitely not the case. believe in yourself.

152 Name: Anonymous Post Date: 24/04/04 10:53

Hey Train,
Being that clueless is a crime, ya hear.

154 Name: Train Man ♦ SgHguKHEFY Post Date: 24/04/04 10:54

Sorry to make things complicated . . . _⌐|O
I'm the one with zero experience.

We plan on seeing each other the second week of May

164 Name: Anonymous Post Date: 24/04/04 10:58

Don't you think you should see her like right now?
Please hurry up and go in for the kill.

168 Name: Train Man ♦ SgHguKHEFY Post Date: 24/04/04 10:58

She's going on a trip from the 29th
and returning on the 4th so I could see her on the 5th maybe

I reckon she'll be a bit tired from her trip
so I'll be careful not to push it

170 Name: Anonymous Post Date: 24/04/04 10:59

>>164
savour it. take some time to savour the sweet lightness of your emotions.
once you start dating for real then you won't be able to savour this kind of
emotion.

173 Name: Anonymous Post Date: 24/04/04 11:01

say hello to me, who's been promised a date by a woman for over three
months but she always puts it off

174 Name: Train Man ♦ SgHguKHEFY Post Date: 24/04/04 11:01

It's as if I'm dreaming . . .
If this ends up being some sort of set-up then I'll die, for real.

175 Name: Anonymous Post Date: 24/04/04 11:01

>170
I understand completely---
It's all rosy and romantic in the beginning but then it ends up going down
the drain
but if you don't want any regrets . . . savour it man, savour it.

>173
She's probably savouring the magic, dude.

180 Name: Anonymous Post Date: 24/04/04 11:04

>>173
Yep, sounds right.
I was asked out by a girl once, 'Let's have a drink,' she said
and I took it for real but then she said
'Couldn't you tell I was just trying to be polite?'

181 Name: Train Man ♦ SgHguKHEFY Post Date: 24/04/04 11:06

I admit, a month ago, I had long scraggly hair, wore glasses, couldn't

care less about my clothes and made my way to Akihabara three times a week
My life was basically all about playing games, watching anime and hanging out on 2-Channel

Lately I've got to know myself as someone who quite enjoys dressing up and going out . . .

---

183 Name: Anonymous Post Date: 24/04/04 11:06

>>180
tell her you fell for her strong ethos and take-control vibe

---

188 Name: Train Man ♦ SgHguKHEFY Post Date: 24/04/04 11:08

thanks everybody, for real
I never thought I could change my life on 2-Channel

---

192 Name: Anonymous Post Date: 24/04/04 11:12

You can't see her this week (today or tomorrow)?

---

194 Name: Anonymous Post Date: 24/04/04 11:14

If this leads straight to wedding-land then hey, can you imagine a better couple to toast as newlyweds?

---

195 Name: Anonymous Post Date: 24/04/04 11:15

We're heading into film and TV drama and novel territory here.
Mind you, I've had my share of imaginary scenarios roll around in my head like
a rental video shop that only I could see or
helping a beautiful kimono-clad lady fix her sandal strap at the station or calling a weird office by mistake but
none of these scenarios lead to success stories, dude.

---

200 Name: Train Man ♦ SgHguKHEFY Post Date: 24/04/04 11:17

>>192
she has to work so she can get her days off
dude, I really wanna see her as soon as possible . . . (´－`)

You know what, somehow I'm not afraid of women any more. . .

---

202 Name: Anonymous Post Date: 24/04/04 11:18

>>200
you were afraid of women?

---

203 Name: Anonymous Post Date: 24/04/04 11:19

once you start going out with them . . . you will find out the truly scary
things in their strange nature . . .
I throw that one down to test the waters . . .

---

206 Name: Anonymous Post Date: 24/04/04 11:22

Even if I'm all alone and have nothing going on, if I can get all stoked and
excited listening to my mates talk about their love life then you know what,
I think it's just fine.
I'll be fine even if I continue to remain all by my lonesome.

---

209 Name: Train Man ♦ SgHguKHEFY Post Date: 24/04/04 11:24

Well then it looks like I'm gonna need some more clothes so
I'm off to get some . . . (´－`)
tho it's still before payday . . . (×_×)

thanks for all your words of encouragement!

laters

Train Man, leaving those words behind, pretty much gave no sign of
hesitation.

Mission
6

The Miraculous
Final Chapter

221 Name: Anonymous Post Date: 24/04/04 12:01

No way . . .
I wasn't here for the most important attack . . .

Train, late as I am, allow me one word.
You are a lucky bastard, you dog.

In my mind, I've already got visions of Miki Nakatani and the rocker you look like lovey-doveying it up.
('A`) Benwa

223 Name: Anonymous Post Date: 24/04/04 12:31

Man oh man . . .
a bomb from day one!
and a supa-powerful one too! (　×　_　×　)

I've been up two nights in a row trying to finish a report and finally got to sleep . . .
and then I wake up to this here . . .
man, I is tired . . .

wishin you happiness, Mista Train

231 Name: Anonymous Post Date: 24/04/04 13:12

What I thought after I finished reading.

Perhaps Train's natural traits are being interpreted as 'laid-back and comfortable' in all situations?

232 Name: Anonymous Post Date: 24/04/04 13:20

>>231
But he was all panicked and dawdling in the beginning so I doubt it?

233 Name: Anonymous Post Date: 24/04/04 13:21

>>231
I wonder . . .
she already knows that he's never been out with a girl before.
walking in circles looking for the bathroom wouldn't be seen as a
'laid-back and comfortable' move, I don't think.

It's more like she's thinking he's cute for being a bit shy and flustered and
kinda off-key, maybe.

272 Name: Train Man ♦ SgHguKHEFY Post Date: 24/04/04 19:27

Hey. Looking through the backlog now.
So I guess there are some people who went for Benoist tea.
Waitresses as maids . . . (¨;∀¨)=3 hot-hot-hot!!!

Umm . . . today we e-mailed each other
'Can't wait to see you'

And we promised to spend next year's Golden Week holidays
together (´—`)

273 Name: Anonymous Post Date: 24/04/04 19:28

>>272
damn! onto next year already are you!

how far have your talks gone jkliojapo_)98898*&^

280 Name: Anonymous Post Date: 24/04/04 19:38

next year you say . . . and planning on spending it together?
are you maybe talking about going to Tahiti and spending your
honeymoon in one of those bungalows on the water?
SOUI!@&)#GOP)()988900-&*^%#$^&*)_'?{

281 Name: Anonymous Post Date: 24/04/04 19:38

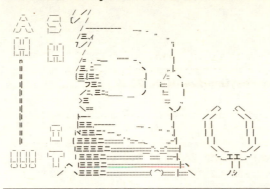

299 Name: Train Man ♦ SgHguKHEFY Post Date: 24/04/04 20:07

Um . . . and I was asked about my plans for the holidays . . .
and I have nothing . . . ＿| ￣|○

301 Name: Anonymous Post Date: 24/04/04 20:08

Hermes was actually a netizen of a thread much like ours but for single
women, Geekitas, and she was going online telling her fellow Geekitas
that she met somebody nice. Her fellow Geekitas probably told her to
send the cups as a thank you gift! Make it Hermes if possible! Advising
her about this and that.
He called to thank me, ah yeah--- or should we order some tea for you.
There must have been posts like that.

304 Name: Anonymous Post Date: 24/04/04 20:10

Train, you cool with cash? You're probably spending a lot on your clothes
and those dates and if you're doing the business then you need some for
the hotel.

311 Name: Train Man ♦ SgHguKHEFY Post Date: 24/04/04 20:28

I can't come out and tell her I'm going to a porn-mag event can I?
＿| ￣|○

For now I told her I was going shopping
It's not a lie, is it?

plus I have no money

---

312 Name: Anonymous Post Date: 24/04/04 20:29

>>311
yeah, right.

---

313 Name: Anonymous Post Date: 24/04/04 20:30

I'm having a dizzy spell

I'm off to meet with Maiko at Ryujin

---

314 Name: Anonymous Post Date: 24/04/04 20:30

anorak back in da house-------!!! ————(ﾟ∀ﾟ)————!!!!!

---

315 Name: Anonymous Post Date: 24/04/04 20:30

>>311
think about what's to come and just lay off the fan-mag events
stick to walking around the cool streets and stuff

---

316 Name: Anonymous Post Date: 24/04/04 20:31

>>311
Isn't it time you grew out of anoraks?

---

317 Name: Train Man ♦ SgHguKHEFY Post Date: 24/04/04 20:32

'Really? Are you going shopping with a girl?'

um what's goin on here . . . (´ー`)

318 Name: Anonymous Post Date: 24/04/04 20:33

To have come this far and still insist on going
to a f@*%ing fan-mag event !!!!

```
  ∧＿∧ _  ￣
 (  'A`/ ＿＝￣ ヾ geek kick !!
  ＼  ヽ ＝ -=／      ＿      .:'.' _ )･｡ﾟ∧∧
   /     .-U=-＿-=— ＝     ', ･,'O  ;#;))∀ﾟ(;;)｡.ζ   ｡
  /  .へ＿  —-＿ —   —+･.(_ ; ,;ヾ ,つ つﾟ
 .|  .|ヾ. -= -./  ￣  ￣〃,      *; ･¥    (_つ/ kapow !!!
  | |     _= /                             し'
  ＼.＼  /  ./
     U (.  ヾ
        |  ./
       .| |
       ノ  )
       ミ/
```

319 Name: Anonymous Post Date: 24/04/04 20:33

Hermes is jealous ah yeaaaaaaaah ————(ﾟ∀ﾟ)————!!!!!

337 Name: Train Man ♦ SgHguKHEFY Post Date: 24/04/04 20:42

for now I replied with 'I always shop alone'

Hmm, if I end up going out with her for real, would I have to stop being a manga obsessive anorak?

will I turn into?
Interests: Hermes
(x_x)

339 Name: Anonymous Post Date: 24/04/04 20:43

>>337
goopity goopgoopgoopgoopggopoooopppoggooop

340 Name: Anonymous Post Date: 24/04/04 20:43

goopitygoop ah yeaaaaaaah *･ﾟﾟ･*:.｡..｡.:*･ﾟ (n'∀')η ﾟ･*:.｡. .｡.:*･ﾟﾟ･* !!!!!

341 Name: Anonymous Post Date: 24/04/04 20:43

>Interests
>Hermes

Ffffffuuuuuuuuuu!!

342 Name: Anonymous Post Date: 24/04/04 20:44

>>337
You!!!! Let me slap you one!!!!

359 Name: Train Man ♦ SgHguKHEFY Post Date: 24/04/04 20:49

If she asks me to leave the manga anorak tribe
that's what I may end up having to do but

if she doesn't then there's no way I could leave it behind
I guess she wouldn't understand my porn obsession . . . _⌐|O
I'm not into the Lolita mags tho . . .

364 Name: Anonymous Post Date: 24/04/04 20:52

you are a porn-mag anorak
you do know that real women don't get wet like they just took a piss

365 Name: Anonymous Post Date: 24/04/04 20:52

seriously, if you start going out with her for real, you'll forget the porn events
and stuff because you won't have the time or the inclination anymore

366 Name: Train Man ♦ SgHguKHEFY Post Date: 24/04/04 20:54

>>365
ah yeah for the experienced advice *·˚˙*:.｡.o.｡:*˚(ﾟ∀ﾟ)ﾟ*˙:.｡. .｡.:*˙˚·*!!!!!

I'll do my best . . .
but don't you think normal games are still ok . . . ?

368 Name: Anonymous Post Date: 24/04/04 20:55

Well I'm sure once you get to know a real woman then you'll probably get to understand what's good about it that beats the mags.
If you still think the mags are better after experiencing a real woman, then I would recommend that you never leave the porn fanzine world.

408 Name: Anonymous Post Date: 24/04/04 21:23

Name: Anonymous Post Date: 05/05/04 20:03

Can I . . . cannnn I just once more?
Can I buy just one more?
Can I use that money?
This will be my last, I swear . . .

But I'm about to have our baby, Mr Train . . .

I'm sorry . . . I haven't been able to . . . shake this off . . .

. . . fine . . . Mr Train, do as you please
. . . but I'm not staying by your side any longer . . .
I don't want to wait all night for you to come home
When you leave to buy your porn mags . . .
I'm done with it . . .
Good bye. I will take care of the child on my own . . .
I'm returning to the train . . . . . .
Mr Train . . . instead of chosing me and our child's happiness . . .
you chose the magazine . . .

watch out man, those mags and events will be waiting for you with open mouths sporting an evil grin

410 Name: Train Man ♦ SgHguKHEFY Post Date: 24/04/04 21:30

she says she's a bit on the tired side so she's retiring early
I'm off tomorrow but I think I'm going to bed early too (´ー`)
We plan on seeing each other the second week of May

430 Name: Anonymous Post Date: 24/04/04 22:08

You're probably already asleep so take a look at this later, Train.

When you're ready, you be the one to tell her you like her!

This is important. All Gods up till now waited for the ladies to come up and open their hearts but judging from the time we spent on this, you will have to be the one that tells her.
And stop apologising to Hermes all the time.
Just don't forget that, will ya.

By the way, this is what I learned from a friend of mine (who the ladies dig)
Tho I myself have yet to utilise said theory . . .

465 Name: Anonymous Post Date: 25/04/04 00:54

Train who we all nurtured and developed into the fiercest soldier.
He is probably about to unleash an intense bombing campaign that will end it all.

You people, start digging deep trenches.
Me, I will head right into the centre of the blast at the moment it explodes to keep the damage from spreading.
Medics, be on the alert to be called in as back-up after the explosion.
It is up to you to save the Geek board.
And it is only you who will be able to deal the blow of 'Encouragement and Approbation' to Train.
I consider it an honour to have shared this time on the battlefield with you.
That's it! (´A`) Benwah

493 Name: Anonymous Post Date: 25/04/04 11:46

We find Train Man calling Hermes when she returns from her trip. He is happy one moment and then ⌐⌐ gasping for his last breath another. The Geeks gather and . . .

---

751 Name: Train Man ♦ 4aPOTtW4HU Post Date: 04/05/04 21:58

I'm gonna go make the call
laters

---

910 Name: Anonymous Post Date: 04/05/04 23:02

come on Train

913 Name: Anonymous Post Date: 04/05/04 23:04

he's probably busy playing a Sailor Moon game

---

914 Name: Train Man ♦ 4aPOTtW4HU Post Date: 04/05/04 23:04

sorry to keep you waiting. Here I go!

Just hung up a little while ago but . . .

She told me what's been going on and . . .
I feel like I'm totally not worthy of even thinking that I could go out with her.
And I felt it big time, that she was a different calibre.

To lay it all out, she went overseas and so she's out there using some foreign language and spending her time in this very elegant kinda way and me . . . what was I doing . . . ⌐|O
I went to that event and was proud about not buying any porn mags and that to me was kinda . . . ⌐| |..............O

Though it's questionable if the final battle is truly gonna happen we picked a date. It'll be this weekend.

Honestly, I've lost my confidence. ⌐| |

---

924 Name: Anonymous Post Date: 04/05/04 23:07

What the hell are you rambling about, Train?
We're not around to push you forward anymore.
You've already been nudged enough times by lotsa Geeks anyway.
Why don't you call up your courage and do it yourself for this final bit.

Said I, on the serious side, tho still worried ('A`)

---

933 Name: Anonymous Post Date: 04/05/04 23:10

>>Train
you've been deregulated haven't you . . .

don't be down on yourself now, you've definitely changed.
you're only a step away from graduating and leaving the Geeks behind.
If you're quitting now then it won't be any different when you meet someone other than Hermes.
When you're talking about being with women, it's about repeatedly pushing yourself from this point onwards.
Don't give up before you've started, don't compare yourself to Hermes and tell her that you will become a man worthy of her love.
All you need to do is focus on what's good about yourself and develop it.

said I, married man that I yam.

934 Name: Anonymous Post Date: 04/05/04 23:10

I may be out of order mouthing off about Train who has turned into a top of the range in-crowd boy but even if you think Hermes is better than you, she wants you.
Not only that, you want Hermes too.
Which means there's only one answer, no?

937 Name: Anonymous Post Date: 04/05/04 23:11

Her specs do seem way up there.
It reminds me of a girlfriend I had lo----ng ago who had very Hermes-like specs.

but hey

I had an inferiority complex too
and you know what, she wasn't even thinking about it.
In the end, I was the one that pulled away after thinking too much about it.
And I regret it.
I don't want Train to go through the same.

940 Name: Train Man ◆ 4aPOTtW4HU Post Date: 04/05/04 23:12

That's right, her specs were way too high for me . . . _| ̄|O

Even if we were to end up together
It's pretty impossible for me and my specs to
keep her satisfied . . .

I was wrong to think wanting to pull myself away from the porn mags and my anorak interests was such an achievement on my part . . . because in fact I was trying to keep her from disliking me, not doing something to have her like me more . . . what a painful discovery . . .

I guess I'll have to keep my hopes way down when I go this weekend (´A`) Benwa

943 Name: Anonymous Post Date: 04/05/04 23:13

You've let me down

---

954 Name: Anonymous Post Date: 04/05/04 23:16

>>940
Whoa, isn't that like a slap in the face for her?
She's not perfect either you know.
She's bound to have her moments of weakness.
Before you mouth off about specs this and specs that why don't you
straighten yourself out and think about not giving up!!!!!!

---

937 Name: Anonymous Post Date: 04/05/04 23:11

I ain't falling for no keep-my-hopes-way-down to freak us out with a crazy
bomb

---

956 Name: Anonymous Post Date: 04/05/04 23:16

>>940
I am one but you're an anorak too, no?
You were really talking about Sailor Moon weren't you?
So just think about Hermes as a different kind of anorak whether it's
teas or foreign languages.
I think if you redirect the energy that used to be poured into Sailor Moon
to Hermes, you'll be able to work out what needs to be done.

---

957 Name: Train Man ♦ 4aPOTtW4HU Post Date: 04/05/04 23:17

**As I thought, coming to this thread gives me that boost of
confidence.** (｀·ω·´)
I'll keep giving it everything.

---

962 Name: Anonymous Post Date: 04/05/04 23:17

>>Train
you better give up the ghost! meet your maker twice!
no, no, go kick the bucket a couple of times!!!!

Romance is a different matter from sports or study.
what you need in sports and study is effort<talent
and in romance, it's effort>talent.
If you're going to give up so quickly, I don't think you'll last long but
you should try telling yourself you won't ever give up. Nobody can say
how this will turn out but you should try the hardest you've ever tried in
your life so you'll have no regrets.

965 Name: Anonymous Post Date: 04/05/04 23:17

>>940
By tomorrow, I think you'll forget that you wimped out today but, do you
really think that the Hermes you fell for really fell just for the superficial you?
And is Hermes the type of woman who can only see what's on the surface?
Train Man, you know best.

22 Name: Train Man ♦ 4aPOTtW4HU Post Date: 04/05/04 23:27

why, are you guys so awesome . . .

32 Name: Anonymous Post Date: 04/05/04 23:30

Let's get this straight.
Hermes just took a little trip overseas and had an average time and came
back, right?
It's something that she worked her way up to but she's doing it all very
naturally.
Going out with Train, too, is something that she's not being forced to do
but something she's doing because she wants to.

Then it all looks cool to me.
You're not coming from the same place which means that you can't do the
things that she does
but you're trying to walk with her now, right.
Don't be so down on yourself.

36 Name: Anonymous Post Date: 04/05/04 23:31

13 Name: Anonymous Post Date: 04/05/04 23:28
without delay

>>Train

Let me lay it out for you. Even before all this speaking English or going overseas or tea business, the fact that you went to Hermes' house is a big huge deal, ok?
It's not like you can go to a travel agent and buy a ticket to her house or anything. Nobody can teach you how to be invited to her place. Speaking English and going overseas, well you can figure those out with a bit of money and time.

We pretty much knew the spec imbalance from the start.
Anime anoraks being freaky weird animals is plain as daylight fact and she's a pretty girl from a nice family. From the beginning, the imbalance was there, a big huge crack that made it tough for you to see the other side.
If you keep babbling on and on you're gonna make me hafta kick yo ass, for real.

---

71 Name: Train Man ♦ 4aPOTtW4HU Post Date: 04/05/04 23:42

thanks everybody, really. Every one of your words goes straight to my heart. Thanks to you, I've recovered and am operating at full tank!
(ˋ_ˎ´) woooooooooo!!!
She said I should bring a big bag because she has loads of presents for me. (´—`)

---

74 Name: Anonymous Post Date: 04/05/04 23:43

He's recovered! (´—`)

---

76 Name: Anonymous Post Date: 04/05/04 23:43

So Train's back on track?
Why don't you think about what you want to do with Hermes, where you want to go and what you want to eat.
Imagine your future with Hermes.

Don't let yourself get the better of you, go out there and grow with Hermes. If you dedicate yourself to Hermes she will welcome you in for sure.

91 Name: Anonymous Post Date: 04/05/04 23:45

hey, have you not noticed?
we just refuelled the world's most powerful bomber?

The countdown to the final battle continued as Train Man and the netizens of the thread fidgeted about restlessly.

---

402 Name: Train Man ♦ 4aPOTtW4HU Post Date: 05/05/04 17:31

Hey, finally returned.
I'm tired from going all over the place . . . ＿|￣|○

got some souvenirs, went around location scouting, dropped in at Akihabara . . .
I was e-mailing her during all this but when I wrote
'I'm location scouting for a next date'
she replied with

(＾3＾)

wassup with the face . . . (´—｀)

I'm ready to go. All I can do is wait for the day of my final battle to arrive.

---

403 Name: Anonymous Post Date: 05/05/04 17:32

kissin in the houssssssssse *･ﾟﾟ･*:.｡..｡.:*･ﾟ(n'∀')η ﾟ･*:.｡. .｡.:*･ﾟ･* !!!!!

---

409 Name: Train Man ♦ 4aPOTtW4HU Post Date: 05/05/04 17:36

pant pant (;´Д`) **pant pant** (;´ Д`) **huff huff huff** (;´ Д `)

414 Name: Anonymous Post Date: 05/05/04 17:44

>>409
Hm? Is that a faulty drip
or perhaps a burst leak?

415 Name: Train Man ♦ 4aPOTtW4HU Post Date: 05/05/04 17:46

One of her holiday photos of her and her friends in pjs
pfioqewi09387*&*&)(lkm

416 Name: Anonymous Post Date: 05/05/04 17:46

>>414
the latter

417 Name: Anonymous Post Date: 05/05/04 17:47

>>415
wha wha wha wha whatchu talkin bout!!!!!

425 Name: Anonymous Post Date: 05/05/04 17:57

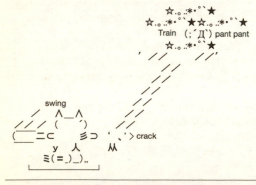

426 Name: Anonymous Post Date: 05/05/04 17:57

(´３`) like 2-Channel

427 Name: Train Man ♦ 4aPOTtW4HU Post Date: 05/05/04 17:59

By the way, at this moment she's in her pjs at home writing to me . . .
e9-opiklp;0-9
When I asked her to send me a photo of that, she said no. (´·ω·`)

452 Name: Train Man ♦ 4aPOTtW4HU Post Date: 05/05/04 18:12

but . . .

I like it when she sends me photos
but it's not as easy sending my photos . . .
coz I'm in an old T-shirt and tracksuit bottoms with crazy hair . . .
I should probably take a couple of photos for times like this . . .

461 Name: Anonymous Post Date: 05/05/04 18:17

>>452
Instead of the old T-shirt and tracksuit bottoms, get yourself some casual
outfits at Uniqlo. With the quality of phone cameras, she won't know the
difference even if you're wearin Uniqlo.
Get Hermes to pick you out a new frame for your glasses on your next date.
Your excuse is that you don't have a knack for picking the right frames.
And your head . . . well, let's just say that with all the other stuff you have
going for you, she'll probably just ignore that.

478 Name: Train Man ♦ 4aPOTtW4HU Post Date: 05/05/04 18:43

What about this: in exchange for me choosing a PC for her
she'll choose my frames . . . sound good? (´ー`)

Do you think Hermes makes frames . . . ?

479 Name: Anonymous Post Date: 05/05/04 18:45

>>478
they do but they cost more than a computer

485 Name: Train Man ♦ 4aPOTtW4HU Post Date: 05/05/04 18:49

To be honest, I've started cleaning my room up a bit
I also gave away most of my posters . . .
I gave away most of my plastic models and figurines . . . but man, I
just have so much stuff and without getting rid of them, I really can't
do anything . . .

---

487 Name: Anonymous Post Date: 05/05/04 18:49

Why don't you think about leaving your parents' house and getting your
own place?

---

498 Name: Train Man ♦ 4aPOTtW4HU Post Date: 05/05/04 18:52

>>487
I've actually been saving for that but
I've used up a lot of what I managed to save in the last few weeks
and it's kinda difficult to manage with my salary now . . .

---

544 Name: Anonymous Post Date: 05/05/04 19:14

- get rid of all anorak-related stuff (posters, porn mags)
- hoover room
- place clothes on hanger and put them in one, maybe two places
- place books and magazines in hard-to-spot location. do not pile
  them up.

don't forget the bed
make sure your bedclothes are washed and fluffed up as you could be
using them later . . .

---

557 Name: Train Man ♦ 4aPOTtW4HU Post Date: 05/05/04 19:24

By the way, let's just say that no way can I invite her to my house.
(´3`)

558 Name: Anonymous Post Date: 05/05/04 19:25

>>557
Can I just say that I get hyper reactive to the word 'Toriaezu'
but basically, I think that's the best way to go

559 Name: Anonymous Post Date: 05/05/04 19:26

>>557
so you're a Gunota

564 Name: Anonymous Post Date: 05/05/04 19:42

>>559
What's a Gunota?

565 Name: Anonymous Post Date: 05/05/04 19:44

>>564
Gunota is what you call a Gundam anorak, (an obsessive of the anime
Gundam) as Toriaezu is the name of one of the lesser known battleships
in Gundam

586 Name: Train Man ♦ 4aPOTtW4HU Post Date: 05/05/04 20:57

she has to like me, I mean, there's no other way to read it

588 Name: Anonymous Post Date: 05/05/04 20:58

>>586
hold on hold on, don't go too far too soon

589 Name: Anonymous Post Date: 05/05/04 20:58

>>586
LOL

590 Name: Anonymous Post Date: 05/05/04 20:59

Your Highness the Virgin One, what, pray tell do you speak of?

591 Name: Anonymous Post Date: 05/05/04 20:59

>>586–588
Even though nobody wrote anything for 30 minutes, here you guys are
suddenly posting simultaneously . . . makin me LOL

596 Name: Anonymous Post Date: 05/05/04 21:04

Let's hear what you've got to say, give us the reasons for your comments

598 Name: Train Man ♦ 4aPOTtW4HU Post Date: 05/05/04 21:04

Well, it's just that unless that was the case she wouldn't be saying
'Can't wait to see you' and 'I want to hear your voice before going
to bed'
to a man.
Yep, definitely. (´ ─ `)

613 Name: Train Man ♦ 4aPOTtW4HU Post Date: 05/05/04 21:11

hey, it's Wednesday already . . .
I have 3, 4 more days . . . ＿|￣|○
Now and then I break into this cold sweat . . .
even now I sometimes think this is all some weird joke

614 Name: Anonymous Post Date: 05/05/04 21:12

you seem a bit on edge. you ok?

615 Name: Anonymous Post Date: 05/05/04 21:13

>>613
dude, you're up and down like a yo-yo!

622 Name: Train Man ♦ 4aPOTtW4HU Post Date: 05/05/04 21:16

I've been all over the place since meeting her . . .
I've been switching between hope and despair all because of her . . .

623 Name: Anonymous Post Date: 05/05/04 21:18

>>622
that's what's fun

---

629 Name: Anonymous Post Date: 05/05/04 21:20

>>622
Hermes is up and down because of you too

---

628 Name: Anonymous Post Date: 05/05/04 21:20

>>622
that's normal. but if you think this all calms down when you start going
out-out with her you're sadly mistaken.

---

644 Name: Train Man ♦ 4aPOTtW4HU Post Date: 05/05/04 21:48

Successfully piloted to showdown location

---

646 Name: Anonymous Post Date: 05/05/04 21:50

here it comes . . . piloted, eh?

---

647 Name: Anonymous Post Date: 05/05/04 21:50

ah yeah----!!!!!

---

650 Name: Train Man ♦ 4aPOTtW4HU Post Date: 05/05/04 21:53

I was just putting the final touches to our next date
After we buy her PC, we decided to go into town (undisclosed locale)
for the showdown

What remains now is . . . going for it
man, I really wonder how it'll go

>>642
thanks dude. will do all that I can (｀·ω·´)

---

662 Name: Train Man ♦ 4aPOTtW4HU Post Date: 05/05/04 22:02

she seems to realise that the place I've chosen is the spot for our showdown, heartily deciding that it was a good place to discuss lots of things

she's gone to bed so I'm gonna do the same
thanks again everybody

laters

---

679 Name: Anonymous Post Date: 05/05/04 22:15

```
 ∧,,,,,∧
 ξ ・∀・ヽ  Go Train go
;' つ旦と
と,,,,,,ξ,,,,,ξ
```

Finally, the date for Hermes and Train Man's showdown has come upon us. The cold weather of the past few days has cleared, blessing the skies with brilliant weather. The sky looks as though it's also raring to go.

---

180 Name: Train Man ♦ 4aPOTtW4HU Post Date: 08/05/04 09:21

now that I'm up

---

181 Name: Anonymous Post Date: 08/05/04 09:26

all bombers in position-----

182 Name: Train Man ♦ 4aPOTtW4HU Post Date: 08/05/04 09:28

man am I nervous . . .

---

188 Name: Anonymous Post Date: 08/05/04 09:38

didn't you watch Sailor Moon today?

---

190 Name: Train Man ♦ 4aPOTtW4HU Post Date: 08/05/04 09:46

In preparation for today, I already did a view-through (･∀･)
But let me watch Keroro ＿|￣|○
I'm leaving around noon so I'll hang out till then and try to stay focused

---

193 Name: Anonymous Post Date: 08/05/04 09:51

Is Hermes cool with not going home tonight?
Have you checked out hotels in the area you're going to?

---

194 Name: Train Man ♦ 4aPOTtW4HU Post Date: 08/05/04 09:54

Even if she was ok with it, I can't imagine a hotel coming into it
Plus she can make it home in her car at whatever time . . .

---

196 Name: Anonymous Post Date: 08/05/04 09:58

Uh-uh . . . I think it would be unnatural for it not to go that way.
It's one thing if you were in school but you're both adults.

---

200 Name: Train Man ♦ 4aPOTtW4HU Post Date: 08/05/04 10:01

>>196
((((;ﾟдﾟ))) oh man
no way jose mannnn wioue098fi9

Sigh . . . I'm feeling a bit down . . . ＿|￣|○

204 Name: Train Man ♦ 4aPOTtW4HU Post Date: 08/05/04 10:01

but man how Nishizawa-san gives me the hots

---

205 Name: Anonymous Post Date: 08/05/04 10:05

Hermes is the only one that should be giving you the hots

---

206 Name: Train Man ♦ 4aPOTtW4HU Post Date: 08/05/04 10:05

Haruna and her voice (*´Д\`*) pant pant

215 Name: Train Man ♦ 4aPOTtW4HU Post Date: 08/05/04 10:13

How can I say this? I keep worrying about Mr Mole and Mr Rubber.

---

221 Name: Anonymous Post Date: 08/05/04 10:18

I hear you. I know that you posted it for times like this.
There's no need to say it.
I've brought it over for you so thank me later.

> 586 Name: Train Man ♦ 4aPOTtW4HU Post Date: 05/05/04 20:57
>
> she has to like me, I mean, there's no other way to read it

---

224 Name: Train Man ♦ 4aPOTtW4HU Post Date: 08/05/04 10:20

>>221
(｀・ω・´) atte----ntion!

I will continue to do all I can possibly do with everything I have

225 Name: Anonymous Post Date: 08/05/04 10:22

>>224
you really have become a man

228 Name: Anonymous Post Date: 08/05/04 10:24

Right, that's the vibe to go forward with.
Lady Hermes likes Train. I like Train too.
So Train, will you be my boyfriend?

230 Name: Train Man ♦ 4aPOTtW4HU Post Date: 08/05/04 10:27

thanks everybody

I still can't believe I've come this far
I think back on my life and wonder what I could possibly have been
doing all this time

232 Name: Anonymous Post Date: 08/05/04 10:28

>>230
If you didn't have your past, you wouldn't have your present, yeah.

236 Name: Anonymous Post Date: 08/05/04 10:33

The new and improved Train is way cool.
But the one that showed courage in the beginning was the
pre-transformation you.
Be confident, Train.

237 Name: Anonymous Post Date: 08/05/04 10:34

Kind of late saying it but aren't you glad you called back then instead of
writing a letter.

238 Name: Train Man ♦ 4aPOTtW4HU Post Date: 08/05/04 10:34

>>232
When it comes to relationships with women, I've experienced being disliked but never liked . . .
and that's suddenly flipped and . . .
To be honest, I thought I was going to be single and a virgin till the day I die
that said, who knows if I'll really be able to break out of this mould but . . .
can things suddenly change like this, for real?

can't help but think about it
I have to clear my mind

---

241 Name: Train Man ♦ 4aPOTtW4HU Post Date: 08/05/04 10:37

I just got a good morning e-mail from her . . .
just you wait, I'm going share all these deep feelings with you . . . (´ ― `)

---

244 Name: Anonymous Post Date: 08/05/04 10:38

I'm sure Hermes is probably stressing right now. Doing her make-up extra carefully . . .

247 Name: Anonymous Post Date: 08/05/04 10:43

I'm feeling tingly all over the place

264 Name: Anonymous Post Date: 08/05/04 11:03

I have nothing to do with any of it but my heart's thumping wildly

---

286 Name: Train Man ♦ 4aPOTtW4HU Post Date: 08/05/04 11:20

Just took a bath
Will leave as soon as I'm ready

I've lost all sense of time and I'm half in a dream. To be honest I'm

half hopeful and half uncertain but I will do what a man's got to do.

Today will probably decide the direction my life will take
I'm planning to jump out of the dark shadows of my previous
existence

Thanks for your encouragement.
I'm gonna show you what I'm made of! (´ー｀)

Off I go!

laters

---

289 Name: Anonymous Post Date: 08/05/04 11:22

Go Tra—in, go tra—in! T-R-A-I-N!

---

294 Name: Anonymous Post Date: 08/05/04 11:23

I'm cheering you on while I bolt my lunch

Good luck with your showdown!

Right, I guess I should start digging the trench . . . ('A`) laters

---

299 Name: Anonymous Post Date: 08/05/04 11:25

. . . . . . with those final words, >>286 disappeared without trace

```
:::::::::: .::::::: .::::::::°.:::::::::::   (_)(_)  :::.。::::::::::::::::::: :::: °.:::::::::::
:::::::。::::::::::: .  .::::::::::::::::::: _ i/ = =ヽi .:::::::::::。::::::::::: . . . .:::::
:::: ::::::::::::::::☆ゞ::::  ／/[|l    」  l|〕 :::::::::::::::°.:::::::::::::。:::::::::::
:::::::::::::::::::::::::: . . .:::: ／ ^ || _,ヽ ||  .::::::::: :::: .. .:::::::::::::
:::::::::°. .  .:::::::   ／ヽ丿    ヽ___／  ::::::: . .::::::::::::::::: .:::::
:..... .... .. .     く ／      三三三∠⌒>:..... .. .   .:...... ... ..
:..... . ∧∧    ∧∧    ∧∧     ∧∧ .... .... .. .:..... .... ..... ... . .
.... .::( 　 )ゝ ( 　 )ゝ( 　 )ゝ( 　 )ゝ Don't ever come
....   i ⌒ ／  i ⌒ ／  i ⌒ ／  i ⌒ ／ back you hear? . . ...
.. 三 | 三 | 三 | 三 |  ... .:::::::::: .::::::::: . .::::
       Attention!   Yes sir!
```

302 Name: Anonymous Post Date: 08/05/04 11:28

good luck dude

---

303 Name: Anonymous Post Date: 08/05/04 11:29

hey
just got up

Go! Train! Give it everything!

---

304 Name: Anonymous Post Date: 08/05/04 11:30

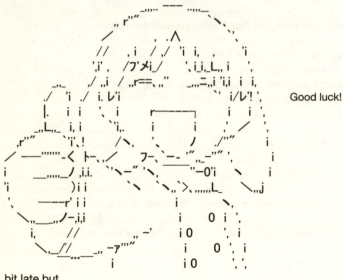

Good luck!

bit late but
the world is there for the taking!

---

307 Name: Anonymous Post Date: 08/05/04 11:31

>Train

I'll pick up your bones for you, so go!

laters

308 Name: Anonymous Post Date: 08/05/04 11:33

Even if Hermes ends up being a no-go
Train is no longer a Geek.
You be shinin', Train.

309 Name: Anonymous Post Date: 08/05/04 11:34

(`·ω·´)ゝ

318 Name: Anonymous Post Date: 08/05/04 11:48

Up up and away you go!

Let's say Hermes has heard about 2-Channel and understands the two
sides of the coin here. if she finds out about this place, she may be moved
to tears.
But I guess since she doesn't have a PC, it's not likely.

I hope today is the happiest day of your life!

Train Man, the computer nerd who shook with fear at the thought of calling
a girl had transformed in two months. Train Man, having gone through what
many would call a drastic transformation, carried the hopes and support of
the netizens of the thread out the door as he walked towards his showdown
with Hermes. No matter the outcome, Train Man and the netizens had no
regrets. Train Man's efforts were pure gold. Go, Train Man!

---

408 Name: Anonymous Post Date: 08/05/04 17:01

I hope the bombing won't start until I get back home . . .
damn it, I can't get any work done!

422 Name: Anonymous Post Date: 08/05/04 18:04

Hey people
I don't know if I have what it takes to survive this next attack . . .
I have a feeling that there'll be a nuclear warhead attached to an
intercontinental ballistic missile.

448 Name: Anonymous Post Date: 08/05/04 20:02

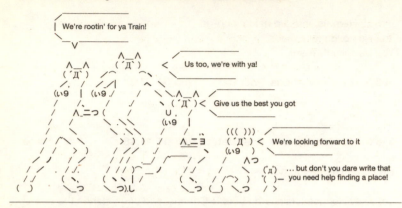

479 Name: Anonymous Post Date: 08/05/04 21:02

I was up all night but I can't go to sleep before Train gets back . . .

550 Name: Anonymous Post Date: 08/05/04 22:27

I dug the trench. All I can do now is wait . . .

('A`) pant

553 Name: Anonymous Post Date: 08/05/04 22:29

What if he's back home already, crying and watching Sailor Moon

602 Name: Anonymous Post Date: 08/05/04 23:15

I just broke up with my girlfriend over the phone. I hadn't heard from her in
3 weeks.
As I read about Train and Hermes I got to thinking about how in the past,
we got excited just like this but once you lose the ability to get excited and
giddy over each other, well, it's over. I'm looking forward to today's attack!

634 Name: Anonymous Post Date: 08/05/04 23:36

Train's not here yet eh . . . man, I rushed home for Train . . . _| ̄|O

682 Name: Anonymous Post Date: 08/05/04 23:51

I'm sure you all understand
but I can't be still with all this hoping and worrying . . .

```
      / /＼⌒＼ hub-bub-hub-bub
    / /  /⌒)Ｊ hub-bub-hub-bub
  ∧∧__∧∧ ＼((∧∧__∧∧
 ((; ´ДД`)))'  ))((・∀∀・ ;)) ＜ Calm down everybody!
 //   ⌒)Ｊ ( ⌒＼⊂⊂⌒＼
.(((OO Ｊ ))        ()＿        )))
 ))_)_)) (;;;;;;;;;;;;;;;) (((_((
```

748 Name: Anonymous Post Date: 09/05/04 00:20

I mean, look at the time.
There's no way that coming clean and some random chatting would take up
the whole day from noon. We're heading into nuclear bomb territory, no?

asioij98348\[;p0=-

760 Name: Anonymous Post Date: 09/05/04 00:25

maybe he's not coming home . . .

917 Name: Anonymous Post Date: 09/05/04 01:02

Imagine if Train writes from the newly purchased PC in Hermes' bedroom
after Hermes goes to bed . . . shit . . . that'd be too much.

918 Name: Anonymous Post Date: 09/05/04 01:02

Dude. I made myself some curry to pass the time . . .
Then it occurred to me:
'I'd love to sit down to a meal with you guys in this thread'
Man, what's going on with me?

I'm digging in . . . . . .

925 Name: Anonymous Post Date: 09/05/04 01:04

I is getting hungry for some curryyyyy!!!!!

942 Name: Anonymous Post Date: 09/05/04 01:08

Just made some curried noodles

---

956 Name: Anonymous Post Date: 09/05/04 01:11

I made some garlic rice.
Thanks for your curry. I'm gonna pour some of it onto the rice, man.

---

986 Name: Anonymous Post Date: 09/05/04 01:19

Bet you Train is thinking about this thread
He will return . . . unless of course, something came up . . .

---

309 Name: Anonymous Post Date: 09/05/04 02:34

I will wait . . . damn it, I will wait!

---

348 Name: Anonymous Post Date: 09/05/04 02:48

can't . . . make . . . it . . .
I'm going to bed . . .

---

350 Name: Anonymous Post Date: 09/05/04 02:48

As we lose one brave soldier after the next in this historic battle . . .
Though burdened by futility and regret, one lone Geek stands up . . .

. . . . and heads to bed

---

427 Name: Anonymous Post Date: 09/05/04 03:28

Sleepysleepysleepysleepysleeeeeeeeeeeeeepyyyyyyy!!!!!!

---

459 Name: Anonymous Post Date: 09/05/04 03:51

Of course I want to hear Train's report but after this one, he's probably graduating from the board . . .

And that's why I'm gonna stay up and wait for him so I can say my last good-bye.

543 Name: Anonymous Post Date: 09/05/04 04:31

I bet Train turns up the moment I leave the board.
I ain't gonna sleep.
But I is so sleeeepy.

Something must be going on. He hasn't made an appearance . . . which leads to the conclusion that just maybe Train's not going to show . . . but just as they were about to give up . . .

568 Name: Train Man ◆ 4aPOTtW4HU Post Date: 09/05/04 04:40

Hey guys. (´ー`) Is this where I pick up the thread?

569 Name: Anonymous Post Date: 09/05/04 04:41

He's back he's back he's back he's back
─────(ﾟ∀ﾟ≡(ﾟ∀ﾟ≡ﾟ∀ﾟ)≡ﾟ∀ﾟ)─────!!!!!!!!!!

570 Name: Anonymous Post Date: 09/05/04 04:41

Yipeeeeeeeeeeeee ──────(ﾟ∀ﾟ)────── !!!!

571 Name: Anonymous Post Date: 09/05/04 04:41

ho---------ly . . . . . . mother of . . . . . . !!!!
khlasfouhpppposssssiiiolhu-=-1y4-0=-8

574 Name: Anonymous Post Date: 09/05/04 04:41

I'm so glad I stayed up.˚･(/Д`)･˚｡

629 Name: Train Man ◆ 4aPOTtW4HU Post Date: 09/05/04 04:47

Thanks for waiting. Shall I start with the outcome?

634 Name: Anonymous Post Date: 09/05/04 04:47

Please . . . outcome . . . yes . . .

---

635 Name: Anonymous Post Date: 09/05/04 04:48

>>629
No no! Keep the main dish for the end!

---

640 Name: Anonymous Post Date: 09/05/04 04:48

never mind the order, just spit it out!

---

647 Name: Anonymous Post Date: 09/05/04 04:49

whatever the Train feels should come first is the best way.

---

651 Name: Anonymous Post Date: 09/05/04 04:49

Finally, we stand at this historic crossroads of the thread where the biggest baddest and soon to be legendary attack will occur . . .

---

665 Name: Train Man ♦ 4aPOTtW4HU Post Date: 09/05/04 04:51

Looks like you all know what the outcome was anyway so I'll do my usual.
If only I wasn't so sleepy

---

667 Name: Anonymous Post Date: 09/05/04 04:51

And finally, the stage curtains open for the final chapter

---

671 Name: Anonymous Post Date: 09/05/04 04:51

you all know what the outcome was?

---

676 Name: Anonymous Post Date: 09/05/04 04:52

>looks like you all know what the outcome was anyway

>looks like you all know what the outcome was anyway
>looks like you all know what the outcome was anyway
>looks like you all know what the outcome was anyway
>looks like you all know what the outcome was anyway

---

694 Name: Anonymous Post Date: 09/05/04 04:54

I beg of you, I beg you to

Let it out bit by bit

I can't settle for anything less at this point!
Kill me softly and slowly!

---

770 Name: Train Man ♦ 4aPOTtW4HU Post Date: 09/05/04 05:03

I'm crazy tired right now, dunno how clearly I can write
but here I go.

Today we met up at her house.
On the train ride over there, I was practising coming clean, making
myself sweat every time I imagined the moment itself. I kept
repeating it the whole way.

I got to the house. It was different from last time, but my hands were
still shaking as I pressed the doorbell. After pressing it for a while I
lifted my finger off slowly and the door opened straight away.

'Hello'

She came out tapping her shoes.
The sight of her made me hot again. (´—`)
Every time I see her she's wearing something different. How many
outfits does she have and well, she does own a lot of light-pink
outfits. Not that it matters because she looks good in them. (´—`)

I get in her car. Seeing her hands on the steering wheel made me a
bit scared, but as I watched her profile, I thought about what a pretty
face she had.

FYI, it was a cool car. You could hardly hear the engine

and there was no real car-smell to the inside

'Could you please wear your seatbelt'
she said, as she slowly took off.

---

783 Name: Anonymous Post Date: 09/05/04 05:05

final attack in the hoooooouuuuussssssssse------
————(ﾟ∀ﾟ≡(ﾟ∀ﾟ≡ﾟ∀ﾟ)≡ﾟ∀ﾟ)————!!!!!!!!!!
Hey! I've taken cover and shit so bring it onnnnnnnnn!!!!

---

793 Name: Anonymous Post Date: 09/05/04 05:06

everybody, let's go together, shall we . . .

---

830 Name: Anonymous Post Date: 09/05/04 05:11

Hey everybody who's watching 'Geek Gets Shot Down in Flames – Call
the Medics' thread, what's upppppp?
This boy is . . .

no more

grblub

---

838 Name: Train Man ♦ 4aPOTtW4HU Post Date: 09/05/04 05:13

Once we got going I thought her driving was very 'her'.
She started up and stopped very gently and softly.
Could be coz the car was a good one.

Shall we go and get your PC first, I said, as I navigated.

I kept staring at her face, which I usually don't get to do on account
of being a bit shy.

When we got to a red light, she seemed to sense my gaze and turned
to me
'Hm?'
she said, cocking her head

854 Name: Anonymous Post Date: 09/05/04 05:15

I think I'm dying here coz I cocked my head a bit too hard

859 Name: Anonymous Post Date: 09/05/04 05:15

'Hm?' she cocked her head
pretty much burning up

Harrumph isau0873497

891 Name: Anonymous Post Date: 09/05/04 05:19

I can feel the lovin in each and every move Hermes makes.
I see. This is what coupledom is about.
I've never experienced it but now I understand.
I'm never gonna look at couples on the train the same again.

903 Name: Train Man ✦ 4aPOTtW4HU Post Date: 09/05/04 05:21

For the sleepy ones, should I just jump to the outcome?

908 Name: Anonymous Post Date: 09/05/04 05:22

>>903
oh no you don't no you don't

910 Name: Anonymous Post Date: 09/05/04 05:22

>>903
Nope. I'm not having that.

913 Name: Anonymous Post Date: 09/05/04 05:22

>>903 Train
You really are such a good guy but you don't need to do that!!!!

Hey! Hey! Hey! Just keep writing it as it happened, yeah!!!!!!

---

914 Name: Anonymous Post Date: 09/05/04 05:22

>>903
Hold on Train!
Go slowly and deeply man, slowly and deeply!
We've got to savour this.

---

926 Name: Train Man ♦ 4aPOTtW4HU Post Date: 09/05/04 05:23

right. I'll just go as usual.

I wonder how long it'll take for me to tell today's story . . . ＿￢|O

---

935 Name: Train Man ♦ 4aPOTtW4HU Post Date: 09/05/04 05:24

Mmm! Just got a goodnight e-mail from her!!!!
─────ヽ(∀｀)人(`∀´)人( ｀∀)人(∀｀ )人(`∀´)人(｀∀)ノ───── !!!
I could just burn up and die

---

942 Name: Anonymous Post Date: 09/05/04 05:25

Curry just might pour out of my pores

---

944 Name: Anonymous Post Date: 09/05/04 05:25

>>935
feel like charging with bamboo spears

---

953 Name: Train Man ♦ 4aPOTtW4HU Post Date: 09/05/04 05:26

ahdfoierijlk;oi@-84l@Hermes

sorry. I'm just gonna reply to her. laters.

957 Name: Anonymous Post Date: 09/05/04 05:26

It's time for Train to graduate out of this thread.
I know you must be sleepy, but push yourself and write the story . . .
some of us spent half a day discussing your situation . . .
hey guys, it was fun hangin out

44 Name: Anonymous Post Date: 09/05/04 05:36

woke up to come and check the thread and whoa, I've been attacked
what's up with this speed, we've gone through a thread already

53 Name: Anonymous Post Date: 09/05/04 05:36

>>44
over half of it was us talking crap while we waited

63 Name: Train Man ♦ 4aPOTtW4HU Post Date: 09/05/04 05:38

Even though it was right after the holidays, the traffic wasn't so bad
We drove into a car park near where we were going and
she quickly backed into a parking spot. She didn't even look back,
which I guess meant that she's used to driving.
'You're good at parking aren't you?' I said
'I'm rubbish with other cars' was her reply.

We left the car park.
There weren't as many people on the pavement as usual so it was
pretty easy for us to walk side by side
after we walked for a bit, she reached for my wrist. I quickly said,
'It feels kind of strange,' as I flipped my wrist and grabbed her hand.
She smiled at me and said 'You're right, this feels much better.'
I was burnin' up inside. When I squeezed her hand, she squeezed back.
This really was the best thing ever

71 Name: Anonymous Post Date: 09/05/04 05:39

'You're right, this feels better.'

Rrrrrooooooooaaaaaaaar

74 Name: Anonymous Post Date: 09/05/04 05:40

aaaaaarrrrrrrrrghhhh
my heart's all squeezysqueakysquashysqueeeezy

95 Name: Anonymous Post Date: 09/05/04 05:43

what's this sensation . . . in my chest cavity . . . a
sloopyslumpyclumpymelty . . .
could this be the final, lethal weapon?

132 Name: Anonymous Post Date: 09/05/04 05:49

you know what, we've all been hanging together with Train here for
14 threads
and when I think about saying goodbye to everybody, I get all emotional.

147 Name: Anonymous Post Date: 09/05/04 05:51

morning mates
now that I got a good three hours of sleep, allow me to take over patrol duty

159 Name: Train Man ♦ 4aPOTtW4HU Post Date: 09/05/04 05:55

We got to the shop. We were holding hands in the shop too but man,
it's kind of embarrassing you know . . . (´ー`)

We went to the laptop corner and I showed her a few of the ones I
had my eye on. For a moment, the old me was about to surface but I
squashed him down and got over it. She said 'I think I'll go with this
one' and picked the one I recommended most.
We picked a modem and also got some leaflets for ISPs. She paid
everything in one go on her card. How cool, I mean, how cool is she.

We got the assistant to wrap it up so we could carry it and I took the
bag.
'Oh, I'm sorry . . . '
'No, don't worry. It's heavy,' I said, picking up both the PC and
modem.

Outside, she grabbed the smaller bag and reached for my hand with her other hand. (´—`)

I'm gonna take a little break now . . . ⌐IO **But I'm not going to bed**

168 Name: Anonymous Post Date: 09/05/04 05:56

she grabbed the smaller bag and reached for my hand with her other hand (´—`)

sdryufjpe347809@@*0-tij

---

172 Name: Anonymous Post Date: 09/05/04 05:57

she grabbed the smaller bag and reached for my hand with her other hand

haha . . . . . .ha . . . . . .ha . . . . .ha . . .

---

174 Name: Anonymous Post Date: 09/05/04 05:57

you wanna hold hands sooooooo much don't you!!!!!!

---

182 Name: Anonymous Post Date: 09/05/04 05:57

>Outside, she grabbed the smaller bag and reached for my >hand with her other hand.
it sounds vaguely familiar like I've heard it before . . . or not . . .

---

191 Name: Anonymous Post Date: 09/05/04 05:59

hey people
can't you see the beautiful couple holding hands over there?

256 Name: Anonymous Post Date: 09/05/04 06:09

just crossed my mind . . .

you think the ladies reading Train will suddenly feel like they really really want a boyfriend?
like how we all sit around gasping for air as we howl about getting it on with the ladies . . .

---

257 Name: Anonymous Post Date: 09/05/04 06:10

>>256
definitely, all the time.

---

258 Name: Anonymous Post Date: 09/05/04 06:10

>>256
pretty sure they do
I'm sure there are a few ladies reading this.

---

261 Name: Anonymous Post Date: 09/05/04 06:10

>257
m(ry

---

276 Name: Train Man ♦ 4aPOTtW4HU Post Date: 09/05/04 06:12

We get back to the car park and put the bags in the boot.
After closing it, she reached for my PC-carrying hand and said 'I'm sorry. It was heavy, wasn't it,' not to me but as if to my hand.
she covered my hand with hers and rubbed the marks from the handle.
hot hot very hot
I also rubbed the hand she used to carry her bag. (´ー`)

When I tried to pay for parking she, of course, said no.
As we headed out of the car park, she said 'Getting hungy?' and we decided to head for the place we'd chosen.
And off we drove.

277 Name: Anonymous Post Date: 09/05/04 06:13

here it comes here it comes
────(ﾟ∀ﾟ≡(ﾟ∀ﾟ≡ﾟ∀ﾟ)≡ﾟ∀ﾟ)────!!!!!!!!!!

286 Name: Anonymous Post Date: 09/05/04 06:14

whoooaaaaaaa ────(ﾟ∀ﾟ)────!!!!!!

287 Name: Anonymous Post Date: 09/05/04 06:14

I can't take it anymore. I'm just running after ya, god knows why . . .

297 Name: Train Man ♦ 4aPOTtW4HU Post Date: 09/05/04 06:14

**damn I's sleeeeeeeeeeeeeepyyyyy!!!!
I'm getting light-headed!**

298 Name: Anonymous Post Date: 09/05/04 06:14

He'll fight to the death
For all of you who've fought through since the 125 bombing
this is the moment of truth

207 Name: Anonymous Post Date: 09/05/04 06:02

* let me make another suggestion *

Train seems pretty tired and his posts do take a long time so
why don't we let him sleep it off for a bit and come back after
he's got something written out and planned his bombing campaign

* just a suggestion (twitch, twitch) *

323 Name: Train Man ♦ 4aPOTtW4HU Post Date: 09/05/04 06:17

Hmm? What do we think of >>207's idea?

324 Name: Anonymous Post Date: 09/05/04 06:17

>>323
up to you, dude

---

353 Name: Train Man ♦ 4aPOTtW4HU Post Date: 09/05/04 06:22

thanks for understanding. I'm gonna sleep a bit first
but I reckon when she wakes up I'm gonna start getting a storm of
e-mails from her because we have to set up her PC and stuff. So
maybe this is the only time I have . . . ?

---

358 Name: Anonymous Post Date: 09/05/04 06:22

Hold on! When exactly are you coming back?

---

375 Name: Train Man ♦ 4aPOTtW4HU Post Date: 09/05/04 06:24

well . . . actually, I think now's the only time for me to write
between now and when she wakes up

---

376 Name: Anonymous Post Date: 09/05/04 06:24

told you all not to slack off! To your positions everybody!!!!!

---

382 Name: Anonymous Post Date: 09/05/04 06:25

don't push yourself, >Train

---

399 Name: Anonymous Post Date: 09/05/04 06:27

Not knowing Train was going to make his appearance 3 minutes later
I was playing a game from 4:37 and just returned . . .
I shouldn't have played the game!!!! Stupid, stooopid, stoooopid me!!!
O 「l_

401 Name: Anonymous Post Date: 09/05/04 06:27

>>375
. . . . . . till death, eh, Train.
bring it onnnnnnn!!!!!!!!!

405 Name: Train Man ♦ 4aPOTtW4HU Post Date: 09/05/04 06:27

I'm gonna have a mega-caffeine-booster drink
laters

429 Name: Anonymous Post Date: 09/05/04 06:30

getting way sleepy (´A`)

439 Name: Anonymous Post Date: 09/05/04 06:31

>>399
me tooooo!
I've finally caught up.
what the hell was I doing standing by from 1 am pressing the refresh button over and over . . .
anyway, I'm just glad to have finally caught up

470 Name: Anonymous Post Date: 09/05/04 06:37

sleepy . . . gonna get some coffee

484 Name: Train Man ♦ 4aPOTtW4HU Post Date: 09/05/04 06:41

All right, I'm back.
I'll start up at 7, ok

487 Name: Anonymous Post Date: 09/05/04 06:42

Annihilation warning ah yeah---------
—ww∧√レv v～(ﾟ∀ﾟ)—ww∧√レv v～— !!

488 Name: Anonymous Post Date: 09/05/04 06:42

I'm not gonna last till 7

---

494 Name: Anonymous Post Date: 09/05/04 06:43

7 o' clock . . . gonna get some grub!!!!

---

497 Name: Anonymous Post Date: 09/05/04 06:43

The cows around here are mooing so loud I can't sleep

---

506 Name: Anonymous Post Date: 09/05/04 06:45

15 minutes . . .
gonna snooze for a bit
laters

---

562 Name: Anonymous Post Date: 09/05/04 07:00

```
∧,,,,∧
ξ ・∀・ヽ  Sparkly Sparkly
．' つ旦と
と,,,,,,ξ,,,,,ξ
```

why don't we all sparkle together and wait for death to turn up

---

575 Name: Train Man ♦ 4aPOTtW4HU Post Date: 09/05/04 07:02

We were eating at a restaurant she recommended.
It was quite dark inside the restaurant. It was the kind of place where you eat sitting on big comfy sofas. I was kinda nervous 	￣￨O Even now, going to places that aren't family-style restaurants or fast food joints makes me nervous.

This was when she gave me some gifts from her travels. Accessories and that, I think.
I saw the HERMES logo and said
'My god . . . you've got me something so expensive again . . . '

'It's not so expensive over there' she said, but it doesn't change the fact that it's still way upmarket.
I thanked her loads and she asked me to try it on so I did. I think it's what you'd call a necklace. It's kind of short for a necklace but . . .

I was having a difficult time putting it on so she helped me with it . . . and her breast came so close to my face it almost touched 09ifdhoi-eru09jdiaquw=
and man, did she smell nice . . .
'It looks good on you' she said, clapping her hands.

then she pointed to her neck and said 'we're wearing the same thing'

I burst into flames

---

576 Name: Anonymous Post Date: 09/05/04 07:02

let me go and check if all's quiet on the front . . .

---

581 Name: Anonymous Post Date: 09/05/04 07:02

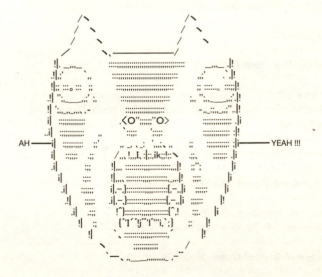

AH ——— YEAH !!!

582 Name: Anonymous Post Date: 09/05/04 07:02

```
o   ┠━━┨  go-ng
(˙ヽ━◎ |  go-ng
/〉. |    |  go-ng
```

584 Name: Anonymous Post Date: 09/05/04 07:02

>>576
run--------!!!!!

589 Name: Anonymous Post Date: 09/05/04 07:03

what is this?

are you trying to kill me?

591 Name: Anonymous Post Date: 09/05/04 07:03

my knees are knocking . . . _| ̄|O

612 Name: Anonymous Post Date: 09/05/04 07:06

the enemy's too powerful

655 Name: Anonymous Post Date: 09/05/04 07:13

Hermes choker as a gift . . . . . . correction, matching chokers . . .
for a guy she hasn't kissed yet and who hasn't told her his feelings. . . not
even officially going out . . . .

what's going onnnn 1209ujmpo9ie9488yipk=-[)*@#&__@$

657 Name: Anonymous Post Date: 09/05/04 07:14

attention all members, attention all members.
this is not drill, I repeat, this is not a drill

687 Name: Anonymous Post Date: 09/05/04 07:18

Train, you asleep . . . ?

702 Name: Train Man ♦ 4aPOTtW4HU Post Date: 09/05/04 07:20

I'm up
I'm writing

---

720 Name: Anonymous Post Date: 09/05/04 07:22

Reconnaissance Unit, I order you to return! A warning has been sounded

---

738 Name: Train Man ♦ 4aPOTtW4HU Post Date: 09/05/04 07:25

After I accepted her gift I listened to her talk a bit about her trip
She talked about people over there, what she ate, the culture and the
language. She told me that she learned a lot just by going there.
When I told her that I hadn't gone anywhere since my school trip, she
told me off a bit. (´ー`)

When we left the restaurant (we paid separately)
'Let's take some photos in the Print Club photo booth,' she said.
I had no idea what she was talking about and replied with a (?_?)
like face so she yanked my hand and we went to an arcade
so, we were going to be taking photos together . . .
to be honest, I hate that kind of thing but
she dropped the coins into the slot and quickly pressed some buttons.
'Make sure you put on a cute face.'
'Wha? Whaaa?' I said while the machine snapped away . . .

When I saw the final photo, you couldn't tell where I was looking
and . . .
She'd pulled a face
'It's not the best but it's a memento'
she gave me half the photos. I think I'm beginning to like the photo
booth already.

---

744 Name: Anonymous Post Date: 09/05/04 07:26

ah yeah againnnnn ————(ﾟ∀ﾟ)————!!!!

746 Name: Anonymous Post Date: 09/05/04 07:26

Print Club photo boooothhheoijwu098)(*@#)OP@_)

748 Name: Anonymous Post Date: 09/05/04 07:26

investing in Print Club photo booths . . .

749 Name: Anonymous Post Date: 09/05/04 07:26

did you perhaps mean to type Puri-Kura instead of Print Club?

752 Name: Anonymous Post Date: 09/05/04 07:27

Print Club photo booth . . .
I've heard this one before apiu!)_(*@U#Poppdopiu*^@%

753 Name: Anonymous Post Date: 09/05/04 07:27

the Print Club photo booth is increasingly the weapon of choice

760 Name: Anonymous Post Date: 09/05/04 07:28

I was amazed by the unexpected direction . . . but wait, is this déjà vu?
fotoboooooteoai02909)@#*UIO_)haahahahhhhhaaaahahahah

827 Name: Anonymous Post Date: 09/05/04 07:38

morning
well I just peeked in to see what was goin on siopjer-989890009)*(@(00-

838 Name: Train Man ♦ 4aPOTtW4HU Post Date: 09/05/04 07:42

We went back to the car then headed to the spot we'd chosen for our
showdown.
She knew what was about to happen too . . .
I could tell we were both getting well nervous.
We started talking less and my clenched fist was getting sweaty.

I hesitantly gave her directions. All the time we were getting closer
and closer to our destination. In the silence I rehearsed my lines over

and over again.

When we got there I could hear my own heartbeat. I was dripping with sweat.
We got out of the car and started walking. Just as I thought, there were couples all around.
'What a nice place,' she said.
'I checked it out,' I said, and she said it was very me to do that. It was a park but compared to when I came in the daytime, there were lots more people, and basically all couples. All the benches were taken.

We walked around the park for a bit with no particular plan. I had no idea how to set the mood.

---

843 Name: Anonymous Post Date: 09/05/04 07:43

showdown----!!!!!!!

---

844 Name: Anonymous Post Date: 09/05/04 07:43

garrrrrr

---

850 Name: Anonymous Post Date: 09/05/04 07:43

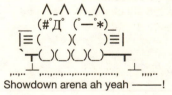
Showdown arena ah yeah ———!

---

866 Name: Anonymous Post Date: 09/05/04 07:46

She knew what was about to happen too
She knew what was about to happen too
She knew what was about to happen too
She knew what was about to happen too
She knew what was about to happen too
She knew what was about to happen too

what?!

868 Name: Anonymous Post Date: 09/05/04 07:46

There is a bomb coming straight for us that no trench or bomb shelter can protect us from . . . . . .

Brave men, I will not let you die alone!!!!

871 Name: Anonymous Post Date: 09/05/04 07:47

I'm reliving that sensation when I was just about to clear the RPG (;´Д`) pant pant

882 Name: Anonymous Post Date: 09/05/04 07:48

I was up all night checking the thread when I found Train Man's 'Just got home' and I was hip-hip-hooraying when I suddenly woke up and checked the log and found out this was a real-time attack!
It was a prophetic dream . . . I kept having a bad dream about checking the log . . .

884 Name: Anonymous Post Date: 09/05/04 07:48

Everyone.
I think after this next attack, I will no longer be part of this world.
Though I am a battleworn soldier from the 125 attack, I think I won't be able to survive this next one.
Allow me these final words.

I love you all
gasppp

956 Name: Train Man ♦ 4aPOTtW4HU Post Date: 09/05/04 08:02

My heart's thumping like mad as I write . . .

958 Name: Anonymous Post Date: 09/05/04 08:02

here it comes . . . . . .

960 Name: Anonymous Post Date: 09/05/04 08:02

'ah yeah' systems complete

---

977 Name: Anonymous Post Date: 09/05/04 08:04

prepare to engage target! prepare to engage target! it's coming, it's coming . . . !

---

978 Name: Anonymous Post Date: 09/05/04 08:04

Colonel! We aren't ready for it!!!!

---

22 Name: Anonymous Post Date: 09/05/04 08:06

Men! Brace yourselves! This is your final battle!

The hundreds maybe thousands of netizens who had been carefully watching the thread all waited with bated breath for Train Main's bomb-bay doors to open. They'd been waiting for this moment for the past two months. Even though there was a chance the entire world would go up in flames, nobody was running. The bomb quietly slips out of the bay doors and falls slowly but surely towards the thread. And then. As it bursts into flames, the thread becomes enveloped in a powerful light like never before.

---

41 Name: Train Man ♦ 4aPOTtW4HU Post Date: 09/05/04 08:08

We walked around for a while before she said
'Look, over there'
she pulled my hand and lead me to an empty bench

We sat down. I wondered if we'd ever sat so close before. Of course, we hadn't. I was so nervous I couldn't even open my mouth.
But, now was the moment.

'I have something important I want to say'

I broached the subject. She just nodded in silence, listening.
But then I found myself unable to speak any further.

I stood up and faced her as she sat on the bench.
'Um . . . I . . .'
I said as words failed me yet again. I was so nervous I could die,
I thought.
Everything that had happened since we met went through my
head . . .

She grabbed both my hands and said
'You can do it!'
'I really like you, Hermes,' I said, finding a lot more courage
than I used that day on the train. My voice shook as I said it.
She stood up. I couldn't look at her face.
**'I like you too, Mr Train. Will you always be by my
side?'**
she said.

---

42 Name: Anonymous Post Date: 09/05/04 08:09

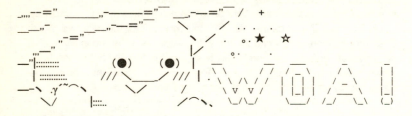

It was a miraculous moment. Train Man had become a legend. A mass of
congratulations arrived.

---

47 Name: Anonymous Post Date: 09/05/04 08:09

ah yeaaaaaaaaaaaaaaaah

48 Name: Anonymous Post Date: 09/05/04 08:09

>>41

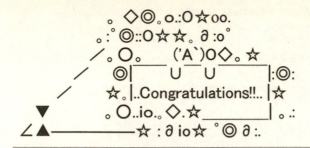

49 Name: Anonymous Post Date: 09/05/04 08:09

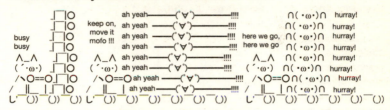

50 Name: Anonymous Post Date: 09/05/04 08:09

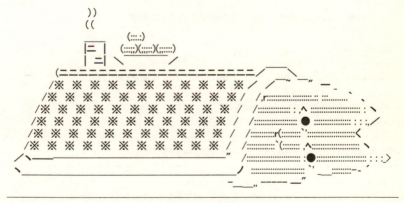

51 Name: Anonymous Post Date: 09/05/04 08:09

bye . . . . . . bye . . . .everybody

52 Name: Anonymous Post Date: 09/05/04 08:09

53 Name: Anonymous Post Date: 09/05/04 08:09

aaaaaaaaaaaaaaaaa
aaaaaaaaaaaa
aaaaaaaaaaaaaa
aaaaaaaaaaaaaaaaaaaaaaaaa
aaaaaaaaaaaaaaaaaaaa
aaaaaaaaaa
aaaaaaaaaaaaa

54 Name: Anonymous Post Date: 09/05/04 08:09

gasp

55 Name: Anonymous Post Date: 09/05/04 08:09

whoa! Right in front of my eyes . . . . . . a bomb!!!!!!
ouch . . . fffff . . . ouch . . .

56 Name: Anonymous Post Date: 09/05/04 08:09

57 Name: Anonymous Post Date: 09/05/04 08:09

here it issssssssss-----------

58 Name: Anonymous Post Date: 09/05/04 08:09

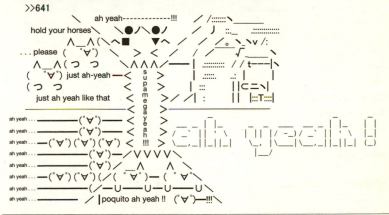

59 Name: Anonymous Post Date: 09/05/04 08:09

>>641

60 Name: Anonymous Post Date: 09/05/04 08:09

Oh no! I've been hit! Eject! Eje . . . .

62 Name: Anonymous Post Date: 09/05/04 08:10

```
          ⊂￣～つ.Д｡)⊃
  ⊂￣～つ.Д｡)⊃
   ⊂￣～つ.Д｡)⊃
    ⊂￣～つ.Д｡)⊃
     ⊂￣～つ.Д｡)⊃
      ⊂￣～つ.Д｡)⊃
       ⊂￣～つ.Д｡)⊃
⊂￣～つ.Д｡)⊃
        ⊂￣～つ.Д｡)⊃
         ⊂￣～つ.Д｡)⊃
```

63 Name: Anonymous Post Date: 09/05/04 08:10

```
ah yeah! ──( ´∀`)·ω·) °Д°)·∀·)⌐─ ⌐)´ˬ`)°∀°)´-`)──!!!!
ah yeah! ──(°∀°)─( °∀)─( °)─( )─(° )─(∀° )─(°∀°)── ! ! ! ! !
ah yeah! ──────(°∀°)────────!!!!
Under   ──||Φ|(|°|∀|°|)|Φ||── arrest ─ !!!!!
```

64 Name: Anonymous Post Date: 09/05/04 08:10

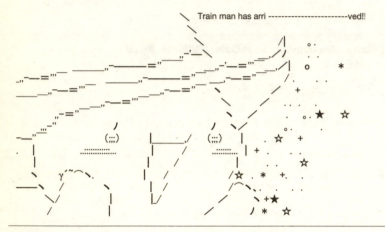

Train man has arri --------------------------ved!!

65 Name: Anonymous Post Date: 09/05/04 08:10

ah yeah for real
'You can do it!'
attack force

66 Name: Anonymous Post Date: 09/05/04 08:10

```
Love is in the airrrr ──────────(°∀°)──────────!!!!!!
everywhere I look around ──────────(°∀°)──────────!!!!!!

in the whisper of the trees by Train
────────────(°∀°)────────────!!!!!!
in the thunder of the sea by Hermes
────────────(°∀°)────────────!!!!!!
Love is in the air ──────────(°∀°)──────────!!!!!!
oh oh oh ──────────('A`)──────────!!!!!!
except for Geeks who just get Benwah
────────────('A`)────────────!!!!!!
```

67 Name: Anonymous Post Date: 09/05/04 08:10

Point of impact!!!

---

68 Name: Anonymous Post Date: 09/05/04 08:10

Ahhhh . . . finally, I've found it
the place where I will take my last breath
thank god (/_·ヽ) way to go Train!

---

69 Name: Anonymous Post Date: 09/05/04 08:10

weeeeeeee---- it's hotting up in here

---

70 Name: Anonymous Post Date: 09/05/04 08:10

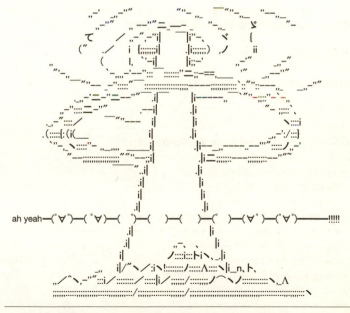

---

71 Name: Anonymous Post Date: 09/05/04 08:10

you've arrived!!!
Don't know why but I can't stop crying!!!!

Way to go Train!!!! Way to go Ermaiz!
sob. Banzai for the Geeks!

---

72 Name: Anonymous Post Date: 09/05/04 08:10

```
        *   .※ ※ ※. *
      *  ※ ☆ ☆ ☆ ☆ ※  *
     *  ※ ☆   ※ ※   ☆ ※  *
    * ※ ☆  ※   ※   ※  ☆ ※ *
   * ※ ☆ ※   ※ ☆ ※   ※ ☆ ※ *
  * ※ ☆ ※  ※ ☆   .☆ ※  ※ ☆ ※ *
  * ※ ☆ ※ ※☆      ※※ ※ ☆ ※ *
  * ※ah yeah─────(°∀°)────── !!!※  *
  * ※ ☆ ☆ ※☆      ※※ ※ ☆ ※ *
   * ※ ☆ ※  ※☆  .☆※  ※ ☆ ※ *
    * ※ ☆ ※   ※☆※   ※ ☆ ※ *
     * ※ ☆ ※   ※   ※ ☆ ※ *
      *  ※ ☆   ※ ※   ☆ ※  *
       *  ※ ☆ ☆ ☆ ☆ ※  *
        *  .※ ※ ※. *
           *   *
```

---

73 Name: Anonymous Post Date: 09/05/04 08:10

congratulatiooooooooonnnnnnnnnnnnnnns

---

74 Name: Anonymous Post Date: 09/05/04 08:10

tfgy290jp-0*()&$%*()

---

75 Name: Anonymous Post Date: 09/05/04 08:10

She grabbed both my hands and said
'You can do it!'

---

76 Name: Anonymous Post Date: 09/05/04 08:10

ah yeah-----! ─────(°∀°)─────!!!!

---

78 Name: Anonymous Post Date: 09/05/04 08:10

way to go!
way to go, Train . . . !

79 Name: Anonymous Post Date: 09/05/04 08:10

Carry the injured to safety! Re-establish the front line! We won't allow needless death!!!!

80 Name: Anonymous Post Date: 09/05/04 08:10

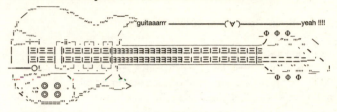

81 Name: Anonymous Post Date: 09/05/04 08:10

You did it Train! Way to go, for real! Take good care of Hermes and make her happy you hear!!
Finally, finally . . . this moment has come upon us . . .

82 Name: Anonymous Post Date: 09/05/04 08:10

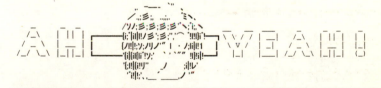

83 Name: Anonymous Post Date: 09/05/04 08:10

ah yeah------------

84 Name: Anonymous Post Date: 09/05/04 08:11

85 Name: Anonymous Post Date: 09/05/04 08:11

ah yeah! ———(ﾟ∀ﾟ)———!!
way to go!
man, is Hermes great . . .

86 Name: Anonymous Post Date: 09/05/04 08:11

no matter how you look at it, this is definitely an ah yeah---
——(ﾟ∀ﾟ)—(ﾟ∀)—(ﾟ)—( )—( )—(ﾟ)—(Aﾟ)—(ﾟAﾟ)———!!!
it's as if 10000 mad crazy runaway motherships slammed into us
runnnnnnnnnnnnnnn —ヾ( )ﾉﾞ ヾ(ﾟдﾟ)ﾉﾞ ヾ(ﾟдﾟ)ﾉﾞ ヾ(дﾟ)ﾉﾞ ヾ( )ﾉﾞ ——!!

87 Name: Anonymous Post Date: 09/05/04 08:11

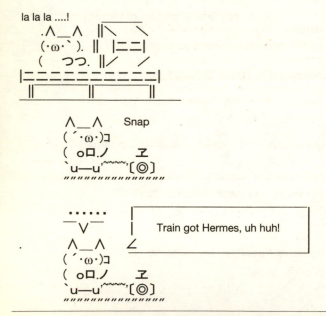

88 Name: Anonymous Post Date: 09/05/04 08:11

ah yeaaaah!!!
way to go!!!!!!!!!

89 Name: Anonymous Post Date: 09/05/04 08:11

way to go Train Man!

---

90 Name: Anonymous Post Date: 09/05/04 08:11

way to go-----------!
well done! well done! well done! well done!!
well done dude! top man!

---

91 Name: Train Man ♦ 4aPOTtW4HU Post Date: 09/05/04 08:11

thanks everybody

---

92 Name: Anonymous Post Date: 09/05/04 08:11

Way to go, for real.
good to be happy, eh . . . . .gulp.

---

93 Name: Anonymous Post Date: 09/05/04 08:11

straight up
ah yeah-----! ─────────────(ﾟ∀ﾟ)─────────────!!!!!!

---

94 Name: Anonymous Post Date: 09/05/04 08:11

   | || ||| | ||| || | whhhoooshhh!

```
 ─────────────
 /::::::Λ＿Λ:::::::::::::::/
/::::::(∩´Д`)∩ ::::::/
/:::::::(          /::::::::/   ta-ta-da-tah peeek-a-boooo
```

---

95 Name: Anonymous Post Date: 09/05/04 08:11

supamega way to go!

96 Name: Anonymous Post Date: 09/05/04 08:11

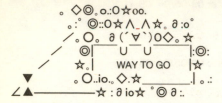

97 Name: Anonymous Post Date: 09/05/04 08:11

Train Man ♦ 4aPOTtW4HU Post Date: 09/05/04 08:08
it's time for you to go down in history, man

98 Name: Anonymous Post Date: 09/05/04 08:11

────ヽ(∀゜)人(゜∀゜)人(゜∀)ノ──── !!! ah yeah

100 Name: Anonymous Post Date: 09/05/04 08:11

ah yeah! ────(゜∀゜)────!!!!
ah yeah! ────(゜∀゜)────!!!!
ah yeah! ────(゜∀゜)────!!!!
ah yeah! ────(゜∀゜)────!!!!
ah yeah! ────(゜∀゜)────!!!!

101 Name: Anonymous Post Date: 09/05/04 08:11

Train a-blooooooooomin'
Hermes a-blooooooomin'
way to go, Train!!!!!!!!!!!!!!
I knew it was gonna be ok, I was absolutely sure but I still cried. ·゜·(/Д`)·゜·。

103 Name: Anonymous Post Date: 09/05/04 08:11

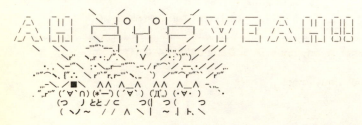

I think I'm gonna cry . . .

---

104 Name: Anonymous Post Date: 09/05/04 08:11

Shit, forgot to get my ASCI ready

---

105 Name: Anonymous Post Date: 09/05/04 08:12

way to go!

---

106 Name: Anonymous Post Date: 09/05/04 08:12

way to go, you really did a great job

---

107 Name: Anonymous Post Date: 09/05/04 08:12

my heart aches

---

108 Name: Anonymous Post Date: 09/05/04 08:12

>>103
I'm already crying

---

110 Name: Anonymous Post Date: 09/05/04 08:12

Right back atcha!

111 Name: Anonymous Post Date: 09/05/04 08:12

was everybody just anxiously waiting?

112 Name: Anonymous Post Date: 09/05/04 08:12

```
           (⌒∨⌒)╱::"＼
        (⌒＼======╱⌒(⌒∨⌒)
     (￣＞::(˚Д˚)<(⌒＼======╱⌒)
       (￣╱=====(＿＞::(˚Д˚)::＜
      ╱((⌒∨⌒(＿╱U::U＼＿)
     ╱(⌒＼======╱  (＿∧＿)`∨⌒) ､@,
    <(＿＞::(˚Д˚)::＜＿Ｌ//Ｊ＼======╱⌒;@@^
    |丶(＿╱======＼＿)(＿＞::(˚Д˚).⊃|╱`
    | 丶.(＿∧＿) // (＿(╱======＼＿)
    |  ＼Ｌ|.Ｊ  ///／(＿∧＿)
    |   `.:7      ╱Ｌ"Ｊ
    丶 ╱      :::╱
    ╱￣＼(„˚Д˚)⌒丶  ＜ Train man, way to go you bastard!
    丶===╱./∧ᵉ＼=ᵗ╲
     ╱∠/|  |丶＼
    (＿￣|╱＿U"U ∨`"
```

you really did it you fucker!

113 Name: Anonymous Post Date: 09/05/04 08:12

Now we're all ready to face death!!

114 Name: Anonymous Post Date: 09/05/04 08:12

way to go Train

115 Name: Anonymous Post Date: 09/05/04 08:12

Way to go Train, and all you guys here in the thread, you don't give up!
I guess the real (´A`) Benoist moments are yet to come, but thought I'd
just comment..

117 Name: Anonymous Post Date: 09/05/04 08:12

(Д) ° °

118 Name: Anonymous Post Date: 09/05/04 08:13

way to go, and good job!

119 Name: Anonymous Post Date: 09/05/04 08:13

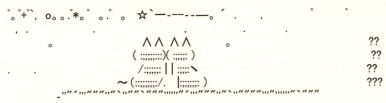

??
??
??
???

All happiness to you

121 Name: Anonymous Post Date: 09/05/04 08:13

What a girl to be there for you when you're about to come clean.
Hey Train, you better step up and be there for her from now on.
All in all, way to go. From a 25-year-old virgin

122 Name: Anonymous Post Date: 09/05/04 08:13

didja get together
did they get together?!?!

123 Name: Anonymous Post Date: 09/05/04 08:12

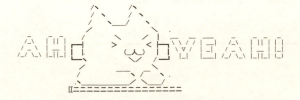

124 Name: Anonymous Post Date: 09/05/04 08:13

Good for you for not choking!
≷≥ ̄ ̄ ＜ ̄ .|≷≥ Honestly, I was touched.
It was well worth waiting up for

---

127 Name: Anonymous Post Date: 09/05/04 08:13

you bastard!
I've never met a man who has shown this much progress and maturity!
way to go, you bastard!

---

128 Name: Anonymous Post Date: 09/05/04 08:13

Pulled my heart strings, tears are fallin
don't know why, really really
I'd like to say well done to you.
Way to go Train
thank you
Valhalla is coming into focus . . .

---

129 Name: Anonymous Post Date: 09/05/04 08:13

 One coupling confirmed!

---

130 Name: Anonymous Post Date: 09/05/04 08:13

get your bear--ings ─────────
```
          ∩ _ ∩
  ─────ヽ( ･(ｪ)･ )ﾉ─────
       ( (    ) )
        U ‾ U
```

131 Name: Anonymous Post Date: 09/05/04 08:13

stay by my side forever
p . . . pro . . . ..propo . . .

---

132 Name: Anonymous Post Date: 09/05/04 08:13

and that was how god was born

---

133 Name: Anonymous Post Date: 09/05/04 08:13

good boy, good boy
```
     ∧＿∧
    ( ´∀`)∧∧
    ( つ つ('Д`)、
    ｜ ｜ ｜( : )
    (＿)＿)ｕ~ｕ
```

peek -a-
```
     ∧＿∧          ?
    (∩∀∩)          ∧∧
    (    )         ('ρ')
    ｜ ｜ ｜         ( : )
    (＿)＿)         ｕ~ｕ
```

```
        ∧＿∧
ah yeah —(゜∀゜)———————— !!!!!
     ⊂    ⊃           (')
     ｜ ｜ ｜            (
       ) )             |
```

---

148 Name: Anonymous Post Date: 09/05/04 08:14

Congratulations ————(゜∀゜)———— Congratulations!

---

149 Name: Anonymous Post Date: 09/05/04 08:14

。·゜·(ノД`)·゜·。
Congratulations Train!
You've gone pink and flowery on us!

---

155 Name: Anonymous Post Date: 09/05/04 08:15

Does this mean that I just witnessed the birth of a god . . .

156 Name: Anonymous Post Date: 09/05/04 08:15

support me forever

157 Name: Anonymous Post Date: 09/05/04 08:15

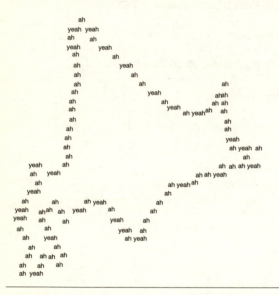

158 Name: Anonymous Post Date: 09/05/04 08:15

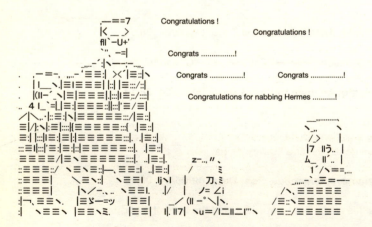

Congratulations !

Congratulations !

Congrats ....!

Congrats ....!   Congrats ....!

Congratulations for nabbing Hermes ....!

161 Name: Anonymous Post Date: 09/05/04 08:16

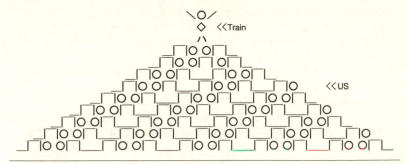

```
            \O/
             ◇   <<Train
             ∧
          ┌─┐IO OI┌─┐
       ┌─┐IO OI┌─┐ OI┌─┐
    ┌─┐IO OI┌─┐   ┌─┐IO OI┌─┐
 ┌─┐IO OI┌─┐   ┌─┐IO OI┌─┐  ┌─┐IO     <<US
IO OI┌─┐   ┌─┐IO OI┌─┐   ┌─┐IO OI┌─┐
  ┌─┐IO OI┌─┐   ┌─┐IO OI┌─┐   ┌─┐IO
 IO OI┌─┐   ┌─┐IO OI┌─┐   ┌─┐IO OI┌─┐  ┌─┐IO
┌─┐IO OI┌─┐   ┌─┐IO OI┌─┐   ┌─┐IO OI┌─┐   ┌─┐IO OI┌─┐
IO OI┌─┐   ┌─┐IO OI┌─┐   ┌─┐IO OI┌─┐   ┌─┐IO OI┌─┐   ┌─┐IO
```

162 Name: Anonymous Post Date: 09/05/04 08:16

>>Train

You are the coolest of the cool.

You're gonna have to keep her happy from now on.

Make sure you keep her laughing and grow old together. Way to go.

164 Name: Anonymous Post Date: 09/05/04 08:16

```
            ┌^ ヽ
Way to go    |  ,*"¨″‴*  y-─,
          ≡  ´∀ `     .:'
        ( ヽ      ( ヽ ≡
 ((    ≡          .:.  ∧,_,∧
       ::         ≡  ':´∀`':,,
       `;;            .:'  c  c.ミ
        U″*‴~″^'ヽ)      u‴*″J
```
Way to go

Wave after wave of congratulations flew in from the netizens, who had cheered Train on from the beginning.

---

126 Name: Train Man ♦ 4aPOTtW4HU Post Date: 09/05/04 08:13

I've got more for you but I'm going to take a break
Writing is bringing things back too clearly

171 Name: Anonymous Post Date: 09/05/04 08:16

Ummm . . . I wonder if it's because I've been up all night
I can't stop crying!
Bawling here
Haven't cried in a long time!
How can something happening to a stranger stir you up so much

200 Name: Anonymous Post Date: 09/05/04 08:20

If Train is watching Pretty Cure at this stage of the game, I'll give him mad respect

203 Name: Anonymous Post Date: 09/05/04 08:21

>200
The man watched Keroro before he went out yesterday

There's no way he wouldn't be watchin

215 Name: Anonymous Post Date: 09/05/04 08:22

```
( ,゚ヽ゚ )
   \,; シュボッ
     ().
     |E|
```

(゚ヽ゚)y─・~~~   < way to go, Train

218 Name: Train Man ♦ 4aPOTtW4HU Post Date: 09/05/04 08:23

I'll carry on after Pretty Cure (´ー`)

220 Name: Anonymous Post Date: 09/05/04 08:23

>She grabbed both my hands and said
>'You can do it!'

This is killer.
I think it's a sign of Lady Hermes' kindness.

226 Name: Anonymous Post Date: 09/05/04 08:23

>>218
As we thought.

227 Name: Anonymous Post Date: 09/05/04 08:24

>>218
oh you, why I oughta . . . . . . (·∀·) !! awesome!

228 Name: Anonymous Post Date: 09/05/04 08:24

It's not my place to say it but let me say it anyway.

Hey Train, if you end up hurting Hermes, all of us buried here aren't gonna stand for it. You go and make her a happy girl.

231 Name: Anonymous Post Date: 09/05/04 08:23

yes yes

(´—`) looks to me like an awesome smile

235 Name: Train Man ♦ 4aPOTtW4HU Post Date: 09/05/04 08:25

>>220
If I think about it, I'm gonna boil over

244 Name: Anonymous Post Date: 09/05/04 08:27

Pretty Cure . . . is that some kind of cousin of a manicure?
Seriously, don't know what that's about . . .

251 Name: Anonymous Post Date: 09/05/04 08:28

>>244
I'll be serious for just a moment. It's an anime title

266 Name: Train Man ♦ 4aPOTtW4HU Post Date: 09/05/04 08:31

I'm watching the screen but I'm not taking anything in

---

272 Name: Anonymous Post Date: 09/05/04 08:32

So this is the first time I've watched this Pretty Cure show.
The girl with the long black hair is cute.

---

332 Name: Anonymous Post Date: 09/05/04 08:43

. . . hey, I just woke up but what's this going through 2 threads from 5am?
not to mention Train watching Pretty Cure.

Anyway, way to go, Train, before even reading the log.

---

358 Name: Train Man ♦ 4aPOTtW4HU Post Date: 09/05/04 08:47

My brain is not taking anything in . . . _| ̄|O

---

365 Name: Anonymous Post Date: 09/05/04 08:48

>My brain is not taking anything in . . . _| ̄|O
No worries, dude.
You're gonna automatically start afresh anyway

---

375 Name: Anonymous Post Date: 09/05/04 08:50

all right . . . this thing . . . ain't something you should own up to
I mean when you said anime, I figured it was something like Doraemon or
Dragonball Z but . . .

Train, I'm not gonna tell you to quit but make sure Hermes doesn't find out.
Any average person would pull away in fright, for real.

---

393 Name: Anonymous Post Date: 09/05/04 08:52

Proof that there are only a few true-blue Geeks amongst us.

Remember this. You have seen the true face of a Geek.

And go and read the log one more time.

---

416 Name: Train Man ♦ 4aPOTtW4HU Post Date: 09/05/04 08:55

So after I heard her words, all the memories of hardship and difficulty just vanished into a vast whiteness and then I felt a sharp tingly thing in my nose then all this water started pouring out of my eyes and nose.
And so though I wanted to tell her
'Thank you'
and
'Let's always stay together'
No words were coming out of my mouth
but I kept trying over and over again to say it
but I just couldn't
That's when she moved towards me and hugged me.
'It's all right, it's all right,' she said, rubbing my back.
Though I struggled to put all my past struggles into words, all I could warble out was
'piujenk)(*@#f9u'
can't believe it ＿|￣|○
way too excited, you know . . .

The Geeks struggle to regain their composure after Train Man's renewed attack. And instead of waning, his attacks gain even more strength.

---

423 Name: Anonymous Post Date: 09/05/04 08:56

>>416
a sudden ah yeaaaaaah
―――(゜∀゜)―(゜∀)―(゜)―( )―(゜)―(∀゜)―(゜∀゜)―――!!!!

429 Name: Anonymous Post Date: 09/05/04 08:56

resuming a-suddenlyyyyyy ah yeaaaah ―――――(゜∀゜)――――ｯ!!!!

430 Name: Anonymous Post Date: 09/05/04 08:56

just when I thought I could relax, the man attacks out of nowhere!!!!!

431 Name: Anonymous Post Date: 09/05/04 08:56

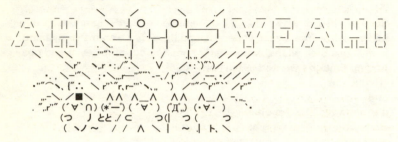

Resuming with an out of the blue attack!!!!

433 Name: Anonymous Post Date: 09/05/04 08:57

Looks to me like somebody's launching an all-out attack during an armistice

436 Name: Anonymous Post Date: 09/05/04 08:57

So suddenly

Is this Pearl Harbor?

437 Name: Anonymous Post Date: 09/05/04 08:57

I love Train for just waltzing back in as if nothing had happened-!

456 Name: Anonymous Post Date: 09/05/04 09:00

Lady Hermes is really such a nice girl, isn't she?

458 Name: Anonymous Post Date: 09/05/04 09:00

>>416
You . . . you cried too . . .
Train, you is too cute. You make me wanna hug you.

You people shouldn't gang up on such a cute Train over Pretty Cure, ya
hear? ｡ﾟ(ﾟ´Д｀ﾟ)ﾟ｡

463 Name: Train Man ♦ 4aPOTtW4HU Post Date: 09/05/04 09:00

'People are watching' she said.
Sure enough. There were couples on benches on both sides . . .
she began to pet my face which by now was all scrunched up and a
wild mess
**'You saying you liked me made me like you even
more'** she said, as she got up onto her tippytoes and kissed me
a few times around my sideburns. Just when I thought time had
stopped, the tap in my nose and eyes started to gush uncontrollably.
I gritted my teeth and tried my best not to let any noise escape from
my mouth.
'I'm sorry. No girl has ever treated me so kindly' was what I really
wanted to say but those weren't the words that came tumbling out.
She just nodded and wiped what could have been either snot or tears
from my face with some tissue paper.

I have no idea how much time passed but when I finally lifted my
head I saw that her eyes were bright red . . .
I let out a confused 'Ah . . . ' as I looked into her face
'Watching you made me cry' she said as she wiped some
tears from her face with the back of her fingers.

This blow opened up the floodgates connected to the Geeks' tearducts
which had long been arid as the land on Mars.

466 Name: Anonymous Post Date: 09/05/04 09:01

'You saying you liked me made me like you even more'
rrrroooooooaaaaaaaaaaaaaaaaarrrrrr

469 Name: Anonymous Post Date: 09/05/04 09:01

･∴･(⊃Д`)･∴･

472 Name: Anonymous Post Date: 09/05/04 09:02

(⊃Д`) waaahhhhh

477 Name: Anonymous Post Date: 09/05/04 09:02

a kiss already.

It's over and done with, I can rest in peace

478 Name: Anonymous Post Date: 09/05/04 09:02

I may have to cry toooooooo

479 Name: Anonymous Post Date: 09/05/04 09:02

･∴･(⊃Д`)･∴･

480 Name: Anonymous Post Date: 09/05/04 09:02

(⊃дС) waaaahhhhh

481 Name: Anonymous Post Date: 09/05/04 09:02

I like you tooooooooooooooooooooooooo

482 Name: Anonymous Post Date: 09/05/04 09:02

ah yeah yeaaaaaah
──(°∀°)─(°∀)─(°)─( )─( )─(。)─(A 。)─(。A。)────!!!
knows no boundaries ah yeaaaaaah ──────(°∀°)──────── !!!!

483 Name: Anonymous Post Date: 09/05/04 09:02

damn . . . . . . this stings, man . . .
in my mind, I've cast myself as Train

garrrrrrrrrrr (´A`) waaah

484 Name: Anonymous Post Date: 09/05/04 09:03

```
                     ,--'"           /    r'  |j.!
            `. `--  --. ,'" .' .--.,--`.
           |   i--.'"                 `.
           |    |.--/ミ,/:=:\,._
       _,--'-- ."":======:"".      .--,  ., `._
      !  7/:======/∧:=:.,:=============ヽ-¡`)
      |  '/:====/:_;∠!∧:ヽ\ヽ:ヽ=:,ヽ|/:ヽ
      i  'i';::/レ/     ヽ)ヌ\_>_ヽ,レ∧:i::::¡
here it isssss──|  W'∧|(   0 !! 0  ヽヽ|ノ/|::|::::|──────!!!!
      |  ヽ/ >:,,,  ' ヽ,   _ノ /`-i::|::|:::::|
      i   !       `"!!! _,)ヽ!|./:::|
   --,/`..' --,`\ C===ニ)  ノ,- `*'|/:====|
   ⊃_4'  \         --`, __,,_ ヽ!:::::::|.|
   =--'-,`.'-`._         -` ` ,'" " `._.|:|
      ,->,.-i-⊃--..__         ヽi
    (,ノ'"/'`\            --`.          \
      /  `,      ヽ,.,.-- "`〈  `.,____,⊃,人
    i              i  '/'`| :|::::::::::i
```

can't take it no more. I'm gonna cry too. waaaahhhhh

485 Name: Anonymous Post Date: 09/05/04 09:03

What a good woman Lady Hermes is.
Don't matter whether you're an anorak or a Geek, make her as happy as possible and find happiness for yourself.

490 Name: Anonymous Post Date: 09/05/04 09:04

I'm a single male but I've never come across a woman like this. Looks like god does exist after all. He must be looking after the courageous ones who try hard.

498 Name: Anonymous Post Date: 09/05/04 09:04

ah yeah----
────(´∀`)·ω·) ゚Д゚)゚∀゚)·∀·)￣—￣)´_ｽ`)−_)゚э゚)´Д`)゚-´)────!!!!

tears comin' for real.

Definitely, this attack has gone way beyond 125.

499 Name: Anonymous Post Date: 09/05/04 09:04

'Watching you made me cry'
Me done it too.

500 Name: Anonymous Post Date: 09/05/04 09:04

At this point, everything's cool. It don't matter what your hobbies are.
What matters is that there are two people who like each other, that's it.

I'd really like to have some sort of snot-like liquid wiped off my face!!!

511 Name: Anonymous Post Date: 09/05/04 09:06

>>Train
What time was it when it happened?

518 Name: Anonymous Post Date: 09/05/04 09:07

I'm all teary-eyed too. I see now that all this time Train spent feeling
unsure of himself and even his whole life till now was all in preparation for
finding happiness with Hermes.

520 Name: Anonymous Post Date: 09/05/04 09:08

>'I'm sorry. No girl has ever treated me so kindly' was what I really wanted
>to say but those weren't the words that came tumbling out.
>She just nodded and wiped what could have been either snot or tears
from my face >with some tissue paper.

This is the best part.
It's the moment when she embraced Train's whole way of being.

529 Name: Train Man ♦ 4aPOTtW4HU Post Date: 09/05/04 09:09

>>511
Honestly, I don't really know. We got to the park around 10pm . . .

Oh man, thinking about it is making me wanna cry

557 Name: Train Man ✦ 4aPOTtW4HU Post Date: 09/05/04 09:11

There's still some more

---

559 Name: Anonymous Post Date: 09/05/04 09:11

It looks like these two might even get married.
This kind of couple where each cares deeply for the other is bound to last
a long time.

Of course, this is just my brain projecting ('A`) honeymoo

---

565 Name: Anonymous Post Date: 09/05/04 09:12

>>557
ahyeahyeahyeahyeaaaaaaaah

---

566 Name: Anonymous Post Date: 09/05/04 09:12

shit. I think I'm leaking some kind of fluid from my ear

---

568 Name: Anonymous Post Date: 09/05/04 09:12

we have been forewarned

---

573 Name: Anonymous Post Date: 09/05/04 09:12

Hey, let's go and replenish the arsenal!!
Check the barrage!
What we've been afraid of is upon us! The H-bomb-class doomsday
device!!

---

595 Name: Anonymous Post Date: 09/05/04 09:15

I don't live in Tokyo so I'm not so familiar with this kinda stuff
but are there really sweet girls like this around Tokyo?

---

601 Name: Anonymous Post Date: 09/05/04 09:17

>>595
more mature than sweet

605 Name: Anonymous Post Date: 09/05/04 09:17

cute and sweet with an older sister vibe

(;´Д`) you there? are you still out there? are there enough of you to go around? or was Hermes the last of the breed? arrghhhhhhhhh

---

609 Name: Train Man ♦ 4aPOTtW4HU Post Date: 09/05/04 09:18

got mail--!! ——————(ﾟ∀ﾟ)——————!!!
she's up way early!

hold on a sec
let me take care of this first

---

645 Name: Anonymous Post Date: 09/05/04 09:25

>when I finally lifted my head I saw that her eyes were bright red . . .
>I let out a confused 'Ah . . . ' as I looked into her face

I like this bit coz it's so very Train

---

678 Name: Train Man ♦ 4aPOTtW4HU Post Date: 09/05/04 09:32

'I keep thinking about last night'

---

682 Name: Anonymous Post Date: 09/05/04 09:33

What part of it is she thinking aboutttttttt
_|￣|…………O

---

687 Name: Anonymous Post Date: 09/05/04 09:33

holyyyyyyyyyyyyyyyyyyy!!!
my arm! my arm!!

700 Name: Anonymous Post Date: 09/05/04 09:35

From carpet bombing to targeted bombing. And then moving into position
to strike a final blow . . .

733 Name: Train Man ✦ 4aPOTtW4HU Post Date: 09/05/04 09:42

Once we both calmed down we decided to leave the park.
When we got back to the car she said 'Shall we talk over here?'
so we moved to the back seat of the car.

Right about now I realised something strange was going on. One of
my contact lenses had fallen out without me noticing.
'One of my contact lenses is missing'
As soon as she heard this
'Oh no, let's go back to find it' she said as she pushed herself out of
the car but I stopped her and told her mine are disposable.
Since it felt weird to just have one contact lens in, I took it out.
'Ha ha ha, I can't see a thing,' I said
'Not even my face?' she asked, leaning in towards me.
Though I could see, I said 'No, I cc . . . cc . . . can't see'
after which she reached her arm around my neck and pulled in so
close I could feel her breath.
'Can you see me now?'
I just nodded in silence.

736 Name: Anonymous Post Date: 09/05/04 09:43

ah yeah! ——————(ﾟ∀ﾟ)——————— !!

737 Name: Anonymous Post Date: 09/05/04 09:43

>she reached her arm around my neck and pulled in so close I could feel
her breath.
>she reached her arm around my neck and pulled in so close I could feel
her breath.
>she reached her arm around my neck and pulled in so close I could feel
her breath.

738 Name: Anonymous Post Date: 09/05/04 09:43

holyshiiiiiiiiiiiiii------

739 Name: Anonymous Post Date: 09/05/04 09:43

Somebody please, kill me now!!

741 Name: Anonymous Post Date: 09/05/04 09:43

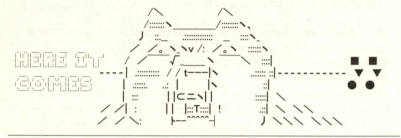

753 Name: Anonymous Post Date: 09/05/04 09:44

Shit------- here it comes, the final blow . . . here it comes, get down in the shelter, the shelter!

808 Name: Anonymous Post Date: 09/05/04 09:53

This is reminding me of Private Ryan.
From the moment we land, we are met with a barrage of gunfire killing one Geek after the other.
Bombarded by gunfire, the bloodied bodies of Geeks keep falling one by one.
The voices of those calling 'Medi-------c!!' abound.

Benwah.

861 Name: Train Man ♦ 4aPOTtW4HU Post Date: 09/05/04 10:01

I don't know how long we stayed in that position, in each other's faces but neither of us said a word . . .
I did feel the softness of something pressing up against my arm though . . .

After a while her fingers travelled up and started stroking my lips.
I found myself saying 'that tickles' but she didn't listen and instead
said, 'and now for you, Mr Train?' and closed her eyes.

Inside,
ah yeah-------!
——(´∀`)·ω·) ˚Д˚)´∀`)·∀·)￣￣)´_ﾆ)–)˚∋`)´Д`)˚—˚)——!!!!

I reached for her hair and leaned in to kiss her right by her ear.
'Ooo!'
she said, scrunching up her shoulders. I was kind of surprised too
'Not there,' she said and laughed at me. ＿|￣|○

---

865 Name: Anonymous Post Date: 09/05/04 10:01

>I did feel the softness of something pressing up against my arm though . . .
>I did feel the softness of something pressing up against my arm though . . .
>I did feel the softness of something pressing up against my arm though . . .

---

872 Name: Anonymous Post Date: 09/05/04 10:02

>>861
'Not there'

ooooooooo ——————— ;´Д` ——————ゞ

---

880 Name: Anonymous Post Date: 09/05/04 10:03

Evacuate immediately, evacuate now . . . . point of impact

---

886 Name: Anonymous Post Date: 09/05/04 10:04

I reached for her hair and leaned in to kiss her right by her ear.
'Ooo!'
she said, scrunching up her shoulders. I was kind of surprised too
'Not there,'

help me kiss location

889 Name: Anonymous Post Date: 09/05/04 10:04

mediiiii----------------c!!!!!!!!!

893 Name: Anonymous Post Date: 09/05/04 10:05

>>886
good one. lol.

903 Name: Train Man ♦ 4aPOTtW4HU Post Date: 09/05/04 10:07

Well, since she had kissed me in that general area
I figured that I was supposed to do the same to her ＼(´Д｀)／

939 Name: Anonymous Post Date: 09/05/04 10:14

Traaaaaaaaaaaaain
No teasin' with this interval shit . . . just spill it, please, just spill ittttttttt

24 Name: Train Man ♦ 4aPOTtW4HU Post Date: 09/05/04 10:24

'Right here'
she laughed as she placed her index finger on my lips.
'I guess we've lost the mood haven't we?'
I said, laughing too
'Oh well,' she laughed.

When we settled down after a while she said
'All right, I'm ready' and closed her eyes.
'Here I go' I said and took a deep breath and moved my lips close to
hers.
I think I stayed there for 2 or 3 seconds . . .
I couldn't believe that something so soft existed in this world . . .
After I pulled away, we looked at each other . . . well, basically it
was more like we were staring into each other . . . I could see myself
reflected in her pupils.

And then she suddenly blurted out in a whisper
'Oh, you're making my heart throb'

and kissed me over and over again.
And as if in return, I kissed her back.

---

28 Name: Anonymous Post Date: 09/05/04 10:25

ah yeaaaaaaaaah ────(´∀`)·ω·) ゚Д゚)·∀·)￣─ ̄)´_ゝ`)────!!!!

---

30 Name: Anonymous Post Date: 09/05/04 10:25

>>24
```
            *   .※ ※ ※.  *
        *  ※ ☆ ☆ ☆ ※  *
      *  ※☆  ※ ※   ☆※  *
    *  ※☆ ※  ※  ※  ☆ ※  *
   *  ※☆ ※   ※※ ※   ※ ☆ *
 * ※☆ ※ ※☆   .☆ ※   ※ ☆ ※ *
 * ※ ☆ ※ ※☆      ☆※ ※ ☆ ※ *
 * ※ah yeah──────(゚∀゚)────── !!!※ *
 * ※ ☆ ※ ※☆      ☆※ ※ ☆ ※ *
 * ※ ☆ ※   ※☆  .☆※  ※ ☆ ※ *
   *  ※☆ ※  ※※☆※  ※ ☆ *
    *  ※☆ ※  ※  ※  ☆ ※  *
      *  ※☆  ※  ※   ☆※  *
        *  ※ ☆ ☆ ☆ ※  *
          *   .※ ※ ※.  *
             *    *
```

---

39 Name: Anonymous Post Date: 09/05/04 10:26

2nd viewing

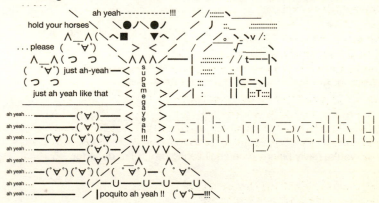

---

44 Name: Anonymous Post Date: 09/05/04 10:26

ah yeah ——————(°∀°)—————— !!!!

ah yeah ——(°∀°)—(°∀)—(°)—( )—( )—(。)—(A 。)—(。A。)————!!!

ah yeah ——(° ∀°)—(° ∀)—(°)—( )—( )—(。)—(A 。)—(。A。)——
—!!!

ah yeah —(´_ゝ`)´_>`)···)°∀°ξ ;;;;)´A`)´—`)·ω·`)`Д´)O皿O)´∀')·(ェ)·)—!!!!

a twisted ah yeah! ——————(° ∀°)—————!!!!

54 Name: Anonymous Post Date: 09/05/04 10:26

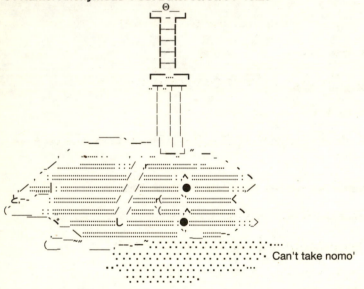

Can't take nomo'

69 Name: Anonymous Post Date: 09/05/04 10:28

man, you're really planning on annihilating us . . . I'm done for . . .

34 Name: Train Man ♦ 4aPOTtW4HU Post Date: 09/05/04 10:25

My body's giving up!

I'm going to sleep. I'll carry on later today.

laters

The Geeks were relentlessly battered and pounded down. After Train Man left, a momentary calmness took over the thread.

---

61 Name: Anonymous Post Date: 09/05/04 10:27

stand down for now . . .

91 Name: Anonymous Post Date: 09/05/04 10:31

All right, I'm going to bed! See you later!

We're this close to the final assault and turning into mere shadows of our former selves . . .

92 Name: Anonymous Post Date: 09/05/04 10:31

I wonder when Lady Hermes started liking Train.

108 Name: Anonymous Post Date: 09/05/04 10:35

'Making my heart throb'
such beautiful words . . .

109 Name: Anonymous Post Date: 09/05/04 10:35

He's really turned himself into a stealth bomber
He left us no time to issue air-raid warnings and all but wiped us out

I reckon if he's heading to bed now, it'll be another 4-6 hours
but I bet he's too frazzled to sleep so I say he'll be back in 4 hours

111 Name: Anonymous Post Date: 09/05/04 10:35

>>102
That Train, man, he really pushed himself hard
He returned from his date and went without sleep to attack us

It was definitely something that I stayed up for this but Train is not too shabby either

---

134 Name: Anonymous Post Date: 09/05/04 10:50

Train's dark side is something to be reckoned with . . . this really hurts

wonder what I've been doing till now . . .

---

158 Name: Anonymous Post Date: 09/05/04 11:10

you know what, when we all read Train's first report
all of us and I mean all of us told him to go with it . . .
even if we were to factor in the desperate nature of all Geeks,
thank god Train wasn't derailed on account of some negative comment from us
of course, it's all because Train was the most passive one of us . . .

---

160 Name: Anonymous Post Date: 09/05/04 11:15

In the beginning I didn't think he would develop into a such a mind-blowing bomber
I mean when he first reported about saving those ladies he did say he might have to betray us but even back then I thought he was way ahead of himself.

To think things like this really happen in the world.

---

180 Name: Anonymous Post Date: 09/05/04 11:48

Hermes has some child-like elements but
judging from her paying for parking and holding down a job
well, she is a real woman, a really nice catch.
She was meant to meet Train . . . . . . it's gotta be destiny.

Congratulations Train.

I thought you might cry when you told her how you felt, and you really did
And it's great Hermes accepted your kindness and returned it with joy!
I always heard that happiness grows when shared by two but now I know
it's true. I'm getting weepy.

---

197 Name: Anonymous Post Date: 09/05/04 12:15

Got quiet in here.
As though the intense brutal air strike never happened, the surviving
soldiers huddled together in the silence, thankful. Had the bombing begun
early that morning? That, too, was now a long-lost memory.
But still, looking out over the field there was a mountain of skeletal
remains.
Random body parts, hands, legs, fingers, hair, eyeballs . . . . . . what a
destructive force.
The damage sustained by the survivors was in itself horrible to see.
Next to me stood a Geek Soldier who continued aiming his M92 out into
the emptiness though he had no bullets.
Mumbling 'ah yeah' like an afterthought. Not even a blink. Grinning from
ear to ear. I listened to the sorrowful clicking noise of his trigger echoing
through the battlefield.
Beyond his gaze was the land he was fleeing to.

He said, 'Will resume within the day'
I can't think of anything. The roar of the explosions is even now vibrating
in my head.
He will, as promised, resume his attack in a few hours.
Has the Command Centre been annihilated?
But I . . . I can . . . still move . . . . . . and will keep on . . . till the end . . .

---

201 Name: Anonymous Post Date: 09/05/04 12:20

I've finally caught up . . . .but man, how many threads do you need to go
through in one night!
I'm late, but way to go Tren. Really happy for you.
I'm just as happy as if it was happening to me. You made me cry too.
Oh yesss sireeeeee, I cried, man, you made me cry. May you be happy for
a long time to come!!!

---

205 Name: Anonymous Post Date: 09/05/04 12:26

An apparently trivial catalyst plus

lots of courage plus
some backseat driving + meddling
and Train's own perseverance and development
gave birth to a miracle

take care of her forever.

---

264 Name: Train Man ♦ 4aPOTtW4HU Post Date: 09/05/04 13:49

just woke up. it's muggy today isn't it?
slept really badly. Couldn't shake the exhaustion at all.

But then I woke up to find a couple of hot e-mails.
Is this the way couples go about things? (´—`)

She managed to set up her PC and internet on her own. (´·ω·`)
there goes my chance to shine . . .

She says she wants to hear my voice so that's what I'm gonna do.

laters

---

266 Name: Anonymous Post Date: 09/05/04 13:49

ah yeah---------!!!

---

277 Name: Anonymous Post Date: 09/05/04 13:52

Oh my god, this is the first time I'm experiencing Train Man in real time . . .
. . . oh no, I'm getting kinda nervous . . .

---

278 Name: Anonymous Post Date: 09/05/04 13:52

Coffee and two packs of Marlboro
Ready to roll.
A puff before setting out on my journey to a sweet death.

283 Name: Anonymous Post Date: 09/05/04 13:57

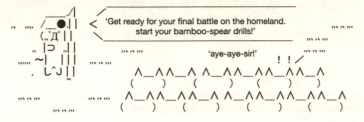

'Get ready for your final battle on the homeland.
start your bamboo-spear drills!'

'aye-aye-sir!'

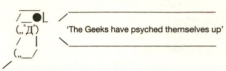

'The Geeks have psyched themselves up'

We've got to defend ourselves.

---

301 Name: Train Man ♦ 4aPOTtW4HU Post Date: 09/05/04 14:08

It should be Sunday every day

---

302 Name: Anonymous Post Date: 09/05/04 14:09

Sunday every day ah yeah-!

---

334 Name: Anonymous Post Date: 09/05/04 14:17

EVERYBODY, ARM YOURSELVES!
USE THIS !

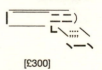

[£300]

---

337 Name: Anonymous Post Date: 09/05/04 14:19

>>334
is that a hairdryer?

341 Name: Anonymous Post Date: 09/05/04 14:19

Woe is I who gave up at 4 yesterday and went to work today only to return once again.

Mr Train, congratulations.
So you, who I've been watching over, are finally leaving the lair.
It's been like a soap. Sometimes it makes me want to bless you and other times it gets me down. It's got my emotions all stirred up.
Please take good care of Lady Hermes.

But let me just say this one thing to you.

You ffffuuuuu you really betrayed your people!!!!!

On that note, let me shove you into the couples board where you can freely googoo and gaga all you want!
And copy this for when you return to the dark side.

by K-Man

399 Name: Train Man ♦ 4aPOTtW4HU Post Date: 09/05/04 14:52

this may take a while

400 Name: Anonymous Post Date: 09/05/04 14:53

>>>399
it's fi--------------ne.
take your ti------------me.

409 Name: Anonymous Post Date: 09/05/04 14:55

The two months I've spent here really were a lot of fun.
I felt a bond like I've never felt. I'm sure memory fades but I don't want to forget what happened here.

413 Name: Anonymous Post Date: 09/05/04 14:56

Auxiliary forces have arrived! We are ready for the final battle!

461 Name: Anonymous Post Date: 09/05/04 15:23

I've been up since yesterday morning—I just clocked 32 hours.
I somehow managed to survive the real-time attacks too.
I've been posting how long I've been up every so often.
This thread is Train's history but it is also mine.
Ok, it's a bit forced but give me that much yeah.
I'm not going to bed now because if I do that I won't be able to sleep tonight.

I'm gonna go and get some curry now
laters

476 Name: Train Man ♦ 4aPOTtW4HU Post Date: 09/05/04 15:34

just hung up

I'm so happyy

483 Name: Anonymous Post Date: 09/05/04 15:35

yeah . . . . . . happy . . . . . . that's great . . . really great, man . . .

(´A`) Benoist

484 Name: Anonymous Post Date: 09/05/04 15:35

here it comes here it comes here it comes

487 Name: Train Man ♦ 4aPOTtW4HU Post Date: 09/05/04 15:36

sorry to keep you waiting. Was I going to carry on where I left off this morning?

489 Name: Anonymous Post Date: 09/05/04 15:36

oh yeah
give it to me

533 Name: Train Man ♦ 4aPOTtW4HU Post Date: 09/05/04 15:47

I think we were kissing for about 2 or 3 minutes.
Some time had passed and after I cooled off I said
'I still can't believe it. I keep thinking this is a dream.'
She reached up with both her hands and pinched my cheeks
'See, it's not a dream, is it?'
'I huznt uurt aaa iiiz naaa a dweeaam'
I wanted to say 'It doesn't hurt but it's not a dream' but it didn't
come out right because she was pinching my cheeks.
Watching me, she burst out laughing.
Then she made me laugh too.

After we finally calmed down we started talking about
all the stuff we couldn't talk about before.
Why we fancied each other and things that were on our minds.
We talked and talked but never ran out of things to talk about.

539 Name: Anonymous Post Date: 09/05/04 15:48

540 Name: Anonymous Post Date: 09/05/04 15:49

they're all casual and stuff now

543 Name: Anonymous Post Date: 09/05/04 15:49

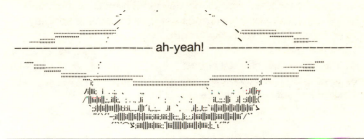

544 Name: Anonymous Post Date: 09/05/04 15:49

> She reached up with both her hands and pinched my cheeks

This kind of stuff happens for real? ('A`)

555 Name: Anonymous Post Date: 09/05/04 15:51

My first real-time attack! I will do my best to survive . . . (° Д° ;)

558 Name: Anonymous Post Date: 09/05/04 15:52

>>555
good luck rookie!

586 Name: Anonymous Post Date: 09/05/04 16:00

This is a first for me
glued to 2-Channel all day like this

589 Name: Anonymous Post Date: 09/05/04 16:01

Almost 12 hours has passed since the battle began . . . I may be . . .
almost . . . reaching the end of the line . . .

601 Name: Train Man ♦ 4aPOTtW4HU Post Date: 09/05/04 16:04

She told me that during the whole train incident, she didn't think
of being attracted to me or anything like that.
Though she did say 'Now that I think of it, maybe I was already drawn
to you' but at the time she basically thought 'didn't know there were
any brave guys these days' and didn't think much more of it. Since
she had the chance to buy the Hermes teacups cheap she thought
they would be perfect as a thank you gift.

She didn't think I'd call that day either.
She was really glad I was so blown away by the gift.
When I asked her out to dinner, she didn't think much of it and
assumed it would end up being a one-off.

On our first date, while we were talking over dinner she thought
'I want another chance to talk to him'
It wasn't that she started to fancy me then and there but it was more like
being on the same wavelength. And she felt comfortable talking to me.

And then she talked to her friends about me. The girlfriend she
brought on our second date asked 'You like him don't you?' and that
made Hermes realise perhaps she did. But to make sure, the
girlfriend came with her on the second date.
This'll go on for ever if I tell you about everything we talked about in
the car.

---

603 Name: Anonymous Post Date: 09/05/04 16:04

```
                        ∧∞∧       < Never fear!!!
          = /卍\=ᄀ(´'─')つ   ))
          = ( ∈э,____+∪_____||≫
          =    ♂      ─―==⊃='(((
              ∧∞∧
  = /卍\=√(´'─'),.   ))
  = (∈э,____∪_____||≫
  =    ∂    ¬∠=\='' ((
             <Ь
                        √∞∧       < The air force is here to back you up!
          = /卍\=ᄀ(´'─')つ   ))
          = ( ∈э,____+∪_____||≫
          =    ♂      ─―==⊃='(((
              ∧∞∧
  = /卍\=√(´'─'),.   ))
  = (∈э,____∪_____||≫
  =    ∂    ¬∠=\='' ((
             <Ь
                        ∧∞∧       < All attack units in formation!
          = /卍\=ᄀ(´'─'),.   ))
          = ( ∈э,____+∪_____||≫
          =    ♂      ─―==⊃='(((
              ∧∞∧
  = /卍\=√(´'─'),.   ))
  = (∈э,____∪_____||≫
  =    ∂    ¬∠=\='' ((
             <Ь
```

609 Name: Anonymous Post Date: 09/05/04 16:05

No problem, Train. Could you answer one question.

Did we make a difference?

610 Name: Anonymous Post Date: 09/05/04 16:05

>the girlfriend she brought on our second date asked 'You like him don't you?' and >that made Hermes realise perhaps she did.

girlfriend=god

615 Name: Anonymous Post Date: 09/05/04 16:07

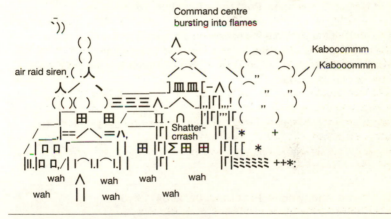

617 Name: Train Man ♦ 4aPOTtW4HU Post Date: 09/05/04 16:07

I think you get the idea of our chat in the car, no?
We talked for about 2 hours . . .

618 Name: Anonymous Post Date: 09/05/04 16:07

As I thought, the girlfriend was sent to size you up! What a minx!

620 Name: Anonymous Post Date: 09/05/04 16:07

people, now's the time to arm yourselves for real!
all yours, yeah!

[£100]

---

624 Name: Anonymous Post Date: 09/05/04 16:08

wassup. inflation?

---

634 Name: Anonymous Post Date: 09/05/04 16:09

The gods of the story are the geezer on the train, the one who asked for the teacup brand name and the one who told Train to call.
You know what. It's kinda like when Christ was born and the three kings went to check him out.

---

640 Name: Train Man ♦ 4aPOTtW4HU Post Date: 09/05/04 16:10

umm . . . I'm gonna continue

---

641 Name: Anonymous Post Date: 09/05/04 16:10

Oh no, Lady Girly Hermes is way too cute (＊´Д｀)
Hey Train, it's not like you haven't heard this before but take her hand in yours and never let her go!
If you fuck it up then you will deserve to die 10,000 times over!
Somebody already wrote this before but respect her for the longest time.
I wish you happiness you fucker!~ (´—｀)

---

643 Name: Anonymous Post Date: 09/05/04 16:11

127 Name: Anonymous Post Date: 16/03/04 22:37

I knew it! The cups have a deeper meaning!
The ones who misinterpreted just a bit are kind of gods too

686 Name: Train Man ♦ 4aPOTtW4HU Post Date: 09/05/04 16:21

Talking for two hours took it out of us
We were speechless for a while . . .
'Do you want to go somewhere?'
she said, breaking the silence.
I agreed
'Where do you want to go?'
she asked, and I thought about what would be open
I did think of somewhere else but I calmed myself down and said
'Do you want to go to a diner?'
'Well now that you mention it, I am a bit hungry'
she laughed.

As she got ready to move up to the front seat
I said 'Just one more' and reached for her arm and stopped her
and gave her a light cous
but then she said
'A little more'
and kissed me three or four times.
Then she wiped her lipstick off me

---

693 Name: Anonymous Post Date: 09/05/04 16:22

si----gh ───────── ;´Д` ─────────

694 Name: Anonymous Post Date: 09/05/04 16:22

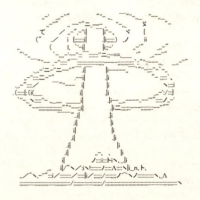

695 Name: Anonymous Post Date: 09/05/04 16:22

and gave her a light cous
>cous?

---

705 Name: Train Man ♦ 4aPOTtW4HU Post Date: 09/05/04 16:23

I don't mean cous . . . ＿￢|Ｏ
a peck, a mouth-to-mouth kiss ヽ(｀Д´)／ arrrgh

---

793 Name: Train Man ♦ 4aPOTtW4HU Post Date: 09/05/04 16:37

So we ended up driving back to her part of town and decided to eat at
the local diner. She said she hadn't been there 'in a really long time'

 . . . and here's a killer line from our drive there
'I feel lonely being so far from you while I'm driving'

and we're talkin maybe about 10 or 20 centimetres of space (´—`)
so we held hands while we were at red lights.

We finally get back to her part of town and go to the diner.
She quickly ran into the bathroom to check her make-up--
she told me that the harsh lighting exposed too much,
not that I gave a damn (´—`)

I waited couldn't wait for her to return
and flipped through the menu but couldn't work up an appetite
so I decided she could choose.

She came back after about 15 minutes and I asked her
'Could you order for me too?'
and she ended up ordering the Japanese dinner set for me.
Wow, she knew exactly the kind of food for someone who didn't have
much of an appetite . . .

827 Name: Anonymous Post Date: 09/05/04 16:43

>so we held hands while we were at red lights.

déjà vu again!
Train is definitely on the way to being a god.

832 Name: Anonymous Post Date: 09/05/04 16:45

c'mon guys, hurry up and arm yourselves!
all yours, yeah!

[£2000]

856 Name: Anonymous Post Date: 09/05/04 16:51

big huge bomb headed our way!!

876 Name: Anonymous Post Date: 09/05/04 16:55

the end will be here very soon.
Standing here at this point brings me down.

As you'd expect. I'm on drugs, yeah. but I'm gonna go to the hospital tomorrow and tell them
'I just experienced something that gave me peace of mind'

I hate to part with Train and all my people I've fought alongside.
ヽ(･∀･)ﾉ damn it I blabbed some soft shit on 2-Channel

913 Name: Train Man ♦ 4aPOTtW4HU Post Date: 09/05/04 17:02

this will be the last of it

The moment to face the end had arrived.

874 Name: 731 aka Train Man Post Date: 16/03/04 21:31
  My hands are frozen! ＼(｀Д´)／

614 Name: 731 aka Train Man Post Date: 17/03/04 23:00
  HELP ME WITH DINNER

364 Name: Train Man ♦ SgHguKHEFY Post Date: 27/03/04 23:49
  AND SHE REALLY DRESSED UP FOR THE OCCASION . . .

775 Name: Train Man ♦ SgHguKHEFY Post Date: 23/04/04 23:39
  How can I say it, it's like we both know that the next time we see each
  other, we will be facing the final battle.

This short but eventful two-month period looks to be coming to a close with
the next blow.

---

917 Name: Anonymous Post Date: 09/05/04 17:03

final attack warning coming atcha--- ─(ﾟ∀ﾟ)─!

---

919 Name: Anonymous Post Date: 09/05/04 17:03

so at last we've come to the final battle
kinda deep, no?

---

920 Name: Anonymous Post Date: 09/05/04 17:03

today is the day our comrade is taking that glorious flight out into the world.
let us all bless his journey and slowly return to the darkness.

---

13 Name: Anonymous Post Date: 09/05/04 16:55

all you people better arm yourselves before Train comes back!
use this! I'm keepin it nice and cheap for you, yeah!

[£3000]

---

14 Name: Anonymous Post Date: 09/05/04 16:58

stop putting the price up will ya

24 Name: Anonymous Post Date: 09/05/04 17:08

the most powerful one ever is coming at us

26 Name: Anonymous Post Date: 09/05/04 17:08

air raid! air raid! enemy aircraft approaching!

31 Name: Anonymous Post Date: 09/05/04 17:09

Do not close your eyes until you take your last breath, all of you!

40 Name: Anonymous Post Date: 09/05/04 17:10

I'll die with a smile on my face if I meet my maker now

45 Name: Anonymous Post Date: 09/05/04 17:11

The almost one month I've spent since 125 is coming to a close (´A｀)
Benoist
I've taken all that I can from the real-time attacks (´∀｀) ohyeah

54 Name: Anonymous Post Date: 09/05/04 17:12

>>40
Ah.
I've got no regrets either.
I had a good life.
From here on in Train and Hermes will be the architects of a new world.
Leaving the world in their able hands gives me much joy.

87 Name: Anonymous Post Date: 09/05/04 17:14

We can all see the same light, no?

91 Name: Anonymous Post Date: 09/05/04 17:15

Behold the soft and warm light . . .

94 Name: Anonymous Post Date: 09/05/04 17:15

I'm glad we made him call that day . . .

97 Name: Anonymous Post Date: 09/05/04 17:15

>>91
Oh . . . . . . feel the embrace . . . . . .

108 Name: Anonymous Post Date: 09/05/04 17:16

I hate to think of parting ways with Mr Train
As I cheered him on, I think I fell for him
I wanted to pop his cherry too

139 Name: Anonymous Post Date: 09/05/04 17:18

my heart won't stop thumpin like crazy

144 Name: Anonymous Post Date: 09/05/04 17:19

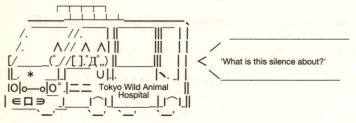

159 Name: Anonymous Post Date: 09/05/04 17:19

I'm scared! Somebody help me!

167 Name: Anonymous Post Date: 09/05/04 17:20

We are all about to bear witness to the birth of a legend!!!!!

195 Name: Anonymous Post Date: 09/05/04 17:22

If the next post is going to be his last, must be taking him time to get it all
together?

Just as the collective nerves of the thread netizens were fraying . . .

205 Name: Train Man ♦ 4aPOTtW4HU Post Date: 09/05/04 17:23

too many posts . . . I swear, what is going on ╲(ﾟДﾟ)/ whoa!
hold on a sec . . .

---

213 Name: Anonymous Post Date: 09/05/04 17:23

too many posts . . .
hey! I think it's going to be bigger than we thought!!!!

218 Name: Anonymous Post Date: 09/05/04 17:23

I heard him load up!!!
It's gonna be a big one---!!!!!

---

228 Name: Train Man ♦ 4aPOTtW4HU Post Date: 09/05/04 17:24

We talked about how things would be from now on
To be exact, we talked about where to go on dates and
how she would go around telling her friends she had a boyfriend
and where we would go next week.
We took photos to load up into her PC

And before we knew it, it was 4 in the morning.
'It's nearly morning' I said
'You're right. Shall we go?' she replied, and stood up.

She said she would drive me home.
'It's not a good idea to have you walking the streets alone at night,'
she said. (´ー`)

---

251 Name: Train Man ♦ 4aPOTtW4HU Post Date: 09/05/04 17:25

We drove along while I gave her directions.
'Oh, right here,' I said.
'Thank you so much for driving back,' I said as I got out of the car.
She said
'A parting gift' as she opened both arms.

I hugged her tightly and repeated
'Thank you, thank you so much'
She hugged me back and said
'So happy for you, so happy for me.'
And we kissed each other.

She pecked me lightly 3 or 4 times
and then looked straight in my eyes and said
'Can you kiss like a man?'
I just nodded.

---

254 Name: Anonymous Post Date: 09/05/04 17:25

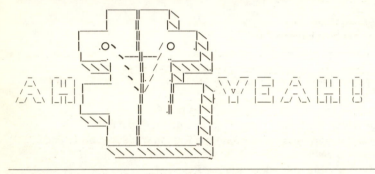

---

260 Name: Anonymous Post Date: 09/05/04 17:26

a man's kissssssssssss?

---

261 Name: Anonymous Post Date: 09/05/04 17:26

manly kiss ah yeah-----! ———(ﾟ∀ﾟ)———!!

---

264 Name: Anonymous Post Date: 09/05/04 17:26

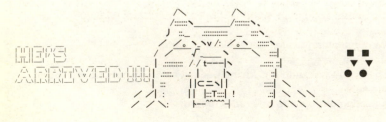

---

265 Name: Anonymous Post Date: 09/05/04 17:26

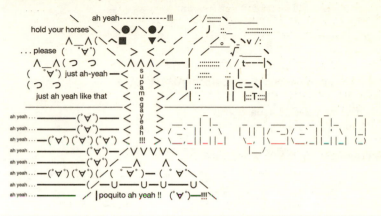

271 Name: Anonymous Post Date: 09/05/04 17:26

a manly kiss comin atchaaaaaaaaaaa-------!!!!

274 Name: Train Man ♦ 4aPOTtW4HU Post Date: 09/05/04 17:26

'I'm going to use my tongue so don't be surprised'
She tilted her head just a bit and placed her lips on mine.
I honestly had no idea what I was supposed to do.
Her tongue slipped out from the tiny space between her lips.
I welcomed her with the tip of my tongue.
We lingered and felt each other out,
as if making sure we were both really there.
Don't need to say it, this was all new to me.
Is this what it's really like?

I don't know how long we were locked together
but by the time we came up for air, I was a slobbery mess
'aah . . . I'm sorry . . . ' she said
'No, no, there's no need to apologise.'
'Well,' she reached out and tried to wipe my lips again but I said
'I want to keep it just like it is for a while'
after which she told me off
'don't be silly' (´—`)

> **She got back into the car and after saying good night she sped off.
> I stood there until I couldn't see her car anymore.**
>
> **That's about it.** (´—`)

---

286 Name: Anonymous Post Date: 09/05/04 17:27

here it is! the celestial apparition!!!!
the doomsday device!!!!

288 Name: Anonymous Post Date: 09/05/04 17:27

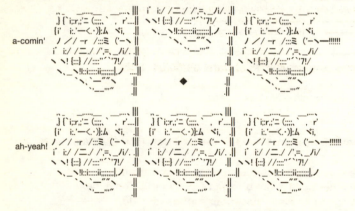

---

289 Name: Anonymous Post Date: 09/05/04 17:27

one of the all-nighters here . . . just woke up . . . .
to a sudden deluge of bombasoikpokr0-9807)*(@#lp0

290 Name: Anonymous Post Date: 09/05/04 17:27

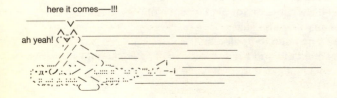

291 Name: Anonymous Post Date: 09/05/04 17:27

. . . as I was saying, but whoa, what about a mannnnnnnnnnnnnnn kissssssssssssss

292 Name: Train Man ♦ 4aPOTtW4HU Post Date: 09/05/04 17:27

all done

The final blow that Train Man landed completed the emotional rise and fall of the two and seemed like a bright light from God, purging all the Geeks. There wasn't one left who harboured the will to fight.

293 Name: Anonymous Post Date: 09/05/04 17:27

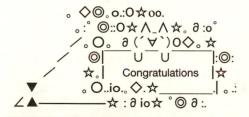

298 Name: Anonymous Post Date: 09/05/04 17:27

ah yeah----- ──────;y=-(ﾟ∀ﾟ)･｡'.'──────ｿ!!!!!

305 Name: Anonymous Post Date: 09/05/04 17:28

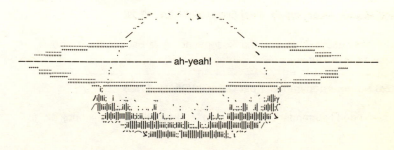

308 Name: Anonymous Post Date: 09/05/04 17:28

fu--------------ck.
Hermes,
love yaaaaaaaaaaaaaaaaaaaaa!!!!

322 Name: Anonymous Post Date: 09/05/04 17:28

Way to go Train
Really, truly, truly

325 Name: Anonymous Post Date: 09/05/04 17:28

Congratulations Train! And thanks for sending us back to the shadows
with a skip in our step

326 Name: Anonymous Post Date: 09/05/04 17:28

I surrender! I surrender so please stop . . . asopi390_(*OPKlkiopo)(@#

327 Name: Anonymous Post Date: 09/05/04 17:28

till the end . . . . . . you're landing all your punches

328 Name: Anonymous Post Date: 09/05/04 17:28

Way to go Train. Really. Congratulations.
Grab hold of that happiness for all of us
And thank you very much.

329 Name: Anonymous Post Date: 09/05/04 17:28

the end, eh . . .

thank you

333 Name: Train Man ♦ 4aPOTtW4HU Post Date: 09/05/04 17:29

love > my people

336 Name: Anonymous Post Date: 09/05/04 17:29

I can now, with no regrets, rise to heaven
Train Man, congratulations . . . thank you . . .

341 Name: Anonymous Post Date: 09/05/04 17:29

>>333
thank you

344 Name: Anonymous Post Date: 09/05/04 17:29

Thank you Train!

I can finally be reunited with my long -departed mother

345 Name: Anonymous Post Date: 09/05/04 17:29

aaaaaaaaaaaaaaaaaaaaaaaaaaaaaaaal love ya tooooooooooooooo

346 Name: Anonymous Post Date: 09/05/04 17:29

way to go, Train . . .

Congratulations . . .

taste all the world's joy for me

350 Name: Anonymous Post Date: 09/05/04 17:29

>>333
me too>Train

358 Name: Anonymous Post Date: 09/05/04 17:29

>>333
love ya>Train

365 Name: Anonymous Post Date: 09/05/04 17:30

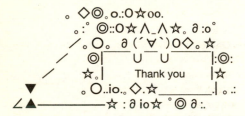

366 Name: Anonymous Post Date: 09/05/04 17:30

>love > my people
>love > my people
>love > my people
>love > my people
>love > my people
>love > my people

370 Name: Anonymous Post Date: 09/05/04 17:30

>>333
I love ya too

373 Name: Anonymous Post Date: 09/05/04 17:30

congratulations > Train
I love ya too.
Thank you! Be happy!

378 Name: Anonymous Post Date: 09/05/04 17:30

Train, congratulations for real!
You've only just begun.
The real story is to come.
The story of Train and Hermes.
Who nobody can come between.
Be happy!

383 Name: Anonymous Post Date: 09/05/04 17:31

I'm so happy for you Train. ･ﾟ･(ﾉД`)･ﾟ･

395 Name: Anonymous Post Date: 09/05/04 17:31

Mr Train, I'm really happy for you. Congratulations.
You made all that cheering worthwhile. Hope you're happy for a long time
to come.

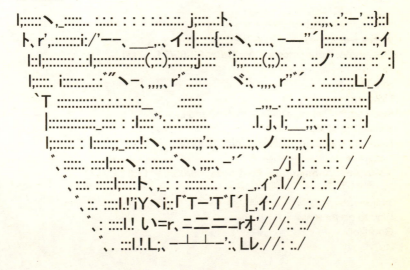

389 Name: Anonymous Post Date: 09/05/04 17:31

Train, way to go for real.
keepin it real till the end.
Loads of stuff's goin to happen, but keep on keepin it real, yeah.

399 Name: Anonymous Post Date: 09/05/04 17:31

Sometimes I get this thought.
As the days fly by am I really happy with each day?

Every day I go for my goal, do what I need to do
by doing fun stuff and satisfying my appetites.

It all connects to the future . . . but what exactly is the future?
If people die and consciousness dies with them, then what meaning does
any of this have?
Even if you satisfied all your appetites while you were alive, won't it all be
meaningless when you die?
I feel all empty but I can't say how.
But still, I choose to go on living each day

One day we'll reach the goal beyond the light.
That place Train managed to get to.

I promise I'll get there too. (´∀`)

400 Name: Anonymous Post Date: 09/05/04 17:31

>>333
I love ya too
Hope you will always walk with her hand in yours
pulling her along
Here's to the both of you making it work.

401 Name: Anonymous Post Date: 09/05/04 17:31

Train
Way to go for real.
Good job.

420 Name: Anonymous Post Date: 09/05/04 17:33

No way, how wonderful is this.
When you first started, honestly, I didn't think you had a chance.
same wavelength was the key, wasn't it.

I was kinda down with work and that but I'm gonna reload tomorrow and
kickstart myself.

423 Name: Anonymous Post Date: 09/05/04 17:33

I've only been reading up till now but allow me this one post.
Train and Lady Hermes, congratulations. I wish you a lifetime of
happiness together. Over the past two months I've been able to reaffirm
the love I feel for my husband of 10 years and know that I can share
forever with this man for whom I felt consuming love a decade ago.
Good luck to Train and all you Geeks.
If I'm reincarnated, I'll be sure to come back as a Geek.

450 Name: Anonymous Post Date: 09/05/04 17:34

>>423
I absolutely don't recommend it

432 Name: Anonymous Post Date: 09/05/04 17:33

congratulations Train!!!!!! It was the best fucking attack ever . . . . . .
grrr . . . gasp . . .

418 Name: Anonymous Post Date: 09/05/04 17:32

I'm still alive god damn it.
Hey Train, if you can still write in, tell me this,
What happened to that big bag you brought because she had loads of
gifts from her trip that she wanted to give you?

443 Name: Train Man ♦ 4aPOTtW4HU Post Date: 09/05/04 17:34

>>418
She had already organised it all in a large paper bag

442 Name: Anonymous Post Date: 09/05/04 17:34

Good bye
I'll never forget you all...
Go in peace

---

451 Name: Anonymous Post Date: 09/05/04 17:35

Man oh man, way to go Train
I held myself back from posting and it really paid off
The story went your own special way
I don't feel up to cooking tonight
and since I don't have a girlfriend to cook for me, I guess it's cup noodles for me but

final words, grab hold of that happiness !

---

479 Name: Another Geek Bites the Dust Post Date: 09/05/04 17:36

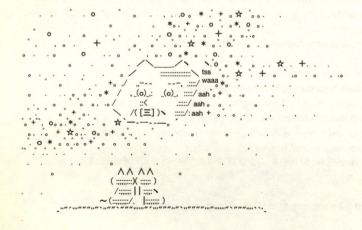

483 Name: Anonymous Post Date: 09/05/04 17:36

Don't think anyone remembers but
I'm the '1 when you return' guy.
way to go from me.

491 Name: One of Us Post Date: 09/05/04 17:37

Dudes. The past two months' worth of expended energy and might, in
yer face!
http://www.geocities.co.jp/Milyway-Acquarius/7075/

497 Name: Riceball Post Date: 09/05/04 17:37

>>Mr Train
Make sure you don't start taking her for granted.
That's where I messed up asdfopiokl)(*@#^#$!})
Wishing you a life of happiness.

love from a riceball

517 Name: Anonymous Post Date: 09/05/04 17:41

I saw the flash site One of Us created
got chills man

528 Name: Train Man ♦ 4aPOTtW4HU Post Date: 09/05/04 17:42

I'm checkin out the Flash

537 Name: Anonymous Post Date: 09/05/04 17:43

Congratulations and thanks, Train.
Go at your own pace and deepen your relationship.
For some reason, I'm feelin a bit lonely but
I'm gonna try hard too.

538 Name: Anonymous Post Date: 09/05/04 17:43

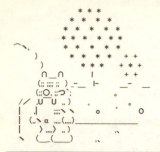

---

540 Name: Anonymous Post Date: 09/05/04 17:43

Train.
Don't let her go.
No matter what happens.

You're going to experience all kinds of things from now on.
Just remember us every time you think you've fucked up.
What you did here and what you were told here.
And remember what you went through just so you could be with Hermes.

Happiness to you. Laters.
 . . . shit
Just checked One of Us's site . . . can't stop crying. (ТДТ)

---

547 Name: Anonymous Post Date: 09/05/04 17:45

I've prepared something

Graduation Diploma

Mr Train Man
As Chief Representative
of the Geek Board, on the 4th day in
May of the 15th year of the Heisei Era,
I declare you as a graduate of the
Geek Board.

---

550 Name: Anonymous Post Date: 09/05/04 17:45

>>547
I think you've got the diploma, dude

---

557 Name: Anonymous Post Date: 09/05/04 17:47

>>547
I'm moved you went to the trouble of making that thing with your own hands.
I can tell that you're not used to this stuff and did your best.
You're making me all weepy.

---

598 Name: Anonymous Post Date: 09/05/04 17:54

>>547
But wanting to congratulate Train, that feeling is conveyed
Big time big time. Train gets it. So do we.

---

556 Name: Anonymous Post Date: 09/05/04 17:47

offering kindness to others . . . a heart that never gives up . . . an innocent
heart
being considerate and mindful of others . . . having the attitude and
courage to move forward

you've helped me come to terms of all of that and more
I'm going to keep stepping forward one step at a time ('∀`)

---

583 Name: Train Man ♦ 4aPOTtW4HU Post Date: 09/05/04 17:52

F'n amazing Flash . . .
This is . . . . my story .. . ...

At ground zero, one finds not the burnt remains of a fallen township, but
scores of smiling netizens cheerfully waving their hands.

587 Name: Anonymous Post Date: 09/05/04 17:52

Ladies and gents, the ever buzz-worthy 'Train Man'
has taken his final bow in this thread
Please offer a generous round of applause and hurl some abuse at our
main man Train Man ♦ 4aPOTtW4HU to wish him well

May you be blessed with happiness forever and let us hope that you spill
some of that lovin' over into our lives.

Way to go! Train Man ♦ 4aPOTtW4HU

589 Name: Anonymous Post Date: 09/05/04 17:52

I don't have to carry a gun anymore . . .

Let me return. Back to my home.

All men, disarm now.

596 Name: Anonymous Post Date: 09/05/04 17:54

That's right! The main man in this amazing story is none other than you,
Train!

603 Name: Anonymous Post Date: 09/05/04 17:55

way to go Train!
Let me post this bit to commemorate the day.
Don't forget to give us a wedding report.

605 Name: Anonymous Post Date: 09/05/04 17:56

I'm quitting the arms dealin bizniz.
thanks to those who bought from me.
I got some stock left so I'm leaving it here for you.

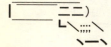

[£50]

606 Name: Anonymous Post Date: 09/05/04 17:56

Kanagawa Unit, returning home!
For Train we offer our cannon salute!
We wish you and Hermes happiness! Good bye!

608 Name: Anonymous Post Date: 09/05/04 17:56

I guess no more threads will start after this one . . .

613 Name: Train Man ♦ 4aPOTtW4HU Post Date: 09/05/04 17:57

kinda lonesome, no?

616 Name: Anonymous Post Date: 09/05/04 17:57

Starting with One of Us and followed by all the Geeks that gathered here
in the thread. Also the cool guys and girls that offered Train some advice.
Glad to have met you all here in the thread.

Above all.
Train, well done. And, way to go.
I was mostly reading and not posting, but I had lots of fun. Thanks.
All the best with Hermes.

This thread may have ended here but Train and Hermes' story will keep
going.

618 Name: Anonymous Post Date: 09/05/04 17:58

Nagoya 8th Regiment Communications Soldier, returning to home base!
I'd like to share my heartfelt joy at surviving with all my people here

619 Name: Anonymous Post Date: 09/05/04 17:58

>>613
You're leaving us for http://love2.2ch.net/ex

634 Name: Train Man ♦ 4aPOTtW4HU Post Date: 09/05/04 17:59

>>619
whaaa------------------- ──────。˚(´Д`)゚。──────ン!!! -----!!!
but I'm ready for my new beginning.

---

635 Name: Anonymous Post Date: 09/05/04 17:59

Train . . . .
You're way . . . . . .
ready to . . .
graduate . . .

Way sad and lonely. (;Д;)

---

636 Name: Anonymous Post Date: 09/05/04 17:59

Just got back from my second job
I kept checkin on my mobile but haven't been able to read it all
I said it before I left for work but I'll say it again
Congratulations Train & Hermes!!
And thanks to Train & Hermes, One of Us, all Geeks including myself,
other single men and women!! And well done!!

During the first real-time attack, I thought no way would things ever go
this far but after witnessing such an incredible feat, I feel as though I need
to push myself further.

And finally, all happiness to Train and Hermes!

---

641 Name: Anonymous Post Date: 09/05/04 18:00

But if they do end up getting married or something . . . I'd love to find out
one way or another . . .

Oh, I guess someone could just pick up a Train report from the couples
board . . .

---

652 Name: Train Man ♦ 4aPOTtW4HU Post Date: 09/05/04 18:01

You don't have to forget Hermes and Benoist
If you do, all of this stops making any sense

Even if something happens, I'll deal with it, ok (´ー`)

---

657 Name: Anonymous Post Date: 09/05/04 18:02

I was following things all chilled out but
the part where Train told her he liked her made me cry . . .
and then the Flash site made me cry some more.
All happiness to you, Mr Train!

---

661 Name: Anonymous Post Date: 09/05/04 18:02

>Even if something happens, I'll deal with it, ok (´ー`)

Well said, Train! Train! You da man---!

---

682 Name: Anonymous Post Date: 09/05/04 18:04

With this the curtains descend on the Train thread we had all followed over
the last two months.
Come to think of it, we were constantly obsessed with Train . . .

---

685 Name: Anonymous Post Date: 09/05/04 18:05

I've watched many Geeks who transformed into gods and took flight but why
is it . . . . . . that this time, I'm incredibly sad to see him go . . . . . .。(°´Д`°)°。

---

644 Name: Anonymous Post Date: 09/05/04 18:00

>>628>>Train
help me   give advice

---

696 Name: Train Man ♦ 4aPOTtW4HU Post Date: 09/05/04 18:06

advice? . . . hmmm . . .
to have loads of different kinds of courage and to ask for advice

701 Name: Anonymous Post Date: 09/05/04 18:07

Dear Train,
I hope to see you again sometime here on this board
You'd probably come back to quietly offer your advice to some Geek who,
much like yourself in the beginning, is muddled and lost . . .
I won't say goodbye. Till we meet again!
Here's to you Train, and all our comrades!!

713 Name: Anonymous Post Date: 09/05/04 18:08

When I first came across a Train post in real time,
I didn't think it was anything special.
Watching him hum and hah over calling or not calling
made me want to beat some sense into him.
When he had dinner with Hermes and her friend
I doubted there would be a follow-up date.
But right after that . . . Train shot out at lightning speed
straight like an arrow down the path towards the answer, the right answer
Congratulations Train, thank you Train.
You are truly a man now . . .
Don't turn around as you walk away. Even if you get lost . . .
for you have the couples board gang waiting for you
and more importantly, a girlfriend . . .

714 Name: Anonymous Post Date: 09/05/04 18:08

You're all too good to be true.
Moving. Tear-jerking.

722 Name: Anonymous Post Date: 09/05/04 18:10

I'm not crying because of the bombings but because I have to say
goodbye to Train.

730 Name: Anonymous Post Date: 09/05/04 18:11

man, I can't take it anymore
I'm leaving this net-café to go pretend like I've been rained on

Train, much happiness to you . . . and thanks for everything over this long
period of time.

Geeks, we were all able to contribute to Train's happiness. It'll be all right. Let's keep believing the day will come when we, too, will morph. Let's go on reaching out to all the gods that come our way.

And finally, sorry for the long message.

---

731 Name: Anonymous Post Date: 09/05/04 18:11

Thank you Train Man. Thanks to hot springs, rubber bands and moles and everybody else. And finally, a parting gift from a remaining geek.

---

732 Name: Anonymous Post Date: 09/05/04 18:11

Things moved fast after that dinner with her friend.
Judging from the way Hermes behaved, too.
If you add what we now know about how Hermes felt, it gives that day a lot more weight.

way to go >Train

---

734 Name: Anonymous Post Date: 09/05/04 18:11

What it means for one person's heart to truly connect to another person.
I think Train delivered the answer.

---

735 Name: Anonymous Post Date: 09/05/04 18:11

Train, you hold one person's happiness in the palm of your hand
Of course, that person is Hermes
promise us that you will never let any of it slip out of your hand!

---

737 Name: Anonymous Post Date: 09/05/04 18:12

Hey hey, Train.
Don't forget us, ok?

748 Name: Anonymous Post Date: 09/05/04 18:14

I am honoured to have walked alongside Train and all of you in this thread.
May good fortune fall on Train and all you guys. me 2 yeah

---

749 Name: Anonymous Post Date: 09/05/04 18:14

can't stop crying

---

770 Name: Anonymous Post Date: 09/05/04 18:17

I'm all emotional and teary like I was at graduation . . .

---

786 Name: Train Man ♦ 4aPOTtW4HU Post Date: 09/05/04 18:19

I just went and posted on the couples board.
shoulda written something better . . . . . . _|⎺|O

---

800 Name: Anonymous Post Date: 09/05/04 18:20

> 169: Lover is Anonymous: 09/05/04 18:16
> first post here (´—`)

looking forward to being here. will give it my best for a long time to come.

---

795 Name: Anonymous Post Date: 09/05/04 18:20

Since Train has finished giving us the report, I'm going to upload
something I was working on back when Train and Hermes were still in the
heat of the battle (back when I was hoping against hope all on my own)

I joined the war effort about a month ago and though your bombs did
send me back into the shadowy depths of my Geekhood, watching you
mature over these two months made me want to offer heartfelt
congratulations too.

You who could barely walk in a straight line in the beginning, were raised
by the netizens into a valiant soldier who bombed the hell out of us then
rose through the ranks and finally to graduated. I hope you and Hermes
stay happy together for a long time.

You are all younger than me and I do have a nagging big-brother overprotective tendency but to be honest, I'd really like to scream out

" " ∩ ⌐⌐
　⊂＾(｀Д´)　＜I want a Hermes too...!
　`ヽ_つ ⊂ﾉ
　Squirmy Squirmy

(I love this AA)
All of you, be proud of yourselves. You all have the ability to develop a Geek into a combatant.

And to all Geeks, if you ever have difficulty taking that first step, think back to this thread. And remember all the netizens that cheered Train on. It's just as Train said in 696. >to have loads of different kinds of courage >and to ask for advice. Yes, we are not alone. We will follow Train's tracks!

I've been working myself up for some speed-dating at the weekend. I'll go down fighting!

Utterly Geekoid single male in his early 30s,
with apologies for the long post and ramblings

---

811 Name: Anonymous Post Date: 09/05/04 18:21

Hey Train, get moving will ya.
Make sure you don't let go of her hand now you grabbed it.
No need to turn back.

Your happiness. Let's just say that would be a great parting gift.

---

813 Name: Anonymous Post Date: 09/05/04 18:22

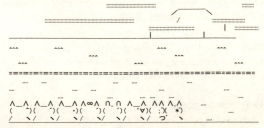

In the end, Train represented our collective hope . . . . . .

The time for Train Man to leave the lair had arrived.

840 Name: Anonymous Post Date: 09/05/04 18:27

It's almost time . . . no?

841 Name: Anonymous Post Date: 09/05/04 18:27

>Train
Good job, and keep going. Be there for each other.
Been here watching over you since your birth. deep, man.
Your progress, your evolution was something real. The past two months
have been special. Thank you. I wish you a world of happiness.

Train and all you lot, let me just say that you're my mates and I love ya.
∴·(´Д`)·∴。

850 Name: Train Man ♦ 4aPOTtW4HU Post Date: 09/05/04 18:28

thank you everybody
may good fortune find all the Geeks in the world!

855 Name: Anonymous Post Date: 09/05/04 18:28

>>850

well put!!!!!!!!!

858 Name: Anonymous Post Date: 09/05/04 18:28

suppose the time has come

864 Name: Anonymous Post Date: 09/05/04 18:29

may you be happy for a long time to come

laters

871 Name: Anonymous Post Date: 09/05/04 18:30

Hey Train. Thank you. Thank you. Goodbye.
I'm gonna try hard so I can get to that side!

878 Name: Anonymous Post Date: 09/05/04 18:31

shit, there are only 100 more to go. This is really making me cry.
I don't know what to do with this loneliness and weepiness and happiness
all bundled into one. I've never felt this way before.

880 Name: Anonymous Post Date: 09/05/04 18:31

shit . . . I'm starting to really feel kinda lonely . . .

Train---be well!

I'd really like to one day get there too . . .

891 Name: Anonymous Post Date: 09/05/04 18:32

Let us know when you get married.
all happiness to you. laters

900 Name: Train Man ♦ 4aPOTtW4HU Post Date: 09/05/04 18:32

I guess it's ending, huh . . . . . .

When I told her that I'd sought asked friends how to tell her I liked
her, she said
'what wonderful friends'

908 Name: Anonymous Post Date: 09/05/04 18:33

>>900
friends you can't introduce to her

909 Name: Anonymous Post Date: 09/05/04 18:33

Train 900 you,

. . . by friends . . . you mean . . . us?

heyheyheyheyheyheyheyheyyyyyy, you gave me goosebumps, dude!!!!!

910 Name: Anonymous Post Date: 09/05/04 18:33

we're your friends, eh . . .
thanks.

912 Name: Anonymous Post Date: 09/05/04 18:33

∴･(⊃Д｀)･∴

914 Name: Anonymous Post Date: 09/05/04 18:33

>>900
mm

∴･(⊃Д｀)･∴ waaaaaaaahhhh!!!

915 Name: Anonymous Post Date: 09/05/04 18:33

>>900
Hermes knows about usssss!

hot damn.

916 Name: Anonymous Post Date: 09/05/04 18:33

Train, Hermes . . . thanks

(･ω･) laters

922 Name: Anonymous Post Date: 09/05/04 18:33

>>900
｡∴･(/Д｀)･∴｡ weeeeeepyyyyyy

you is makin me cry

---

926 Name: Anonymous Post Date: 09/05/04 18:34

Couldn't pronounce the brand name
Trippin at key moments

Lots happened

Those who continuously prayed for god's good fortune to shine
Those who believed it would never be

There were many

There is a beginning and end to everything
Congratulations, Train

---

927 Name: Anonymous Post Date: 09/05/04 18:34

Oops, forgot to thank you on account of being dead and all
Mr Train and Lady Hermes, congratulations
If you let this all go to your head and cheat on Hermes and make her cry
we're gonna come and get you, yeah?

well well, I wish you all the best
Guess I'll drown my sorrows

---

928 Name: Train Man ♦ 4aPOTtW4HU Post Date: 09/05/04 18:34

If anything happens
I'll use a name that'll be easy to spot

---

936 Name: Anonymous Post Date: 09/05/04 18:35

Hey Train, thanks
all happiness to you

---

937 Name: Anonymous Post Date: 09/05/04 18:35

Ringin the departure bell (RRRRRRRRRRRR

944 Name: Anonymous Post Date: 09/05/04 18:35

arg gur am rrr how come I'm crying over seeing a stranger off?

945 Name: Anonymous Post Date: 09/05/04 18:35

we've come to the end, finally . . .

948 Name: Anonymous Post Date: 09/05/04 18:36

well, let's see Train off, shall we?

949 Name: Anonymous Post Date: 09/05/04 18:36

finally

950 Name: Anonymous Post Date: 09/05/04 18:36

adios amigo

951 Name: Anonymous Post Date: 09/05/04 18:36

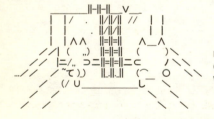

rrring
Coupledom-bound Geek land train
Watch the doors, ready to depart

952 Name: Train Man ♦ 4aPOTtW4HU Post Date: 09/05/04 18:36

Man . . . just when I thought my tears had dried up . . . . . .

953 Name: Anonymous Post Date: 09/05/04 18:36

Train . . . thanks for the dream ｡ﾟ･(ﾉД`)･ﾟ･

954 Name: Anonymous Post Date: 09/05/04 18:36

50 to go
all you guys, Train. Be well.

---

963 Name: Anonymous Post Date: 09/05/04 18:36

On platform 2, Happiness-bound train, ready for departure
Please step into the car as the train is very crowded

---

970 Name: Train Man ♦ 4aPOTtW4HU Post Date: 09/05/04 18:37

You're giving me £10 . . . . . . what should I write?

---

971 Name: One of Us Post Date: 09/05/04 18:37

```
ヽ('A`)ノシ(^3^)ヽ('A`)ノシヽ('A`)ノシ(×_×)(´—`)ヽ('A`)ノシヽ('A`)ノシヽ('A`)ノシ(^3^)(/Д`)ノシ
ヽ('A`)ノシ                                                              ヽ('A`)ノシ
(´—`)     Train Man, Hermes – thank you, it was a lot of fun       ヽ('A`)ノシ
ヽ('A`)ノシ                                                              ヽ('A`)ノシ
ヽ('A`)ノシ        'Train Man, wishing you happiness with Hermes'       ヽ('A`)ノシ
ヽ('A`)ノシ                                                              ヽ('A`)ノシ
ヽ('A`)ノシ          Greek Shot Down in Flames Board Moderator        (×_×)
ヽ('A`)ノシ                                                              ヽ('A`)ノシ
ヽ('A`)ノシ(^3^)ヽ('A`)ノシヽ('A`)ノシ(´—`)(×_×)ヽ('A`)ノシヽ('A`)ノシ(^3^)ヽ('A`)ノシヽ('A`)ノシ
```

>Train Man
I'll log it all for the Flash site.

If there's anything you want me to edit out of the log like links or certain
words then send me an e-mail or post a note will you?

If you do end up getting married, then let me know when you feel like it.

I'll post congratulations on the site. Train! 。・゜・(/Д`)・゜・。 waaaaah!

977 Name: Anonymous Post Date: 09/05/04 18:37

983 Name: Anonymous Post Date: 09/05/04 18:38

Hey, let's all watch Train leave and give him our sincerest, deepest bow

that's all we can offer to top off our compassion, no?

986 Name: Anonymous Post Date: 09/05/04 18:38

Train, everybody, thank you for everything!
Hoping that we'll meet again one day!!

996 Name: Anonymous Post Date: 09/05/04 18:39

Final post, Train, all happiness to ya!

997 Name: Train Man ♦ 4aPOTtW4HU Post Date: 09/05/04 18:39

997

998 Name: Anonymous Post Date: 09/05/04 18:39

if I hit 999, then I'm ready to declare my love . . . who am I kidding, no one to declare it to!

999 Name: Anonymous Post Date: 09/05/04 18:40

Train, just fill up the final three

1000 Name: Anonymous Post Date: 09/05/04 18:39

run towards the glory in store for you!

1001 Name: 1001 Post Date: Over 1000 Thread

This thread has gone over 1000.
No additional posts are possible so please start another thread.

Sorry. I may end up betraying you guys.
I'm no good at writing so don't know how well I can tell this story.

Damn. This thread's got something going on . . .
May the force be with you . . .

The Train Man saga launched by these seemingly banal words has finally
come to a close. Train Man, who learned to courageously take that first step
and to believe in himself initially said 'anyway, the point is that you guys really
need to get out more.'

Off we step into the brightly lit abyss.

Post-fin

'You Were Trying So Hard ....'

After Train Man's departure, the netizens of the thread start to fear something.

---

458 Name: Anonymous Post Date: 16/05/04 12:19

One day . . .
H: 'Hey Mr Train, did you post something on a bulletin board
           online?'
T: 'What? What do you mean by something?'
H: 'Umm . . . my friend was telling me about it . . . and I'm
           wondering if . . .'
T: 'I don't understand. What was your friend saying?'
H: 'Well . . . that our story is featured on a bulletin board called
           2-Channel . . .'
T:

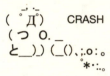
（ ﾟДﾟ）   CRASH
（ つ O. _
と＿)) (＿(),;.o:。
　　　°＊･:。

---

459 Name: Anonymous Post Date: 16/05/04 12:20

(((((;ﾟДﾟ))) wawawawawaw

now way can we have that

---

462 Name: Train Man ♦ 4aPOTtW4HU Post Date: 16/05/04 17:56

long time no see. got a little report for you.

---

463 Name: Anonymous Post Date: 16/05/04 17:57

Train heeeeeeeeeeeeeeeeeeere!! ─────(ﾟ∀ﾟ)─────!!!!

---

466 Name: Anonymous Post Date: 16/05/04 17:59

ah yeah!

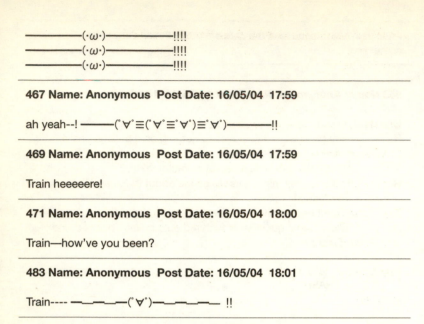

————————(·ω·)————————!!!!
————————(·ω·)————————!!!!
————————(·ω·)————————!!!!

467 Name: Anonymous Post Date: 16/05/04 17:59

ah yeah--! ————(゜∀゜≡(゜∀゜≡゜∀゜)≡゜∀゜)————!!

469 Name: Anonymous Post Date: 16/05/04 17:59

Train heeeeere!

471 Name: Anonymous Post Date: 16/05/04 18:00

Train—how've you been?

483 Name: Anonymous Post Date: 16/05/04 18:01

Train---- ——–——–—(゜∀゜)——–——–— !!

484 Name: Anonymous Post Date: 16/05/04 18:01

did something happen?

490 Name: Train Man ♦ 4aPOTtW4HU Post Date: 16/05/04 18:02

This thing you've been worried about, that she would find out about
the postings, well, you don't need to worry about it anymore. I
showed her the entire log last night. I really wanted her to see
everything.
I was confident she would read it and understand.
All I was worried about was that I was risking exposing her
identity.

It took a long time to read everything but she was really surprised
and said 'There really are such good people out there, huh'

I'm watching the thread as I write but man, does it move fast!
Let me post this first.

498 Name: Anonymous Post Date: 16/05/04 18:02

you serious?

---

505 Name: Anonymous Post Date: 16/05/04 18:03

whaaaaaaaaaaaaaaa!!!!! you showed her???

---

516 Name: Anonymous Post Date: 16/05/04 18:03

Hermes is the best . . . . dewy-eyed.

---

517 Name: Anonymous Post Date: 16/05/04 18:03

you showed her!

---

518 Name: Anonymous Post Date: 16/05/04 18:03

my god . . .

---

522 Name: Anonymous Post Date: 16/05/04 18:04

>>490
really . . .
is that what Lady Hermes said . . .
that day, that time when we cheered you on . . . did not go to waste.

makes me happy happy.

---

535 Name: Anonymous Post Date: 16/05/04 18:05

have you come clean about your anime fetish?

---

536 Name: Anonymous Post Date: 16/05/04 18:05

This means she knows about Keroro and Sailor Moon and Pretty Cure . . .

---

548 Name: Train Man ♦ 4aPOTtW4HU Post Date: 16/05/04 18:05

About coming out about my anorak-ness, I didn't really address that part but she has anorak-like tendencies herself so I was pretty

confident that she'd be able to accept my leanings. I can't divulge what exactly her fetish is as that may expose her indentity . . .

---

621 Name: Anonymous Post Date: 16/05/04 18:11

Is Lady Hermes . . . there with you???

---

647 Name: Train Man ♦ 4aPOTtW4HU Post Date: 16/05/04 18:13

I'm at home now so she's not here.

---

726 Name: Train Man ♦ 4aPOTtW4HU Post Date: 16/05/04 18:27

Yesterday I went over to her house around midday. So I could show her the log.
I also wanted to check to make sure her PC was working OK. And I took the teacups again.

Her mother was home this time. I was supa-dupa nervous . . .
'Hello.'
'Hello, come on in . . . make yourself at home.'
'Nice to meet you asd98@#^*#_+K_ihui'
I was dead nervous in the beginning so I don't remember what exactly we talked about . . .
But her mother seemed like a sweet person. Since she was going to make tea for us, I handed her the teacups.

I made it up to her room that day.
I was kinda taken aback because her room definitely had a semi-anorak vibe floating through it but I pretended not to be shocked because she was coming out to me in her own way that day.
I'd love to be able to give you the details but . . .

I quickly got to the point
'That thing I've been talking about wanting to show you . . . '
I was confident but still nervous . . .
'Yeah. Show me, show me.'
She seemed really interested . . .

730 Name: Anonymous Post Date: 16/05/04 18:27

ah yeah!

---

746 Name: Anonymous Post Date: 16/05/04 18:29

went right for the jugular didn't ya

---

747 Name: Anonymous Post Date: 16/05/04 18:29

and that's how the location of our slaughterhouse was exposed . . .

---

793 Name: Anonymous Post Date: 16/05/04 18:34

hey you lot
there's a chance Hermes may be checking this thread later on.
Behave like gentlemen, please.

(;´Д｀) huffpuff

---

837 Name: Train Man ♦ 4aPOTtW4HU Post Date: 16/05/04 18:39

'Have you heard of 2-Channel?'
I needed to explain before I showed it to her.
'The bulletin board?'
'Right, the anonymous bulletin board. It's a vortex of all kinds of
people and their feelings,' I said, to which she replied with a '?' on her
face. I got all lyrical about the dirtiness of anonymity and the flip side,
the beauty of it.
In reality, my explaining went on forever.

'Remember when I said I asked friends for advice? I was talking
about these people.'
Then I told her a bit about the thread.
And I owned up to writing a blow by blow account of our relationship,
from the moment we met till the day I poured my heart out to her. She
didn't say anything right away and I was relieved.

'The record includes my hearfelt but dirty thoughts as well as some
secrets but I'd really like you to read it,' I added, as I handed her a

CD-R of the log. I brought both the log and the edited version but
I decided to let her read the real log first.

---

840 Name: Anonymous Post Date: 16/05/04 18:39

real log?

---

841 Name: Anonymous Post Date: 16/05/04 18:39

da da da . . . real log???

---

842 Name: Anonymous Post Date: 16/05/04 18:39

realloioipokllooooo log??!?!?

---

843 Name: Anonymous Post Date: 16/05/04 18:40

(゜д゜)

---

845 Name: Anonymous Post Date: 16/05/04 18:40

>I decided to let her read the real log first.
>I decided to let her read the real log first.
>I decided to let her read the real log first.
>I decided to let her read the real log first.
>I decided to let her read the real log first.

---

847 Name: Anonymous Post Date: 16/05/04 18:40

omg, the real log . . . lol

---

849 Name: Anonymous Post Date: 16/05/04 18:40

rrrrrrrrrrrrrreal lllllllllllllllllog????

---

850 Name: Anonymous Post Date: 16/05/04 18:40

real log he says
you sure thats ok? (;´Д`)

865 Name: Anonymous Post Date: 16/05/04 18:40

you showed her the real deal, raw and in the flesh!

Real log. That would be the uncensored version of the posts. On the Flash site, the dirtier posts had been edited out just in case Hermes found out and came to the site. Feeling as though their depravity had been exposed, the netizens became flustered.

---

867 Name: Anonymous Post Date: 16/05/04 18:40

you say you showed her the real log to start with? wouldn't you usually work your way up to it? Wouldn't you first show her One of Us's site and then show her the real log? No matter how you look at it, once a Train, always a Train . . . you make me hot.

---

872 Name: Anonymous Post Date: 16/05/04 18:41

>>837
it looks like you're not just any old couple. it's like you've already got some deep trust going . . .
If it was me, I couldn't even show my family or friends my posts . . .

---

919 Name: ◆N/WAG/OonQ Post Date: 16/05/04 18:45

>>Train
way to go

---

984 Name: Train Man ◆ 4aPOTtW4HU Post Date: 16/05/04 18:55

After reading for about 2 or 3 minutes, she moved the scroll bar all the way to bottom and said 'There's . . . so much here'
'Yep, there's two months' worth.'

We decided to put my screen name as a search and read through.
The posts about the train incident gave us a little jog down memory lane.
She laughed out loud at 'It says Hermes. Guess they're some household goods brand.' I thought I was in the clear . . . after she

read the part about me calling her and asking her to dinner, she said
'You were trying so hard . . . '
'No kidding,' I replied, and we smiled.
Then she told me that seeing how hard I had tried made her heart flutter.

---

991 Name: Anonymous Post Date: 16/05/04 18:56

ah yeah--- ——————————(°`∀°)—————————— !!!!!
She's giving you points for all your hard work . . .
I guess that's the way it is for two people in love with each other . . .

---

286 Name: Train Man ♦ 4aPOTtW4HU Post Date: 16/05/04 19:24

In the middle of this, her mother came in with tea and biscuits.
They were homemade again . . . (´д°) They were yum.
and yeah, I asked for Benoist tea . . . (´—`)

As she got to the end she said
'It reads like a novel'
as if it was somebody's else's story
When she finally finished reading, she sighed and said
'I'm glad I got to know what you were thinking about. Thank you.'
And then
'Why didn't you tell me sooner?'
'But really, I'm so happy it turned out this way,' she said and
squeezed my hand. And then as if signalling a kiss . . . the vibe shifted
suddenly and . . .

I reckon it ended up being a positive thing.
Other than the fact that men are pervs.
She did say that it was because of people cheering me on that I was
able to work up the courage and that was how we ended up
together.
And finally, she said
'Why are these wonderful men Geeks?'

---

297 Name: Anonymous Post Date: 16/05/04 19:25

>And finally, she said

>Why are these wonderful men Geeks?

('A`)

---

318 Name: Anonymous Post Date: 16/05/04 19:27

ah yeah *:.。.。:*･ﾟ(n'∀')η゜･*:.。.。:* 彡 ☆

---

357 Name: Anonymous Post Date: 16/05/04 19:31

>'But really, I'm so happy it turned out this way,' she said and squeezed my hand. >And then as if signalling a kiss . . . the vibe shifted suddenly and . . .

Train. Train.
You is far ahead . . . so far ahead . . . I can barely see you any more . . . . . .

---

359 Name: Anonymous Post Date: 16/05/04 19:31

comin right atcha

---

366 Name: Anonymous Post Date: 16/05/04 19:32

Train, you're a bullet train

---

367 Name: Anonymous Post Date: 16/05/04 19:32

>>357
I imagined a Geek running for dear life after Train . . . lol

---

387 Name: Anonymous Post Date: 16/05/04 19:35

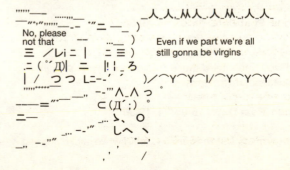

No, please
not that

Even if we part we're all
still gonna be virgins

---

409 Name: Train Man ♦ 4aPOTtW4HU Post Date: 16/05/04 19:37

She really gave me a hard time about my anime obsession and porn mags.
'Sailor Moon . . . wow, it's been so long since I saw it . . . '
'Why do you need those magazines?'
'Well, I'm just a healthy male' I said, skirting the issue, to which she replied
'I see . . .' _| |.......O
and then came this hot-hot line
'But with me around, you don't need those magazines anymore, right?'
She hit the nail right on the head _|⌐|O
Before I knew it, I said
'I won't buy them anymore'
And that shouldn't be a problem.
But that was the first time I was scared of her.

And then she got into a huff about what I quoted as being spoken by her. Maybe I misheard but at a few points she said
'I didn't say that'
Or about her boobs
'They may not look like much, but they are a C (said while sticking chest out)'
Or about my catching a glimpse of her underwear
'Perv'
She also said 'I don't look like Miki Nakatani'
She was, of course, just being modest.

---

414 Name: Anonymous Post Date: 16/05/04 19:38

>>409
>'But with me around, you don't need those magazines anymore, right?'
rrrrrrrrrrrrrooooooooooaaaaaaarrrrrrrrrrrrrrrrrr

---

419 Name: Anonymous Post Date: 16/05/04 19:38

>'They may not look like much, but they are a C (said while sticking chest out)'

she's too cute

---

432 Name: ♦N/WAG/OOnQ Post Date: 16/05/04 19:39

>>Train
God has spoken . . .

---

449 Name: Anonymous Post Date: 16/05/04 19:39

>'They may not look like much, but they are a C (said while sticking chest out)'

I can't take it . . . can't take it any more . . . _|⌐|O

---

450 Name: Anonymous Post Date: 16/05/04 19:39

shit
that kind of dialogue

gets me all hot and bothered

---

452 Name: Anonymous Post Date: 16/05/04 19:40

> 'Perv'

Can't take it no more . . . . . . more than all the bombings
this very banal word is stabbing me deep in the heart, non-stop . . .

---

466 Name: Anonymous Post Date: 16/05/04 19:41

Diggin the C-cup puts us in a very warm place and comes dangerously close to hotness. But remember that there are many women out there who are not close to being Cs so don't put down your weapons yet.

---

476 Name: Anonymous Post Date: 16/05/04 19:41

>'I won't buy them anymore'

Did you keep what you had?

---

490 Name: Train Man ♦ 4aPOTtW4HU Post Date: 16/05/04 19:41

'But with me around, you don't need those magazines anymore, right?'
This is a great hint-hint nudge-nudge line but at the same time, she's putting on the pressure.
Not that I was pressured into giving up my porn mags . . .

---

495 Name: Anonymous Post Date: 16/05/04 19:42

doesn't matter dude, just give up the mags
and give me what you got

---

506 Name: Anonymous Post Date: 16/05/04 19:43

I won't buy porn mags anymore!
Give me another chance!
I'm sorry! I'm sorry!

---

504 Name: Anonymous Post Date: 16/05/04 19:43

>>490
hey, couldn't you have given her some line like

but sex and wanking are two different things, right?

---

516 Name: Train Man ♦ 4aPOTtW4HU Post Date: 16/05/04 19:43

>>504
Um, yeah, well, ah, yeah, um, I . . .

525 Name: Anonymous Post Date: 16/05/04 19:44

>>516
huh? wha wha wha what's up?

---

526 Name: Anonymous Post Date: 16/05/04 19:44

>>516
what is that mumbling stumbling . . .

cou . . . could it be . . . . . .

---

579 Name: Train Man ♦ 4aPOTtW4HU Post Date: 16/05/04 19:47

I haven't done it yet. What can I say, I'll be showing her this site too so . . .

---

591 Name: Anonymous Post Date: 16/05/04 19:47

>>579
you serious?
Lady Hermesalicious, wanna go out with moi?

---

593 Name: Anonymous Post Date: 16/05/04 19:47

she's gonna be checkin us out (´Д`)

---

600 Name: Anonymous Post Date: 16/05/04 19:48

What?! You're gonna show her this site?!

Well, er, Train Boy, everybody else may be posting their dirty little thoughts here but I will continue to cheer you on . . . ha!ha!ha!

---

607 Name: Anonymous Post Date: 16/05/04 19:48

hmm . . . as we thought . . . Hermes will be visiting this site . . .
hold on, I'm gonna go get changed

609 Name: Anonymous Post Date: 16/05/04 19:48

pleased to meet you sweet Hermes girl

---

611 Name: Anonymous Post Date: 16/05/04 19:49

As soon as Train posted that he'll be showing the site to Hermes, the number of posts drastically decreased! lol

---

614 Name: Anonymous Post Date: 16/05/04 19:49

checkin us out here!

would you like some curry?

---

621 Name: Anonymous Post Date: 16/05/04 19:49

What? Showing this site too?

ar . . . rr . . . take good care of Train Boy, please.

---

627 Name: Anonymous Post Date: 16/05/04 19:49

The moment I read that Hermes would be visiting the site, I got down on the floor and sat with my legs tucked under me like a good Japanese boy for some reason

---

634 Name: Anonymous Post Date: 16/05/04 19:50

Hey Train, don't lose sight of that happiness
you finally got in your hands
and don't make any mistakes you can't take back

---

650 Name: Anonymous Post Date: 16/05/04 19:50

real-time Train Man in da ho-------use ──────＼(ﾟ∀ﾟ)/────────!!!!
all happiness to ya! Don't give Lady Hermes anything to cry about!!!

The anonymous netizens, who all remained nameless and faceless and whose whereabouts also remained unknown, rallied behind Train Man whether called for or not and at times partied on in the thread regardless of Train Man's presence. What they did was something very simple: they offered to help somebody who needed help. It was a simple gesture stemming from a sense of common courtesy we all carry within ourselves.

Seeing the flustered Train Man made the netizens rally round him, which in turn gave Train Man the courage and strength to dial Hermes' number.

Those netizens who cheered Train Man on. Those who came in contact with the story and reacted by cheering Train along or applauding him are all made from the same thread and spirit.

| Hermes: 'Such good people they were'

The Mammoth Book of Best New Manga

Edited by Ilya

The essential collection for every manga fan, *The Mammoth Book of Best New Manga* contains over 500 all-new pages of original comic strip stories in every genre you can think of – and quite a few more besides.

True-to-life drama, sci-fi parable, medieval fantasy, updated Chinese myth, historical, romance, time travel, comedy, horror, funny animal and, oof, sometimes all of it happening at once! Contributors include Andi Watson, Michiru Morikawa, Selina Dean, Keiiii, Tiggy Bandit, Neil Cameron, Asia Alfasi, Craig Conlan, Cosmo White, plus a host of other bright young talents.

Publication: October 2006
1-84529-353-3
£7.99

Coming soon in Robinson paperback

Not in the Guidebook: Weird and Wonderful Mysteries from Google Earth

James Turnball and Alex Turnball

Just as you thought the world had been fully explored, here are truly astonishing sights on planet Earth that no guidebook takes you near. Drawn from the web site googlesightseeing.com, these satellite camera discoveries include The Plug Holes in the Mediterranean, Arizona's Boneyard, Australia's Extraordinary Flying Car, The Hole in the Coast of Mexico, and Face of Jesus Found in the Sand.

They are the hole-in-the wall gems that you'd never stumble onto on your own, but which the cameras did. Extraordinary natural formations, offbeat man-made marvels, or the simply uncategorizable – all are glitches in the matrix of how we expect to see the world.

Publication: November 2006
1-84529-466-1
£8.99

Coming soon in Robinson paperback

The Mammoth Book of the
Funniest Cartoons of All Time

Edited by Geoff Tibballs

A bumper volume of more than 400 of the funniest cartoons
ever published. They include the finest gems of cartoon
humour, spanning every decade. Also included is a brief
biography of each artist.

Includes work by all the great favourites, such as Matt, Larry,
Ed McLachlan and Mike Baldwin, as well as over 50 other
remarkable talents. The collection is arranged by theme, from
sport and sex to the long arm of the law.

Publication: August 2006
1-84529-429-7
£7.99